Dear Reader,

Are you like me? Do you have 'reading moods'? Sometimes I like a story with an element of mystery in it, on other occasions I enjoy a sexy read; there are times when I love my romance novels spiced with a little humour and others when I look forward to a warm and involving family-centred story. How about you?

Each month, I work hard to provide a balanced list for you, to ensure that every *Scarlet* reader's taste is catered for. As you can imagine, this is quite a difficult feat, particularly as I may suddenly be offered four similar stories – four tales of romantic suspense, for example, all at one time. So far, from your letters and questionnaires, it seems that we're getting the mix just right. But do let us know, won't you, if there is anything you particularly want to see more of on *your* list. Or is there something you think is missing from the *Scarlet* list? In the light of the current interest in Jane Austen, would you like *Scarlet* to include some Regency romances?

Keep those letters and questionnaires coming, won't you?

Till next month,

Sally Cooper

SALLY COOPER,
Editor-in-Chief – *Scarlet*

About the Author

The Mistress, **Angela Drake**'s first *Scarlet* novel, was very popular with readers, and we are sure that you will thoroughly enjoy *Woman of Dreams*.

Angela is a Chartered Psychologist currently practising as a freelance consultant. She is the published author of several romance and mainstream novels and has also written for the young adult market.

In her spare time, the author enjoys reading, going to the cinema and listening to music.

Angela is married with one grown-up daughter and lives in Harrogate with her husband and other assorted pets!

Other **Scarlet** *titles available this month:*

WICKED IN SILK – Andrea Young
NEVER SAY NEVER – Tina Leonard
COME HOME FOREVER – Jan McDaniel

ANGELA DRAKE

WOMAN OF DREAMS

Enquiries to:
Robinson Publishing Ltd
7 Kensington Church Court
London W8 4SP

First published in the UK by Scarlet, 1996

A copy of the British Library Cataloguing in
Publication data is available from the British Library

ISBN 1-85487-714-3

Printed and bound in the EC

10 9 8 7 6 5 4 3 2 1

PROLOGUE

Twenty years ago, when Zoe was six years old, her mother had taken her to a fortune teller. The woman was old, with deep cracks of skin framing her eyes and fanning downwards from her mouth. She had long black hair tied in a knotted silk scarf and huge gold earrings that twinkled in the dim dusty light of her hot little room.

Zoe had been fascinated, staring into the crinkled face with its glinting penetrating eyes. Magnetized and held. Just sufficiently afraid to feel a tiny thrill of excitement.

Her mother had sat with clasped hands, questioning urgently in her breathless rushing way. Then falling gradually silent as the woman looked up from her cloudy glass ball and began to speak.

Long slow sentences. A ripe black treacle voice. Zoe had watched the deep red lips move, attending more to the lulling rhythmn of the words than their content, which for a child was mainly baffling.

Her mother, however, had listened intently; shoulders hunching, knuckles clenching. At the end she had rushed from the room sobbing noisily. A perplexed Zoe, trotting in pursuit of her wailing parent, had twisted round for a last glimpse of the strangely magical woman who had the power to conjure up so much noise and grief.

Spring into Summer

CHAPTER 1

François Rogier stared into the glistening yellow pool at the base of the pan, turning down the gas jet and flicking his wooden spoon at precisely the right moment to promote a rapid thickening which transformed the small smooth lake into a opaque fluffy mound. A second deft flick transferred this little work of art onto a warmed plate to nestle within a garland of sliced tomatoes and sprigs of parsley.

'Leonore, your egg is ready.'

The child was sitting at the table, bent over an exercise book, writing with painstaking care. She turned her face up, puzzled for a moment as she emerged from a distant world of her own. She looked at the plate, looked back at her father and smiled.

Carefully she counted each slice and sprig. 'Seven and seven,' she said. She cocked her head on one side, bird-like. 'That's very lucky.'

'Indeed?' he commented drily, wondering who had told her that.

Leonore reached for the pepper mill, her small fingers strong and firm as she grappled with the stiff grinding mechanism. A small shower of brown speckles landed on the scrambled egg. Leonore picked up her fork and lowered it daintily into the eggy mixture.

She was a very adult child. Preferred coffee to orange juice at breakfast time, fresh pasta to chicken nuggets at supper.

But then she had lived on her own with her father for two years, a period representing a third of her life. And her father was a man of care and precision, the sort of man who had the patience to attend to the details of things.

'May I look at the work you've been doing?' François enquired. He asked in a manner suggesting that if she were to say 'no', he would respect her wish for privacy.

Leonore nodded, smiling and pleased.

François looked at the childish handwriting: distinctive, bold and primitive. It reminded him of the energetic, mainly incomprehensible, images displayed in Poppy's chic Manhattan gallery. Work produced by supposedly mature adults.

He thought suddenly and sharply of Poppy – standing in her gallery, illuminated by a slash of brilliant sunlight from the huge skylight windows, a gilded halo around her blonde head. He closed his eyes briefly, hunched his shoulders against the pain.

Don't think of her, he told himself, aware of an ache like an iron bar in his chest.

He forced his concentration back to Leonore's chunky script. She had written two long strings of words: a column of English nouns on one side of the page, their counterparts in French on the other. He noted that her spelling was completely accurate in both languages, something it gave him extreme pleasure to see.

6

It was only in the last year that Leonore had begun to speak fluently and with confidence. He had begun to fear that she might never speak at all.

Right from the beginning, when Poppy had first known she was pregnant, she had been determined that her child – always referred to as 'he' – should be brought up to be bilingual, acquiring the languages of French and English simultaneously, in equal measure. Just because her son would be born and brought up in England, that was no reason for him to be denied his French inheritance. He would speak French as easily and competently as any child born and raised in Paris or Lyons.

'After all, darling,' Poppy had protested prettily to François, 'you abandoned your family and your country to be with me. It's the least I can do to make sure our little one speaks your language like a native.' She had paused, elegant and capable hands clasped around her swollen belly. 'French,' she had declared, 'the language of chivalry. The language of love.'

An enchanted, infatuated François had gazed at his wife with unbridled indulgence.

She had continued her bright, sharp declarations. 'I shall start straight away – as soon as he's born – talking to him in French and English.'

For Poppy, her embryonic baby's mind had been an empty page, simply waiting to be written on. Fresh, receptive and uncomplicated.

But the son she had been confidently expecting turned out to be a girl. And the empty page of the child's mind proved to be far more complex and resistant than Poppy could ever have dreamed.

In the daytime, whilst François was absent, Poppy had

talked and sung to her baby constantly. In the morning the baby had heard only English, then in the afternoon the stimulating entertainment had been all in French. Poppy's own French was impeccable. She had begun learning at school when she was nine and spent many holidays in Languedoc with her parents' friends, honing up her conversational skills and her accent. There came a time when she could fool even some of the locals.

The baby Leonore had watched and listened to her mother with attention and delight. She had begun the usual childish experimentations with words at around nine months: imitating sounds, echoing phrases, flexing the muscles of her throat and mouth in order to achieve a replica of her mother's voice.

As recognizable words began to emerge, so Poppy would gently correct any crossover between the two languages. It amused, but then concerned her, that Leonore's developing speech seemed to be heading into a charming mixture between the two. An infantile, idiosyncratic *franglais*.

Kindly, but firmly, Poppy insisted on the appropriate language at the appropriate time. She demanded accuracy also; not in a harsh way, just quietly repeating the required sounds. And when François came home at supper time, Leonore was required to demonstrate her newly acquired achievements.

François had become uneasy. He saw the growing anxiety in the baby's huge blue eyes. He tried to talk to Poppy about it. She was gay and dismissive. 'You wait, darling, in a year's time we shall have a little girl who will be able to hold her own in London or Paris.'

In a year's time they had a child who was more or less silent.

And it was not until some time after Poppy eventually left that Leonore had begun to make a hesitant attempt to sketch out ideas in words instead of the drawings which had become her main means of communicaiton.

That Leonore was now beginning to express herself in writing gave François enormous pleasure.

Leonore broke off a chunk from the warmed baguette on the table and wiped carefully around her plate, weaving the bread in and out of the sprigs of parsley as though on a slalom course. She licked the remains of egg from the bread with a dainty kitten tongue. 'Mmm, good!' she said, glancing again at her father.

He tapped the exercise book. 'This is good, too, Leonore.' He reached out and touched his daughter's soft blonde fringe with fingers full of tenderness. 'So, Miss Peach is giving you homework now, is she?'

Leonore shook her head. 'She says children should play and do what they like when they get home.'

'Does she, indeed?' François raised quizzical dark eyebrows.

'Yes.'

François was inclined to agree. The pressure would pile on soon enough. What would Poppy have thought of that philosophy, he wondered? What would Poppy think of Leonore's life now? An ordinary little girl attending the local school, mixing with children whose parents were in the main neither rich nor smart.

'I just did the words because I wanted to,' said Leonore, taking the book back from François and stashing it in her zip-up folder.

'Mmm,' François nodded absently, his mind once again lodged in a small exclusive art gallery in Manhattan.

9

'Yesterday Miss Peach had a bright green shirt and parrot earrings,' Leonore mused. 'And red high heels.'

François pulled himself back from thoughts of Poppy. His dark eyes sparked with amusement. The exotic-sounding Miss Peach had been a regular feature of conversation in the past months since she had taken on the role of Leonore's language tutor.

Leonore had been receiving special tutoring in English for some time now, ever since her headteacher had requested a meeting with François in order to discuss the little girl's worrying quietness.

Starting school at four and a half years old, six months after Poppy's dramatic exit from the family, Leonore had spent her days in the classroom sunk into long silences which had appeared to her teachers to border on mute-ness.

The headteacher had spoken to François calmly and quietly. She had talked about Leonore being 'troubled', in need of 'help'. She had let drop the word 'psychologist'.

François had drawn in a breath, wincing, angry. He had been adamant. 'Leonore needs nothing except time. And love.'

The head teacher had seen the ferocity of determination in the father's glance and refrained from pressing the issue. The psychologist was not called upon. Instead, arrangements were made for Leonore to join in with a small group of children of varied nationalities, all of whom were learning English as a foreign language. A visiting tutor arrived twice a week to teach them.

Slowly, painfully, Leonore began to experiment with speech all over again. This time there was no Poppy, listening out for every little mistake, and after a shaky start the learning process began to proceed steadily. When Miss Peach arrived on the scene it took off like a soaring arrow.

François looked at his watch. 'Nearly time to be leaving, little love.'

Leonore packed her furry pencil case in her folder and smiled up at her father. Love and understanding flowed between them. 'Teeth,' she said, solemnly.

He heard water running in the bathroom, imagined her brushing vigorously.

Such energy she had. Such vitality: boundless, surging with the optimism of childhood.

He had a swift sense of the weight of his own thirty years sitting heavily on him. Dear God! Sometimes he thought he could not have made a greater mess of things if he had deliberately set out to do so.

Through the connecting walls he heard his neighbour's dog launch into a frenzy of barking, bracing itself for the ultimate outrage of the post erupting through the door.

François grinned to himself, imagining the small dog quivering with furious indignation. The barks reached a climax, died away into short growling grumbles and then subsided. Another half a minute and his own mail would arrive.

He looked down the long hallway to the front door, eyeing the brass mouth of the letter box, bracing himself. He disliked the arrival of the mail. It rarely brought any joy these days. Merely bills, statements of accounts, circulars. Letters from Poppy which made his eyes wet.

Galloping down the steps, Leonore grasped the envelopes as they inched their way into the Rogier household.

11

'One for Daddy,' she announced, handing François a thick cream-coloured envelope. 'Two for ME!'

She laid her communications on the table like trophies. There was a cream envelope identical to the one François had received. And a bright pink one addressed in immaculate italic script in vivid purple ink.

Leonore hesitated between the two, delaying the pleasure, uncertain which to select first.

François stared down at the paper in his fingers, registering Poppy's leggy loopy writing. With a flash of insight, he knew what was inside even before he saw it. Instantly he reached a full understanding of the meaning of the word 'heartstopping': the tightening inside the chest wall, the liquidy sweep in the stomach, the raw answering response deep in the gut.

He willed himself to be still; a sheet of calm untroubled water for anyone to look on and see only clear light at its base. Straining to keep his fingers from shaking, he made a sharp tear along the envelope, opening up a jagged gap.

The card inside was thick and stiff. Embossed in thick shiny blue letters.

An invitation. A wedding to take place in a skyscraper gallery. A marriage between his wife Poppy (for that was how he still thought of her) and her lover Liam.

He breathed in, holding the air, then slowly allowing his rib-cage to contract. For François, it seemed that a huge black line had been slashed through the most exciting chapter of his life, a brutal full stop placed at its finale.

And now he must face Leonore's response. She was holding the card at arm's length, considering, her head cocked in its chaffinchy pose. Quietly, with great dignity, she turned the card over and laid it face down on the table. Picking up the pink envelope, she opened it and pulled out the paper inside.

She turned her face up to François, a smile curving her features, her eyes beaming out excitement. 'Miss Peach is having a party. She wants me to go. And you, too, Daddy. Can we go? Can we?'

They looked into each other's eyes. Relieved, able to smile freely again.

'I can wear the tunic Mummy sent me . . .' Leonore broke off. She did not like to speak to him about Mummy. Or about the new tunic. There were things that made Daddy very sad. Maybe she should just leave the tunic in its tissue paper until she was too big to wear it.

'Of course we'll go. And your tunic will be just the thing for Miss Peach's party,' François told his daughter, sweeping her up and swinging her around.

He glanced down at the wedding invitation cards, thanking God for a friendly tutor and her unknowing intervention at a most timely juncture.

CHAPTER 2

A few hours earlier in Rome's Fiumicino airport, whilst François and Leonore slept in a darkened London, all was activity and noise; a buzz of voices in a world medley of languages. It was a Monday morning and light was just seeping into the sky. The vast departure complex hummed and seethed like the final Saturday afternoon in Harrods or Bloomingdales before Christmas.

A tiny figure, jewel-bright in pillar-box red, shouldered her way through the throngs of towering Scandinavian businessmen stocking up on whisky in the duty-free shop.

As the blond giants stared down, so she smiled slantingly up – and pathways melted open for her. Male attention was instantly caught; masculine chivalry and courtesy swiftly aroused. Her shoulders were only slender, but the mental energy driving them was not to be trifled with.

She was in a rush, had left things a fraction too late for comfort. Her plane had been boarding for twenty minutes now. The final call had already been repeated twice.

She made a habit of this – cutting things marginally fine so as to treat herself to little fizzing thrills of internal

14

anxiety. It was the way she liked to live. Just a little on the edge.

In some curious way, tempting fate gave her a sense of being in control of things, of taking charge of her own destiny. It made her the kind of person entirely the opposite of her scatty superstitious mother, who had been driven by life's everyday challenges like a piece of goosedown in a gale.

The girl at the check-out watched with a weary lack of enthusiasm as a tall blond giant rolled his numerous bottles towards her. She reached for the credit card he flourished, ignoring his attempts to joke with her in gauche Italian when the plastic failed to register. Resignedly, she stared at the card and began to key in its number. Made an error. Started again.

The till squeaked in protest. The exhausted girl went laboriously back to the beginning.

The bright red shoulders behind the blond giant bristled with agitation. Immaculately drawn red lips twitched with what appeared to be silent swearing.

Over the loudspeaker a suave voice informed passengers for London Heathrow that their aircraft was about to leave.

Exasperated, yet laughing in mockery at her own discomfiture, the young woman in red abandoned her bottles of Frascati and Orvieto and made a dash for the departure gates.

A steward and stewardess looked up, calmly waiting to greet her as she clattered on her high heels down the long flight of steps leading to the tarmac. Beyond them in the darkness the plane crouched, growling urgently, engines impatient, egg-shaped discs of light beaming from its

15

sleek belly. She had a sense of being about to enter a dragon.

Running up the steps, her heart began to pump. Anticipation of flying always did that to her, for all that she was a seasoned traveller.

'Sorry, sorry,' she told the steward standing at the door of the aircraft. 'Have I held everyone up?'

'No, no.' He smiled reassuringly. Like all cabin staff, he was a master of suppressing whatever emotions might be pounding through his veins.

He indicated her seat. Row five. A window seat. She settled down, unbuttoning her jacket, smoothing her short skirt over slender curved thighs, noting with pleasure that the aisle seat beside her was empty. Good. She would be able to spread herself a little. Relax, sleep at ease.

She reached for her belt, hauling in the excess unrequired to accommodate her tiny frame.

Serene now, she waited for the doors to close, the safety demonstration to begin, the long slow trundle down to the take-off strip.

A figure erupted into the aircraft, hurling himself along the aisle, then swooping down beside her as though drawn by a magnet.

She flinched.

'Here. Your wine!' He was grinning broadly, flourishing a shiny plastic bag in front of her nose.

She registered the man who had been ahead of her at the check-out. The one with the credit card that had caused so much trouble.

The air around him stirred and bristled as he pulled off his sweater and stuffed it in the overhead locker together

16

with his and her carrier bags, clinking with bottles. He was all energy and vigour, making his presence well and truly felt.

She smiled to herself, registering the sort of man who harboured no doubts about his effortless ability to draw women into his circle of charm. And not Swedish or Danish. This man was as English as damp cloudy springs and rolling green meadows.

She got out her wallet and extracted a small wad of notes. 'Thank you,' she told him, proffering them.

'No, no!' he protested, gallant and expansive, waving the notes away.

'Oh, yes!' she said softly, dropping them into his lap, then turning her back on him and staring determinedly out of the window. No way would she permit herself to be patronized, however tasty the patron. Through the reflection in the thick shiny plastic she could see him flinging himself back into his seat, a lazy smile of irony curving his full mouth.

The aircraft sauntered meekly to the main runway, paused, aiming its nose dead centre between the dainty rows of lights, then, with a huge roar, hurled itself forwards and up.

She felt her back pressed against the seat. And at the same time felt the dry fingers of her fellow passenger brush lightly against her own as they lay, deliberately relaxed, on the arm rest.

'Best bit of the flight,' she heard him murmur. 'Most dangerous. Highest risk factor.'

She smiled. Refused to be drawn into a dialogue. Leaning her head against the back of the seat, she closed her eyes.

17

The steward came along with coffee and sandwiches. A choice of alcoholic drinks. Her travel companion tapped her lightly on the knuckles. 'Drink?'

She shook her head. Kept her eyes tightly shut.

·It had previously been in her mind to read for a while on the first stages of the flight. Maybe glance over her outline for the next day's work.

Now, with the possible threat of having to chat – and threat it was, despite the obvious attractiveness of her neighbour – she found herself determined to get some sleep.

Perversely, as her determination increased, so the likelihood of sleep seemed to elude her.

Damn. She breathed deeply, recalling exercises from yoga classes some years before. She filled her lungs. Expanding, expanding. Holding. Then letting go. Slowly, slowly. And then again. And again . . .

She was walking along a broad road. A highway, a motorway, an autoroute or an autobahn – it could anywhere in the world.

She glanced behind her, but there was nothing to see – just darkness. And yet the ground below her was glistening and dazzling, hurting her eyes like piercing daggers of sunlight. By the side of the road great swathes of corn swayed, bowing down and then lifting themselves up as though a great machine had swept by demanding their submission.

She walked on. It was so lonely. There was not a person in sight. Not for miles and miles.

The atmosphere became heavy with foreboding. The swathes of corn ahead began to steam. Fire spread from

18

their roots, spreading and blossoming into vast rippling curtains of flame, yellow and red and orange.

She put her hand to her eyes. Her hair felt hot, her eyelashes scorched like a burned-out match.

Thick black billows of smoke rolled towards her and her stomach clenched with fear. Through the boiling mass of flame, she made out the shape of a plane's tubular aluminium body lying on the road ahead. Silver belly exposed and scorched, it had the appearance of a shot bird.

The wings were flexed and distorted, one of them partly buried into the ground, the other tilting up to a sky obscured by filthy choking smoke. A trail of oil slithered over the wing's top surface, slimy and evil.

All around the grounded plane the air seemed to be full of moans, one long sigh of pain.

She stood very still. Her legs had become heavy, refusing to move.

A man stumbled from the smoke. He was black from the oil and soot. Black hair and eyebrows. Eyes like the night sky, luminous and deep beyond all imagining. But pale milky skin, with a moon-like sheen.

'Oil,' he shouted. 'Oil burning! Run. Get away!'

She struggled, longing to respond. Her legs were disobedient, sunk in buckets of sand. She wanted to flee, to escape the nightmare. And at the same time, she was drawn and pulled towards her rescuer. He was safety. He was her only salvation. But she was stuck . . . rooted . . . her legs fastened the ground.

The oil had slithered off the wing. Curving around the man, it began to move towards her, a venomous snake sparking up into livid flares of creeping fire like a flaming pipe shot through with holes.

The man was mouthing desperately, frantic to save her: Zoe. Zoe! But his voice simply floated away to be swallowed up in the smoke.

She was weeping now. The snake of fire was nearly on her, its tongue flicking with incandescent viciousness. As she looked with final appeal to the unknown man, she saw that he was weeping, too . . .

Faces were leaning over her. Male faces. Terrifying strangers.

'You were kicking me nearly to death,' a dry voice informed her, springing her back into consciousness.

She stared around her, registering a plane that was airborne, thrusting calmly through peaceful, flame-free skies. Her heartbeats slowed from their violent sprinting jerks. The breath steadied in her chest.

'And moaning like hell,' her blond travel companion added. 'Get her a brandy, will you?' he asked the concerned steward. 'And one for me, too.'

'That must have been a pretty frightening dream,' he commented. 'Fear of flying, perhaps?'

She shook her head. 'No. Not at all.' Never before, anyway.

The blond man laughed. 'You can have pretty spectacular dreams twenty-five thousand feet up.'

He was trying to be kind. To make a joke of it all.

She sipped the brandy. She tried to persuade herself that the grasping tentacles of the cruel dream were sliding away, slowly setting her free.

The brandy was liquid fire in her stomach, but her body and limbs were icy cold. Squirming in her seat, she tried to get a view of the aircraft's wing. She could

20

see nothing but the grey outline silvered by moonlight. The main body of the wing was tilted away, shrouded in darkness. Struck with new panic, she commanded her eyes to pierce the darkness, to see things that it was impossible to see.

In the end she had to give up. There was no way of telling if a doom-laden trail of oil was snaking an evil secret path in the darkness. She attended, instead, to her reflection in the plastic; it shocked her. The face was ghost-like, drained of life. The eyes were huge orbs of terror, beaming out from the dark shutters of her hair. She did not recognize herself.

She shivered. The brandy trembled in the glass.

'Hey, there! Are you OK?' The blond man turned to her. Suddenly his arms were around her, his hands holding hers, grasping tightly and steadying the violent shaking she was powerless to control. He murmured all manner of silly nonsense, calming her as though she were a trembling kitten, flung out into the terrors of a stormy night.

She was grateful for his attempts to soothe her, but her body was metallic and rigid in his grasp.

She felt herself shot through with dreadful warnings. She tried to pin down this newly awakened fear, to wrestle with it and banish it from her mind. But it twisted away from her, wriggling free and settling somewhere deep in her innermost thoughts. *Take care, Zoe! Something dreadful is coming!*

She held herself steady and taut within the frame of the blond man's arms. She was absolutely still now, again in control. But in the dimmed cabin lights, her cheeks were streaked with tears.

21

CHAPTER 3

The little dog's stiffly vertical hackles subsided. Satisfied with a job well done, the presumptuous postman once again dispatched to try his luck elsewhere, he returned to the feet of his mistress and awaited his reward.

A soft white hand reached down, the long russet-painted nails tickling spiky white hair and the pink skin beneath. 'Good boy, good boy. I wonder how much it would cost to have your bark cosmetically removed.' The voice was deep and gravelly, languid with affection. As he looked devotedly upwards, a piece of toast appeared from the pine canopy of the table, luscious with chunky butter.

Marina, his goddess who lived her life on a plane around five feet higher than her dog, licked her fingers as she contemplated the postman's likely offerings and the events of the next seven hours at work. Neither prospect was cheering.

Getting up from the table, she scooped china cup, saucer and plate to one side and reached for the pack of cards which rested on the dresser, wrapped loosely around with a swathe of magenta silk.

'Well, now, shall I do a reading?' she asked the dog,

whose name was Risk because he had been about to launch himself across racing lanes of traffic in Oxford Street at the age of six weeks when Marina had spotted and seized him. 'Well?' she repeated.

Risk looked up. Concluding that the likelihood of further toast was poor, he replaced his nose on his paws.

'No opinion, eh?' Marina unwrapped the cards and shuffled them with practised skill.

'Just a quick one,' she reassured Risk. 'A simple consequences spread. A little peep into what might be in store.'

Risk lifted his head again. Registered the folding of the scarf and the subsequent tumbling of the cards through his mistress's fingers. His stare seemed to her baleful, tending to reproach.

'You don't approve, dog, do you? But I think I'll carry on anyway.'

Already her experienced hands were setting out the cards in a precise formation. Six of them revolving in a lozenge shape around two centrally placed cards, the one overlapping the other.

As a young woman, Marina had first encountered the Tarot cards in the makeshift booth of a garrulous fortune teller on a seaside pier. The tools of the teller's trade had also boasted a waving bronze pendulum on a piece of fraying satin ribbon and a clouded grease-streaked crystal ball that looked as though it could do with a good wash.

Marina had regarded the latter paraphernalia as little more than a joke. The cards, however, had provoked a prickling spark of curiosity, a tiny electric jolt of excitement. A twist of fear.

Such strange, arousing, arcane images she had seen spread before her on the teller's brown baize cloth. Lurid painted cartoons. Caricatures depicting commanding figures of ancient gypsy myths, with such evocative names as The Magician, The Hermit, The Lovers. The Fool and The High Priestess. The Hanged Man. Death.

Over the years, Marina had gradually come to an understanding of the messages hidden behind the picturesque surface of the cards. She had learned to connect with and decipher the different stories they recounted and foretold. Slowly, each card began to yield up its store of secrets.

Sometimes, Marina fancied that the cartoon figures and images could almost assume the power of a living presence. But this was a private and personal view, not to be shared with anyone else.

'See,' the fortune teller had declared to the young Marina, turning over the cards she had commanded her customer to select from the pack. 'The High Priestess! That's a good card, a wonderful sign.'

'Oh.' Marina had been cool and cynical. 'How so?'

'It means you're a person with a lot of intuition. You know things about the world, you can read people's characters.' She paused, drumming on the table with nicotine-stained fingers whilst Marina reflected that the teller might have a point. She was pretty sure she could read this particular woman's character like a book. The teller was nothing but a trickster and a charlatan. A trader on human gullibility.

'You'll be doing a lot of studying this coming year,' the teller said. 'Learning things. Things about people.'

Marina's bold confidence had suffered a slight set-back. It was the end of the summer of her twentieth year. She had been on the point of starting her final year as a psychology student at one of England's great civic universities. She took her studies very seriously. Worked long hours. And this year would be the hardest so far. Finals came at the end of it. Nine three-hour written examinations.

A great deal of study. A great deal to learn about people.

The teller had turned over two more cards. 'Now! Look at this. The Empress! My word, you're going to be a lucky lady.'

'Another good card?' Marina had asked, making sure to lace the remark with sarcasm, as by now she was finding herself caught up in the teller's obvious excitement.

'The Empress will bring you abundance, my pet. She will bring you love. A good deal of money. And children. Beautiful children to be a joy to you for all your life.' The teller smiled, triumphant as though she herself had arranged for all this good fortune to fall into Marina's lap.

Marina had sharpened up her wits. She knew from her studies that reading cards or tea leaves, looking into crystal balls and organizing one's life by the stars, failed in the main to meet the exacting standards of impartial and rigorous scientific enquiry.

She saw now how the teller's excitement was all manufactured, a commercial gimmick necessary to her trade. Her spiel was too smooth, too pat. She had memorized simple meanings to each card, and those were what she trotted out every time, regardless of the individual hopes and fears of the person who sat opposite her.

The individual client was of little interest to her. And why should they be? She could earn her five shillings easily enough by reciting a few lines in response to the cards she turned up. A sharp-eyed parrot with an ounce of wit could probably do as well.

Marina looked down at the cards. The third one, as yet ignored and unexplained, depicted a plump and vacant man staring out from the card with leery challenge. At his feet was a tiny toy-like dog, protective and wistful. Underneath the unappealing cartoon figure was his title, proclaimed in bold, flowing script. The Fool.

'And what about this? The Fool?' she demanded of the woman, angry now because for a moment she had allowed herself to be taken in. 'You're not going try to convince me this is a good card, are you? Surely it must contradict all you've said before?'

The teller jerked her head up and her cheap *diamanté* earrings flared with splinters of light. 'Don't you presume to doubt the cards. You think you know a lot, young woman. I can see that in your face. But it can dangerous to mock the cards. Oh, yes.'

'All right, then. Convince me. Give me a reason not to mock!' Marina sat back, arms folded over her breasts. Glinty and challenging.

'The Fool is not what you might think. He has depths. He brings possibilities.' She stared hard at Marina and the young woman's skin prickled with some strange unknown sensation.

26

'Such as?'

'Stepping out into a new future.'

'Hmm!'

The teller jabbed a menacing finger at her listener. 'This time next year you'll win a special prize, young lady. I can see a great hall full of people. They're applauding, wishing they were as clever as you. And you'll have money, too, riches and luxury.'

Marina told herself this was all so predictable. Simply feeding suckers what they wanted to hear.

As if the woman could read her thoughts she abruptly changed tack. 'But just you take care not to be tempted too easily. You can be headstrong, rush into things. It could lead to you into trouble.'

Something you could say about ninety-nine per cent of the population, Marina reassured herself, whilst becoming more unnerved by the minute.

Enough was enough. She got up to leave. 'Very interesting,' she told the Tarot reader smoothly with all the condescension she could call up.

'And this time next year you'll be married,' the woman said, as Marina swung back the curtain shrouding the entrance to the cabin and breathed in the clear sweet air beyond.

Marina had given a snort of irritated disbelief. And then, heart thudding, had broken into a run, putting as much space between herself and the silently speaking Tarot cards as she could manage.

The following year she had gained a First Class Honours degree, presented to her amidst much pomp and applause in the university's great hall. Very shortly afterwards, she had accepted the offer of a research post at Cambridge, and not long after that had impulsively married the irresistibly attractive leader of her team after a six-week courtship.

Then subsequently had learned a number of bitter lessons.

Today, on this grey Monday morning, embarking on her own Tarot reading, Marina looked with curiosity at the cards she had dealt herself. There was a small flutter in the heart region as she registered a spread reminiscent of the one she had seen on the pier thirty years before. The High Priestess, The Empress, The Fool, all three were once again in a position of prominence. And, lying beside them, two other highly significant cards: The Devil and Death.

For a moment she tensed, then schooled her body to relax.

The Death card used to put the wind up her when she first started Tarot reading. And indeed, she still viewed it as a card to be treated with caution and respect. But Marina had never carried out a reading where the Death card foretold the death of the person coming to the cards for an answer to their questions. Sometimes a close friend or relative of the questioner had died, but these had invariably been old people, already sick and weakened.

The Death card was not necessarily a bringer of doom, rather a foreteller of change. A messenger who spoke of casting off the old and building afresh. Not so much death, as rebirth.

A rebirth, thought Marina, crinkling her eyes and squinting down at the cards. For me? Can the time really be coming when I can pack in my dreary job selling rich pampered women absurdly expensive clothes and spend my days doing things I enjoy instead?

Death. A new start. A new job, then? Hah! She grimaced, mocking herself. She, Marina, a woman of fifty. At fifty it was hardly a glass ceiling of opportunity barring the way to a woman's success in the job market. More like a thicket of thorns.

She turned back to her spread. The Priestess. What was she doing here today? The Priestess: a patient gifted teacher, an aid to study. An intuitive mind, endowed with a knowledge of life. The Priestess presented one with the prospect of important life-influencing decisions to be made.

But there was The Empress next to her. A 'good' card, the creaky old fortune teller on the pier had said. But Marina had come to see the Empress figure in a rather less flattering light. An emblem of fecundity and abundance the Tarot wisdom said. A vamp, said Marina. A sybarite. A hard-boiled materialistic bitch.

And sitting smugly beside her, there was that wildest of all cards: The Devil. The embodiment of mischief. The master of temptation, entrapment and bondage.

The lurid image of the Devil, horned and claw-footed, grinned out at her, mocking her for enslavement to something or someone up to no good. The Devil tempted her with thoughts of passion, the dizzy infatuation of falling for a pretty face regardless of the character beneath. Oh, not a good card at all.

When Marina read the cards for other people, she liked to frame her analysis into a simple story to illuminate the meaning she foresaw. So what was the story here?

29

The High Priestess, that wise teacher, in the primary commanding position in the spread, told her that she was about to embark on some quest, some journey of discovery. Along the way was some unsuitable alliance, a lover of luxury and materialism. She was moving out into an uncertain, unknown future. There was a new start ahead, but danger. Infatuation with someone quite unsuitable. Bonds devilishly hard to break. And danger. Some terrible kind of danger.

Marina paused, chilled, suddenly burdened with foreboding. She sensed something dreadful lying ahead. How could she see The Fool, The Devil and Death cards together without seeing danger?

There was a sudden intense sensation of unease. What she had called up this morning with the cards was not good. In fact, it was positively disturbing.

She paused, sighing, frowning. Not only were the cards not encouraging, somehow they did not seem to fit properly either. The story they told her was cloudy and confused. Off beam.

In a rush of impatience, she swept the cards up and replaced them in their silk scarf.

You stupid woman, she told herself. Reading cards. Imbuing grotesque pictures on pieces of paper with life and significance.

It was nonsense. She knew that. Not in her heart of hearts, but in the scientific part of her mind which had been trained up like a mental athlete all those years ago.

She exclaimed out loud in exasperation.

Risk sprang up, eyeing her, a low growl of dismay in his throat. Risk hated her to be upset, could not bear his mistress to seem in danger of toppling from the pinnacle of goddess-like omnipotence on which he had placed her.

'I am growing into a crazy wrinkled old woman, who believes in mumbo-jumbo and engages in dialogues with her dog,' Marina told him.

Her firm tones elicited his full approval. Sensing that she was once again secure on her high lofty throne, he felt free to race into the front room and protest loudly at the effrontery of the neighbours, who were daring to exit from their own door and walk down their own path, separated from his own territory by no more than a few twigs of privet hedge.

Marina pursued him and clasped her hand around his yapping mouth, rendering him dumb. 'Shut up. You'll scare them off. And they look nice. I want them to be our friends.' She released his throbbing indignant muzzle and he looked up at her reproachfully, defiant growls still rumbling in his throat.

Marina stared out at her new neighbours with interest. The tall dark man, his sculpted classical features remote but in no way cold. His little girl, walking beside him with such grace, her face turned up to his, glowing with loyalty and affection.

This man is a tower, thought Marina. A tower of strength and and stability, a fortress and refuge for his defenceless dependent child.

Marina found herself strongly moved by the current of love flowing so transparently between this man and his daughter. And with that emotion came a sudden glinting flash of insight.

Of course! The message in the cards had not been meant for her at all. It was designed for her mysterious neighbour.

Sometimes it happened like that. You asked the cards a question and they were insistent on ignoring it and answering another one instead. Or answering a question for someone else.

She knew she was right. She felt it in the quickening of her pulse, the tiny flares of electricity that jabbed in her nerves. There was no doubt.

Watching the man steer the girl protectively onto the inner part of the pavement, safe from the traffic, Marina folded her long arms tightly around her chest and felt a chilling concern about what lay in store for him – and his innocent child.

CHAPTER 4

The room was fragrant with hothouse roses, dozens of them, crammed into ornate Chinese vases standing plump and dignified on a polished oak floor. It was a room of light and space, a room which managed to combine elegance with flamboyance – a riot of colour with a sensation of warmth and peace at its heart. There was a great sweep of windows looking out due south, creamy walls hung with brilliantly coloured rugs and huge gilded mirrors from centuries long past. Canary yellow curtains cascaded from ebony poles, the fabric spilling over onto the wooden boards like the spray from a mountain torrent. Cushions of finch green frolicked over sofas which had fat little rolls of cream velvet for arms, and crimson tassels for fingernails.

François paused in the doorway, surveying the scene. He had envisaged a prim little gathering, a handful of dedicated and earnest teachers drinking sherry and then departing for a hefty English Sunday lunch of roast pork and apple crumble. Instead, he was confronted by a merry swirling throng, sipping champagne and nibbling fragile canapés topped with shiny caviare, olive paste and other exotica.

33

'Come on, Daddy!' Leonore tugged at him.

Maybe I should have worn a tie, François thought, recalling the stiff pre-lunch cocktail parties in 1970s' Paris, when he had still been in short trousers and his mother had required him to be an immaculate accessory to her flawless chic.

He put a hand up to his open-neck black silk shirt and then ran it through his hair The thick tufts flew up like a ruffled eagle's feathers before settling over his forehead in soft spiky strands.

'Where's Miss Peach?' Leonore exclaimed impatiently, standing on tip-toe and peering through the laughing crowd. 'I can't see her!'

She took a glass of orange juice from a tray deftly balanced on one hand by a young waiter, picturesque in satin-backed stripey waistcoat and black bow tie. From the tray supported on this young conjurer's other hand, she selected a stick skewering a central gherkin, wrapped around with anchovy fillets. 'I wish I could see Miss Peach,' she said, licking the salty skin of the anchovy with a pink tongue.

'She'll appear soon enough,' François reassured her, accepting a glass of champagne from the waiter following on. Automatically he dipped his nose to the rim of the glass, inhaling the bouquet before he drank. Eyes, nose and taste buds told him that this was no good imitation. This was the real thing: vintage champagne, rich and buttery, voluptuous and yet refined. Classy and cool with an acidy sting in its tail.

He gave a twisted smile, observing the rich, pampered company casually swilling down this nectar, and reminding himself that a third of the world's population had never even sampled the luxury of using a telephone. And yet that thought in no way diminished the beauty of the wine in his glass. Holding it up against the stream of southern light, he was astonished at its clear and simple purity.

A thing of beauty is a joy forever.

He drew in a long breath, glanced down and laid a hand briefly on Leonore's warm glossy head after which he helped himself to a canapé of inky squid, nestling in a lake of avocado mousse. Placing it reverently on his plate, he surveyed it with interest. A little work of art. Edible still life.

'Snacks for sparrows,' a voice chimed in his ear.

François turned. The speaker confronting him had startlingly blue eyes gleaming from a shaggy mane of yellow blond hair. There was a lazy grin on the classically regular features, and yet the expression in the eyes was unmistakably challenging.

François found himself straightening his spine, holding his body still, bracing himself internally. It was a gesture of automatic defence he could readily discern in others; children in a playground, dogs in a park, politicians in a debate. A response he had captured on film countless times.

He looked around the glossy assembly. The cut of the mens' shirts was unmistakably expensive, the women were wrapped up in silk and suede. They stood in their little groups for no more than a few minutes at a time, forever moving on to seek new contacts. They reminded him of shoal of restless tropical fish. They reminded him of the kind of people who turned up at Poppy's gallery.

35

'Nothing so mundane as sparrows,' François commented, swinging round and staring hard into the blue eyes. 'Peacocks, perhaps?'

The blond man threw back his head and laughed. 'Fair point.' He flung out an arm, almost toppling an approaching waiter. With a scoop of one large capable hand, he transferred the remaining contents of the tray onto his plate. 'Need to stock up, it could be sometime before the next waiter's along,' he commented. 'They're like London buses, are waiters, hunt in packs.'

François gave a faint smile for the sake of politeness. He could feel the tightness in his lips and disliked himself for his inablility to relax and go along with whatever flow was in progress.

'Have you known Zoe long?' the blond man asked.

'Who's Zoe?' asked François.

The blue gaze sharpened for a moment. 'Our hostess.'

'Ah! Miss Peach.'

'The very same!' The blond man's voice had slowed to a laconic drawl and François fancied his glinting eyes said, *Keep off*.

'Miss Peach!' Leonore cried suddenly, shifting from one foot to the other in excitement. 'Miss Peach. I'm here!' She launched herself forward like a small missile. An urgent missile in a flowery tunic, her hair gleaming like the pearly pelt of a beaver pup.

Miss Peach bent down and kissed the top of Leonore's head. Her arms, slender and quickly darting, went around the child. 'Leonore. My sweet little love!' she exclaimed.

The hairs at the nape of François's neck prickled like those of threatened dog. Who was this young woman to

36

call Leonore her sweet little love? Such an affectation. Hypocritical. Gushing and false.

My sweet little love. It was what Poppy had always called their daughter. And look where that had led. Leonore rarely saw her mother from one autumn to the next spring.

His observant gaze moved over Miss Peach, coolly appraising. As a professional photographer, François was always at work in his head, assessing a potential subject, noting features that would become luminous on film, planning a composition.

There was something instantly vivid and intense about this gazelle-like woman. It was not a mere question of richness of colour: the sable hair cut in starkly geometric style, the porcelain pale skin, the flash of flirtatious red nails. There was some inner quality of energy, some taut and fizzing quality that intrigued him.

And all of this was conveyed in the woman's gestures and body posture, for he hadn't yet seen her face. That was still bent towards Leonore, who was looking back with an animation it warmed François's heart to see.

'Zoe loves kids,' the blond man commented to François, chummy and man to man. 'I suppose she has to, teaching the little devils for hours at a time. It would drive me simply mad.'

François could believe it. He guessed that guns, claret and labradors would be much more in blue eyes' line of country. He gave a twisted smile. There was something about this man which was beginning to grate more than he liked to admit.

'Put the kid down, Zoe, and come and give some attention to the rest of your guests! Let me do the

37

honours.' The speaker turned to François, beaming and supremely confident. He raised beautifully curved and questioning eyebrows.

'Rogier. François Rogier,' François volunteered quietly.

'Charles.' No other name was offered. 'Zoe! Come on! Talk to the grown-ups. Meet François.' He leaned across and took the woman's arm. He was all smiles and gaiety, utterly in command.

Zoe Peach detached herself with reluctance from Leonore and put her head up.

François stared down, registering a heart-shaped face and huge slanting eyes. Zoe Peach was all cheek-bones and fraily transluscent skin. Her hair dipped and swung as she tilted her head, and her long silver earrings glinted like moving water.

François found himself on the point of reaching for his camera in an entirely automatic gesture. But he had left it at home. Leonore had been quite firm on that point. He had not even been permitted to put it in the car.

Those lips, he thought, narrowing his eyes in assessment. So curiously tender and childlike. Bare of any scrap of lipstick, they were the soft fleshy pink of nature and the lower lip was disproportionately full and slightly puckered like that of a child. It gave her face an air of vulnerability, which was probably entirely spurious, yet utterly alluring.

But it was her eyes which claimed and held him. Perfect ovals, lustrous and haunting. And of a most unusual and compelling aquamarine.

Leonore's Miss Peach was, in a word, visually mesmerizing.

François found himself vaguely jarred. He had expected a brisk bright young person, competent and professional. Someone he would take to in a detached kind of way, grateful for her efforts to bring out his daughter's stifled linguistic potential.

He had not expected someone who would – stir him.

His concentration faltered. A half-eaten canapé slid from his plate and Zoe Peach bent to pick it up.

The neckline of her Persian blue satin shirt fell open. He tried to pull his eyes away. But it was impossible to ignore the creamy drop of her breasts, the rosy dark tips of the nipples standing out against the white lace of her plunging bra.

Gazing down on this vividly female image brought a responding ache to his groin, sweet and sharp. He looked away, cursing himself, shocked by this instant surge of animal desire.

Crouched on one iridescently stockinged knee, Zoe Peach tilted her chin and glanced straight up into his eyes. There was a smile of welcome on her face, a smile of amusement, too, at the ridiculousness of the situation: a sophisticated young hostess grubbing around on the floor for flakes of squashed pastry and smoked salmon. Kneeling at the feet of one of her male guests.

François pulled himself together, instructed his hormones to behave themselves and extended a hand of greeting.

Her hand, coming up to meet his, suddenly stilled and fell away. There was a throbbing pause. The inky pupils of her eyes enlarged. Her gaze linked in with his own and he had an image of buried memories struggling to surface.

He saw that the breath was coming into her chest in tiny painful gasps and for a moment he feared she was on the point of keeling over limp and prone.

He reached down, placed his hands under her armpits and gently brought her into an upright position. She stared up at him, her lips parted slightly. The expression in her eyes baffled him, awakening prickles of unease.

François saw that Leonore was watching Miss Peach anxiously. There was that troubled look in her eyes he used to see just after Poppy left. *Is it my fault?* Leonore had the sensitivity of a highly tuned radio receiver, picking up and analysing the faintest signals of human emotion.

Charles, in contrast, seemed to have noticed very little on that score. Grabbing fresh glasses from a passing tray, he placed one in Zoe's hand, drained the other one and helped himself to a second. 'This girl serves the best champagne north of the Thames,' he told François, grinning like a cat in a dairy.

François fancied that, for 'this girl', the perceptive listener should subsitute 'my girl'. Charlie Whoever-he-was was eager to stake out the ground around the intriguing Zoe Peach. No subtleties here. The message was loud and clear. *Keep off!*

Zoe Peach had closed her eyes momentarily. She was taking very deep breaths, holding them and then exhaling slowly. Opening her eyes once more, she appeared to have overcome whatever feelings had disturbed her. She smiled brightly, her eyes dancing with life and merriment. 'Leonore, I mustn't forget to tell your daddy how well you're getting on with your French.'

'I've noticed,' said François. 'Thank you.'

Zoe Peach went on to elaborate a little. Technical points on the acquisition of language. The need to build on the learning in stages, consolidating each new task and idea through a variety of interesting exercises.

François attended carefully. He began to form the idea that under the zippy, colourful exterior there seemed to be a razor-sharp intellect. It struck him that this young woman was not what she seemed, that she was somehow cloaking the essence of her personality behind a vividly painted screen of glamour.

Yet even as the competent professional words proceeded from her sweet full mouth, he had the impression that a part of her mind was preoccupied with something else. In addition, he was disconcertingly convinced that it had something to do with him.

Her eyes would mostly avoid his. Then suddenly her glance would connect up straight into his pupils and with that connection would come a shock, because behind her eyes was a silent scream of pain.

François was not a fanciful man. Quite the opposite. He had always regarded himself as one of life's pragmatists. Someone who got on with the here and now, the problems that were out in the open to be seen, assessed and tackled.

But looking down at the vivid and outwardly composed Zoe Peach, he was convinced that he was in the presence of some stirring inner turmoil.

Leonore stood between the two of them, listening with an expression of great concentration. As Miss Peach drew to the conclusion of her enthusiastic thumbnail sketch, Leonore scratched the tip of her nose and looked thoughtful. But before she could voice the question that was forming on her lips, Charles took Zoe firmly by the arm and bore her away to be swallowed up once again in the swirl of her guests.

François thought it was time to leave. He felt suddenly tired, disinclined to mingle.

'Let's go to your favourite Italian reataurant, get a pizza inside us,' he said to Leonore.

'Tagliatelle,' said Leonore. 'The green sort. With red peppers in the sauce.'

'Hot chocolate fudge cake to follow,' said François.

'Pineapple with cream,' said Leonore.

They went down the broad white steps between the stately columns. A father and his daughter. Outwardly laughing and carefree, yet in their inner hearts fiercely clinging to each other in their separarate loneliness.

In the busy cosy reataurant, François placed their order and then sat back, watching Leonore sipping fresh lemon juice through a curly straw. She was as neat and fastidious as an oriental cat, neither spilling nor dribbling a drop.

Like Leonore's, his mind was still at Zoe Peach's very smart party. Questions revolved slowly in his head. The issue of why a young woman, surrounded by all the trappings of seemingly considerable wealth, should spend her days tutoring the more needy members of the school population? The question of why that woman seemed to enjoy the company of a lustily macho escort who appeared to be somewhat challenged in the human sensitivity area?

But those issues, however intriguing, were no more than idle speculations. There was one central puzzle of

42

much greater significance to which his thoughts kept returning. A puzzle that became increasingly disturbing the more he examined it.

The question of why the sight of him, François Rogier, should arouse such naked terror in a woman who had never set eyes on him before.

CHAPTER 5

'Allow me to take you away from all this,' proclaimed Charles, surveying the aftermath of Zoe's lavish hospitality with a grimace. Lounging on one of her excellently comfortable sofas, he was wondering how the hell he was going to persuade her to come out on a date with him. It was two weeks since their auspicious bumping into each other in Fiumicino's departure complex; still she was resisting anything beyond a quick drink at the local wine bar after she finished work. And even then he'd virtually had to kidnap her before she'd agreed.

'It's Sunday,' said Zoe.

'What of it?' Charles raised his long legs to enable one of the catering firm's minions to insert a carpet sweeeper in the space beneath.

'Once upon a time it was a day of rest.' Her words were lightly tossed out. Noncommital.

Charles frowned. He was never quite sure what to make of Zoe's clipped comments. For instance, her latter remark was probably nothing more than a casual, automatic response to his own equally casual remark. On the other hand, she could be making a point: mocking the ever-more liberal customs of an age where every day was

44

a potential for profit; mocking those who supported such customs; mocking those who resisted; or simply mocking *him*.

'Rest is for old has-beens,' he told her. 'The great city of London never sleeps. There's a whole feast of entertainment out there, just waiting to delight us.'

She smiled. She shook her head.

Charles felt like he used to as a little boy when someone managed to thwart him. He reflected that it was quite a considerable time since anyone had truly thwarted him. The feeling was not good.

Zoe gave a little sigh. She shook off her strappy platform shoes and tucked her gazelle-like legs beneath her.

Charles tried to persuade himself this was a good sign. Discarding any items of clothing was always a good sign in women. But this gesture of shoe removing was encouragingly domestic and intimate, calling up the prospect of a charming 'night in', snuggling together by the fire and nibbling toast. Well, maybe not toast. That rather reminded him of various nannies and their supper-time snacks. He hurriedly changed the menu to malt whisky and a few of the left-over salmon canapés.

Zoe Peach was the most gorgeous girl he'd laid eyes on in months. No trace of the bimbo about her, yet not a raving intellectual either. At least she hadn't started reading Shakespeare to him yet, which was what had driven him from the bosom and bed of his last girlfriend. 'Well, if you don't fancy going out, what *would* you like?' he asked with elaborate patience.

For you to go away and leave me in peace, thought Zoe. She was exhausted. She was like a puppet whose stuffing had been removed before its poor husk was tossed to one side.

She had a full programme of teaching the next day. Four different groups of different children in four very different schools. And she had not yet completed her preparation. Of course, she could give her language tutorials standing on her head. But that wasn't the point. Children learned best when they were most motivated, which meant most stimulated. One had to feed them the information in the most entertaining way possible. And *that* required planning.

'Well?' Charles insisted.

'I'm whacked.' she told him gently. 'Go find someone more frisky and obliging to play with, Charles.'

He paused, considered. Eventually he stood up, finally realizing that he was not going to get his own way. Not tonight, at least. 'Tomorrow, then,' he decreed. 'Dinner. The theatre. Drinks afterwards.'

Zoe sighed.

'We are friends, aren't we?' Charles said, winning and boyish, his thick yellow forelock lurching becomingly over one eyebrow.

She nodded.

'It must have been fate we met like that,' he said, standing over her, inclining his body slightly. 'In deeply romantic Rome. Drawn together over the purchase of two litres of best malt whisky.'

Another nod.

He put his face down to hers, put on his most seductive voice. 'On the plane, I really got the feeling there was something going between us.' He recalled her delicate body in his arms, so fragile yet so tense. Tantalizingly desirable.

46

Zoe held herself rigid. 'I was grateful for your help,' she said stiffly.

He was baffled. Intrigued. He had never met a woman like this; one who seemed untouched by his sexual magnetism. He prided himself on the languid ease with which he attracted women. They fell into his arms and his bed like skittles. But Zoe Peach was showing no sign of being skittled. Neither was she furiously resisting, a condition which, in his view, was always indicative of a pretty swift and total capitulation to follow on.

Maybe she was a dyke. The idea kept crossing his mind, so desperate was he to find a reason for this sudden decline in his pulling power. He felt like a six-cylinder hot performance car that has had its engine stolen.

Staring now into the cleft of her blouse, inhaling the spicy peppery fragrance which rose up from her, he knew for sure that her failure to fall under his spell was nothing to do with a want of femininity. Zoe Peach was 22-carat solid female.

He looked down at her, a still silent figure, her eyes staring ahead, lost in some world of her own.

Charles was suddenly impatient. His mind started running through the list of companions he could call up on his mobile from the car.

Whatever thoughts Zoe Peach was thinking, they didn't look too jolly. 'I'm off,' he said. 'I'll call you in the morning.'

She looked up. Smiled absently.

Charles touched the crown of her head. 'Penny for them,' he said lightly, magnificently misjudging the mood.

* * *

47

Zoe stretched. Her left leg was numb; it felt as huge as a punch bag. As she rubbed it, the veins crawled and tingled with the renewal of the blood supply.

She looked at her watch. Half-past eight. It was two hours since Charles had left. She had been sitting on the sofa for a whole two hours doing nothing, half-awake, half-drowsing. Her mind had been swimming with thoughts of the past, speculation about the future.

Since the night of the terrifying dream on the plane, she had found herself inhabiting a new internal world. Fanciful notions of tragedy and disaster swarmed through her head like glinting shoals of killer fish. Every day she listened with anxiety to the news bulletins on her car radio, scanned the newspapers from cover to cover. Every day she trembled to learn of some shocking air disaster that would confirm the prediction of her dream. And she was convinced that it *was* a prediction. The image had been so powerful, so vivid. It must surely have been sent as some kind of warning.

But for who? She had been afraid for herself at first, terrified as the plane from Fiumicino came in to land at Heathrow. She vaguely recalled going so far as to clutch violently at Charles Pym, thus unleashing another set of problems to deal with. He had smiled at her with such intimacy. 'You're safe with me,' he'd murmured, all velvet charm.

But the landing had been as smooth as butter, and it had dawned on her that maybe the dream was not a purely selfish omen. The more she thought about in the days that followed, the more she had become convinced that the dream was not for her at all, but a warning for someone else. Maybe not just one person, maybe the whole crew and passenger population of some huge aircraft. She felt a need to take action. Face her responsibilities. Warn someone.

She could hardly sleep at nights, racked with indecision as to what she should do. She had tentatively broached the issue of premonitions in the staff room of one of the schools she visited, vaguely hoping for some guidance. But there had been a general consensus that 'all that kind of thing' was merely hysterical nonsense cooked up by charlatans or pathetic neurotics. There had been a good deal of raucous laughter and tales of dotty old aunts who went to clairvoyants and seances and thought they saw spirits.

Zoe had realized the scepticism and opposition she would arouse by sharing her experience with those who had no knowledge or belief in the power of the human mind.

After a week or so of indecision she had found herself drained and weary, like someone struggling against some unknown, untreatable infection. She had considered cancelling her party. But that would have been such a negative thing to do. And what would have been the point? She always gave a party in the last week of February. That had been the time of her mother's birthday. Her sweet, scatty, indulged mother who had made a lifetime's work of giving parties.

In fact, the party had helped. At first, anyway. Being with her friends, circulating, laughing, playing the role of the perfect hostess. For an hour or so, her mind had been so full of the fluffy logistics of feeding and amusing fifty or so people that it had emptied itself of those heavy images of tragedy and death.

And then François Rogier had appeared and her mind had screamed back into painful alertness. Her stomach had lurched and recoiled, her veins had fizzed with electricity.

It had never occurred to her that the crystal-sharp image of the man in her dream would translate itself into reality. She had thought of that figure as a symbol. Some kind of healing icon, sent to deal with the aftermath of a tragedy. To salvage and comfort.

Now, it seemed that perhaps François Rogier himself might be the one at risk. Or perhaps Leonore. She groaned out loud. No, not Leonore. Please, God! Not sweet, lovable little Leonore.

She sprang up. There had been enough mental agonizing. Enough procrastination. She went through into the hallway and picked up the fat directory of yellow pages.

Slowly her finger slid down the lines of print.

CHAPTER 6

Marina heard sounds through the kitchen wall. Tiny snuffly sounds, augmented by an occasional fluty wail.

'Damn!' she said, tearing at a triangle of blackened and scraped toast, and chewing determinedly. Internal chompings temporarily cancelled external disturbances.

But once the toast was dispensed with, there was no way of avoiding the sad little sonata proceeding next door.

Marina sighed. She didn't want to hear a child crying in distress. Not this morning, or next week, or ever. She was becoming far too sensitive. In her younger days, she had rarely given a thought to the pathos of life: people sleeping on park benches, children going without hot dinners or affection, dogs flung from cars on to motorways. And when she had reflected, it had been in a rational, practical kind of way. Think about it, do what you can to help, forget about it.

Nowadays she couldn't even watch the corniest old films on TV or hear a snatch of Mozart's *Magic Flute* without dissolving into tears.

She laid her head against the wall which divided her kitchen from the one next door. Yes. There was definitely a child crying on the other side. She supposed there was no way the child could be any other than that glowing, swan-like little girl who walked down the path each morning, gazing adoringly up at her father.

Marina sighed again, more heavily. She would have to go round and check things out. One couldn't ignore the grim facts of children ending up neglected, beaten, starved or murdered, owing to the prim connivance of neighbours who preferred to turn the other ear rather than risk transgressing the boundaries of politeness and invading the sacred sanctity of *the family*.

And then, of course, regarding this particular family, there was the question of what the cards kept telling her.

'Hell!' said Marina very loudly, causing Risk to spring up from the cushioned comfort of his shamefully luxurious basket and launch into a machine-gun burst of barking.

'Oh for God's sake!' Marina grumbled, grabbing her keys and trying to sprint down the hallway before he had the chance to grab her hem in his routine efforts to prevent her reaching the outer door and abandoning him.

She shook him off, but his teeth had already made a small rip in the black cloth. She bent down and tapped his nose. '*Magic Flute!*' she whispered to him, narrowing her eyes in threat.

Risk stiffened. He laid his ears back, then turned and slunk away back to the kitchen.

'Just so you know who's boss,' Marina said, sliding around the door, already planning what little treat she would give him when she got back.

Standing and confronting the front door of her next-door neighbour's house, she felt an absurd reticence about ringing the bell or banging on the wood. Impulsively, she stepped sideways and peeped furtively into the front room window.

A man's puzzled face stared back at her.

Marina's heart trundled a little more energetically than usual. She smiled, raised her hand and waved. It was a ridiculous gesture in the circumstances, the brief shivery oscillation perfected by the older royals.

The man appeared at the door. 'Good morning,' he said pleasantly.

Seen close to, he seemed tremendously tall and impressive. And his eye contact was impressively unswerving. Marina took to him instantly. She told herself that this man couldn't possibly be a bully or a heartless child molester, knowing full well that it was precisely such crude and sentimental assessments that allowed the most horrific crimes to flourish unfettered.

'Please – do come in,' he said. It was clear he had recognized her as his neighbour.

She followed him meekly down the hallway, marvelling that a house which was the mirror-image of hers could project such a different atmosphere. Drinking in the dazzling light and space, she made an instant decision to redecorate her own hallway in lovely bright pinks and creams and chuck out all her dusty memorabilia.

He took her into the front room. Unlike her own, which was clogged with a 1920s' boudoir piano and huge stereo speakers that could serve an ocean liner, this room was all air and empty corners.

I'm smothered by the clutter of the years, thought Marina. In my house and in my head. Maybe my heart too.

'Would you like coffee?' her neighbour asked.

She hesitated. Cosy socializing hadn't been on her agenda.

'I've been meaning to make some,' he explained, 'but my daughter's been crying in the kitchen and I thought it was tactful to leave her on her own.'

'Ah.' Marina looked at him with intense interest. 'Yes, I heard her. That's why I came,' she said quietly.

His soft dark eyes became brittle with wariness and he no longer looked so friendly. She had an ugly vision of herself seen through his eyes: an intruder, a trespasser on delicate ground which had nothing to do with child abuse or neglect.

Years ago she would have been excruciated by this situation, squirming with hot embarrassment and desperate to get away as fast as possible. Today she felt no social unease, merely a growing curiosity. But then, in the days of her youth, she had felt and done all kinds of things entirely alien to her now. Twenty years ago she had been inspired to cut her husband's clothes into jigsaw-like fragments and dump them outside his tutorial room in black bin-liner bags.

'I'm sorry to seem interfering,' she said. 'I just hate to think of people being unhappy.'

'Better to interfere than turn a deaf ear,' he said correctly.

'Yes. I do believe it is.'

He jabbed his long fingers against his forehead and pulled them through his hair in a swift savage movement. 'My little girl rarely cries. Just sometimes she needs to let go. I suppose it's because her mother . . .' He paused. 'I suppose it's because she misses her mother. I certainly do.' He gave a Gallic shrug and departed to the kitchen.

Marina sucked in these drops of information with the eagerness of one daily condemned to hearing very little besides the droning of understimulated women on the subjects of their hormone therapy, their brilliant children and their bunions.

So! It was as she had suspected – her neighbour had no wife. He was a man abandoned. But in what circumstances? Had his wife died tragically young? Had she gone off to some far-flung place to 'find herself' – very popular amongst the young? Or had she simply gone off with a new lover? It was hard to imagine a man magnetic enough to be a serious rival to her neighbour. But then, love was no respecter of reason.

This mateless man, Marina thought fancifully, hearing the rush of water and the rattle of a kettle lid, has such style about him, such refinement and restraint. He is like an exquisite marble statue poised on a lonely pedestal. Smiling at her own shameless romanticism, she closed her eyes and pictured him thus, his little girl nestling at his feet.

She then reminded herself of her cards' insistent message that he was about to topple off. The thought made her wince. Those bloody cards; she wished she could kick them into the middle of the next millennium.

The little girl came in, silent and shoeless. Her eyes were shiny-rimmed and pink like an albino rabbit. She smiled up bravely at Marina. 'You live next door, don't you? Your dog's always barking.'

'I'm sorry.'

'I like dogs.' She regarded Marina with an air of taking in every tiny detail. 'I'm Leonore Rogier and my daddy's

55

name is François. When I'm bigger we're going to have a labradog – dor,' she corrected herself.

Marina gave this some serious consideration. 'My dog's got a tail rather like a labrador.'

'What's the rest of him like?'

'Most peculiar. Would you like to meet him?'

Leonore nodded vigorously. And then she smiled. The room seemed to grow brighter.

François Rogier produced excellent coffee and offered spiced biscuits that appeared home-made but must surely have come from a local delicatessen. The men in Marina's life had always been totally helpless in the face of puzzling things like raw flour and an oven.

'Daddy made these,' Leonore volunteered obligingly to end further speculation. 'Sometimes he puts faces on made of icing.' She looked at her father and smiled, both child-like and maternal.

She might as well have said, *My daddy's the best in the world*. The emotion was utterly transparent.

François Rogier flashed Marina a glance. *There now, are you satisfied?*

Marina relaxed. She dipped a biscuit in her coffee and felt her day much brightened by these proceedings. She undid the ties of her black Victorian cloak, procured with much wheedling from the stern wardrobe mistress of a dying theatre twenty years before, and let Leonore try it on.

Whilst Leonore strutted and swirled, she and François swapped views on the local neighbourhood: the best shops for crusty bread, the most likely places to find unlikely herbs, the restaurants they had sampled recently. They spoke in careful sentences, neither one of

56

them inclined to betray too much of themselves.

He told her that he was a freelance photographer. Most of his work was taken by newspapers and magazines, but he co-operated on book projects as well. Biographies, travel diaries.

'And you?' he enquired politely.

'Fashion consultant,' she told him.

'Ah.' He nodded.

'Translated, that means shop assistant,' she explained. 'I spend my days helping women to undo and do up zips and lying shamelessly about how much the clothes on our racks suit them.'

Now he smiled.

There was a time when things were very different, she thought, suddenly wistful. *But I had my chance. My mistakes were all my own. And now, after everything, I think I'm basically happy again.*

She stood up. She thanked François Rogier for his hospitality and then took Leonore back to her own house to meet Risk.

'His breath smells of fish,' said Leonore, sitting up against one of the piano legs with a dopey-looking Risk lying between her legs, paws scratching the air as she tickled his cream and ginger tummy. She bent down. 'And his coat smells too. All lovely and doggy. I wish he was mine.'

'Think of all the barking,' said Marina.

'We wouldn't mind,' said Leonore.

'You and Daddy?'

'Mmm.' Leonore grasped one of Risk's paws and kissed it. 'I don't think my mummy would like a dog,' she said.

'Very sensible,' agreed Marina. 'They lie on your bed when you're not looking and chew the heels off your shoes and eat your letters.'

Leonore's eyes registered each of these remarks and then she said, 'My mummy's going to be married again.'

Marina heard the solemnity in the child's voice, the tremor behind the outer calm.

'To Liam,' Leonore said.

Marina drew in a long silent breath, feeling she was in the presence of something awesome here. She considered things she might say in response and then decided that they were both trite and unnecessary.

There was a long pause. Leonore stroked Risk's ears with great concentration and tenderness. 'I've got an invitation,' she said. 'Daddy's got one, too.'

'To the wedding?'

Leonore nodded. 'It's in New York. That's where Mummy lives.' She moved her hand over Risk's belly in long sweeps and he closed his eyes in bliss. 'It takes a long time to get there. You can watch videos on the plane.'

Marina's body jerked. Air travel, flying. The whole incredible idea of being enclosed in a steel box thousands of feet up in the sky scared her to death. It always had. And when a fellow student had been killed flying out to Cuba to work with abandoned children (everyone had warned she'd get herself shot for meddling with political dynamite) she had felt some grim justification for her irrational terror.

A flight, she thought. Little Leonore and her intriguing enigmatic father. Her pulse quickened. *A quest, a journey, danger . . .*

58

Dear God!

Risk turned his head and looked at his mistress. Rolling over onto his front and staggering clumsily to his paws, he moved to stand beside her, leaning his head against her leg.

'He loves you very much,' said Leonore, impressed. 'If I come to visit a lot, will he love me a bit, too?'

'Definitely. He's a dog with the most superior of tastes,' said Marina. 'And you must visit as much as you like. I get lonely sometimes on my own.'

'I like your house,' said Leonore, looking around her. 'Lots of old things.'

'Yes. Me for one,' Marina agreed.

Leonore observed her with new interest. She made no attempt to contradict the remark.

Curious, she approached the tottering pile of long-playing records stacked on the floor near the 1970s' stereo equipment, which Marina realized must look ancient and totally baffling to a child. The equipment had been Colin's pride and joy. Like everything which took his interest, he must have the best, the most sensitive, esoteric, prestigious on offer. Not for Colin the instant gratification of nipping into the local electrical shop and buying a ready-made packaged sound system. His precious equipment had been assembled after months of painstaking research, scouring the hi-fi magazines for technical reviews, selecting each separate piece of equipment.

The complete system had been a technological work of art. A miraculous scientific symphony of woofers and tweeters, costing a fortune.

She laid her hand on the plastic cover guarding the

precious turntable. Ah yes, this system had been Colin's pride and joy. Until a year or two had passed and technology had advanced and he had needed to update it all.

Marina was painfully aware that the only reason for allowing her mind to race through all this past garbage was solely to keep it from racing through the image of Leonore and François climbing innocently into a plane with the intention of crossing the Atlantic.

A part of her desperately wanted to recall the details of the Tarot reading which had first drawn her full attention to her neighbours. Another part shied away from the details like a horse from a dangerous hurdle.

A quest, a journey. Danger.

'*The Magic Flute,*' Leonore read from the record sleeve lying on the top of the heaped pile. She traced her finger over the evocative cover picture of a white-columned palace standing out against a navy starred sky. Each column was decorated with the body and head of a most evil and ferocious-looking beast.

'It's music,' Marina explained. 'A story with music and singing.'

'Is it frightening?' Leonore's finger tentatively laid itself against a monster's jaws.

'Very. If I put it on, Risk will run upstairs and hide under the bed.'

'Why?'

'Because those fierce creatures on the picture sometimes roar and howl on the record and it terrifies him out of his wits.'

'Poor Risk! Don't put it on.'

'I hardly ever do. In fact, I only have to tell him

I'm thinking about it and he starts behaving like an angel.'

Leonore took time to consider this fully. She glanced at some of the other record sleeves but they didn't they seem to hold the allure of *The Magic Flute*. 'I think I'll go back to Daddy now,' she said. 'Can I come again soon?'

'Of course. Daddy'll be lonely without you,' Marina said drily.

Leonore looked up at her. Marina saw that her eyes were troubled and heavy with the burdens of a child's responsibility for the happiness of their parents. She cursed herself for the stupidly thoughtless remark.

'Goodbye,' Leonore said from the step. She turned away, then twisted back. 'When you get *much* too old,' she said with great kindness, 'as old as my *grandpère* who lives in France, I'll look after Risk for you.'

CHAPTER 7

A few miles away in Covent Garden, Zoe descended the iron-railed stone steps leading to the basement apartment of a tall Georgian house. The shiny brass plate beside the door said simply: Theodore Dowlan – Consultations exclusively by appointment.

The advertisment in the yellow pages had been rather more evocative. 'Clairvoyant, palmist and healer', it had proclaimed. 'Serious, genuine readings undertaken for discerning individual clients. Daytime and evening appointments available.'

She pressed the old-fashioned brass bell, thinking that it seemed rather incongruous in this up-to-the-minute street where every other door was guarded by an entry-phone system.

But she supposed clairvoyants worth their salt would have no need of one.

It was the kind of thought which would normally have made her laugh, but today she was jagged and uncertain. Hungry for reassurance. Standing outside this place of mystery, she found herself sickeningly fearful of sinking deeper into the sucking sands of a fear that seemed both outside of herself and deep within. Totally out of her control.

A man opened the door. Smallish, dapperly suited, balding, with a neat pointed nose and beard, he projected an image quite the opposite of what she had vaguely expected.

'Miss Peach? Do come in.' He took her through a small lobby into a room overlooking the garden at the back of the house.

He seated himself behind a huge gleaming desk and gestured to her to sit opposite him.

This must be him, thought Zoe, still with the feeling that the man in front of her was some kind of butler or secretary and that the real Theodore Dowland would soon materialize, tall, inscrutable and prophet-like, to displace him.

'You're filled with nervous tension,' he told her. 'You were born under the Zodiac sign of Aquarius, weren't you? Artistic, temperamental, imaginative, sometimes too much so for your own good?'

She nodded dumbly. 'Yes. How did you know that?' she wondered, alarmed.

He ignored the question and continued with his theme. 'You have internal scars,' he told her.

Zoe gaped at him and felt her mouth dry.

'You have known great sadness in your life. Yes?'

'Yes.' She felt transfixed, an animal staring into the eyes of its pursuer.

'Don't be afraid,' he told her. He placed his fingers together and lowered his head a little. Zoe had an impression of some intense internal concentration taking place. 'I see the sadness connected to your parents,' he said eventually. He looked at her, his eyes sharp.

Zoe licked her lips. Pressed them together.

'Your mother is dead,' he said.

She nodded, feeling the colour leave her face.

'And your father, too. Yes?'

'Yes.' *How did he know? Oh God!*

'You're alone in the world.'

'No!' Her protest was hot and genuine. 'I have lots of friends – ' She stopped short. She mentally stood back, suddenly able to see herself through eyes other than her own. She saw her busy professional life, her full social life. Her extensive travelling. People revolving around her constantly. Not a moment permitted for loneliness to rear itself and swallow her up.

He nodded. She had the feeling he did not believe her.

'What kind of reading did you come for?' he asked, spreading his hands and laying them palm down on the leather top of his desk.

'Reading?'

He gave a patient smile. 'I read cards. I read palms. I consult a crystal ball. Some clients have a preference for one or other particular mode of getting in touch with their inner psyche.'

Zoe swallowed. 'I don't really know. I don't know much about – this kind of thing . . .'

He looked at her thoughtfully. 'I can tell you're speaking what you believe to be the truth. But I would suggest otherwise.'

'What?'

'You may know nothing about the world of the occult and all its maps and pathways. But I would suggest that you have a considerable unconscious capacity for psychic divination yourself.'

'Oh, God!' Zoe groaned. She looked around her

helplessly, as though longing to escape.

'No, don't fight it. Let yourself be soft and pliant. Be steady in your inner self,' he said soothingly. 'Be calm and draw on your spiritual strength.'

She breathed deeply. 'What makes you say I have psychic powers?' she demanded.

'You have an aura around you,' he said simply.

'That means nothing to me.'

'Let me explain. Each individual transmits his or her own essence into the outer world. An essence in psychic terms is perhaps what most people would call the personality or the unique chemistry of an individual, as demonstrated through their physical, mental and emotional characteristics.'

'Yes. I understand. Go on.'

'You carry a powerful aura of secret knowledge. I could see it around you as soon as I saw you standing outside. I could sense it as you followed me into this room. And I can feel it now.' He paused. 'Psychic power is not a force of evil. There is no need to be frightened of it.'

Oh, yes, there is, she thought. She wondered how much he could see of her inner fears. One moment she had an unnerving conviction that he could see and understand everything about her. The next she was convinced that the whole set-up in this luxurious consulting room was a sham. A very clever, very professionally managed and convincing sham. But total falsehood, nevertheless.

'You're dressed in purple,' he commented softly. 'Purple is an unusual choice of colour for a young person. In fact, it's a colour rarely worn in modern times. Look around you when you go out and you'll see for yourself.'

'I love colour,' she said, feeling a vague need to make a protest. 'Reds, pinks, greens, blues.'

He smiled. 'Those with special psychic abilities usually do. They're not afraid to be surrounded with light and transparency. They're bold. They don't need to cloak their uncertainties in the greys and blacks of the conventional world.'

She looked pointedly at his own neat dark suit.

He smiled. 'Men are unlucky. For our business purposes, we have to look like all the rest. Safe and ordinary. Many of my clients are very fearful when they come here. They need to be reassured.'

She nodded abstractedly. Her attention had been caught by the crystal ball placed centrally on his desk. It was nothing more than a solid sphere of glass about the size of a large orange; its overall appearance disappointingly grey and cloudy. A dull unremarkable object, sitting squatly on a simple circular wooden base.

And yet her eyes were unable to leave it. As she stared into its heart, it began to brighten and then to glow with a silver liquidy light. A transluscent ribbon of blue appeared around its edge; dense and deep blue like the evening sky just after the sun has set.

She gazed at it, captivated.

'What do you see?' he asked.

'Light,' she said, concentrating fiercely. 'And a haze. A blue haze. So blue.'

'You are seeing an aura,' he told her. 'Only those with psychic powers see an aura so readily.'

'There's something in the centre,' she said, her veins

66

prickling with heat. 'A dark shape. I can't see what.'
Her heart began to bang against the wall of her chest.
She drove every ounce of mental effort into the centre
of the ball. There was a person there, she was sure of it.
But who? Who? The central shape swelled a little, grew
sharper. And then, without warning, it slowly dis-
solved.

She looked up at Theodore Dowlan in dismay. 'It's
gone. Just cloudiness again.'

'And the aura?'

'That's gone, too.'

'You can't expect to see with perfect clarity the first
time you look into a crystal. To see as much as you did is
highly unusual.'

Zoe felt nauseous and dizzy. The ball looked innocent
enough now. Just a dead weight of dull glass sitting on a
desk. She wished she had ignored it. She wished she
hadn't seen its tantalizing images. And she most fer-
vently wished that she hadn't come here to consult this
so-called psychic.

'What you have told me confirms that you have
considerable psychic powers,' Theodore Dowlan observed.

'No! I'm just an ordinary person.'

'No one is an ordinary person,' he said. 'Every person
is unique and special.'

Zoe looked hard at him, reflecting on that last comment. She had been on the verge of being completely
swayed by the seemingly majestic authority of his divination. Impressed beyond doubt. Now she was reassured
to hear him falling back on corny clichés. *Every person is
unique and special.* What a handy stock phrase to have up

one's sleeve when in difficulty. No doubt it was one he used regularly to impress his more gullible clients.

'Yes, I know that's a trite and clichéd phrase,' he said, shattering her short-lived confidence to doubt him. 'It's also true. And I would advise you to take serious notice of the very special qualities you've been given.'

'We're going too fast,' she said panicky.

'We have just an hour. I'm not one of those charlatans who wastes time with meaningless introductions and platitudes. What did you expect?' he asked calmly.

'I don't know.' She looked at him with appeal.

'You came for reassurance. All my clients come for reassurance.'

'Yes.' Help me, help me, she was pleading silently.

'You came because you wanted someone to tell you that your psychic powers are mere phantoms. Nonsensical notions to be firmly stamped on.'

She nodded. 'Yes.'

'You wanted to convince yourself that something the deeply hidden part of your mind is telling you is untrue.'

'Yes.' She had been going to keep it all secret. The dream, the horror, the fear. Now, suddenly, she was desperate to unlock the gates of her vision and set it free. But something held her back. If he couldn't divine it, then she wasn't going to share it with him. It was too precious.

He leaned back in his chair, his bright glinting eyes watching her.

She was convinced that some power was at work. Some force circulating within the room.

She hung her head, closing her eyes for a moment. When she looked up, she saw that the man on the opposite side of the desk was not a part of that power. He was frowning, perplexed and pondering. In this particular case, his mind had not extended into her thoughts. As far as her dream was concerned, he was still ignorant and excluded.

In a sudden bright shaft of intuition, she understood that the dream belonged only to her, locked away inside her, secret and inviolable. She also realized there was only one other person in the world with whom she could contemplate sharing it.

'You mustn't reject the psychic powers at your disposal. Denying them will only make things worse,' Theodore Dowlan said smoothly. 'You must go along with the flow of your ideas. Open your mind to them and allow them to enable and guide you.'

'I think I understand that now.' she agreed.

'So shall we go on, then?' He leaned forward expectantly.

She stood up, suddenly convinced about what she must do. There was only one man in the world she must open her mind to, and Theodore Dowlan was not he.

'No, I don't think so.' She took out notes and laid them on the desk in payment. 'Thank you for your help,' she said, composed and distant.

He followed her to the door. She sensed a slight anxiety emanating from him in rippling waves.

'I'd like you to go away and meditate on what we've talked about. I'd like you to come again in another day or so,' he said.

'Perhaps.' She doubted it.

Relieved to be once again in the fresh air, scenting the

spring wind, she walked swiftly away from him up the steps.

She could have sworn his eyes were boring into her back.

CHAPTER 8

There were five children in Zoe's first session of the morning. Five very individual children between the ages of five and nine, brought together by their need to develop their skills in the speaking, reading and writing of the English language. All of them had at least one parent who was not a native of the UK, and all except Leonore had only recently come to Britain.

Zoe waited for them in the medical room. A grey-blanketed camp bed took up most of one wall. There were precision weighing scales in a corner of the room and beside these a huge first-aid cupboard, neatly stocked with pills, creams and bandages for accidents and emergencies. It was the only space in the cramped school not already in use.

Clearing a mound of papers and cardboard boxes from the small table which provided the only space suitable for teaching purposes, Zoe started on the task of setting up her travelling puppet theatre: a colourful assembly of brightly painted wood panels with genuine velvet curtains to draw across the stage. The puppets, which she had lovingly handcarved, dressed and painted, sat propped on a chair, limp and passive. Not until the children arrived would life, song and dance be breathed into them.

But the children were late this morning. The whole school was in the assembly hall for a talk on road safety. Corridors and rooms were eerily empty and silent.

Zoe looked at her watch. She tapped her fingers on her knees. Restless, she got up, went to the window and looked out. She sat down again. Her eyes moved across to the green folder lying on the top of her open document case. Impulsively, she reached out and slapped the lid shut to make it disappear.

She hadn't thought there would be time to consider the contents of the green folder this morning. In fact, she hadn't wanted to consider them at all before she took them out to show to the only person who had a right to see them.

Two handwritten sheets. That was all there was. No more than a few lines to encapsulate the dream that had buried itself in her mind like a slug in an apple. It had occurred to her, whilst she was writing the words down, that perhaps to capture the shifting images in black and white would somehow put the whole episode in perspective. Strip it of its power.

But it hadn't.

She heard the doors of the assembly hall open. There was a growing buzz of chatter, the clumping of an army of young feet. The door flew open and a boy of five erupted through it.

Stefan Kussek was from Prague. A few months previously he had come to live in London with his Czech grandparents. Quite what lay behind this unusual family arrangement, no one in school seemed sure. Zoe gathered there was some legal battle going on about Stefan's being able to remain in Britain on a long-term basis.

Stefan spoke very little English. He appeared strangely unmoved by his separation from his family and his country. He was like a terrier puppy: cheery, curious, pugnacious and generally unsquashable.

He dashed across to the chair on which the puppets lay, grabbed one eagerly and waved it in the air, making its head wag frantically. 'Look right, look left, look right, look left,' he chanted excitedly, his voice rising to a screeching crescendo.

She smiled, put out a hand and gently steadied his flailing arm. 'When must you always look right and look left, Stefan?'

He looked at her, pushing his lips out. 'Cross road,' he said, frowning with the effort of remembering how to say things in English.'

'That's it! Alway look before you cross.' She gave a playful tug at the puppet's dangling wooden foot. 'You like him?'

Stefan nodded vigorously.

Zoe raised her eyebrows. Teasing him, questioning him. Urging him on to say more.

'Yes. I – like – the – puppet,' he said with dogged deliberation, frowning because she was getting her own way in making him speak English. With the other teachers, he managed to hold out for much longer.

'His name is Benjamin,' said Zoe. 'That's a very long name, isn't it?' She smiled. Her eyes twinkled with challenge as if to add that she didn't expect for a moment that Stefan would be able to remember such a long and complex name. She turned away from him, making a show of tweaking the fabric of the mock theatre's curtains.

'Ben-ya-meen!' Stefan said indignantly. He frowned, not quite satisfied. He tapped her briskly on the shoulder. 'Ben-*juh*-meen.'

Zoe whipped round, eyes open wide. 'Good! Good! Excellent!'

'Ex-say-lent,' Stefan echoed experimentally. 'Clever boy! Yes? Clever boy, clever boy!' His voice soared to a shriek.

Zoe laid a calming hand on his shoulder. 'Very clever boy.'

The other children were arriving now, sliding in shyly, smiling up at their teacher, looking forward to the session ahead.

Zoe noticed that Leonore Rogier was looking strained and pale, her small face pinched as though with cold. Yet today was mild and sunny. Zoe felt a fresh twinge of disquiet.

She settled the children in a semi-circle around her and then took up the puppets one by one, introducing them to the fascinated audience, repeating each puppet's name, encouraging the children to attempt an imitation of her words.

Her small group listened intently. They watched every movement Zoe made. In her canary yellow blouse and skirt, with her bright green shoes and swaying gold earrings, Zoe was a vision as brilliant and eye-catching as the principals in a pantomine.

The children loved her. They loved her quickness and brightness. They loved the way she smiled and joked and never shouted or lost her temper. And curiously enough, in Miss Peach's lessons, no one was ever rude or difficult. There was never time because she entertained them so much; kept them constantly busy, talking and thinking. She had their affection and loyalty gathered into the palm of her hand.

At the end of the session, the group replaced the puppets on the chair and began to gather up their bags, books and pencils. One by one they trooped out happy and stimulated, clutching their small blue note-books in which Zoe had written down words for them with her special pen filled with bright purple ink.

But Leonore and Stefan hung back, reluctant to leave.

Zoe beckoned Leonore to come and stand beside her. 'What is it, little love?' she asked, laying her hand lightly on the girl's slender shoulder. 'What's the matter today?'

She was more than a trifle concerned about Leonore; the little girl had done virtually no written work during the session and had not volunteered a single remark of her own free will.

Leonore stared ahead, saying nothing. Zoe sensed that the child was shrinking into herself, withdrawing into the silent world in her head. She decided to refrain from pressing and coaxing, merely allowed her hand to remain resting reassuringly on Leonore's hunched shoulder.

Stefan was hesitating in the doorway, slithering to and fro around the edge of the door like a snake. Eventually his small body disappeared, but only for a moment. He was instantly back again, sidling backwards and for-wards, his bright eyes slipping from one corner of the room to the other.

Suddenly Leonore gave a sharp gasp of desolation and flung her arms around Zoe, burying her head into her chest. Her grasp was a stranglehold filled with all the ferocious strength fuelled by powerful childish emotions. Small choking whimpers escaped from her.

Zoe put her head down to hear better. 'Little love,' she murmured, stroking Leonore's hair.

Seeing his teacher fully occupied, Stefan decided to seize the moment. In one fluid movement he shot out his arm and made a grab for the puppet that had attracted his attention earlier on.

Zoe, who rarely missed any of the childish antics which took place in her teaching zone, flung out an arm in response, catching the hem of his shirt with two fingers and putting a swift brake on his thoughts of escape.

As though he had been assaulted by a flung plank, the child dropped like a stone to the floor and shrank into a tight ball. His arms curled like snakes around his head, creating a tight armoury of defence. Clearly he had expectations of some severe retribution.

Gently disengaging Leonore, Zoe stooped down to the small boy. 'Stefan,' she said gently. 'I'm not going to hurt you. Stefan. It's all right.'

Just as she was considering making a gentle attempt to prise the rigid armouring from around the child's ears, he leapt up like a crazed cornered animal and let out a bloodchilling scream. Then another, and another.

Leonore stared at him, both concerned and fascinated as the shrill protests of panic and anguish reverberated through the room.

Zoe saw that she had to act quickly. She also saw that whilst Leonore was dismayed, she was not afraid. 'Leonore, go to the Head's room and ask her to come, will you?'

Leonore nodded and ran off, leaving Zoe to grapple with the enraged and terrifed little boy whose limbs were now wildly flailing; arms beating the air, feet kicking out viciously.

Zoe gasped with pain as the hard soles of his shoes connected with her shin bones. Pulling Stefan's hot squirming body against her, she eventually managed to haul him on to her lap.

He lay there, tense and rigid, still clasping the puppet, a look of fiercest desperation and mutiny on his face. The legs and head of the puppet, damp and creased with the sweat from Stefan's hands, lolled from his vice-like grip.

Zoe wrapped her arms around the tormented little boy and rocked him in steady rhythm. By the time the Head arrived, Stefan was perfectly still and quiet, his thumb in his mouth, his eyelids drooping with emotional exhaustion.

The Head, a capable practical woman in her early forties, sized up the situation instantly. She disengaged the child from Zoe's arms and laid him on the camp bed, covering him with the blanket. 'This is nothing new. We've been having quite a few problems with Stefan recently,' she commented. 'And you're going to be late for your next group. It's time you were off. Don't worry, I'll get someone to come and sit with him.'

But Zoe was worried. She sensed something badly wrong in Stefan's life. It seemed too easy just to leave him to sleep off his distress. 'We should get him some help,' she told the Head.

The Head nodded, smiling, conveying the impression she had seen this kind of thing so many times before. 'I'll speak to his grandmother this evening when she comes to collect him. Don't worry,' she repeated to Loe reassuringly. 'We shall do all that's necessary.

Zoe hesitated. Wanted to press further. But of course the Head was quite right. It was not Zoe's place to recommend what should be done for this child's emotional welfare. She was merely a visitor to the school. A tutor on the move. Her job was teaching language. Pastoral responsibilities rested with the full-time staff, those teachers who cared for the children every day of the week.

'Go on!' the Head insisted. She turned to Leonore, who was looking from one person to the other, quietly absorbing all that was said, wondering about all that was not said. 'Help Miss Peach carry her things to the car, Leonore, will you?' the Head requested briskly.

Zoe walked out to her car, Leonore trailing behind her with an assortment of bags. Zoe thought of the troubled small boy lying on the bed in the medical room, clutching a wooden puppet, and had a hollow sense of having in some way failed to do as much as she should have for him. Of having failed a small child who had been crying out for her help. She was also stabbed with the now horribly familiar sense of something dreadful being about to happen.

Dear God! It's me that needs the 'help', she thought ironically.

Glancing down into Leonore's pale face, she was reminded that here was another child who seemed in need of comfort.

Leonore looked back at Zoe, her eyes wide and full of some strange wordless pleading.

Side by side, they loaded Zoe's equipment into the

78

boot of her car. Zoe made a few playful remarks, but Leonore was grave-faced and silent as she gamely lifted up the box of puppets and handed Zoe her bag of books and papers. And the moment the lid had clunked shut, she turned sharply away and almost ran back into the school.

Watching the small fleeing figure, Zoe suddenly knew it was time for action. Today, she told herself. Today I'll do it. This afternoon. Before Leonore arrives home from school.

CHAPTER 9

François spread the prints out on the desk. Lavish luscious colour photographs of the lavish luscious interiors of the homes of an assortment of celebrities. Extravagant swags and swathes formed a backdrop for a variety of beautiful faces who smiled with creamy assurance into the lens of François's camera.

François had that rare knack of enabling his photographic subjects to be completely themselves, to reveal their inner personality traits on film – even if they would have preferred not to.

A senior editor at one of Britain's glossiest magazines had already paid him a considerable sum for his previous set of shots, and for this current collection she had made the promise of even more. A further shoot was arranged for next week. Some stately home in one of the shire counties. François was not quite sure where. Nor did he particularly care. When the time came to do the work he would turn up punctually and in due course turn in a stunning set of shots. But these glamorous assignments gave him little artistic or personal satisfaction. He would never have chosen to do these kind of shoots, if it had not been for an urgent need for the kind of money Poppy had expected from the divorce settlement.

His lawyer said he had been mad to go along with all her extravagant requests. A luxury flat in Covent Garden where she could have Leonore to stay when she was in London, sole rights to the red BMW convertible François had bought on their fifth wedding anniversary. And on top of that, all of the canvases she had acquired in the course of her art-dealing activities; paintings which had been financed with François's money, because he had been so keen to help establish her on her chosen career.

The lawyer had sighed heavily and frequently and told François that he should contest his wife's outrageous demands. And, indeed, François often reminded himself that it was Poppy who had left. He had loved and cared for her and she had left him. Of her own free will she had deserted him for the love of another man. There was no need for him to be generous. Some men would probably even have resisted being fair.

But François had not had the heart to fight her. He had never denied her anything throughout all their time together. The old habits and loving feelings still persisted, even in the face of Poppy's rejection and a childish display of what he had eventually and sadly had to admit was simple greed.

The lawyer had, in time, given up his counter-suggestions, had shaken his head in resignation and got on with the task of finalizing the legal details of his client's astounding generosity.

And now François was saddled with mortgage repayments which threatened to cripple him if he didn't pull out all the stops to earn every penny he could get. Turning work down on the grounds of artistic fulfilment was a luxury he couldn't afford. If a job paid good money, then it must be done.

He lit a cigarette and inhaled thoughtfully, looking down at the brash gleaming photographs. Rows of perfect celebrity teeth grinned back at him, ice-white and glinting. He exhaled with a rush of irritation and then, recalling his daily resolve to give up smoking, viciously ground the glowing tip of the cigarette into the base of a heavy glass ashtray. Moving to the table piled high with camera equipment and boxes of film, he reached into his work holdall and pulled out a slim black folder.

Gently he slid out a further set of prints and spread them on the other side of the desk, as though in opposition to the ones already in place.

These prints were in monochrome. Solemn, stern pictures. Twenty portraits he had taken during a recent visit to a local nursing home for the elderly.

A gallery of faces, grooved and gnarled like the bark of ancient trees, stared fixedly into the lens of his camera. The emotions caught here were raw and bleak. There were few smiles, rather intimations of bewilderment and resignation. There was anger, too, and bitterness, and starkly naked fear.

And yet, despite all the pain, there was something about these photographs that excited him. He knew that he had captured some universal quality of human experience in these pictures, feelings that would surely touch a nerve in every observer who looked at them.

The human worth of these images far outstripped that

of his roll call of glitzy celebrities, yet the money he would get for them would in no way reflect that. The bristly wrinkled faces of old nobodies waiting to die would fetch comparative peanuts.

Automatically he reached for another cigarette, lit up, inhaled. His gaze drifted, following the haze of blue smoke, tracking up the length of the high window. Beyond the glass he registered the flash of a bright yellow car. It slowed down, a slab of metallic custard seemingly intent on parking outside his small strip of garden. He could hear the purr of a precision engine, a little growl before it was turned off and extinguished.

The woman who got out was as glowing and colourful as her car. A scarlet wrap was thrown across her shoulders and long silver earrings flashed beneath her thick curtain of dark hair.

For a moment François allowed his eyes to run over her, drawn and intrigued. Then suddenly, recognition dawned.

Zoe Peach! Leonore's favourite language tutor.

François ran a hand through his hair, cursed softly. The second cigarette rapidly joined the first and he wafted his arms energetically to dispel the curls of smoke.

He was standing at the open door even before Zoe Peach had reached the gate.

She looked at him. He saw her hesitation, how she drew back a little, her eyes wide like a startled deer.

He beckoned her forward. 'Come in. Please.'

She walked ahead of him into his study. He smelled her sharp peppery perfume, the warmth of her skin. The air in the room seemed to brighten, to move and flicker around her.

François registered his responses to this woman with interest. 'Is there some problem with Leonore?' he enquired in level neutral tones.

Zoe Peach turned and looked up straight into his eyes. She shook her head. 'She's a little quiet at the moment,' she commented eventually.

François had the feeling she was struggling with some difficulty. Eddies of uncertainty flowed from her. And yet she had struck him before as a supremely confident young woman, even to the point of brittleness.

'Is she still making good progress?' he asked.

Zoe Peach frowned. She seemed to be in an almost dreamlike state. 'I'm sorry?' She stared at him, obviously having lost the thread of their previous brief interchange.

'Leonore,' he prompted. 'Are you pleased with her work?'

'Yes. Oh, yes, she's doing very well. She has a natural ability with languages.'

'I agree. She just had a bad start, that's all.' He smiled, wondering what the hell was behind this visit. 'I was half-expecting you to tell me that her work had suddenly dropped off. Deteriorated.'

'She has been exceptionally quiet recently,' Zoe Peach agreed, emphasizing her previous point.

'Yes. Can't you guess why?' He gave a lazy smile, amused to find himself enjoying the opportunity to tease her a little.

She blinked.

François was suddenly exasperated. He wanted to grasp Zoe Peach's shoulders and rattle her back into full alertness of the present. 'Leonore has got the idea that if she speaks up too readily, then she'll no longer need to come to your group. If she's too clever a girl, you'll throw her out – that's how she sees it. And she'd hate that. Because you're one of her favourite people.' He spoke with dry irony.

Zoe Peach took a few moments to digest this information. 'Of course! Why didn't I think of that?'

In the face of her continuing unease, François was suddenly wary himself, beginning to form a theory as to the most likely reason behind this odd visit. 'You were probably thinking other things instead,' he said icily.

She flinched visibly.

'Well. Weren't you?'

Her head shook in a tiny gesture of helplessness in the face of this cold unprovoked attack.

'People are always *thinking* things about children from split families,' he elaborated, a thread of menace and warning underlying his even tones. 'They think a lot and then they begin to get worried about the children's welfare and then they jump to all sorts of conclusions.'

Zoe Peach shook her head vigorously. 'No.'

'Oh, yes. And I've come to the conclusion they frequently think the very worst about a set-up where a little girl lives alone with her father.' His cool eyes pierced her own troubled ones.

She coloured, parted her lips in silent protest. 'No. I never thought anything like that.'

'I'm glad to hear it.'

'I've always had the impression that you and Leonore were very close. Very contented together.'

'Quite.' He raised his eyebrows. He was not smiling. 'Well, Miss Peach, if you haven't come to talk to me about Leonore's progress or concerns about her welfare, then isn't it time you told me what you have come for?'

She clasped her hands together tightly. She seemed unable to speak. She put up a hand to her eyes. Walking away from him as though drugged, she went to stand by the table. Her glance moved down to the photographs. She stood for a long time, perfectly still. 'These are beautiful.'

He was not sure to which set she was referring.

'This is your work, then? You're a photographer?' she said.

'Yes.'

'Yes, of course. Leonore told me.'

Zoe picked up a print, showing a smiling blonde young woman. A top fashion model, posing in her fashionable flat, wearing simple denim jeans and a plain white T-shirt which merely served to accentuate her golden radiance.

'She photographs marvellously,' Zoe commented. 'Although she's even more stunning in the flesh.'

'She's a friend of yours?' François enquired.

'Mmm. I see her at parties sometimes.'

'You move in exalted and exotic circles,' François commented, not bothering to conceal a certain sarcasm in his tone. Looking at Zoe Peach standing there so immaculate, so expensively turned out, he felt his rage swirl within him towards all the spoiled women he had known. He thought of his mother: always demanding, wanting, getting. His mother must alway have new clothes, new jewels, fresh amusements, everyone's attention. On and on, more and more. And then Poppy. It seemed that he had never succeeded in giving her enough, even though he had offered heart and soul.

His anger was like a spiked rod, tormenting him. And perversely, he wanted to turn the point of the spike on Zoe Peach. He wanted to hurt her, because she touched him in some tender spot, and because she was *there*.

She looked up at him, connecting instantly with his dark inner mood. Her eyes were wounded.

He was thrown off balance, as though he had lashed out at her physically with no reason or warning.

'I have a lot of connections from the past,' she said hesitantly. 'My mother knew a lot of people. That's no sin.'

'I'm sorry,' he said quietly.

She smiled, a long slow smile, her lips indescribably sweet, so that he felt a total bastard.

'Do you believe in dreams?' she asked suddenly, jerking him into new guardedness. 'The power of dreams?'

He shrugged. 'I've never given it a thought.' He looked at her curiously. She had turned deathly pale, her eyes huge shiny pools in her delicate face.

'Premonitions,' she added, her voice unsteady in her throat.

He gave a dismissive laugh, making his opinion on these matters painfully clear.

'No, please! Please listen to me.'

He heard a strange note of naked need in her voice and inclined his head, giving her his full attention.

'I had this dream,' she began.

He had the impression that it was a huge effort for her to speak. It was as though she were forcing herself to plunge into a lake of icy water or make a parachute jump from an aircraft.

'Go on.' He realized that he had to give her a little help. Whatever was troubling her was deeply serious. As far as she was concerned, at least.

'There was a terrible accident. A fire . . .' She looked up at him, terrified and pleading.

'Yes?'

'An air crash.'

'Yes?'

'You were there.'

'What?'

'In my dream. You were there.' Her body was shivering with suppressed feeling.

His emotions were suddenly strongly roused. Sympathy, curiosity, irritation. And a huge bolt of sexual attraction which momentarily stunned him. 'There are plenty of dark-haired men around who might fit my description,' he said with light dismissiveness.

'It was you,' she insisted, her face growing flushed. 'I saw you quite clearly.'

He sighed, exasperated.

'I saw you in my dream, before I met you,' she announced flatly.

'That's nonsense!'

'No. It's true.' She turned up her face, staring into his eyes. 'That's why I was so shocked when I saw you at the party.'

He was on the point of making some disdainful jibe but, glancing at Zoe Peach's stricken expression, he stopped himself.

'I saw you so clearly in my dream. Just as you are in life,' she said.

'You've known Leonore for some time. We're father

and daughter. Maybe you'd seen similarities without realizing.'

'No. In fact, I don't think you look very alike.'

François reached for his cigarettes. She shook her head when he offered one. 'Do you mind?' he said curtly. 'I think I need something to steady my nerves through this crazy conversation.'

Her head drooped. 'I'm sorry. There was no other way to tell you.'

'Probably not. But why bother to tell me at all?'

She gazed at him, frowning. He noticed that her skin had the delicacy of bone china and was amazed to find himself longing to reach out and touch it.

'To warn you,' she said, in a voice filled with surprise that he needed to ask.

'Warn me! *Merde!* This is really going too far.'

'Are you planning to fly in the near future?' she cut in.

He couldn't believe this. 'Leonore and I are going to New York for a wedding. I don't lead the kind of life that includes the luxury of sailing across the Atlantic for a brief visit,' he said sarcastically, instantly regretting it as he watched her face.

'You mustn't,' she said. 'You mustn't fly.'

'To the States. Anywhere? Ever again?' he asked, his flippancy laced with mounting incredulity and anger.

She sighed, then turned away from him. 'I don't know. I just know you mustn't fly to this wedding.' She faced him again, determined and defiant now. 'At least don't take Leonore. You owe her that, not to put her in any kind of danger.'

François's dark eyes snapped with fury. 'For Christ's sake, this has gone on long enough.'

She jerked around to face him. 'You must listen to me. This isn't just a silly whim. I went to see someone . . .'

'Indeed?' He was icy cold. 'Someone who understands this kind of thing, I suppose.'

She blinked as if tensing herself for a physical blow.

'Crazy dreams and hysteria?' he suggested.

She shook her head sadly. 'No, they're not crazy. This man didn't think so, at any rate.'

'He's a charlatan, then.'

For the second time in their encounter she put a hand up to her eyes as though warding off a blow. Her glance fell away from him and rested again on the photographs.

François watched her, tracking her gaze. He raked back the hair that fell across his forehead in a sharp irritable gesture. '*This* is reality,' he said brutally, sweeping his arm over the bleak monochrome photographs. 'These people have no room in their lives for dreams and fantasy. They're too busy confronting reality, trying to survive. Desperately resisting death.'

She stiffened. Suddenly she began to shake violently. She wrapped her arms around herself. He heard her whispering through white lips, 'Help me. Please, help me.'

François stepped forward, appalled to witness such naked distress. It was as though he could smell this woman's pain and fear. Something cool and unyielding in him, a barrier that had lain there like a hard slab ever since Poppy left, slid softly away. He reached out to Zoe Peach and took her in his arms.

CHAPTER 10

Poppy Rogier, soon to be Poppy King, surveyed the results of several days spent arranging and hanging canvases around the stark white walls of her penthouse gallery. She and her assistant Gaby had worked nonstop, checking the measurements of each canvas, deciding which artist's work could be placed alongside each other and how much space could be allotted to each individual work. Poppy had considered the effects of colour and texture when hanging the canvases, trying to create interesting contrasts and yet maintain an overall balance which was pleasing to the eye.

Biographical notes on each of the artists whose work had been chosen for the exhibition were elegantly printed on thick white card. And each individual picture was carefully labelled with its title and catalogue number. The price was clearly, but unobtrusively, marked.

Poppy stood back, surveying the total effect. The light, of course, was superb, supplied by six huge roof windows framed in honey-coloured oak. The sun poured in as though sent straight from heaven, as well it might; the rent for the gallery was appropriately astronomical.

She breathed in and smiled. She was more than

91

pleased with her achievement; she was elated, buzzing with excitement. She was both convinced and determined that this exhibition was going to bring her to the forefront of the art-loving public's attention. It was also going to demonstrate to the most prestigious of New York's art critics that the King Gallery was one to sit up and take notice of.

Poppy closed her eyes, imagining the reviews, seeing the procession of talented artists coming along to her with their work, desperate for their paintings to be included in one of her exclusive exhibitions.

She saw herself carefully assessing canvases as the creators looked anxiously on. Just thinking about it gave her an anticipatory thrill of power at the prospect of evaluating artistic worth; weighing it in the balance against the likely response of the influential critics, together with the all-important issue of commercial demand. Dealing in works of art was a complex business. In order to carve a niche as a successful exhibitor and entrepreneur, one required a good many skills – and a very hard head.

Passing into the long passage-like store room which ran behind the length of the gallery, Poppy glanced at the jumble of canvases stacked along the wall. A number of them were paintings initially considered for inclusion in the forthcoming exhibition, but now rejected. The others represented her stock, the canvases that sold like hot cakes and generated a steady income. Unlike the abstract representations that were hanging on her walls, these pictures were traditional landscapes and attractively recognizable portraits depicting the human form and the animal kingdom.

One of Poppy's best-selling lines was a series of paintings of female nudes. These huge canvases, some of them approaching life-size, were lusciously textured and gloriously rich in colour. The flesh tones of the subjects, bathed in autumn-gold sunlight, were breathtakingly lifelike, and each portrait breathed sensuality; speaking of warm evenings in Tuscany, of mulberry-coloured wine the texture of velvet, and nights spent in leisurely love-making.

The canvases, were in fact, painted for Poppy by a young housewife and mother; an obscure, unknown artist living in a depressed post-industrial city in the north of England.

Her paintings sold to customers from all over the USA. They were hung in villas in Spain, tavernas in Greece and palazzos in Venice. She painted horses, too, great sturdy cobs with flashing eyes, gleaming buttocks and swishing tails. They were almost as sexy as the female nudes. And certainly sold equally well.

But Poppy kept all of these paintings hidden away in the stock room. Sensitive they may be; suffused with life and colour, and in no way distasteful or offensive. But there was no question of displaying them in her gallery. These works were too straighforward, too simple, too easily understood. They were not of the elegant and baffling chic that was necessary to tantalize the discriminating customers and critics visiting the King Gallery.

It rankled a little with Poppy that this steady source of profit (Poppy's, not the artist's) had been discovered for her by François. He had been doing a shoot for a magazine, running an article on inner-city dereliction. The young artist and her husband had been drinking together in a local wine bar as François, at the next table, looked through his previous day's prints. They had expressed interest. A conversation had developed.

He had taken a sample of the young woman's work back to London with him and Poppy had spotted the marketing potential instantly. 'Utterly spontaneous!' she had commented. 'Totally simplistic and naïve, of course.'

'They're painted from the heart,' he had observed. 'Unlike those effete and cunningly calculated daubs done by some of the artists you like to encourage.' François had smiled whilst demonstrating this cruel and vice-like grasp of English vocabulary.

'They'll sell,' Poppy had responded, ignoring the barb. 'How many more has she got?'

'A cellar full. She's been painting for years.'

Poppy recalled her dismay to hear this. Cellars were meant for wine storage, not canvases; they could all be ruined.

But when her contact in Paris had sold the samples straight off for considerable sums, she had been delighted that there had been a ready-made store to plunder.

Surveying one of the canvases now, more than a year later, Poppy recollected that she had never been entirely straight with the artist regarding price. The offers for the orignal canvases had been fair, although modest, but the mark-up for herself and the agent had been unusually large. It was something that had caused one of the rare rows between her and François when it came to his notice.

She recalled his anger now, saw him pacing the room,

94

pushing his hair back, stopping himself reaching for a cigarette.

It was odd, thought Poppy, how François had become the sort of man who must always champion the underdog. She had not realized there was this facet to his personality when she first knew him. She had assumed he was like her. Practical and realistic.

She had also assumed that, because he resembled his mother in the regular beauty of his features, he must be like her in personality. Annette Rogier was a cool, thoroughbred Parisian. She was a law unto herself and very determined to get what she wanted. Rather like Poppy herself, in fact.

And so François had seemed, too – at the beginning. When Poppy had first met him, he had known exactly where he wanted his career to go. And he had been thrillingly fearless, venturing forth on shoots to collect illicit pictures of those in the Paris underworld whom the press wanted to expose. Vicious people who exploited the weak: children and animals. On more than one occasion, having been spotted by his target, he had come home bruised and bleeding. But he had always got the photographs he wanted, and hung on to them, lending weight to the process of justice.

Poppy realized now that she had confused determination and ambition with a desire to forge ahead and make a great deal of money. François had had the first but not the second. Oh yes, he had provided her and Leonore with a very good life-style. But he had never been interested in serious money.

In the end, thought Poppy, he had turned out rather like his father, dark and mysterious and very French.

Henri Rogier had retired early from practising law in Paris with plans to bury himself in rural Provence. At which point Annette had found herself a highly ambitious Spanish politician with a lot of old money and eventually married him.

It was almost as though history were repeating itself.

Poppy brought herself back to the here and now, and brushed a finger over the painted head of a fiery chestnut stallion. The oil was thick and ridged like the carved icing on a wedding cake. She had no problem with the view that the little housewife in the dreary northern city (never visited by Poppy) would be more than satisfied with the payments she had received. After all, what would a person with her kind of life find to do with vast sums of money? Poppy had asked herself secretly.

Well, the problem was drawing to a natural close now. The accumulated store of pictures had been sold and the artist could only supply half a dozen new ones a year. It wasn't sufficient to meet the demand. And, in any case, people were beginning to make murmurings about looking for something new. Poppy would have to look around and find some alternative source of steady income. The artist would have to find a less high-powered buyer who was happy to to deal with less demanding customers.

Leaning against the wall, Poppy had a sudden swift vision of her ex-husband's face. She imagined the disapproval on François's chiselled features to hear of such a plan. He would make comments about exploitation, using people. It didn't occur to François that, in the world of enterprise, one gave people their chance and, when they could no longer come up with the goods, one moved on and offered someone else an opportunity.

That was Liam's philosophy also, and she had come to realize that she and her future husband were splendidly in tune on so many of the issues that had slowly alienated her from François.

As she reflected on the absent Liam, who was in Los Angeles meeting with prospective sponsors for one of their most promising young artists, her hardworking assistant Gaby came in carrying the mail.

'More wedding replies,' Gaby said, dropping her bundle into Poppy's outstretched hands. 'And plenty of stuff from England, by the looks of it.'

Poppy searched swiftly through the bundle, looking for Leonore's handwriting. A little spark of guilt sprang up to reproach her as she was reminded of the way in which she had chosen to leave her child in order to be with her lover.

Leaving Leonore had been the hardest part of the whole upheaval of separation. Leonore was such a beautiful, docile child. She was not showing signs of the cleverness and achievement Poppy knew she had in her, but that would come in time. At least, it would if François could be persuaded to be a little firmer with their daughter. François was far too liberal, in Poppy's view, becoming ever less interested in the fierce competitiveness necessary for surviving in a modern world.

Thinking of Leonore's perfect oval face and her huge speaking eyes, Poppy felt a rush of maternal affection. Together, she and Leonore had made a perfect duo, their striking blonde beauty perfectly matched. It had always made her heart swell with pride when she took Leonore out with her. And naturally she missed her little girl dreadfully.

Liam sometimes urged her to fight François over the custody arrangements. Liam knew some of the sharpest lawyers in New York and they were convinced she would have a good case for having Leonore with her much more frequently than the odd week in the school vacations.

But Poppy did not see things quite that way. As a child, she had started attending boarding school when she was only five. Her father had been offered a posting in Hong Kong and her mother wanted to go out there with him immediately, selecting suitable accommodation and engaging a retinue of servants. Poppy's parents had decided not to uproot their child; she would go away to school and live with her grandparents in vacations.

Poppy recalled that both she and her mother had become used to seeing each other for no more than short periods in the year. It had not seemed cruel, nor painful or unnatural. Not after she had overcome the initial searing grief. And the situation for her and Leonore was really no different.

Recognizing Leonore's handwriting, Poppy slit the envelope with a silver knife and took out the card inside. She was pleased to see that Leonore's ability to form her letters was improving and that her little drawings were charming.

Leonore wrote to say that she and Daddy would be coming to Mummy's wedding on an aeroplane. To illustrate this, Leonore had made a sweet little sketch of a grey plane with red stripes flying through a bright blue sky. There was some news about a boy at school called Stefan who shouted a lot and a lady next door with a dog who was frightened of a magic flute. Poppy scanned swiftly down the lines, hopeful of finding something more interesting. 'I think Daddy shud get marrid,' Leonore informed her mother, her writing getting smaller and smaller as she ran out of space. 'To Miss Peach. She is pretty and smiley and I lyk her very much.' The last two words had a thick line drawn beneath them, and after them Leonore had added, 'A lot.'

Poppy stared. She could not believe what she saw, nor what she felt. Disbelief, a nasty jolt of uncertainty, anger. And, astoundingly enough, jealousy.

'Miss Peach!' she exclaimed, making Gaby turn round curiously. 'Gaby,' she said sharply, 'get my hus . . . ex-husband on the line, please. As soon as possible.'

Zoe sat facing Charles across a tiny table in a packed and expensive restaurant in the West End. Charles had already polished off his Mediterranean fish soup with garlic croutons, and was now savouring his Sancerre and anticipating the comfit of duck which would arrive once Zoe had made her way through a half-sphere of melon filled with Cointreau-soaked raspberries.

He thought Zoe looked irresistible and enchanting, her hair so glossy and dark against her china-pale skin. Her skin seemed to become more silvery and luminous each time he saw her. He just wished she would eat a little more heartily. And more quickly.

Zoe spooned up the melon, finding it an effort to chew and swallow each small portion. In the short weeks since her dream, her appetite had gradually decreased. Since her encounter with François Rogier that afternoon, her interest in food seemed to have completely vanished.

But she was making an effort, having a strong sense of the need to keep up her strength for trials she was sure were coming. Besides, she had no wish to offend Charles who had been extremely kind and attentive over the last few days, his ceaseless efforts to entertain her being one of the few distractions which kept her from endless brooding.

She felt at ease with Charles. He was amiable and amusing, low-key and relaxed. He was also utterly sure of himself. With Charles there was no time wasted on self-doubt. He had no inclination for philosophical ponderings. It would never occur to him to spend so much as a moment considering the wide divergences in the human condition or life's unfairnesses. As far as Charles was concerned, life was a banquet, and he had every intention of enjoying it to the full.

Zoe found nothing particularly unusual or disturbing in this laid-back attitude to life. In fact, it was one she found curiously reassuring. Charles's way of looking at the world was one with which she was familiar, for his opinions, his personality and aspirations were remarkably similar to those of the men who had formed her mother's social circle in Zoe's childhood. They had all been carefree, too, brought up with comfortable wealth and the bright prospects which came from influential connections.

In addition, there was a simplicity and transparency about Charles which made him an ideal companion because she never had to wonder what he was thinking or worry that he might be hiding his true feelings.

'Bought a new yearling this morning on behalf of one of my clients,' Charles told her. 'Black stallion, eighteen hands. A real goer.' He looked at her through lazily seductive eyes. 'The horse, that is, not my client!'

Zoe was interested. She had a natural affection for

animals, although she didn't keep one herself. Her life-style meant that an animal would be too often on its own. 'I haven't ridden for ages. Must be years,' she told Charles, recalling hectic gymnkhanas and brave, wild-eyed ponies.

'Well, that's something else for me to put right in your life,' he informed her, narrowing his eyes suggestively, unashamedly hinting at intriguing and intimate issues unconnected with horses.

'I thought you were at the office this morning,' Zoe smiled, noting the bait and failing to rise to it.

'Sure. I did the deal by phone. I'd already been down to the stables with my client a couple of times last weekend.' He stared hard at her. 'I told you, don't you remember?'

She gave a small start. 'Yes, of course. I'm sorry.' She found her heart speeding up. She must try her utmost to concentrate on the realities of life instead of spending her time locked in the world of her head, half-attending to what people said, instantly forgetting.

She returned to her efforts with the melon. Already the vivid imagery in her mind was active. Around her, in reality, were pink tablecloths and twinkling cutlery and Charles's agreeable solidity. But in her head she saw only a vivid picture of François Rogier's stern and priest-like face, the way he had scorned her that afternoon with anger and contempt on his long curved lips.

And then, how his disdain had softened, how his eyes had darkened and filled with compassion as he moved to enfold her in his arms, holding her close, allowing her to feel truly safe for the first time in what seemed like an age.

She could not remember how long they had stood there beside his display of arresting photographs, fastened together, motionless and silent. There had been utter stillness and peace. And then, with the lightest of touches, his lips had begun to brush against her hair, his fingers press against the bones of her spine. She had felt his lips moving over her face, his breath warm against her temples. She had closed her eyes and raised her head, offering him her own lips, soft and willing, slowly parting to receive his kiss . . .

She shook herself alert and back into the present. Recalling the pressure of François Rogier's firm and sternly insistent mouth, a wave of warmth swept across her breasts and throat. She put her hand up to the collar of her buttermilk silk shirt, pulling it around her heated skin, desperate to hide the signs of an unexplainable desire.

She picked up her spoon once more and toyed with the little mound of raspberries.

Charles put his hand out and laid it over hers, a great bear-like paw furred with glistening golden hairs, playfully imprisoning her own delicately boned, crimson-tipped fingers.

He squeezed a little, making her look up. She was confronted with a mane of yellow hair, a lazy smile, a sharp blue gaze.

He shook his head in mock despair. 'For Christ's sake, Zoe, either eat that stuff or ditch it. I'm desperate for my duck.'

At the end of the evening Charles drove Zoe back to her house. Lively and athletic, he jumped from the car and ran around the bonnet to open the passenger door in old-fashioned gentlemanly style.

She swung her legs out in the graceful manner of a ballet dancer. Charles observed the slim, curved calves with the expert eye of one who knows all there is to know about a filly's fetlocks. Offering his hand to pull her to her feet, he speculated idly on the shape of Zoe's thighs beneath the clinging green satin skirt.

He waited for her to ask him in, although he had already decided against accepting the charmingly courteous invitation which he knew would be forthcoming. There had been two previous overtures of this sort following pleasant dinner engagements. Zoe had made him exquisite amaretto-flavoured coffee and offered him fine old brandy. She had settled him at one end of the vast sofa, put on a compact disc of Schubert Piano Impromptus, and settled herself at the other end.

There had been no question of any light-hearted snogging, the kind of thing that invariably led to other more interesting activities at that time of night when one was nicely relaxed and replete with excellent wine.

Somehow it seemed unthinkable to pounce on Zoe Peach. She was out of bounds, untouchable. He could not say why this was, nor could he understand his own reactions. After all, he was one of the most experienced operators around, a man who could get to grips with a woman in every sense of the word, without any delay.

Zoe Peach would go out with him. Spend time with him. Talk, listen, and give the most promising signs of interest and growing affection. But still he could not bring himself to initiate the physical intimacy he craved. A chaste kiss on the cheek was as far as he had gone, aside from the curious incident in the plane, that is. When they said goodnight, she always permitted a brotherly kiss. She put her beautiful moulded arms up around his neck and gave every appearance of yielding femininity. But then she took her arms away and stepped back from him. *That was nice*, she seemed to be telling him, *but that was all*. And somehow it was unthinkable to press for more.

He was simply amazed at his own reticence. With some of his girls, he had his hands around their bottoms before he had even got to know their surnames.

Charles found himself totally baffled. If his friends knew what was going on, or rather *not* going on, they would be equally amazed, laying bets as to how soon it would be before he managed to get Zoe Peach well and truly laid.

Tonight, however, she did not even ask him in.

Looking down at her, he saw that she was abstracted again, in her own private world, standing there on the pavement like a beautiful and priceless statue – deaf and dumb. It drove him crazy. *She* was beginning to drive him crazy, tantalizing him most deliciously so that he couldn't resist coming back for more of the same.

'Tomorrow night?' he asked lightly.

She looked up. It was as though she had completely forgotten who he was. 'Yes,' she said. 'Give me a call,' she added vaguely as though suggesting that perhaps she might have other things to do once she had time to consider.

Charles touched her cheek lightly. He made no effort to kiss her. And, getting into his car, it occurred to him that perhaps things might be moved along by his taking someone else out to dinner instead the following evening.

Zoe went straight into the bathroom, turned on the bath taps and began to take off her clothes. Beneath her bright green skirt and creamy shirt she wore only a stark white lace bodysuit. Easing down the straps, she peeled the garment away from her breasts. Turning, she caught sight of herself in the mirror, the swell and curve of her high breasts, the erect pink tips of her nipples.

The dark image of François Rogier flashed again across her inner vision and she was pierced with a painful stab of longing. She put up a hand to her forehead. Her fingers were trembling. She had never imagined that hot naked desire would intrude to add an extra complication to her escalating anxiety. And even hot desire, as if that were not important enough, was eclipsed by her sense of a future destiny irretrievably linked with this deeply reserved and enigmatic man. The very idea of it powered her with an intense exhilaration, a throbbing and thrilling anticipation.

She slipped into the warm scented water and lay down, resting her head against the edge of the bath. She would have a long and soothing soak; afterwards, she would prepare herself a warm milky drink with freshly grated nutmeg sprinkled over it. Following that, she would settle into bed and read for a while; nothing taxing, an engaging thriller by one of her favourite writers.

She would, in fact, perform those simple rituals that were well known to promote swift and restful sleep.

Zoe longed to sleep. But recently she had come to fear sleep, with the prospect of losing a grip on her consciousness and exposing herself to further horrifying dreams. But, at the same time as fearing sleep, she was even more terrified at the prospect of enduring those endless hours when oblivion eluded her, leaving her drained and exhausted in the morning.

An hour later, switching off the light and finally abandoning herself to the lonely darkness, she tried to close her mind to all conscious thought, to let herself simply drift, so that anxiety and fear would lose their grip and slide away from her like oil poured on to warm flesh . . .

She was at home with her mother. It was a beautiful day and the two of them were sitting companionably in the garden of the Gloucestershire house. It was a calm, still day, the air hazed with a faintly shimmering August heat. Mother and daughter chatted of this and that; the guests who would be joining them for dinner that night, the clothes that would be needed for the cruise they were taking together in the autumn.

All was relaxed tranquillity until her mother suddenly shattered the easy calm with her worry and fuss because a magpie had flown out of the wood beyond. A single magpie with no sign of a mate.

'Oh, dear!' she exclaimed, pink and flustered. 'Oh, dear!'

Zoe smiled patiently at her dear, sweet, utterly irrational parent!

'One for sorrow,' her mother chanted, 'two for joy . . .
Oh, Mr Magpie, where's your wife?'

Zoe was laughing openly at her now, indulgent and
affectionate.

'Don't laugh,' said her mother. 'A magpie on its own is
so unlucky. Oh, dear. One magpie. And flying straight
towards us like that. That's terribly unlucky. The very
worst.'

The scened changed. Many hours had passed. Her
mother had gone out in the car to meet a friend arriving
at the station. Zoe was in the cool dining-room, setting
out the supper table, polishing the glittering crystal.

Suddenly she was drawn out of the house by some
secret, irresistible force. She was on a bicycle riding
along the country lanes. Tall grass sighed in the wind
as she swept past. She was propelled faster and faster, as
though some unseen thread were drawing her along.

A long dark shadow passed her, sending up a black
cloud of smoke, choking and blinding her. She pedalled
on, powerless to stop. Rounding a corner, she saw her
mother's car, a tiny speck crouched against the side of the
road, creeping along like wounded insect.

And then rounding the corner in the opposite direction
the long dark shadow reappeared, throwing itself over
the road. A huge black vehicle followed, lurching and
screeching, stealing the light from the whole of the
landscape and creating a stifling blind darkness.

There was noise and confusion. An explosion and fire.
Black smoke. Billows and billows of it. Zoe was pedalling
with all her might but her legs were no more than lead
pillows. The pedals were motionless, the cycle chain
locked and still.

She felt herself fall, connect with the sticky warm tarmac. Looking up, she saw her mother's pathetically injured car, the metal bruised and twisted, great white scars marring the bright blue paintwork.

And then, she saw her mother, slumped at the wheel, her wide-open eyes sightlessly staring, a complex lattice work of blood gleaming on her face and neck.

Zoe heard groans, terrible moans of pain. As she watched in transfixed horror, the huge black vehicle began to turn red – the bright scarlet of newly shed blood. It set off again, its engine roaring and furious like the roar of a crazed bull. Zoe saw that it was a bus. A London bus, penned-up and angry in a traffic jam.

She sensed a low, nagging dread. She tried to move. She was pinned to the spot, powerless. A figure ran out from the Gloucestershire hedgerow, straight into the traffic jam. The tiny wiry figure of a child. It was a little boy, sobbing with rage and frustration. He ran at the bus, butting it like a goat. But the bus was stronger. It reached out and swallowed the child up into its growling belly, and he was flattened. Ground to dust.

Zoe was weeping, trying to pedal forward and save the child, because it was a small boy she knew. It was little Stefan Kossek. But she couldn't reach him. The smoke cloud was swelling and billowing and she could see only darkness.

Around her she smelled pain and death, but could not do anything except weep.

A man came running from the smoke. He was black from the soot and fire. Black hair, black eyebrows. Zoe fastened her eyes on him and saw that he was her only salvation from the disaster that was about to swallow her.

'Zoe,' he called. 'Zoe.'

She called back, but her voice choked in her throat.

He held out his arms to her. 'My darling,' he said. 'My poor wounded darling.'

CHAPTER 11

François stood at the window of the fourth-floor offices of *Now* magazine. Behind him his editor, Mary Cartland, looked through his latest collection of celebrity photographs.

'These are great,' she said eventually.

François leaned moodily against the thick plate glass. To the east he could see down the river as far as the Dartford Bridge, an exquisite and delicate piece of engineering, bisecting the skyline. Huge monolithic glass buildings put up in the 1980s reared up from the banks of the river. Their smoky blue and greenish-grey surfaces shone serenely in the pale sunshine, a vast glass sea in which the reflection of soft white clouds gently drifted.

'We'll run them next week,' Mary said. 'How soon can you let me have some more?'

François shrugged. He was tired. He had hardly slept the night before. The episode with Zoe Peach had completely thrown him. And, what was worse, he had had to admit to himself that it was not her astonishing revelation of a premonition involving himself and Leonore which had most unnerved him.

For a brief moment he relived the sensation of her exquisite body resting in his arms, the explosion of a symphony of feelings he had not experienced since the early days with Poppy, and with Zoe the explosion had been stronger and more arousing than it had been with Poppy even at the beginning.

He ran a finger around the moist inside of his roll-neck collar. At the same time, his other hand was inevitably creeping down to the pocket of his jacket in search of a cigarette. Impatiently, he clasped his hands behind his back, recalling that, whilst Mary was far too polite to say so, she hated people to smoke in her office – and quite right, too.

'François?' Mary prompted.

He turned. 'Sorry. Thoughts elsewhere.' He gave a rueful smile which made Mary Cartland's heart jerk. Not for the first time she wondered if François had any idea of his effect on women. He seemed hardly aware of his dark esoteric male magnetism. And she supposed it was that very unawareness that accentuated his charisma.

Mary swept her hand over the row of glossy prints. 'Your heart isn't in this work, is it?'

François shrugged. 'One doesn't turn down work that pays the kind of money this does.'

Mary smiled. 'We all have to compromise,' she said briskly. 'Your work is beautifully professional. A real circulation booster. And just because things are to the popular taste, that doesn't mean one has to scorn them, François.'

He sighed. The idea of trailing off to charm more egotistical celebrities depressed him, but Mary was absolutely right in what she had just said. He smiled at her, wry and dry. 'I'll try to be less arrogant.'

She gave a brief ripe chuckle. 'I'll call you later on and give you the details of the shoot at Hartsford House. But right now, I suggest you push off home and get some rest.' She peered at him, convinced that the fine lines of strain she could see around his eyes and mouth had not been visible before. 'You look dreadful – as though you've been up all night with the cat on the landing.'

François frowned, puzzled.

'A very old saying of my father's,' Mary explained, 'which just goes to show how ancient I am.' She smiled, opening the door and ushering him through, holding herself back from offering his beautiful tight buttocks a loving pat and feeling hugely pleased with her restraint.

François bought a ticket at the underground station. Instead of his usual practice of loping down the escalator three steps at a time, he stood on the wooden-slatted step immobile, allowing himself to passively sink down. He wanted to shake himself like a dog, shake off this troubled mood and get back to his usual rational self. Cool and detached. Unemotional – except as far as his sweet little Leonore was concerned.

He was reminded that, at the moment, Leonore was edgy and upset, too, worrying that Zoe Peach would banish her from the language group if she put on too much of a spurt, worrying about Poppy's forthcoming marriage. Well, he presumed that was one of his daughter's worries, although she had never said so directly.

To make matters worse, Poppy had been on the phone the evening before. And on the rampage. Usually, when she called, she spent most of her time chatting to Leonore; attempting to charm her child in that faintly desperate and vulnerable way that parents do when they have virtually rejected their offspring. But this time Poppy had speedily concluded her conversation with Leonore. It was François she had wanted to speak to.

François felt his face set into grim lines. Cold rage towards Poppy stirred in his heart. It struck him that this emotion was of longer standing than he had been prepared to admit before yesterday's conversation made it impossible to ignore. In fact, for a number of weeks, instead of feeling wistfully regretful on Leonore's part for Poppy's departure, he had found himself becoming much more inclined to anger and disapproval regarding the way his ex-wife had deserted his daughter.

He couldn't help thinking that these negative feelings had been sparked off by the connection he had sensed between Zoe Peach and Leonore at Zoe's party. There had been such a clear spark of feeling between them, a warm glow of affection that he doubted he had ever sensed in the atmosphere when Leonore was with Poppy.

And it was on the issue of Zoe Peach that he and Poppy, separated from each other by thousands of miles of ocean and a an ever growing emotional gulf, had become embroiled in an icy and acrimonious telephone interchange.

'François!' Poppy had spoken his name as though it were an accusation. The angry disapproval in her tone had reminded him so strongly of his mother that he had felt himself transported back in time; a little boy who had unknowingly sinned and must now be admonished. 'François!' she insisted, unable to tolerate so much as a split second of silence.

'I'm here, Poppy. Go on.'

'Leonore's sent me a very odd letter. Are you sure she's all right?'

'Leonore is fine, Poppy,' he had said wearily. *As well as a kid can be when her mother's run off halfway around the world and more or less ignores her.*

'She says there's a child in her class who's always screaming.'

'Yes, there's a kid in her language group who has some problems, apparently.'

'She'll never learn anything if she's with disruptive children. Really, François, this insistence on educating her in a state school is ridiculous. It's gone on far too long. I put her name down for Queen Anne's Preparatory the week she was born. It's high time she took up her place there.'

'I know how you feel about this,' François said patiently. 'But she's extremely happy where she is.'

'Her spelling is still a disgrace,' Poppy said hotly.

'No,' François countered quietly. 'Leonore's spelling is perfectly acceptable for a child of her age.'

'I don't want her to be *acceptable*,' Poppy yelled, completely losing her cool. 'I want her to be *exceptional*, the best.'

'She is,' François said softly. 'Your own child always is.'

'Oh, for God's sake!' Frustration vibrated down the phone.

'Look, Poppy, Leonore is getting along perfectly fine. And it's not only me who thinks so. The Headteacher is very pleased with her and so is her language tutor.'

There was a short silence. 'Is that Miss Peach?' Poppy enquired, and François could tell she was making a tremendous effort to sound calm.

114

'Yes.' François had held himself rigid, refusing to allow his mind to fill with the fragrance and the whole essence of Zoe Peach. It was as though Poppy might see into his thoughts and instantly set out to trample the tender shoot that he could not bear to see brutally torn from the ground.

'François!' There it was again, his mother's voice. Why had he never noticed the similarity before? 'François! Are you and Miss Peach . . . involved in some way?'

François had been stunned. It had never occurred to him that Leonore's innocent scribblings would arouse any particular interest in Poppy's mind, let alone what sounded like suspicion and severe displeasure.

It had never occurred to him, either, that his two encounters with Zoe Peach might constitute anything that might be called an involvement. But now that the words had been spoken, he knew they carried a ring of truth.

Anger had heated up. How dare Poppy interfere with his life? She had all but wiped him out with her infidelity and desertion. What possible right had she to question his new friendships?

He allowed the silence to lengthen, knowing that Poppy would be infuriated. 'I have my own needs, Poppy. And my own friends,' he ventured enigmatically. 'And you have Liam.'

'I have a right to know who you're consorting with when *my daughter is involved*,' Poppy snapped menacingly, goaded beyond all endurance.

François had a curious sense of becoming finally severed from Poppy, the strong silken cord that had bound the two of them together drawing out thin and frayed before snapping in two.

'Well, you'd be delighted with Zoe Peach as a consort for either myself or Leonore. She's very intelligent, very well educated, speaks several languages fluently and has the kind of friends who look as though they've just popped out of London's top drawer. Exactly the sort of person you'd approve of, Poppy.' He hadn't quite believed his ears as he heard himself make this droll speech. Maybe Poppy hadn't been too impressed either as she'd let out a choked cry of rage and hung up on him without delay.

And François had been left feeling not only finally cut adrift from his ex-wife, but in some way irrevocably linked to Zoe Peach.

Walking down the road to his house, he attempted to put both Zoe Peach and Poppy out of his mind. Speculations and brooding about relationships led nowhere as far as he was concerned. Relationships were for living and experiencing in the here and now. Constant reflecting only led to unnecessary anxiety or degrading inertia. He had first-hand knowledge of both, had been been through all that kind of pain just after Poppy had dropped her thunderbolt about leaving him.

Besides Leonore, there was only room in his life for work. Work, professionalism, attention to detail, perfection – those were the secrets of survival. If he filled his diary with assignments, and employed only the highest of work standards, then, together with all the love and care he lavished on Leonore, there was no time left to reflect.

On reaching home, he tossed his leather portfolio on to

the desk and sprang upstairs to change from his charcoal-grey tailored jacket into the battered black leather one he had bought in the King's Road ten years previously.

He was surprised to hear a sharp rapping on the front door. He stood for a moment, uncharacteristically struck with a faint stab of alarm.

It was his neighbour Marina who stood on his doorstep, a striking figure with her wild silver mane and long long legs encased in blue jeans surely as old and battered as his King's Road jacket.

'I've got Leonore around at my place,' she announced shortly without preamble.

'It's only just after two.' François was alarmed. 'What's wrong? Is she ill?'

'No, not ill. She's asleep, actually.' Marina craned over the small hedge that divided their two front paths. 'Perfectly safe, I can see her from here, tucked up on the sofa in my front room.'

'What the hell's happened? Oh, God! And I wasn't here for her.' That Leonore should have been in distress or some kind of danger whilst he was absent! The very thought sent a heavy thud of pain through his heart, seeming to throw all other concerns into perspective.

'These things happen,' Marina said, observing him with a dry expression. 'Parents can't be on call twenty-four hours a day the whole year round.'

'So – what's been going on?' François demanded.

'She knocked on my door around an hour ago. She'd been home first to see if you were in. And, being a sensible kid, she came straight round to me when she found you weren't.'

'But why did she come out of school?'

117

'It took a bit of time to find that out,' Marina admitted. 'She was very quiet and withdrawn. She just wanted to sit in my kitchen and cuddle the dog.' Marina recalled her shock at seeing the child standing there behind her door; the hunched defensive stance, the girl's white, stricken face. And then there had been this awful silence, with Leonore unwilling to make a sound for over half an hour.

'I left her to it, huddled up by my Aga cuddling the dog. It made his day. Anyway, in her own time, she suddenly wanted to talk.'

'Yes?'

'She had a curious little tale to tell. About her teacher – a Miss Peach.'

François swore softly.

'Apparently, Miss Peach stirred up quite a bit of excitement by fainting away on the floor in the middle of giving a lesson. Leonore went to fetch the Head.'

'And?'

'The Head phoned for an ambulance and Miss Peach was carted off. Leonore was all set to go out to the ambulance and wave her goodbye. But the Head, in her wisdom, wouldn't allow her. I suppose it was wise to be cautious.' Marina raised her eyebrows, clearly on the side of warm childish impulse as against sensible adult restraint.

François stared. Then he laughed. 'I can imagine the scene. I'd guess Leonore was pretty frustrated.'

'From the way she described it to me, that's a bit of an understatement. Apparently she raged and wept and then seized her chance and dashed out of the gates during the dinner break when the supervisors were at

118

the other end of the playground. No one knew she'd gone until the afternoon register was taken. She's a sharp little operator, your Leonore.'

'Mmm.' Got some of her father's rebellion in her, thought François, recalling one or two hair-raising bolts of his own from more than one school.

'Leonore's plan was to go to the hospital and find Miss Peach to make sure she was OK. But she soon realized that she didn't know which hospital she might have been taken to, or indeed where any of the nearby hospitals are.'

'Aah – poor pet.'

'So she came home, hoping you'd be on hand with transport to oblige.' Marina eyed him speculatively and gave a low chuckle. 'And if I'm any judge of human nature, I should think you're heartily relieved you weren't.'

'Yes . . .' François tried to smile, give the appearance of passing off the whole incident as something fuelled by nothing more than a piece of childish impulse. Instead he felt a sickening unease. Leonore's reaction seemed out of all proportion to the seriousness of the incident and this, in itself, was worrying. But even worse, Zoe Peach might be truly ill. Damaged, in some way.

He felt his neighbour's sharp glance assessing him, her eyes shrewd and speculative. 'I think Leonore will probably sleep for a couple of hours; she's used up so much energy worrying,' Marina commented, seeming to be leading up to something.

François looked down. 'Yes.' His voice was low and weary.

'So if you wanted to . . . go out anywhere, I'd be more

than happy to look after her until you get back. We get on famously, Leonore, me and Risk!' Marina paused.

'Are you telling me that Leonore would like me to go and check on Miss Peach?' François asked.

'Yes. In fact, if you don't, I think you'll have trouble on your hands once she wakes up.' Marina's smile was slightly wicked, making Fraçois wonder what else Leonore had said to Marina, what else Marina had guessed.

'You're right,' he said briskly, his mind made up. 'I'll go on the bike, it'll be the quickest way of getting around in the rush hour.'

'No rush, Leonore will be perfecly safe with me,' said Marina calmly. 'Just think about yourself for a change.'

François was already moving down the hallway, grabbing his crash helmet, reaching for his keys.

He turned, registering that last remark, amazed at his neighbour's powers of perception.

CHAPTER 12

Zoe sat slumped in the corner of her sofa. Her room and the street outside were quiet. All she could hear was the occasional swish of tyres over wet tarmac. Rain had been coming down steadily for more than an hour now and the light beyond the windows was yellowish and soupy.

She leaned her head back and felt sleep begin to creep up on her. She steeled herself to resist it, to stay fully awake and make her brain work. But her legs felt like tubes of sand, her mind distressingly imprecise.

They had offered her tranquillizers at the hospital. They had said there was nothing clinically wrong with her. She had simply fainted from exhaustion and stress. It was not at all uncommon, nothing to worry about. Her heart function was normal, her blood pressure normal, there was no clinical evidence of anything outside the normal.

During her examination in the busy Casualty department, she had toyed with the idea of seeking advice on her current mental state, being entirely open and frank about the two premonitions she carried in her head. She had felt a need to express her total conviction of their significance, and because of that her constant dread of the future. Noting the doctor's harassed face, the way in which he had to dash from one cubicle to another, juggling patient's needs like a conjuror with brightly coloured balls, she had decided to say nothing.

Each time she recalled the way in which she had passed out in front of her pupils, no doubt frightening them to death, she had felt a terrible fraud. Despite all her anxiety and fear she saw herself in the role of some ineffectual and hysterical woman in a Victorian melodrama, one of those droopy heroines who made a habit of fainting in order that their hero would swiftly materialize to save the scene.

There would be no hero on her scene tonight, Zoe thought grimly. Charles had phoned with profuse apologies to say that he wouldn't be able to see her that evening as something quite unavoidable had come up. Naturally he could hardly bear to wait another day to see her – but that was life, wasn't it? – and he'd pick her up tomorrow at eight.

She felt herself horribly alone. Drained, bewildered and exhausted with no one to turn to, no one with whom she could share her ongoing, seemingly unending nightmare.

She sighed, felt herself drifting, was unable to fight of the dull fatigue . . .

She woke up, alarmed. There was a terrible banging and ringing rattling in her ears. For a moment she could not think where she was, what time it was. The room seemed to have grown very dark. She got to her feet, found herself unsteady and stumbling.

She glanced at the clock on the mantlepiece and saw that it was only just past three-thirty. The darkness must all be in her mind.

The knocking and ringing had stopped. There was a horrible hush. She went into the hallway, standing like a startled deer, sensing the air, listening. She felt sick apprehension. She was entirely alone in the house.

She jerked herself into action, fought down the panic and attempted to crush it with scorn.

She saw a shadow beyond the thick glass of the front door, its bulk splintered into black needles by the sunburst rays carved into the plate.

Gingerly she opened the door. The diffuse figure crystallized into one powerful male form: a man, dressed all in black – black leather jacket, black jeans, a black roll-neck shirt. He filled her vision. He was very tall, a truly arresting presence with his dark hair and black eyebrows, his stern face.

'François!' she whispered, relief and joy welling up in great waves. 'Aah!'

He eased his way in, clasping her swaying figure around the shoulders and supporting her with his calm strength.

He felt her body rigid with tension and fear and was filled with compassion. The sense of mingled protectiveness and desire which rose up in him was so sweet it made him gasp.

'*Ma pauvre petite*,' he murmured, automatically switching to the language of his early childhood. '*Reste tranquille. Calme, calme.*'

He sat down in a large armchair beside the fireplace and pulled her down on to his knee because he knew that she needed to be held, that she could not endure her lonely struggles for one more second. She was like an injured dog, yearning for the reassurance of protecting

123

arms, the steady beat of a sympathetic heart beneath its ears.

She folded herself into him, moulding her bones into his.

He said nothing, simply stroked her hair and her face, over and over again, his hands supremely gentle.

'Am I going mad?' she asked eventually. 'Deranged?'

'No,' François responded firmly. 'You're experiencing something I don't begin to understand. But you're not mad. Simply frightened beyond endurance.'

'Yes,' she agreed softly. 'Thank you for that, François, for trying to understand . . .'

He sighed. He doubted he would ever understand. But he did not doubt *her*. She intrigued him, fascinated him. And he wanted to become a part of her life. An astonishing thought. It gave him intense joy to realize he could still feel such emotion towards another adult human being. Another woman. He had decided some time ago that all those wonderful feelings were dead.

'Have you had another dream?' François asked. 'Another premonition?' The word grated in his throat. He hated the whole idea of it; things outside rational explanation, fanciful speculating, hocus-pocus.

Zoe's breathing slowed and deepened.

'Trust me,' he said.

'Last night I dreamed of my mother. She died four years ago. She was killed, driving her car.' There was a silence. Zoe put up her face and looked at François, staring straight into his eyes. 'I was into my twenties then, but I was still a girl.'

François's brows pulled together as he focused his

concentration on her strange acquamarine eyes and her low, very pleasing voice. He had the impression of that there was a tale she was going to tell him. One that had perhaps waited far too long to be told. He tightened his arms around her. 'Go on.'

'My father died before I really knew him. He was the founder of a building firm, always working, never at home. He left my mother with a great deal of money – and me. I was ten. I knew straight away that it was my job to look after my mother. For ever. I knew this in my bones, because of the way she was: always needing someone, never truly grown up. And, besides, my father had spelled it out to me very clearly the day before he died. "You must look after your mother, Zoe. Promise me."'

'These slender shoulders,' François murmured, his hand caressing the delicate bones. 'Such a heavy burden to put on them. And at ten years old.' He thought of Leonore, only a few years younger than Zoe had been when given this task. How would Leonore feel to be put in charge of *his* whole happiness whilst she was still a child herself?

'It didn't seem like that,' Zoe said. 'It seemed as though I'd been given a mission, something terribly exciting and heroic. You see, I'd always loved being with my mother. She hated being solemn, she liked to be entertained and have fun. And after my father died, she was able to indulge those tastes to the full. She adored throwing parties, going to the theatre, the ballet, the opera. She loved travelling and buying beautiful clothes. And I was her dear little companion.'

'Didn't you have a life of your own?'

'Her life was my life. Her friends my friends. It never occurred to me to think it odd, or to be unhappy.'

'Go on.' François was racking his brains to guess the connection between this sad story of Zoe's strange early life and her breakdown in school that morning. He wondered if she herself saw a connection, and if she did, whether she would be able to share it.

'I saw myself being with my mother for ever,' Zoe continued. 'I had no serious longstanding relationships with men and I never felt that I missed anything. All my friends had "relationship", but I was happy to be a girl on my own. It wasn't until after my mother's death that I became . . . involved with a man.' Her eyes connected with his, dark and hunted.

'And?' he whispered gently.

'It was a painful experience – and it didn't last long.' Her voice held traces of uncharacteristic bitterness.

François bit back the questions he burned to ask. Braced himself against the arrow of jealousy that pierced him to hear her talk of a love affair.

She leaned against him, as though suddenly exhausted. He wondered if he should stop her talking and persuade her to go to bed and rest.

'You're very patient, listening to all this,' she said.

'Why did you need to say it?'

'What I've just told you links up with my dream. It was a ghastly re-living of my mother's death. I don't remember ever having this dream before, although I've often imagined the terrible, unthinkable moment that she died; gone over and over it, trying to persuade myself she would have known nothing, felt nothing. It would all have been over with in a split second.'

'Were you there when she died – in reality?' François interposed softly.

'No. And I never saw her body, nor even the wreck of the car.' Zoe released a long shuddering breath. 'But last night I lived it all. I saw the runaway tractor mow down her little car and pulverize it. I saw her poor cut face and her shattered, mangled body.'

'Dear God!'

He heard her swallow, prepare herself for yet further revelations. 'And then . . . you see . . . there was this terrible picture in my head. I couldn't get the image out of my mind. All morning it was there. Horrible, crushing.'

François felt the breath halt in his lungs.

'You must understand,' she said with heartbreaking appeal, 'I feel as though my previous life has been some kind of preparation, that I was shaped in some way for a very precise time in the future. A part of some complex destiny that's about to become reality.'

He sighed. Suddenly she had lost him, gone off on this idiosyncratic and irrational train of thinking which he was unable to comprehend or follow.

She turned up her face to his, her eyes dark with pain. 'Please, François, don't be angry again. Please. I can't help these thoughts. Dear God, I only wish I could.'

He felt her face bury itself into his chest. Her arms, which had lain still and lifeless as she spoke, now wound themselves around him.

'Make me forget,' she said abruptly, astonishingly. 'Make me feel safe.'

Her hands moved sensuously over his ribs, hungry for closeness, for greater knowledge of his flesh and his whole physical being.

127

He held her very close. Gently he touched her face, her eyes, her mouth, her throat. They had met no more than three times. They knew nothing of each other. And yet there was a strange fittingness about what was going to happen. Electric anticipation passed through his nerves like a bolt of lightning. And he sensed an identical response in her. They fitted together; heartbeat to heartbeat, limb to limb.

It was unthinkable. And yet inevitable. He sensed the urgency of the air in the room, thick with their mutual desire.

She was breathing in shallow gasps, staring into his eyes.

With gentle lingering fingertips, he touched first one and then the other of her breasts. He felt a swift jerk of feeling dart down her spine beneath his other hand and knew that he had the power to please her, to take her on a journey of blissful enchantment that would indeed make her forget everything else.

His own desire was mounting. He slipped his hands inside her blouse and explored the velvety skin of her waist, reverently tracing the delicate framework of her ribs.

As his fingers touched the smooth swell of her breasts, she moaned, pressing the sensitive pads of his fingers deeper into the warm flesh. 'Aah, François, François.'

He looked down at her, lying in his arms, her face rosy and abandoned, her filmy blouse sagging open, her breasts bared for him to kiss.

It seemed to him that a lifetime had passed since he had loved a woman, truly desired a mate.

The reawakening of such powerful desire, so long

damned up, filled him with elation. He felt himself poised on the edge of something dizzily dangerous which would alter his life. The patterns of his former world would dissolve and new ones would form. Bending his head, he moved his lips against her breasts, sucking on the erect rose-pink nipples.

Neither of them spoke.

François gasped aloud at the intensity of his wanting.

He lifted her bodily in his arms and placed her gently on the floor. She groaned softly. Her hands reached out, running over his chest, exploring in wonder, then reaching further, coming to the fastening on his jeans.

Smiling at her sudden hesitation, he put his hand over hers and wrenched the zip down in one swift movment.

To his dismay, she gasped and tensed. Her eyes filled with sudden alarm.

Instantly he held himself perfectly still. She was like a animal scenting danger; one false move and she would flee away.

He rolled over onto his back, put up his hand slowly to her lovely white throat. He smiled at her with great tenderness. 'Don't be afraid, darling. There's nothing to be afraid of.'

She bent and kissed him, her mouth warm on his, but the lips trembling with apprehension. 'I want you so much,' she whispered, tears glistening on her eyelashes. 'But you see, before . . . everything seemed to slide out of control . . . I was terrified. Of pain, of being hurt.'

Her eyes were huge with desire and fear and he cursed any man who could have treated her with such a lack of sensitivity. 'Oh God, Zoe, my sweet one. I shan't give you any pain.'

Slowly, slowly he took her hand and guided it gently over his belly. Her fingers brushed against his swollen shaft and he groaned internally with the searing pleasure he felt. He held himself rigid, the power of his will driven into the submission of his responses in respect of her alarm.

She looked at him with a flash of understanding. He was not going to drive into her, a hot engine of desire. He would harness all of his own urgent impulses until she was ready. He would be endlessly patient. He would coax her with exquisite gentleness. 'Oh, François,' she groaned. Suddenly she knew that he was her only love. Her love forever; stretching back into her past and ahead into her future.

Only him.

Her eyes were huge with love. Surging waves of fresh desire lapped in her breasts and her belly.

He watched her. He was a man of experience. She felt the magnet of his sensual knowledge. And softly the fear fell away from her.

She pulled his jeans over his hips, exposing his nakedness. She rolled the fabric down his thighs and calves, pulling off his shoes as she did so. His feet were long and slender; beautiful like all the rest of him.

His eyes never left her face as she leaned down to him, kissing his knees, the inside of his thighs. She sat up again, looking at him with wonder. And then, marvelling at her own newly found spontaneity, she found herself reaching out to him, caressing the taut, silk-skinned shaft, adoring him.

'Now,' he breathed, burning for her.

She was still wearing her absurd little silk skirt. He

wrenched it up over her buttocks and pulled down the flimsy white panties. Her eyes sharpened with longing. She lifted herself, straddled him, felt him pierce her, sliding in with slow firm authority. There was a long low sigh of mutual bliss.

He realized immediately how inexperienced she was. She seemed entirely innocent of the slow lapping strokes of lovemaking, the thrusting rhythms and the gradual acceleration to a crescendo of pleasure.

He was determined that she should experience the most intense satisfaction.

With deft and exquisite mastery he lifted her from his hips and laid her down on the carpet. He found a cushion, slipped it beneath her buttocks, spread her legs wide and entered her again.

'Slowly,' he said. 'Slowly, slowly. Come with me, darling, We're dancing, lifting, flying.'

She was ready now, her body and mind a throbbing receptacle. He thrust deeper and deeper until she cried out in ecstasy, her muscles throbbing against him.

He was on the verge of his climax, poised on the edge of the cliff, but he forced himself to wait. Looking down at her face he saw joyful abandonment moulding her features, ecstasy moving across her lips and cheeks like great sweeps of moving sunlight over a far landscape.

She stared at him wonderingly, those amazing acquamarine eyes spinning with radiance.

She arched herself up to him, every pulse in her body throbbing. He slid his hand beneath the base of her hairline and pulled her head towards him, bringing their mouths together once more. Their tongues joined, bringing another burst of surging connection.

131

He could feel the tender folds between her legs sparking with fresh pleasure.

His own climax would not wait. He groaned deeply driving into the darkness of her femaleness, his pleasure spinning out to an eternity.

Lying beside her, coming gradually down from the peak of ecstasy, he found himself suffused with an aching tenderness.

She watched him, her eyes never leaving him. Gratefulness, akin to worship, spilled from her quite openly. She would not conceal it from him even if it had been in her power to do so.

He kissed her hair and her eyelids. He kissed the moist skin of her face and then her breasts and the shallow mound of her stomach. There were streaks of blood on the insides of her thighs, sticky and metallic.

He stroked his finger over the skin and showed her the rusty smudges.

She smiled, shaking her head. 'You didn't hurt me. Oh no.' She touched his face with reverent fingers. 'You showed me how to live again.'

'Why didn't you tell me?' he asked gently.

'That I was a virgin?' She sighed, giving a rueful smile. 'I was ashamed to confess my inexperience.'

He shook his head in disbelief. Such a precious gift she had given him. He bent to kiss her lips with exquisite tenderness. Once again he wanted to ask all kinds of questions but held himself back, respecting her right to keep silent on matters that might be too painful to share – even with him.

She took his hand and placed it to lie on the cleft between her breasts. 'The man I told you about,' she said softly, as though she had delved into his mind and understood exactly what it was he needed to know, 'I believed that I loved him and that he loved me. You see, François, I was very naïve then. It took me a while to realize that he simply regarded me as easy game. A poor lonely little rich girl who needed to have her education extended by getting laid.'

François stroked the damp tendrils of hair away from her face. 'And?'

'I didn't get laid!' A smile of mischief lit her features, fuelling him with a fresh surge of love.

His fingers traced around the curve of her lips. 'You're making a joke of it. But he frightened you didn't he?'

She closed her eyes, and a vein in her temples throbbed. 'He was so hot and so quick. So rough. I felt that I was being attacked.'

'My poor poor sweet darling? How could any man treat you like that?' He gathered her close to him and kissed her cheeks and her forehead and her hair.

'We were both guests at a country house weekend party. I let him come to my room . . . I was such a fool.' She gave a huge sigh. 'I suppose I led him on, as the saying goes. And then when he started running out of control I lost my nerve. I hit out at him. I told him if he didn't let me go I'd scream the place down.' She let out a long breath. 'Just thinking about it makes me go hot with shame.'

'Why? You did the right thing.'

'Yes. But I felt as though I'd acted like a little tart. Leading a man on and getting him all hot for me, then shouting for the fire brigade because I couldn't stand the heat.'

'No, *chérie*, you were brave. Wonderful.'

'That wasn't how he saw it. He called me a mean little bitch and a cock teaser.' She spoke the words with brutal frankness.

'The bastard!'

'Maybe.'

'And after that?'

'I steered very clear of men.'

François said nothing but simply held her close in his arms, his heart expanding with love and sympathy. Long moments passed. He felt her heart beating and her breath warm against his chest. And then, very slowly, her hands began to stroke him; his chest, his arms, his belly. Her head moved over his body and her lips began to trace the path her hands had taken, sliding down between his thighs and caressing his swelling shaft until he gasped with pleasure and could not hold back another moment before being inside her once more.

This time there was a raw, almost savage intensity to their lovemaking. He thrust deep inside her as she welcomed him without reserve, raising her hips to take him in as fully as she was able, drawing him into the darkest most secret places of her body and her mind.

As he drove into her, so she went with him, moulding to the rhythm, tightening her muscles around him and giving him the deepest pleasure he could imagine.

In time they shuddered together in unison – he groaning, she crying out, as they reached a throbbing climax.

She gave a long sigh. She had a sense that her body had turned to liquid, lapped with warm waves of satisfaction.

He looked into her amazing eyes, pressing his mouth on hers, gently silencing her tiny yelps of ecstasy.

He felt a strange, quiet contentment, fanning out from the heart of him, reaching out and drawing his lover into its protective circle.

He took her hand, holding it with gentle pressure as the intensity of their pleasure slowly subsided.

He too had the feeling of having experienced some kind of re-birth. He had rediscovered the ability to love a woman fully, from the heart; and, in doing so, had rediscovered a part of himself that he had feared was dead.

She stared into his eyes with an almost childlike directness. 'I didn't know it could be like that. Making love.'

François cradled her head in his hands. 'Neither did I.'

CHAPTER 13

Marina watched over the sleeping Leonore.

Listening to the soft rhythmic tempo of the child's breathing, she found herself infinitely soothed. She tilted her head this way and that, examining the many different ways in which the late afternoon light illuminated the curves of Leonore's sculpted facial bones, changing her skin from ice-cream pallor to warm fleshy apricot. Smiling, she admired the girl's long curved eyelashes resting perfectly still, their curled tips just touching the little mound of flesh rising over the high arched cheekbones which were an exact replica of her father's.

There is something about the casual, heedless serenity of a child's sleep that gives one hope, thought Marina. Even with fifty on the clock.

As she watched and listened, she found her own breathing falling into harmony with Leonore's. All was peaceful.

All shall be well and all shall be well and all manner of thing shall be well.

This calm, comforting philosophy from somewhere in her past stole uninvited into her head.

'Now where did those words of wisdom spring from?'

Marina asked Risk, who was blissfully slumbering on the sofa beneath Leonore's protective arm. 'Presumably from the vast sump of my memory – and attempting to dredge *that* is becoming a progressively tricky business.'

Risk opened an eye, found his mistress much as normal and closed it again.

'*All shall be well . . .*' murmured Marina, pondering. Who the hell was it had dreamed up those reassuring words? Some slaughtered saint, some martyred prophet?

The answer was on the tip of her tongue, perched on the knife-edge of her brain. The more she struggled to recall, the more the memory eluded her.

Another memory intruded instead, words from some long forgotten academic text popping into her mind centre stage. 'A temporary absence of the ability to recall a name or phrase will often be rectified by focusing the thoughts elsewhere. The information that so stubbornly resists all attempts to be retrieved will later most likely present itself quite spontaneously.' Marina could see the words leaping up from the page as clear as though they were there in front of her.

She remembered her days as a psychology undergraduate when she would devour reference books in the library and had had the ability to recall whatever she wanted from them with barely the whisker of an effort. Then she had been twenty. Now thirty years had passed and millions of her brain cells had perished in obedience to perfectly normal ageing processes.

'My faculties are blunted. I used to be proud of my brain and now I'd like to hide it in a long overcoat like a pair of old veiny legs,' she grumbled to the heedless, sleeping duo.

She had always been fascinated with the caprices of human learning, the initial looking and listening, the subsequent remembering and forgetting.

And there was something deeper. The intriguing notion of memory going beyond each separate individual and extending to a collective mesh of experiences shared by all of those inhabiting the earth. A sharing of the joys of birth and love, the pain of disease and wars and death.

And, most fascinating of all, memory transcending time, moving not only through the past, but into the future.

Premonition. Prediction. Telling the future. What psychologists referred to as precognition.

That last thought triggered more old memories, taking her back around a quarter of a century to a time when her days had been filled with fascinating work projects, her evenings crammed with fun and her nights spiced with sex.

She remembered how she had used to get a little tipsy at the end of extended dinner parties with the claret-swigging set she and Colin had knocked around with at the start of their marriage. Over waxed pine tables lit with fat candles from Habitat and littered with half-empty bottles, she would expound her fanciful theories on the quirks of the human mind to their swinging intellectual friends and provide hilarious entertainment.

Everyone laughed at first and found her talk of extra-sensory perception and the paranormal splendidly entertaining. Stretching the point a little, thought some of them; the ones who were pursuing careers in the more established and orthodox sciences. But, then, Marina's subject was psychology and for those in the pure fields of physics and chemistry that new science (as it was then) was in itself something of a joke.

Marina would remind them that her studies were not to be taken lightly. She had won a prestigious research scholarship in order to prepare a PhD thesis. Just because her chosen subject concerned the paranormal, just because her investigations involved those who claimed psychic powers such as clairvoyance, telepathy and precognition, did not mean that her work was not serious.

And, gradually, the patronizing scepticism turned to curiosity when she demonstrated an unnerving talent for putting her findings and theories into practice. Very soon she had become renowned for her clever knack of predicting things which would subsequently come true. Just little things at first: the sex of an expected baby, the precise date of a forthcoming event, the location of a place which would become important to the person on whom she was concentrating her predictive efforts.

People began to observe her with a new – and faintly wary – respect. Beyond the raised eyebrows and the murmurings of 'hocus-pocus' was a good deal of barely concealed vying for her opinion on all manner of issues.

Those who had been most disdainful and reticent in public, phoned her up in private, seeking confidential 'consultations' on their personal lives, inviting her insights into their future fortunes. She knew she should resist. That she was playing with fire, possibly risking her whole professional reputation. But curiosity and the irresistible magnet of gaining power over other people's hopes and fears proved too tempting. Resistance had crumbled.

Senior tutors, research directors, the odd professor or two came knocking on her door, eager for her to harness her inexplicable abilities on their behalf.

They came to her with their personal ambitions, their health problems, their guilty adulteries and burning hearts. Souls were stripped naked before her eyes.

Telling herself it was all in the interests of science, she purchased a hypnotizing pendulum, a crystal ball and a set of Tarot cards to help her in her new project.

Her appointment diary began to fill. Satisfied clients spread the word. Requests for her divinations widened out from friends and university colleagues to a more general public. It was not long before she became aware of a difficulty in finding the time to fit in her PhD preparation. Moreover, and most pleasingly, her bank balance had run into four figures – in the black.

It had all been a delicious ego trip. For a time.

Leonore shifted, Risk grunted and Marina was instantly back in the present. Leonore's eyes snapped open. She gazed gravely at Marina and then smiled.

'How does the world look after a good nap?' Marina enquired.

Leonore stared around her, struggling to disentangle herself from the tentacles of sleep and start rebuilding the world of the here and now. 'Nice.' Her brows pinched together. 'Where's Daddy?'

'He's gone to make sure Miss Peach is OK.'

Leonore nodded. A smile lapped over her lips like soft tiny waves sucking at the shoreline.

'Are you hungry?' Marina wondered.

'Yes.'

'For what?'

Leonore pursed her lips in deep consideration. 'An egg. Baked in a little dish with some cream and some butter. And tiny pieces of fried bread to eat with it.'

'Good heavens!'

'I'll show you,' Leonore said. 'Daddy puts chives on top. We've got them growing in the garden.'

In Marina's kitchen they got out eggs and cream and Marina attempted to light her ancient gas oven, her Aga being more ancient still and only fit for warming soup overnight and preparing slow-cooking stews over the period of several days.

She opened the oven and was relieved to find the inside clean, even though the crusted dust of years fell from the side of the door like a small stiff bootlace once disturbed. Half a taper and several small explosions later, combustion was achieved and some chilly looking blue flames spluttered fitfully in the oven's depths.

'I don't cook much,' Marina confessed to a fascinated Leonore. 'Let's go out into the garden and cut some parsley and chives. I think we might have a long wait until this oven gets up to full speed.'

Leonore poked amongst the clay pots bunched together in haphazard groups outside the french door which led from Marina's kitchen into her long thin garden. Her small efficient fingers ploughed through thriving velvety moss and an assortment of very sprightly looking weeds in the hope of identifying something she recognised which could be chopped and sprinkled on to an *oeuf en cocotte*.

Marina looked down the length of the lawn, thinking that it would soon be time to hoist the mower out of the shed and spend the best part of a morning coaxing it into life.

In the early evening of a late April day, the garden glowed with a vivid green intensity as though some celestial colour button had been activated by a godlike finger. Buds had swelled from a delicate hazing over stark branches into fat knobs like babies' fingers. The grass, dampened by earlier rain, sparkled.

Marina lifted her face and breathed in the damp air.

'Here!' Leonore exclaimed in triumph. 'Look, Marina.'

Marina bent down, poising her scissors over some emaciated and weary parsley. 'So, tell me about the mysterious Miss Peach,' she said, squinting and taking aim.

'My daddy is going to marry her,' said Leonore. 'You should chop your parsley down when it starts getting long stalks like this. It won't hurt it and it'll grow back nice and bushy.'

'I'll try to remember,' Marina said meekly. 'And does your daddy know about this? Getting married?'

Leonore smiled with the smooth serenity of childish certainty. 'Just me. I'm the only one who knows. As well as you, Marina.' She smiled up at her new friend with shining confidence. And Marina, filled with the warmth of guileless regard and affection, had a sudden presentiment that what Leonore willed would happen.

She snipped about in her chives, a pleasingly obliging herb which thrived despite the most determined attempts to neglect it, and asked, 'What about Miss Peach? What does she think about all this?'

It seemed to Marina that, in Leonore's eyes, Miss Peach's role in life was clearly and simply to fall in with her father's needs and wishes. A quite proper thought for a daughter to cherish. But the question had needed to be asked.

Leonore gave no immediate answer. 'Perhaps the oven will be up to speed now,' she suggested.

'Indeed,' agreed Marina.

Bearing their herbs, they returned to the kitchen. A pleasant aroma of heat emanated from the oven, inspiring Leonore with keen and hungry anticipation and Marina with huge relief.

They put the little egg-filled dishes in the oven and, whilst Marina set the table, Leonore applied herself to cutting up tiny triangles of bread in preparation for the frying of crispy croutons.

'I don't think Miss Peach knows,' said Leonore. 'Not yet.'

Marina glanced at the old clock on the wall. Four hours he had been gone. She would be surprised if Miss Peach did not know a thing or two about François Rogier by this time.

Stop it, she chided herself; this frivolous approach to the serious things of life.

She dropped the sculpted morsels of bread into the pan where they sizzled plumply.

She looked at the top of Leonore's glossy head and felt a rush of affection. And then she had a sudden memory of her Tarot reading of some weeks before and there was a sickening jarring.

She thought of Leonore and François flying out to New York to watch a mother and a wife bind herself to a stranger. That event had to be significant. The cards had said so. And the grave issue of marriage was clearly very much on Leonore's mind.

Stop that, too! Marina told herself fiercely. The cards have no power. The cards can tell nothing. And in themselves they can do nothing. All they can do is seduce the mind into playing tricks. They're mischievous and capricious. But in the end they're powerless.

She teased the edges of the bubbling bread, lifting them to inspect their degree of crispness.

'Are they ready?' Leonore asked eagerly.

'Nearly. Not long now.' Marina wrapped her free arm around the girl's shoulders and Leonore leaned into her, soft and moulding.

No, the cards were not to be feared, Marina informed herself silently. It was the power in one's own mind that was truly frightening. Pictures had winged through the atmosphere and planted themselves in her mind during those days when she used to carry out her 'consultations'. The power of prediction they had bestowed on her had been intoxicating. But damn scary, too!

'Mmm,' said Leonore, sniffing the air. 'I can't wait for them to be ready.'

Risk was of the same opinion, sitting up against the oven door, nose poised, expression dopily euphoric.

Warmth stole through the kitchen and wrapped them all in a bonding cloak.

Marina had a sudden memory of the tiny room in a cottage hospital where she had been treated for scarlet fever as a child of five. On the wall had been a little plaque, a tapestry bordered in pink cross-stich with a heartening message painstakingly picked out in dark blue

144

in its centre. She saw it as clearly as though it were there in front of her: *Sin is behovely, but all shall be well and all shall be well and all manner of thing shall be well* . . . Dame Julian of Norwich 1343–after 1413.

CHAPTER 14

Zoe was in love, filled with joy – and a glorious feeling she had never had before of being at the start of some splendid journey. François would show her a new life; with him she would feel and do things she had not even begun to imagine before she met him.

The horror of the past weeks, the sense of being held in a dark cage whilst her mind was attacked by some unseen aggressor, seemed to melt away in the heat of his love and the passion of his love-making.

Each time he came to visit, to spend a few snatched hours with her, she stared into his dark, priest-like features and understood why people did crazy, foolhardy things for love. Suddenly it was quite possible to understand why previously sensible ordinary people would throw up their happy tranquil domestic lives, or crazily abandon their careers or even start a war.

It was like that for him too, each time they were in each other's presence, each other's arms. When he touched Zoe and held her, he felt a sureness about the future, saw her with him for the rest of their lives. And when he looked into her marvellous, luminous eyes he saw an exact image of the love he himself felt. It fuelled his desire and at the same time suffused him with a contentment utterly novel to him.

But Zoe was infuriatingly, albeit enchantingly, vague. She seemed to want nothing more than to live in the moment. To be with him when it was possible, to gently long for the next time when she could not.

For François such an attitude was delightful, and yet exasperating. He was a man who needed to move things along.

'So what are we to do?' he demanded one evening, a few weeks after that first magic time they had made love and bound themselves to one another.

They were eating supper together at her flat. Or rather François was making a valiant attempt to consume some of Zoe's painstakingly prepared herb roast chicken, whilst both of them were hardly able to swallow a thing for the intense excitement of anticipating what was soon to follow.

Zoe laid down her fork. Her hair swung over her face as she tilted her head to smile at him. 'Do? We must go on doing what we are doing. Loving each other.'

'Ah, Zoe, my sweet *amour*. You're so honest, so direct,' he told her, leaning across the table and brushing his lips against hers, his eyes burning. 'With me at any rate, and I love that. I adore it. But we have to make decisions, darling. About our future together.' He reached for her hand and pressed it hard beneath his own.

Zoe did not want to think of the future. Nor the past. She wanted only the here and now with this wonderful man who had the power to fill her world and block everything and everyone else out.

147

'Leonore must be told,' he said, and suddenly his eyes were stern.

'I have the feeling Leonore knows,' Zoe said softly.

'She's a very perceptive child. She senses things. But we must be realistic, Zoe – and we must be fair to Leonore, tell her what plainly what is going on between us. And what we plan to do.'

'Yes . . .' She looked at him with that mute, vulnerable appeal that made his heart feel bruised.

'Can't we just go on a little longer as we are, all being so happy?' she pleaded. Every weekend she, François and Leonore spent a whole day together. They went for walks, they went shopping, they played endless games of Ludo and watched TV and listened to music. François cooked mouthwatering lunches and suppers and they sat around the table in his kitchen where the light fell in shiny pools over the pale sanded-and-waxed floor. It was all so wonderfully warm and harmonious and complete.

For the first time in her life Zoe felt herself part of a real family.

And then, later in the week, François would come alone to her house . . .

Her hand moved in his, a soft curl of appeal, but he was determined. 'There's nothing to be afraid of, Zoe. Being honest with Leonore isn't going to spoil our happiness. Quite the reverse. She adores you.'

Zoe nodded, sighed.

'Very well,' he said, his voice cool, 'we'll go on as we are for another week or so. There's probably nothing to gain in presenting Leonore with any revolutionary plans until Poppy's wedding is over and done with. But after that – then we tell her everything.' His face was set and

148

remorseless, emphasizing his determination for this issue to be faced fairly and squarely.

He heard her sharp intake of breath, noticed how she reached for her glass, took a long drink of wine.

He frowned. Was she still caught up with those crazy thoughts about some disaster about to befall him and Leonore? She had never once mentioned those incredible notions, never so much as hinted at them since the day they became lovers. Surely her mind was not still running on that track.

She had predicted a plane crash. Well, fair enough, there would be air disasters in the future just as there had been in the past. Everyone subjected themselves to possible death and disaster every time they moved a muscle. People died tragic deaths in accidents at home, for God's sake.

He stared at her curiously, unwilling to believe that she might still be a helpless victim of such foolish speculations. Her premonition was the one topic he could not raise with her. He refused absolutely to have anything to do with that kind of thinking. It was time-wasting, pointless and potentially dangerous.

Her hand struggled within his as his grasp tightened. She opened her eyes wide, viewing him with alarm. 'François! You're angry. Don't be angry.'

He looked at her, seeing the fear in her eyes, as though he were in some way rejecting her through his silent musings. Reject her! Dear God, the very idea of it was utterly incredible, made him feel the most heartless and vicious of brutes.

He threw down his cutlery, sprang up and pulled her to her feet, clasping her ferociously in his arms. 'I can't

149

bear another second of waiting,' he told her, half dragging her from the room.

And then the two of them were entwined in her bed with its dark carved headboard and its fine white sheets, drowning in each other's limbs and eyes and lips, losing themselves in the sweet abandonment and release of lovemaking and banishing the rest of the world to a far shore.

As Charles negotiated London's early evening traffic with lazy nonchalance, his thoughts strayed once again to Zoe. He congratulated himself on having allowed quite a few weeks to pass without attempting to contact her.

This commendable persistence in resisting many a temptation to dial her number on his mobile had been considerably assisted by the timely appearance of Lizzi Gluck, a pretty German girl spending a riding holiday at the stables from which he occasionally purchased hunters on behalf of clients.

Lizzi was in England for only a few weeks, out to improve her riding skills and also to have a good time. She and Charles had hit it off at once, the moment they laid eyes on each other over the neck of a stunning grey mare which he was critically assessing.

'A beautiful creature,' Lizzi had said in her husky tones with their appealing mid-European gutturals.

'And she's not the only one,' Charles had quipped, elongating his eyes into seductive slits.

Within hours they had been prone and clasped together tightly in the hay store, thrashing amongst the bales in a robust and amiable coupling that left them breathless and covered in green wispy stalks.

In personality, Lizzi was all that Zoe was not: earthy, direct, and gloriously available. She had a ready supply of fruit-flavoured condoms which she rolled onto Charles with a skill that spoke of copious practice.

And after a heart-pounding four weeks of aerobic exercise in the hay and between the sheets, she had departed to Munich with a big happy smile and barely a backward glance.

'I'll call you,' said Charles, patting her nice firm bottom. But they both knew that he wouldn't. And for both of them that was fine.

Left without a regular bedfellow, Charles had found himself pondering on the disadvantages of brief flings, one-night stands and all those ingenious ways of getting sex which he had always previously believed to be ideal for his temperament and life-style.

'Twenty-eight, old chap,' he had told himself. 'Maybe now's the time to think of a bit more permanence. A girl to keep.'

Like many modern-thinking men who believed they were liberal in their views and espoused principles of sexual equality, Charles's thoughts instantly turned to a girl who had not been 'around'. A girl who had some dignity, some restraint. A girl who was hard to get.

He dug out Zoe's number from his black crocodile Filofax and dialled it whilst negotiating the crazy traffic in Oxford Street.

The answer-phone was on. 'This is Zoe Peach's phone. You're through to the answering machine. Do please leave me a message.'

The sound of her clear, delicately feminine voice made

his heart give a little blip which he found decidedly pleasant.

Smiling, he cut the connection off, leaving no message. Let her guess! And she wouldn't be able to to use the call back facility to find out the number of her caller. His mobile withheld that information.

The first few times he had called and got the answering machine, he was entertained and intrigued. Later on, he became a little irritated. And, on one occasion, calling up from a darkened wine bar in Soho, he had left a somewhat sharp message, something on the lines of wondering where the hell she was and what she was up to.

Shamed to recall this outburst on the following day, he had decided that the obvious next stage in his plan was to call in person at her house to charm, surprise and delight her with his presence, an appropriately expansive floral offering and perhaps a bottle of champagne.

It never occurred to Charles that Zoe would not be delighted to see him. Women had never been able to say no him. Not on a first meeting, nor later on. And certainly not after being left to cool their little heels for a few weeks.

He roared up her house, annoyed to have to park his car way down the street from her front door, where a black BMW motorbike was presumptuously taking up that particular space.

Charles peered at the bike with a critical eye as he passed on his way to Zoe's steps. The registration indicated that it was an early 1980s' model; 1000 cc, gleaming all over with soft leather and thick stainless steel. In pristine condition, the machine was probably something of a collector's item already, thought Charles, looking around him as though to spot the owner of this stylish piece of precision engineering.

Charles remembered that an almost identical machine had been given to him on his eighteenth birthday by a generous uncle who, at sixty, had still sported leathers and helmet himself, hurtling around the country lanes and terrifying elderly lady drivers bound for flower-arranging classes and meetings at the Women's Institute. At least, that was how Charles had liked to think of it.

His own machine had had a short life and a merry one, ending up at the bottom of a West Scotland loch after a particularly lively Hogmanay.

Charles's father had been alarmed and then furious. Had put his foot down firmly and insisted on the next set of his son's wheels consisting of four not two, and being of a rather more modest capacity. Charles had had to put up with a modest Golf GT until he came into his own money on his twenty-first birthday.

He glanced down the road now at his new red Mercedes convertible and, recalling those days of youthful privation, felt a stab of pure happiness.

Juggling an armful of roses with a chunky bottle of well-chilled bubbly, he sprang athletically up the steps and pounded on Zoe's door bell.

Nothing happened. Speculative seconds stretched to a full minute. He applied his finger more firmly on the bell and kept it there. He could hear the steady responding buzz somewhere deep in the inside of the house. And he knew she was in, her quirky custard-coloured car glowed in the road beside the BMW bike.

'Come on, come on!' He felt a spasm of anger, as

though she had guessed it was him, knew that he was wanting her and was deliberately keeping him waiting. Withholding herself.

Pressing his lips together, he dropped the flowers on the step, clenched the bottle tightly under his arm and banged ferociously on the glass panel of the door as though he would wake the dead.

Through the sunburst motif on the glass he saw the splintered outline of her slender frame coming down the stairs. Her hands were fluttering about in front of her as though she were adjusting her jewellery or maybe fastening a button.

He glanced at his watch. Nine-thirty. Surely she hadn't been thinking of going to bed this early.

The thought of bed and the elusive Zoe made his pulse speed up. 'Angel!' he exclaimed as she opened the door, and he brandished his extravagant offering of roses in front of her startled face.

She stared, her eyes wide and questioning, and for a nasty moment he had the impression that she did not immediately recognize him.

'Remember me!' he jested.

'Charles!' She was looking at him as though he might be dangerous.

'Don't I get invited in?' he enquired, jollying her along. With some girls that phrase would have suggested a sly sexual innuendo. But Zoe merely looked strainedly polite and with a watery smile she stepped aside from the doorway, enabling him to pass through.

'Long time no see,' he commented, dropping the roses on the hall table. He thrust the bottle at her. 'Pop this in the fridge, angelic girl. It's been getting all hot and

154

bothered under my hot sticky armpit. You had me sweating out there on the doorstep, I can tell you.'

'Oh! I'm sorry,' Zoe said, looking genuinely concerned.

'It's OK, sweetheart. I could hardly blame you even if you decided to give me the most fearsome bollocking for not putting in an appearance in such an age.' He dipped his head, allowing the thick forelock to fall over his eyes before tossing it back again.

'It's all right, Charles,' Zoe told him gravely. 'There's no need to apologize.'

Charles was inclined to agree there. But he knew the right way to behave in these circumstances. 'Forgive and forget, eh?' He smiled most charmingly, leaned forward and pressed a kiss on her cheek.

She smiled up at him, displaying no definite response to his kiss, either positive or negative.

Grasping the bottle, she went into the kitchen, opened the refrigerator and carefully placed it inside.

Charles followed on, rubbing his hands, smiling to himself, creamily anticipating the coming moments.

Then he saw the table and experienced a bolt of pure shock. In a flash he took in the plump crystal glasses standing together with shimmering dregs of wine lingering in their bowls, the stiffly laundered napkins screwed up and thrown down on the table. A scenario with which he was only too familiar, screaming out its message so brutally: intimate dinner for two, suddenly abandoned for activities more diverting.

As Charles stood gazing at Zoe, deeply reproachful, a dark figure came down the staircase, silky and catlike.

Charles, frozen in disbelief, was forced to look on

whilst François Rogier, long limbs gleaming in black leather, enfolded Zoe in a brief intense embrace before exiting softly, his hand raised in a brief acknowledgement of the untimely intruder.

CHAPTER 15

Zoe lifted her bags and equipment from the car. During the half-hour drive to her first teaching assignment of the day, her thoughts had been exclusively of François. Now, looking towards the front entrance of the school, she thought about Leonore. And then, just for moment, she thought about Charles.

Ahh, poor Charles, he had been so crestfallen and uncomfortable, standing there in her kitchen, cast in the hapless role of gooseberry. For a moment he had looked both wounded and helpless. Being confronted with François so suddenly, and in circumstances which left no room for doubt, had exposed a chink in Charles's cheery armour which made her think of him with a fresh and regretful tenderness.

Children called out to her in happy voices as she went down the corridor to the medical room. 'Hello, Miss Peach. Good morning, Miss Peach.'

'Hello there. Good morning to you,' she responded, her spirits bubbling, her whole being filled with gaiety because she was in love and the entire world was vivid and fast flowing and wonderful and she loved everybody who came into sight.

157

She sensed such an air of camaraderie and enthusiasm in the school this morning. It warmed her heart, gave her surging hope for the future which belonged to the vital children in this school and all the other marvellous young people in countless schools elsewhere.

A boy passing in the other direction offered to take her bags. A girl running up from behind complimented her on her parrot-green suede shoes with their purple buckles. 'Those are great, Miss Peach! Fabulous.'

'They're yours when I've grown out of them,' Zoe promised.

She arrived at the medical room, glowing and breathless. Well, at least she had beaten the children to it, even if there was insufficient time to set up her equipment before they turned up.

Almost immediately they began to filter in. Her little band of eager learners.

She greeted each child by name and presented them with their first assignment of the session: an individual reading task enticingly disguised as a personal letter, tucked into a brightly coloured envelope with one of Zoe's hand-sketched animal cartoons on the front.

The one for Leonore had a small hairy mongrel dog on it, because Leonore had told her that was her favourite kind of dog and one of that exact sort lived next door to her.

'Have I drawn him as you described him to me?' she asked Leonore, holding the envelope and its pencil sketch out for her inspection.

Leonore looked. Zoe awaited her judgement with interest. Leonore had the capacity to be critical, even with those she loved. She would have said 'No' if necessary because, like her father, she had a preference for pitiless honesty over patronizing flattery.

'Yes,' Leonore said. She looked up at Zoe and her eyes shimmered with a child's delight in the sharing of all manner of secret knowledge.

In the face of such clear pure integrity, Zoe felt herself humbled. She touched Leonore's shoulder lightly and at the same time spoke to François in her head: *Yes, my darling, you are right. We must tell Leonore. And soon.*

'Stefan is late this morning,' she commented to her little bunch as they found themselves seats, opened their envelopes and settled to their reading.

There were a few nods. Stefan was not in the same class group as any of the others, nor was he on especially friendly terms with any of those in Zoe's language group. Stefan was something of a law unto himself and so his absence was of little interest to them. In fact, Zoe guessed that the children would be relieved to have a session free from the presence of the unpredictable, volatile little boy who made a great deal of noise and demanded far more than an equal share of teacher attention.

So, where was he? Recalling her dream of some weeks ago, Zoe was unable to quell the feathery flutter of alarm which set her pulses tingling. She breathed deeply, telling herself to be calm and rational, reminding herself of François's refusal to have any truck with such things as the power of dreams to reach into real life. She reminded herself of the cold disapproval that would tighten his beautiful features if he were present to guess at the reason behind her renewed anxiety.

She allowed a few minutes to go by, rehearsing all the

arguments for coolly logical reasoning against impulse and superstition.

Suddenly she could bear it no longer. She must act.

Bending down to Leonore, she said softly, 'Would you go along to Stefan's classroom and see if he's at school today? It's possible he's forgotten that it's his morning to come here to the group.'

Leonore nodded, delighted to be singled out and given a job to do. She smiled up into Zoe's face. 'Yes,' she said eagerly, her face lit with enthusiasm.

Looking down, Zoe sensed again the glowing shimmer of closeness transmitted in the child's clear gaze, an intimation of intimate and mysterious matters unspoken between the two of them.

Leonore was back within a couple of minutes. 'He's not at school this morning,' she told Zoe.

'Ah.'

Leonore looked up at her, her expression curious now. Zoe forced herself to shake off her fears, angry to think that she should have been careless enough to wear her feelings on her sleeve and cause Leonore even the faintest disquiet. 'That's all right, Leonore. Thank you for going to find out. Everything's fine.'

Leonore sat down. From time to time she shot Zoe a swift and perplexed glance.

Holding herself rigidly calm, Zoe managed to go through all the motions required to deliver a faultless lesson.

At the end she allowed Leonore to stay behind for a minute or so, helping her to pack her equipment. 'It's time for you to go to your next lesson, little one,' she said eventually.

'It's playtime,' said Leonore.

Zoe looked out of the window at the stream of children filtering out into the tarmacked play area, a sadly restricted place for two hundred children, with its harshly spiked iron railings forming a protection from the busy road beyond.

'Yes. And you need to be out there playing. Go on.' She ran her finger lightly across Leonore's peachy cheek.

'We're cooking *croquettes de poisson* for you on Saturday,' Leonore informed her. 'With *pommes mignonnettes et aubergines.*'

'I shall make sure to be very hungry,' Zoe responded.

'And *gâteau de noisettes aux fruits* for pudding,' added Leonore, firing an impressive parting shot as she slipped through the door.

Zoe smiled. Leonore's developing skills in speaking and understanding both English and French were deeply satisfying to witness.

But following Leonore's departure, her mood instantly changed; a void seemed to open and Zoe found her mind instantly attacked by all those feelings she had fought to suppress during the teaching session.

She went in search of the Head, poking her head around the door of the assembly hall and then looking in the staffroom where the school secretary, doubling up as general factotum, was pinning up notices on the cork display board whilst keeping a sharp eye on the progress of a frantically grunting coffee percolator.

'She's in her room,' the secretary said helpfully. 'Buried under a mound of paperwork. You know how it is these days.'

It took the Head a while to look up from her work and

161

Zoe stood, quietly waiting. She could feel her heart ticking, tracking the seconds like a clock with a lumpy mechanism and an overloud tick.

The Head laid down her pen, took off her glasses and twisted around. 'Zoe – sorry to keep you. Sit down, please!' She swept a great pile of freshly photocopied sheets from the only available chair. The expression on her face was dogged and resigned.

'Stefan Kussek didn't come to my group this morning,' Zoe said.

The Head frowned. 'Was there some special reason? Have you checked with his class teacher?'

'No.' Zoe paused. 'He's absent, apparently.'

The Head gave a dry laugh. 'Well then, there's your reason.' There was a pause. The Head was obviously desperate to return to the demands of the paperwork.

Zoe cleared her throat uneasily. 'Do you know why?'

The Head's expression sharpened. 'I'm sorry?'

'Do you know why Stefan is absent?'

'No.' She spoke shortly. 'His grandparents haven't been in touch yet.'

Zoe swallowed; showers of saliva were pouring into her mouth, preventing her from responding instantly.

'It's not at all unusual for children to be absent for the odd day,' the Head remarked shortly. 'It could be a dental appointment, or simply a family trip out. We'll no doubt find out tomorrow when he turns up again.'

She swivelled back to her desk.

Zoe understood that the Head was a busy woman, that she did not have the time to concern herself with the over-anxious frettings of a visiting teacher. She knew she should make a quiet exit and leave those with the appropriate authority to make the decisions they felt right in dealing with the children's out-of-school lives.

But even as she told herself these things, Zoe found herself powerless to move, unable to walk away and leave matters unresolved.

The Head, sensing her colleague's stubbornness, swung round and said tartly, 'Zoe, don't you think you're going beyond your brief? You're a visiting specialist tutor. It's neither your job nor your place to concern yourself about the children's private lives.'

'No,' said Zoe. 'I just want to know that . . . Stefan's safe.'

The Head closed her eyes briefly. She sighed. 'Has it occurred to you that maybe you're not very well? It's only a few weeks since you had that strange collapse.'

Zoe nodded, groping for a swift and strong response, but failing to find it.

'If you get yourself worked up over every child you come into contact with,' the Head pressed, 'you'll soon be a nervous wreck. No good to anyone, in fact.'

Zoe flinched, but stood her ground. 'It's just with this one child that I have a special concern.' She broke off. That statement carried no weight, sounded so lame. But how could she put her true concerns into words? She pondered for no more than a split second before realizing that it was an impossibility. 'I'm sorry,' she told the Head. 'I didn't mean to waste your time.'

She moved to the door, decisive once again, already planning what she would do once out of the school gates.

'You really mustn't allow yourself to become so emotionally involved with the children,' the Head persisted. 'I'm sorry to sound harsh, but that kind of attitude can cause a good deal of damage all round.'

Maybe she's right, thought Zoe, although she didn't believe it.

'Perhaps you should take a little time off,' the Head continued more kindly, 'recharge your batteries.'

Zoe closed the door firmly behind her. She ran to her car, took the street map from the locker and identified the location of the hospitals in the area.

She knew that what she was planning to do was out of order, that it would most likely get her into hot water with both the school Head and her own senior colleague in the specialist visiting teacher service.

Her worries went far beyond such considerations. She was driven by an army of vivid, strident fears that shrieked in her head and demanded a response.

Walking towards the reception desk of the hospital she had chosen to call at first, she had some vague idea that she would not find him here. It was as though a quest had been set for her and she would have to negotiate all manner of trials before she reached her goal.

The girl at the desk rifled through a small pile of printouts. 'Kussek . . . yes, he was brought in earlier this morning.' She looked up at Zoe, her face impartial and closed, making Zoe's innards turn liquid with fear. She sensed the very worst about to be told her.

'Is he . . . is he alive?' she whispered.

The girl stared at her. 'Are you a relative?' she enquired, suspicious and faintly accusing.

'Yes,' Zoe responded, astonished at the smoothness of her lie.

'He was admitted a couple of hours ago. Ward A4. Go along the main corridor and follow the signs. See Sister in the office first.'

Zoe set off at a brisk walk. The noise of her tapping high heels echoed in her ears like the rattle of guns. She bent, plucked them off and carried them in her hand, setting off again at a run.

The Ward Sister's office door was open, but the room was empty. Staff at the nursing station seemed unaware of Zoe's breathless presence. One was in heavy discussion on the telephone, the others in earnest dialogue with white-coated doctors.

Unheeding of all matters of protocol and procedure, Zoe ran down the corridor, peering into the four-bedded bays, frantic to find Stefan, to do all she could to save him. She had a conviction that if only she could get to him whilst he was still alive, then somehow the evil that was menacing him could be halted in its tracks, its power destroyed.

She saw him straight away, lying in a bed beneath a long window. She registered a deathly pale face, a motionless, frail body that scarcely formed a lump under the sheets.

Above his head hung an up-turned bottle containing some pale liquid, the clear tube leading from it ending in a thick needle plugged into his pathetically thin arm which lay outside the sheets.

A man and a woman sat on either side of the bed, hunched over the boy's body, the curve of their spines spelling out weary desperation.

Zoe moved softly forward, a tiny but arresting figure in her flared lilac dress and jacket, her dark hair flying around her flushed face, her exotic shoes still in her hands.

The man looked up. Hard lines tracked down his face, marking him out as a man of strength, one who had faced hardship and suffering. Then the woman turned, and Zoe saw that the unseen finger of time had written a similar set of messages on her face also.

There was no suspicion in these faces; rather a sad acceptance of the harshnesses of life and a generous tolerance towards all of the world's other creatures who were potential sharers of the same sadnesses.

Zoe glanced at Stefan. She looked back at the man and woman who must surely be his grandparents. 'He's going to be all right, isn't he?'

'He'd nearly had it,' the man said. 'Another minute and he'd have been right under the wheels.'

'I blame myself,' the woman said. 'I should have made him hold my hand. Been firm. In my day you'd keep them on reins if they were like him. Even at six.'

'Hyperactive,' the man said. 'That's what the doctor thought.'

The woman looked up, her eyes intense. 'I just let go of him for a second. He was pulling at me so hard, straining to get free. He'd got one of those rubber balls, the solid ones that bounce really high – he'd been wanting one for ages. He'd dropped it and it rolled into the road. He just went. Shot. Never looked. The bus had to put all its brakes on to stop.'

There was a long pause. The three of them looked at each other. Then at the sleeping child, snatched from the hot underbelly of a London bus.

'He was thrown back onto the kerb with such a thud. I

thought he was dead then. Truly I did. I'd never have forgiven myself,' the woman said.

'Three cracked ribs,' her husband explained. 'Elbow joint shattered. Internal bruising – they don't know quite how much. Apparently kids are very resilient. He'll pull through.'

'The little devil,' the woman said suddenly smiling. 'We're too old for a lad like him. Young lively kids need young lively parents.'

'Young lads need their dads,' her husband countered warmly.

'Well, his dad's on the next flight to Heathrow, so maybe it's been a good thing out of a bad,' the woman said. 'Split families, it does no good, does it?' she said to Zoe. 'In our day, people stayed together whatever, for the kids' sake.'

Zoe sank down on the foot of the bed. The ferocious rush of mental energy that had fuelled her efforts to find Stefan now drained away with the relief of seeing him alive. She was left limp and depleted.

Stefan's grandparents looked at her with a new curiosity, realizing that, in the white heat of their anxiety, they had been sharing deeply personal views with a complete stranger.

'Are you from the school?' the grandfather asked.

'I'm a visiting teacher, I teach Stefan English.'

'Oh, we've heard about you. The lady with the dolls, he calls you. You people do wonderful work.'

'Thank you.'

Stefan's grandfather leaned forward. 'We haven't told the school yet, so how . . .?' He paused, his eyes puzzled.

'Oh, no. Oh, dear,' said his wife. 'We must do that. So much to think about.'

167

'Yes. All in good time.' The grandfather stared at Zoe thoughtfully, and she could tell that questions were turning in his mind. How had a visiting teacher known of Stefan's accident? How had she known to look for him in a hospital? And why had she come?

Zoe's mouth dried. How could she explain to these people that their grandson's life had been in terrible danger, that he had been granted a truly miraculous second chance?

How could she tell them of the way in which Stefan's life and her own had touched?

Impossible.

She got up. 'I'm sorry to have intruded.'

They shook their heads, indicating that her presence had been more than welcome. But the grandfather's eyes maintained their silent reflectiveness.

Zoe walked away down the corridor, past the nurses' station where the staff were still heavily engaged, past the Sister's room which was still vacated.

Stefan was safe. Just. But he could so easily have been killed.

Zoe understood that a line had been drawn under the authenticity and seriousness of her dreamed premonitions, a heavy and forceful black line that warned her not to give another thought to dismissing them.

Stefan is safe, she told herself, walking briskly through the main concourse and out into the car park.

But others might not be so lucky.

CHAPTER 16

Poppy liked to juggle. This morning, whilst supervising the hanging of her latest collection, it was entertaining to draw up a delicious menu in her head for the intimate supper she was to give at the weekend for her and Liam's friends.

Earlier in the morning, it had amused her to deliver a list of tasks to Gaby, and at the same time consider the finishing touches to the ensemble she would wear at her wedding the following weekend. Moreover, in the midst of all that, she had also been able to glance through the mail, swiftly sorting the vital from the trivial, and simultaneously debating the tricky pros and cons of making a forty-eight-hour flying visit to London to surprise her first husband before marrying the second.

These athletic mental manoeuvres provided Poppy with a way of living that gave her a constant buzz and reminded her of her basic importance in the world.

'*Girl with Clouds* to go next to *Live Energy*, I think,' she directed Gaby, standing back and frowning in deep concentration.

Gaby, perched on a spindly metal ladder, was doing some literal and rather dangerous juggling herself, attempting to grapple with two large canvases framed in thick, satin-finish stainless steel.

She rested the heavy canvases on the top rung of the ladder and looked down at them, wondering which was which. Sneaking a glance at the backs, she was hopeful of finding some useful labelling, or any kind of clue. Both representations looked like the results of several spilled jars of paint over which a playful puppy had pranced.

Poppy saw the young woman's uncertainty and was irritated. She disliked ineptitude in any of its forms. In fact, for some time now she had been thinking of firing Gaby and hiring someone more clued up. Someone with more perception, more sharpness, more style.

'Leave them for now, Gaby, I'll deal with them,' she said crisply. 'Ring round the airports, will you, and get me a reservation on a flight to London this Sunday morning.'

'Shall I get you a return flight?' Gaby asked, relieved to be able to climb down the ladder and release the heavy canvases on to the floor.

'Well, I hardly think I shall be staying in Britain permanently – so that might be just as well,' Poppy commented with a deceptively sweet smile.

Duly crushed, Gaby crept away.

Poppy heard her gushing politely to airport officials and firmed up her resolve for a swift firing. But not until after the wedding. There was far too much to be done. Routine dogsbody things that she, Poppy, simply had no time for. And whilst Gaby was not A1 as an assistant, at least she was available in the here and now.

Poppy was a tiny bit suprised at herself for finally making the decision to fly to London. And rather pleased with herself. She had aired the idea once or twice with Liam.

'It would be nice for them to see me just on their own, before you and I are married, darling, don't you think? They're bound to feel a teeny bit lonely and cut off with the wedding coming up. And, of course, afterwards they'll be very much left to themselves, poor darlings.'

'Sweetheart, you're absolutely right,' Liam had said, fondly imagining that this idea of Poppy's must be some kind of civilized routine divorced European couples liked to go through, the Europeans being such an old-fashioned and polite bunch of people.

'You don't mind, do you, darling? You've no need to feel jealous, you know!' Poppy had said.

Liam had given a whimsical smile and made the appropriate noises about being insanely jealous, although this was nothing like the truth. As a rich and successful self-made man, Liam harboured no envious feelings of any kind towards the aesthetic-sounding François Rogier with his heavy principles and light-weight bank balance.

Poor darling Leonore and poor François, Poppy kept telling herself. They will be so alone. She had got into the habit of repeating that little phrase to herself because a mischievous and discordant voice kept whispering back in Poppy's ear that maybe her little ex-family was not going to be alone at all. They were going to transfer their affections to someone called Zoe Peach. Someone she, Poppy, knew absolutely nothing about, aside from François's uncharacteristically enthusiastic description.

Ever since that evening when Poppy had spoken quite reasonably to François, seeking more information on this

171

new woman in a spirit of human interest and maternal concern for her child, the issue of the mysterious Zoe Peach had kept rearing its ugly head to attack Poppy with a decidedly unpleasant sensation of being usurped.

Gaby returned from her telephoning. 'I've got you an eight-thirty flight. First class, Poppy.'

'Excellent. Where from? JFK?'

'La Guardia.'

'Oh, Gaby, I hate that place and it's hellish getting there. Surely there was something from JFK?'

Gaby flinched slightly under Poppy's impatient and challenging stare, which gave the impression that the pressure on flight availability from JFK airport was all her fault. 'Not at the time you wanted. Not in first class. I've got you a place on the helicopter link to Guardia,' Gaby offered placatingly. 'It only takes five minutes to get there on Sunday mornings.'

'Oh, all right,' Poppy grumbled. 'But I'm sure there'd have been something if you'd insisted. 'You have to be firm with these officials, Gaby.'

Gaby bit her lip with the humiliation of being made to feel a failure, of being told off like a little kid. She didn't think she'd be able to take it much longer at the King Gallery. Poppy had always been a bit of a toughie as a boss, a bit pernickety. But she seemed to be going from bad to worse. And now, in the run up to the wedding, she was so touchy one hardly dared say a word or move a muscle for fear of upsetting her.

Sometimes Gaby wondered if Poppy was truly happy to be marrying Liam. Liam King might be dynamic and power crazy; sexy, too, in a balding, Jack Nicholson kind of way. But Gaby had been fascinated by the photograph of Poppy's little girl and her ex-husband, which was propped up by the fax machine on her boss's desk.

In Gaby's opinion, François Rogier looked simply drop-dead gorgeous with his swordlike cheekbones, his dark brooding eyes and those marvellous long curved lips – so stern and yet, somehow, so very tender. And the kid; she was a real sweetie, cute-looking and smart and totally lovable.

Gaby had spent some long musing moments in front of that family picture. It had made her think hard. Gaby herself hadn't landed a good man yet, just waded through a stream of casual live-in lovers. Looking at that photograph, eloquent with love and trust, made her wonder if the freedom you gained through the fashionable preference for fluid relationships was as great as it was made out to be.

And looking at Poppy's frantic, intense expression now as she spoke rapidly on the phone to Liam whilst checking and signing the letters Gaby had word-processed for her earlier, Gaby wondered if her boss would have been happier if she had never have left London.

Gathering up the letters to fold and mail, Gaby wondered whether Poppy Rogier should have stayed with her ex and her daughter and had a shot at good old-fashioned living happily ever after.

Flying over Manhattan in the all-round-vision helicopter shuttle, Poppy gazed down at the breathtaking panorama spread out beneath; the countless high-rise blocks flashing their glass and steel heads in the dawn sunshine, the glinting river snaking sinuously around their feet. Utterly breathtaking.

As the helicopter dipped and then righted itself, so the great blocks swayed in a gentle dancing response. One of Poppy's fellow passengers clutched at his stomach and snapped his eyes tight shut, blocking out further contemplation of this amazing scene. Poppy smiled to herself, craning her head for a better view. She was always fearless when flying, adored the exhilaration of it all: the various sensations, the speed, the risk.

It struck her that there were perhaps some benefits to be gained in flying from La Guardia.

Pushing her way through the crowds at the airport which reminded Poppy more of a giant bus station than anything else – and a seedy, crumbling one at that – she rapidly changed her mind. At JFK and Heathrow, they knew how to steer the first-class passengers smoothly through all the tedious hurdles to be negotiated before finally getting to their plane. Check in, confirmation of flight times, luggage disposal, passport control, security. It was all done so unobtrusively.

Here, this Sunday morning at La Guardia, everything seemed to be in chaos. The business-class passenger lounge was temporarily closed for some unexplained reason. Queues at the check-in desks were interminable and seemingly static. Many of the passengers waiting in them looked close to fuse-blowing point.

Poppy stared around her in expasperated frustration. Nothing but chaos and mix-up, noise and anarchy: a great stew of people all simmering together. Dire.

A woman pushed impatiently past her, grazing Poppy's leg with the edge of a suitcase and sending a broad ladder, zipping from ankle to thigh, up one leg of her glossy tights.

Why am I doing this? Poppy wondered suddenly, seeing the impulsive journey in a new and somewhat disturbing light. Why am I flying across the Atlantic to snatch a few hours with my ex-husband? she demanded of herself angrily.

In a flash of insight, Poppy was finally able to look into her inner heart and admit the true motivation behind her actions. In setting out to England, the prime focus of her journey was not her 'little family' as she liked to think of them – daughter and ex-husband. In flying to London, the urgent focus of her mission was simply François. Her first lover, the first man with whom she had felt a strong connection.

In her thoughts he rose up, like the young François whom she had fallen in love with whilst hardly fledged into womanhood. She recalled her first sight of him, a young photographer for a minor Paris newspaper, determined to make his way. Tall, leanhipped, gauntly dark and faintly scruffy in his weathered, crinkled black leather jacket, he had projected an air of supreme elegance.

He had seemed to her mesmerizingly different from the cheery, braying young men of her previous acquaintance. François had presence, purpose, weight. She had found his cool demeanour both enticing and compelling. His calm and even temperament had seemed to hint at some dark and exciting turbulence beneath.

But it had been, perhaps, his demonic pursuit of excellence in his work that had most attracted her although, curiously, it had been precisely that dogged integrity towards professionalism which had later frustrated and infuriated her.

175

Over a six-week summer vacation in Paris, François had enslaved and enchanted her, and she had had no doubts in believing that he felt the same way about her.

Her parents had been charmed with him, too, but had not considered him suitable as a long-term mate for Poppy. François, after all, had few assets to offer besides his considerable abilities and personal charm. And photography was hardly one of the solid and worthy professions, like the army or the law.

Her parents' opposition had made him utterly irresistible to Poppy, sweeping away any tiny doubts – of which there had been very few. Braving her parents' reservations, she had married him the following year, following which they had been supremely happy for another two or three.

But, inevitably, the first heartstopping magic had begun to fade and transform itself into something deeper and steadier. And those had been good times, too, she recalled.

Looking back, she had come to believe it was the birth of Leonore that had started the fatal downward slide. For the first time, she and François had found themselves in dispute over basic life issues. Their clash of ideas on child-rearing had opened up a gap that widened slowly into a chasm.

But despite the difficulties, François had remained steadfast in his love and care for her. Even when she had become involved with Liam, he had persisted in loving her. At the time, it had made her angry with him, because she had hated to be confronted with even more guilt.

Poppy stopped dead in the midst of the shuffling

queue, awash with a sea of feelings dredged up from the past.

She felt a shiver run through her body. No, she whispered, no, assuring herself that the old magic François used to work on her had lost its power years ago. Surely!

Poppy's strong and stable convictions were suddenly shaken up, little fragments of confetti in a stiff breeze.

She bent and picked up her bags. The queue was moving briskly forward now. She was almost at the check-in desk.

Could it be that, in my subconscious, I want François back? she thought in utter horror. Am I going to London to try to win him back? The idea, once spoken out in her head, appalled her. Her first marriage was over. Boats had been burned.

Besides which, she loved Liam. She fitted with Liam. They went together, a pair. People changed, moved on, needed to form fresh relationships.

Yes, yes, yes! she muttered fiercely under her breath.

Then to go is madness, she informed herself. Wilful and stupid. Maybe dangerous. Looking around her at the throng of people all bent on dashing around the world, Poppy had sudden thoughts of simply walking away. Going back to the gallery. Spending the day working. Calling up Liam.

She closed her eyes momentarily. She detested doubt and confusion.

The queue propelled her relentlessly forward like a wave about to break on the shoreline.

She took in a deep sharp breath and forced herself to make decisions. She was a strong woman, her own person. Of course she could take a journey to see the man who had once been very dear to her, the father of her child. And it was surely a delightful affirmation of her affection for her daughter that made her want to share some precious moments with her before she committed herself to a man who was not her father.

Poppy stepped up to the check-in desk, laid her tickets out for inspection, placed her bags on the scales and watched them wobble away.

CHAPTER 17

Several hours later in London, evening sunshine threaded its way through the drawn curtains in Zoe's bedroom, planting a golden spear of light on the white cotton cover under which François lay, holding Zoe in his arms.

Their love-making had been slow and lingering. For both of them it had been like some kind of vow, a solemn renewal of the deepening commitment they both felt.

Zoe raised herself on one elbow and looked down at him. He was so precious to her, so dear. She felt tears swelling behind her eyelids just to think of the joy he brought her, the warm lapping waves of pure pleasure. Through all the recent breathless weeks he had given her that, days stretching into the past, yesterday and tonight. And so it would be for all the tomorrows.

That last thought reminded her that she could no longer hold back the secret she must share with him. She must dare to do it; say the things that must be said. Her heart quaked, her whole body was a vast, long sigh. 'Oh, God!'

She realized she had spoken out loud and that it was too late – he had heard, sensed the dark mood.

'What is it, darling?' His arm tightened around her. It felt like a constraint, no longer an embrace.

She wriggled free from him. Sat up and covered her breasts with the lace-edged sheet.

'Zoe. *Chérie?*' His eyes were lazy and amused.

'François, I have to . . .'

'Yes?'

'I have to speak to you again about something that will make you very – displeased.'

He understood immediately. Zoe braced herself for an angry response, but he was merely very quiet, very calm. Dangerously so.

'Well?' His eyes filled with cold disdain even as she watched him.

'I'm sorry, but I've got to say this to you, yet again. You mustn't fly to New York next week. You and Leonore, you mustn't!' Her voice rose sharply. Tears sprang from her eyes and wet her face.

François sprang out of bed. Naked and beautiful, he reached for his cigarettes in the pocket of his jacket, wrenched one from the packet and lit it. He drew in deeply. He had never permitted himself to smoke in Zoe's house before, let alone her bedroom.

He was silent for a time. Then he pulled on his trousers and shirt and threw himself into the chair beside the bed. 'Very well,' he said eventually, 'Am I to understand that Leonore and I must cancel our trip to Poppy's wedding because of some crazy whim? That Leonore, for no good reason that I can possibly think of, must be deprived of seeing her mother again, of witnessing her marriage to her new lover and having the chance to share in an occasion that, though potentially painful, will be invaluable in helping her come to terms with the reality of the present and the future? *Our* future?' he concluded with heavy emphasis, and his face was so harsh, so icy, that for a moment Zoe was almost afraid of him.

Hesitantly, stumbling over the words, she began to tell him about Stefan. She told him in the most minute detail, beginning the story at the point she had discovered the child's absence from school, going through each little conversational interchange with the grandparents at the hospital.

François granted her the courtesy of listening intently. On occasions he broke in with terse and pertinent questions. But all the time he looked at her as though he hardly knew her, as though she were someone not especially close to him, someone he did not especially care for.

Zoe had to keep on speaking, but she could not bear this distance between them. Swiftly, her voice choking in her throat, she crossed the room to stand by his chair. She threw herself onto her knees beside him and clasped her arms around his long legs, burying her face in his lap.

He gave a deep slow sigh. 'Oh, Zoe, Zoe. These dreams of yours, my darling – they have to be put in perspective. You have to rein them in, learn to start controlling them instead of letting them control you.'

She looked up, her eyes watery bright and troubled. 'I can't!'

'Yes!'

She said nothing.

He sensed a wisp of doubt and pressed his point hard. 'If you don't get a grip on these dreams and shadows, Zoe, if you don't grasp them by their frail little necks and

181

destroy them, then they'll destroy you.' He shook her shoulder, not physically rough, but mentally giving her no quarter.

She nodded, meek and mute.

'These fantasies of yours, these shadowy fancies: they could ruin our lives together. You do understand that, don't you?'

She bowed her head. 'Yes.'

He felt like a man who has whipped his innocent puppy. But it was too soon to comfort her yet. 'Zoe, listen to me. Leonore and I are going to this wedding. We are going to board a plane and fly to New York. That is all planned, all decided. Nothing is going to stop us. Not even you, darling.'

A long, sighing pause. 'Yes. I understand.'

He slid his fingers into her hair, massaging the warm scalp, driving the strength of his own beliefs and convictions through his nerves and skin to transmit to hers. 'You can overcome this – obsession, darling. You can!'

She breathed deeply, felt the relaxing power of his touch. She looked up at him, desperate with hope.

'You can do it,' he told her softly. 'And I'll help you. Love is more powerful than any dream or shadow.'

Her eyes seemed to glow and he knew that he had sounded a pure note for her. 'There,' he soothed, stroking a finger from the hairline at her forehead and drawing it down across her cheek. 'Set your mind free.'

'François!' Her voice throbbed with love. Then there was a pause, a sudden feathery flicker of fear over her features. 'François?' Her voice chimed with renewed panic.

François placed his finger over her lips. '*Silence*,' he

told her sternly. 'Not another word.' He pulled back the cover on the bed, lifted her in his arms and laid her gently on the sheet. Then he bent to kiss her and his hand moved with gentle authority over the velvety contours of her waist and hips.

Marina and Leonore were in the kitchen, humming the birdcatcher's song from *The Magic Flute* as they prepared a supper of toad-in-the-hole. Tonight, for the first time, Leonore was to sleep at Marina's house because Daddy was going to stay all night at Zoe's. Leonore appeared pleased and excited, not least at the prospect of sleeping in Marina's tiny guest room, in a bed with an old iron bedstead beneath a lacy cover on which Risk was allowed to sleep, too, provided he stayed on the dog towel.

Whilst Leonore carefully broke eggs into a bowl, Marina skinned the Provençal garlic sausage which François had particularly recommended for the fullest enjoyment of this particular dish. And they sang whilst they worked.

The birdcatcher's song was currently Leonore's top favourite, although she liked the tune better than the words. It worried her to think about a man who roamed the woods dressed up in feathers to fool the birds and played little pipes to entice them from the trees so that he could trap them in his nets and snares.

Leonore had learned these details through her obstinate insistence on struggling through the words in the booklet accompanying Marina's recording of the opera.

'You may find it a bit hard going,' Marina had ventured.

Leonore knew better. 'Zoe says you can practise your reading with anything at all. If you don't know all the words, you just have to get a grown-up to help. Zoe says you can read adverts on buses and street names and signposts and even the backs of cornflake packets.'

Zoe says. Zoe says . . .

Marina smiled to herself. The signs were definitely promising on the François–Zoe romance front, at least if Leonore had any say in the matter.

'Oh poor little birds, getting caught and put in a cage,' Leonore lamented, reaching that part of the song.

'I don't think you should fret too much,' Marina reassured her. 'This particular birdcatcher was pretty hopeless at catching many birds, as far as I can work out.' She was wondering how she was going to explain the next verse of the song, which went into some detail about the birdcatcher's lusty desire to snare somewhat larger and juicier birds – the kind with no feathers or wings.

Sex was always a tricky issue with children, who were either amazingly knowledgeable, which made one feel faintly inadequate and outdated, or else teetering on the brink of understanding, which made them insatiably curious. And, when they were six, it was surely up to their parents to decide how many beans should be spilled.

'And he probably let them go again even if he did catch them,' Leonore said, stirring eggs around a bowl with huge concentration. 'Can we listen to some more songs after supper?'

'Any you like.'

'Risk won't mind, will he, as long as you don't let it go on to the thundery bits or the lions?'

'I don't think he's nearly as frightened as he used to be of that particular piece. We've played it so much he's got blasé.'

'That means "not bothered". It's French,' said Leonore.

'Oh, yes! Of course it is. I keep forgetting you speak such good French. Well, if he's not frightened by *The Magic Flute* any more, we'll just have to find something else to terrify him with.'

Leonore looked up, seized with concern. 'Oh, don't. Oh, poor Risk.'

Marina smiled. 'I'm just teasing.' It was a long time since she had enjoyed extended conversations with a six-year-old. She had forgotten that, in the midst of their radiant imaginings and sly experiments with jokes, they could suddenly retreat into the earnest and literal.

'Will Risk miss me when I go to Mummy's wedding?' Leonore asked thoughtfully.

'Yes.'

'He won't forget me?'

'No.'

Leonore was silent. Her face stilled. The spoon moved in ever-slowing circles within the gleaming egg mixture.

'Are you looking forward to the wedding?' Marina asked.

Leonore nodded, but Marina was not convinced. She watched the little girl doggedly continuing with her task, stirring all her hurt and bewilderment into a couple of broken eggs, determined to be stoical and brave.

What a hurdle for a child to face, Marina thought. To fly halfway across the world to be a witness to the final demolition of one's family. What an ordeal – to stand by

185

and watch another man step into your mother's world, replacing the god-like figure of your father.

Oh, Poppy Rogier, you selfish bitch, taking off and leaving your little Leonore when she was hardly more than a baby. How could you? Marina exclaimed to herself with savage venom. But the truth of the matter – of which Marina was fully aware – was that she was berating herself for irresponsibly leaving her own children. She had never found it possible to forgive herself for this crime, even though they had been well into their teens and perfectly capable of understanding what was going on and dealing with it.

And whilst there had been a period when she was no longer a constant daily figure in their world, she had never neglected to phone and visit and write and invite. And she had still loved them. The problem she had wilfully manufactured, in the wild days of her fading youth, had probably been more hers than theirs. And now they were adults themselves. Fledged and launched and showing every evidence of happiness, fulfilment and worldly success.

But Leonore – sweet, grave, funny, achingly lovable little Leonore was only six. And from what Marina had gathered, had not seen her mother for six months.

'Mummy sent me a dress to wear at the wedding,' Leonore said, still stirring so that the eggs were now a pale cream froth. 'It's blue. And I'm going to have some flowers to hold.'

'Sounds good,' Marina said non-committally.

'Daddy got me a dress, too.' A tiny smile broke through her gravity. 'A yellow one with a green sash. Zoe came with us to help choose it.'

'Well, you'll have to wear the blue one to the wedding and change into the yellow one for the party afterwards,' Marina suggested, instantly grasping the child's dilemma and the impossibility – as Leonore clearly saw it – of not upsetting either parent.

Leonore tapped the handle of the spoon on the side of the bowl and laid it down on the table. She wiped her hands carefully on the towel Marina had tied around her. 'That's what Daddy said,' she told Marina solemnly.

'Well then, it must be the right choice,' commented Marina drily, raising her eyebrows and giving Leonore a wicked wink.

Leonore sat down and rested her chin on her hand.

Such a reflective child, thought Marina. Sensitive as though she were fashioned from air. And so knowing!

Leonore began to hum softly. 'I am the birdcatcher . . . tra, la, la!' Her voice faltered and faded. She looked up at Marina.

'You'll have a marvellous time,' Marina told her, sending up a prayer for it to be true. 'It'll be like a big adventure. You and Daddy flying off together.'

'Mmm.' Leonore seemed to have sunk back into gloom and doubt. She made one more feeble attempt at humming and then fell silent.

Marina added milk to the eggs, poured the whole lot into the well of flour in her mixing bowl and stirred them about. 'Hey! Look here and listen. If I tip up the bowl and beat this sloppy stuff with the back of my spoon, it makes a sound like horses' hoofs galloping over wet sand. Hear it?'

'Yes!' Leonore agreed. 'That's clever.'

She listened for a while, her head tilted on one side as

was often the case when she was concentrating. And then, without warning, she suddenly set free the thoughts that had been penned up in her mind. 'I wish Zoe could come to New York, too,' she said.

Once settled into her seat in the aircraft, Poppy was soon restored to her assured and unruffled self. She leaned back with a small sigh of relief and pleasure.

The cabin staff were smiling and reassuring, the atmosphere in the aircraft calm, efficient and purposeful. Another world entirely to the jumble and disorganization of the airport.

She had a window seat; the place next to her looked unlikely to be taken, so there would be the opportunity to spread herself a little and enjoy a pleasant sense of privacy and exclusiveness.

Once up in the air, with the engines tamed from their initial surge, she was able to relax further. The steward brought her chilled champagne. He was young and dark and very appealing. Italian, Poppy guessed, hearing the faint elongation of certain vowel sounds. He came back later, squatting down beside her in the aisle, enquiring about her comfort, letting her know that if there was anything at all she wanted, then she had only to ask him. Poppy sensed a tiny *frisson* of attraction between them and couldn't help being charmed.

Approaching Britain, the pilot reported that there was very poor visibility for landing at Heathrow and that the aircraft had been given instructions to divert to Newcastle. They were to take an easterly route, flying over the English channel and the North Sea. The weather was likely to be a trifle squally up there and passengers should be prepared for some turbulence. They might be required to fasten their seat belts. But naturally, there was no cause for concern.

Within seconds the steward was again in attendance. 'Nothing to worry about,' he said.

'All the delay. So annoying,' Poppy responded wearily. She suspected that her ankles were beginning to swell. Her bones felt stiff, and she longed to be on the ground again. Striding out. Getting on with life.

The steward offered more champagne. But Poppy's head was beginning to ache now and she ordered tea instead and searched out her aspirins.

Passing up the north-east coast of England, the aircraft encountered vicious winds. And at the same time, when the steward looked out towards the tail of the aircraft, he saw black smoke curling over the wing.

Shortly afterwards, the aircraft disappeared from the radar screens. Later it was officially reported as three hours overdue for landing.

That evening, wreckage was spotted off the Yorkshire coastline by the crew of another flight. A search by helicopters and divers was instantly put into operation.

CHAPTER 18

Sunday evenings had not been the best of times for Charles in recent weeks. The leggy eighteen-year-old he had been casually dating was never available at that time. She had explained why quite reasonably, reminding him that, as she had spent the lion's share of the weekend in his company, it was only fair to share the few remaining hours with her parents before the weekly work grind recommenced. She made it sound like a perfectly good and genuine reason for not being get-at-able.

But Charles was not so sure. He found himself increasingly unable to shake off suspicion about female motives and was constantly on the defensive. Since discovering Zoe with François Rogier – a veritable viper in the love nest Charles fancied he had been building for himself – his confidence had undergone a serious set-back.

And thus he had not been inclined to trust his long-legged eighteen-year-old, pricked with the notion that she, too, might suddenly discover a preference for dark and stern-looking Frenchmen.

But worse, he had found himself increasingly desperate to win Zoe Peach back. He was not pleased about this ambition, recognizing that it was basically a no-hope project. Moreover, a project severely at odds with his view of himself as a cheery cavalier sort of chap who usually got what he wanted, and could count on taking girls or leaving them, so to speak. He saw himself poised at the peak of a very slippery slope.

And he knew that things were very serious indeed when he found himself, almost as though willed by a mind other than his own, driving past her house one dateless Sunday evening. Not just once, not even just twice. He had driven up and down for a good half hour, slowing down as he reached her house, staring up at it hopefully and utterly humiliating himself in the process.

After all, what the hell did he expect to gain from such crazy adolescent behaviour? If he caught a glimpse of her through the window, what then? He was hardly going to pound on her door, upbraid her for sleeping with François Rogier and demand that she come to her senses and jump into bed with him instead.

Zoe had been quite alluring enough when he had considered her more or less his, hovering on the brink of capitulation. But now that another man had taken possession of her – and a man who looked like a formidable rival – his desire to regain the upper hand had become painfully acute. Unbearable, in fact.

This particular Sunday evening he had driven into the vicinity of her house, against all injunctions from his better self not to. He supposed it was the thrill of anticipation at what he might discover that made such a pathetic impulse irresistible. It was like taking a hazardous journey into the unknown. Because, after all, truly fascinating, unavailable women were mainly uncharted territory in the map of Charles's experience.

Even as he turned into the road this particular evening, his heart began to jump about in his chest. A sensation that he found distinctly arousing.

When he saw the black BMW motor-bike parked in the road like a brooding sentinel, he was not sure whether the intensity of his responding sensation was pain or some grotesquely masochistic pleasure.

Parking a little way down the road, he placed a new compilation album of his all-time eighties' favourites into the eight-speaker compact-disc system, reclined the back of his seat, then stretched out his long legs and settled down for a long vigil.

At Marina's house, nine chimes having tinkled from the creaky nineteenth-century French clock on her mantelpiece, all was quiet.

François had given approval for Leonore to stay up as late as she liked on her first overnight visit to the house next door. It was, after all, a rather special occasion all round. For François and Zoe, it meant the luxury to have a whole night together; to be real lovers. For Leonore, it was the first time she had spent a night away from home, with neither of her parents present. And for Marina, a wicked woman who had once run away from her children and responsibilities, it was a wonderful novelty and privilege to have the care and company of her young friend. And for the father of that friend to trust her.

When it came to it, Leonore showed no desire to abuse her bedtime extension. Around eight o'clock, unable to contain her excitement at the prospect of burrowing into the enticing, entirely magical bed in the guest room, she and Risk quietly vanished.

Marina went up later. Child and dog were peacefully wound together, their breathing soft and measured. The sight of all this peace and harmony gave Marina a wonderful warm sensation of contentment.

Unused to such rich feelings, which were in short supply in her current life, she had an instinct to pounce on them immediately before they got a grip on her and began to cause trouble. 'Revolting sentimentality,' she muttered to herself, creeping softly down the staircase.

But some spring had been activated in Marina's thoughts and feelings. The contentment she felt whilst looking down on the sleeping Leonore fanned out and grew. She wanted to grasp this new positiveness and hold it close to her. She hated to think of herself sinking back into the lonely cynicism which was her habitual cloak and her refuge.

She went into the kitchen and cleared the supper things into the sink. As she ran the water and squeezed in liquid soap, she was aware of François's telephone warbling to itself beyond the dividing wall of their houses. She had heard it once or twice earlier on. All these calls on a Sunday evening. François was obviously a popular guy.

She washed the dishes, stacked them in an unsteady heap on the draining board and thought about drying them. Rapidly deciding against such an unnecessary activity she picked up the Sunday newspaper, was instantly overwhelmed by its chunkiness, and tossed it on to the gathering pile of newsprint on her oak dresser.

The Tarot cards in their silk scarf caught her eye. She had neglected them for weeks; deliberately ignored them, in fact, ever since the morning her reading had given her a message about her neighbours – then strangers, now the very warmest of friends.

She recalled the story the cards had told with perfect clarity. A new start ahead, an uncertain, unknown future. Some kind of journey. And danger – terrible danger. Possibly involving Leonore and François.

She poured herself a glass of wine, went through into the sitting room and put on a disc of Fauré's piano quartets because they were beautiful and sharply optimistic without a shred of sentimentality. She listened for a while, the intellectual part of her brain registering the elegance of the music, her feelings now curiously agitated and unharmonious.

She told herself to relax.

Threading through the music came the repeated warble of the phone next door, impossible to ignore. Sipping her wine, Marina frowned. Her earlier positive mood of contentment was rapidly dissolving, to be replaced by an unexplained drone of internal anxiety.

Restless and unable to sit still, she got up and roamed about the room, picking up photographs and ornaments, putting them down again, drawing the curtains on and then drawing them back because she hated to feel enclosed.

Returning to the kitchen for a refill of wine, she found herself unable to resist glancing at the cards on the dresser; felt herself pulled towards them, lured and seduced. In her head she saw herself moving forward to pick them up and take them from their protective scarf wrapping even before it happened.

She stared down at the cards. They lay dead and

inactive in her hands, nothing more than rectangles of cardboard with pictures painted on them. She squinted at them through half-closed lids, doubtful and a little afraid. Then swiftly, before giving herself time to consider further, she brought them to life, shuffling them with deft thoroughness, and laying them out on the table in a simple and basic six-card spread, from which she would construct a simple theory.

She stepped back from the table, her pulse accelerating, hardly able to believe what she saw. Five of the pack's most significant cards had turned up once again, the exact same five that had been there on her last reading: High Priestess, Empress, Fool, Devil, Death. She couldn't recall ever having dealt a duplication of this kind. And there was one extra, truly fateful card. The sixth card was the darkest one in the pack: The Tower.

'Oh, God!' Marina whispered into the darkening silence, for the music had finished long ago. 'What have I dug up here?' It was impossible to reach a different interpretation from the one she had made before on that grey Monday morning when she had asked a question for herself and gained an answer which she suspected was for someone else. But now there was an added horror – a rogue card. And she was convinced beyond doubt that the spread was meant for Leonore and François; possibly also for Zoe Peach, who had become inextricably linked with both of them.

Assessing the positioning of the cards through narrowed eyes, Marina found her attention powerfully drawn to The High Priestess card. She wondered if perhaps the card in its current situation represented, not a set of ideas or a turn of fate, but rather a particular person. She had a sudden strong conviction that The High Priestess card in this spread represented Zoe Peach.

She stood quite still, reviewing ideas and theories. According to the philosophy of the Tarot, The High Priestess figure represented study, learning, knowledge and wisdom. Marina recalled that Zoe was a teacher and also appeared to be something of a 'wise woman', from what she had been able to gather from Leonore.

So, if The High Priestess card represented Zoe, what was she to deduce from the fact that it was standing prominently in the top row of the spread, flanked by Death and The Tower?

Marina touched the Death card with a long burgundy-tinted nail. She still refused to see this as a bad card. This was a tough card, undeniably, but it carried with it great strength and the prospect of a new life presenting itself. So, was the Death card representing some abstract quality in Zoe's life, Marina asked herself, or was it simply representing the person of François? The strong lover standing by his beloved and offering her renewed life.

But then there was The Tower on the other side. Dear God, that was not good, not good at all. The Tower was the worst card in the whole pack. The most unpleasant card to find in a reading, no matter how optimistic the reader and the circumstances. Whichever way you looked at it, The Tower was a bringer of bad news: loss, destroyed illusions, betrayed trust. And, at the very worst, some terrible calamity.

There had been a time when Marina had kept getting The Tower in her own readings. And she had surely suffered: desertion, humiliation, a sense of being washed up and useless.

She took a sip of wine, gazing down at the cards. The story they told tonight was simple enough, the meaning behind it only too clear. There were all the ingredients from the previous reading: uncertainty, a journey, some kind of danger, a possible new start. But added now was some terrible incident, some precise and shocking disaster. And whilst François still seemed to a prime focus in the playing out of this drama, he had now been joined by Zoe Peach, on whom a merciless spotlight seemed to blaze.

Marina's stomach felt decidedly queasy. Why did I do this? she enquired of herself. She had truly believed that she had the card-reading habit well and truly kicked. And now she had fallen for it all over again. And see what she had done. Stirred up a lot of angst for herself.

The house around her seemed thick with silence. The Fauré had finished long ago. Outside, the garden was disappearing into the late evening shadows, the grass turning from green to a sludgy dark blue.

The phone went again next door.

Damn! Give it a rest! Shut up, phone!

Marina took off her shoes and went upstairs again. Leonore was fast asleep, her breathing reassuringly audible and regular. Risk, too, seemed untouched by Marina's growing prickles of disquiet.

He raised his head.

'Are you staying there all night, you wretched inconstant animal? Do nine years of love and devoted care mean nothing? Have you no thought for your poor ancient mistress? Does she have to sleep all alone?'

197

He put his head down again. Breathed deeply with huge contentment.

Marina returned to the ground floor, switched on the television and push-buttoned her way through the channels.

The telephone next door went yet again. And then again. It was going completely beserk.

Marina realized she would have to do something about it. Her nerves were beginning to jangle each time the ripe warblings started up. Three ringing warbles and then silence. Clearly François had the answer-phone switched on. It also seemed equally clear that someone had a decided interest in getting through to him.

Taking the key he had given her from the beneath one of a pair of grotesque but irresistible Victorian china dogs which sat on her mantelpiece, guarding the clock, she went swiftly next door, let herself in, and confronted the disruptive telephone.

The red light was winking frantically, indicating heavy demand. The recording tape must surely have run out by now.

Marina activated the message button. It seemed an eternity for the tape to reel back.

There were some bleeps and then a low growling voice, someone called Liam King. He wanted to know if Poppy had arrived safely. Just checking. Everything fine and relaxed. No worries, huh? Perhaps she'd call him when she finally made it.

Later he was more urgent, wanting to know if Poppy's flight had been delayed, if she'd been in touch at all. But just checking still.

Later he was wanting Poppy to call him back the

absolute minute she got in. Then later he wanted François to call him. As soon as possible. For Christ's sake!

'Someone pick up this goddam phone!' was the final message.

Marina dialled the call-back facility and got the last caller's number. A USA code, a New York number. She scribbled it down on the back of her hand, then dashed back to her own house, suddenly frantic at the thought of imminent disaster.

Risk was in the hall, a bundle of bristling hackles and whining canine anxiety.

'It's all right, it's all right, beloved one,' she lied to him, bending to caress his ears.

Her heart thudding, she went upstairs again. Leonore still lived and breathed. Of course she did. Whatever had happened was unlikely to wound Leonore physically. In other respects – well, that was another matter entirely.

So what was going on here? Poppy Rogier. On a flight from New York. Not expected, obviously. Not arrived, evidently. Oh, God!

The picture of The Tower card was vivid in Marina's head: an exploding mass of stonework with figures flung from it as though struck with some divine thunderbolt. Frantic falling figures, tossed through the air, arms flailing, helpless and doomed.

She dialled the New York number.

Liam King was in a state of despairing frenzy. 'Is that Rogier's place? Is Poppy there? For Christ's sake, has she arrived yet? Where the hell is she?'

'I'm sorry, I don't know. I can't tell you,' Marina said. recoiling at the brutality of honesty. But what was the use of sweet talking? 'Can you fill me in?'

199

Struggling to control mounting panic, Liam managed to produce an account of the day's events as he knew them.

Poppy had got it into her head that she'd like to see her family in Britain. She'd taken the early morning flight from La Guardia. Should have landed at Heathrow around 5 p.m. British time.

'Have you phoned Heathrow?' Marina asked.

'Have you ever phoned Heathrow?' he asked acidly. 'Yeah! I eventually got through to someone who seemed to know more than absolute zero. The flight was sent somewhere up north. It hasn't arrived yet. Vanished from the radar. Three hours late already.'

'Dear God!'

'For Christ's sake, can't anybody tell me what's going on? Don't you have any fucking news-bulletins in that god-forsaken country of yours?'

Get angry, get crazy, Marina thought. Things are going to be pretty hellish for you, Liam King, in the next hours, days, weeks, years.

'I haven't heard the news tonight. I'm sorry. Look, let me try to find out more from this end and I'll call you back.'

'Yeah.' Pause. 'I'm sorry, too. This mess – it's not down to you,' he said lamely.

'It's OK.'

'Where the hell's François, anyway?'

Marina took in sharp breath. 'Out with friends,' she managed with remarkable speed and assurance.

'Yeah. He probably didn't know she was coming. It was going to be a surprise. She's like that, Poppy. Spontaneous.'

200

Arrogant was the word that sprang to Marina's mind. And also, most likely, dead.

Her brain heaved with speculation. Oh, please God, not dead, she prayed.

There was no need for her to make any information-gleaning phone calls. The TV information news service was already running the story of the lost aircraft as its lead item.

In a few terse lines, it was reported that the early flight from New York La Guardia, diverted from Heathrow because of poor visibility, had crashed in vicious squalls off the north-east coast of Yorkshire. The plane's tail had been sighted and also a number of bodies. The search by helicopters and divers was still continuing although, with the loss of natural light, it would soon be called off, to be resumed again at dawn. The seas were reported to be heavy, winds still stiff and the temperature unusually low for early summer.

A help-line number was given.

Staring at the flickering words on the screen, Marina could read in them only doom.

She toyed with the idea of calling Liam back. To say what?

No, she murmured to herself. This is where I hand on responsibility to those most closely involved. Helping is one thing. Taking over the operation is quite another.

With a heavy heart, she dialled the emergency contact number François had given her. Zoe Peach's number.

CHAPTER 19

'Are you hungry, darling?' Zoe asked, sitting up and shaking her head so that the dark strands of hair hung straight again; curtains of polished sable.

'Rather,' said François, mimicking a lazy upper-class English drawl. 'Simply ravenous, in fact.' He switched to a heavy French peasant accent. 'What are you going to cook for me, my little *chérie*?' Rolling on to his back, he stretched up his brown muscular arms and linked his hands behind his head, observing her with wicked provocation.

'Oh!' Zoe's eyes flashed with faint alarm. She had planned to give him a dainty supper of cold meats and tiny vols-au-vent, which had been delivered earlier from the local delicatessen, served with well-chilled champagne. Probably to be enjoyed in bed.

She looked at François and saw that he was laughing at her.

'You're so wonderful to tease, darling!' he said.

'You cruel wicked man. Don't frighten me. You know I can't cook.'

'Of course you can. Anyone can.'

'No. And now that I'm with you, I wouldn't presume

even to try! You're far too brilliant to compete with.'

They stared into each other's eyes for a few moments.

'I love you,' he said softly. 'I adore you. I want you to be with me for always.'

'Yes, I know,' she smiled, kissing him lightly on each shoulder.

'You most certainly should by now.' It was in all his instincts to add that, once he and Leonore were back from Poppy's wedding, nothing would keep them apart again.

But, recalling her lurid fantasies about his and Leonore's journey, he kept his mouth shut. He had no wish to touch that sore spot again. She seemed to lose all reason when a discussion on those lines came up. She become almost another person.

Remembering Zoe like that, a tiny spark of anger flared up and, hating it, he swore to himself in French, silently and with considerable vulgarity.

He slid out of bed. 'I'll open the champagne,' he said.

'How do you know there is any?'

'There always is. Every time I've been to your place, there's always been champagne for me. At exactly the correct temperature. Just waiting.' He turned to her and a silvery glint of connection flashed between them.

She laughed. 'Only the very best is good enough for you, my wonderful François!'

'Which must be why you are always here for me, too, darling.' He touched her cheek with a teasing finger.

Zoe sighed and lay back against the pillows. She heard him in the kitchen, the sound of the fridge door, the chink of glasses, the low 'thwup' of the cork being eased from the neck of the bottle.

He came back, bringing long cooled glasses. Their outsides were misted with tiny droplets of condensation, and a thousand sparkling bubbles leapt from their rims.

He bent to place a glass in her hand, at the same time kissing her lips with lingering tenderness.

They toasted each other. They toasted Poppy and Liam. They toasted Leonore and their future life together.

'Where shall we live?' he asked. 'A new place, I think. Not mine, not here. Somewhere different – mmm?'

'Oh, yes. Oh, how wonderful. Looking for something for the three of us.' Her face glowed with energy and light. 'Making a new home.'

'A new start,' he said.

Enlivened by the idea, they let their imaginations rip. They would rent a little flat in town for François's business needs, and then buy a house out in the country where they would live. A house with russet creeper covering its walls and a big garden surrounding it. Leonore could have a swing and a slide. A dog, maybe even a pony. Or they could go and settle in France. And apartment in Paris, an old house in Provence close to François's father. Perhaps all of those things!

'I can't wait to introduce you to my father,' François added. 'You two will get on so well. I shall feel so proud!'

Zoe laid her cheek on his shoulder. 'Ahh!'

When the telephone rang she made a smiling rueful grimace, rolled over and reached out for it. 'Yes?'

Her face registered faint puzzlement, followed by brief anxiety, then smiling relief. With a little shrug she held out the telephone for François to take. 'For you. Your neighbour. Don't be alarmed, Leonore is perfectly well.'

François raised his eyebrows, took the receiver and spoke swiftly into it. 'Marina?'

Zoe watched him, never took her eyes from his face. The smile died from her eyes, her face, her heart. She sensed some huge change taking place in him, some massive shifts and rearrangements of judgements and alliances.

With the powerful human instinct that enabled her to tune in to the most intimate and personal emotions and also to sense things in the atmosphere, things misty and diffuse, she knew instantly that some terrible and fundamental thing had happened. Panic rose up in her throat, making her feel as though she were choking.

He said little. The occasional low growl, a 'yes', an 'I see.'

Zoe stared at him, a sickening terror threading itself through her guts.

She heard him say 'goodbye', his voice sounding unreal; muffled and drowned.

He turned to her, handed her the telephone. Then he lifted the bedclothes and slipped from them in a one soft gliding movement. He began to get dressed.

'François?' Zoe's voice was no more than a tiny croak, barely audible.

He ignored her, wrenching himself into his clothes. As his wonderful lean body disappeared into cotton and leather, she fancied that he was withdrawing himself from her. Body and spirit.

She left the bed, wrapped herself in a silk kimono, her fingers trembling as she fumbled with the tie. 'Tell me,' she whispered. 'Please, François.' She reached out to him, but dare not touch.

He turned to her. Not to comfort, but to confront, and she shank back, seeing terrible pain in his face.

'Poppy is dead,' he said. 'Poppy, my wife.' He spat the words out as though it were an accusation and his eyes blazed like deadly firearms.

Zoe staggered backwards, landing awkwardly in the chair beside the bed. Her body was shaking and her heart thudding like a tree taking a dreadful battering in a storm.

So this was it. The horrifying culminating reality of the gruesome pictures that had invaded her mind. It seemed that the strength and spirit were ebbing out of her. She felt drained and emptied. And, in some way, guilty. Implicated.

'A plane? She was on a plane?' Zoe whispered, pleading with him to communicate with her.

François stared at her as though she were a stranger. He began to speak to her very rapidly in French. He gave her the necessary information with frightening impartiality and lack of emotion.

'Oh no, oh, God, no!' When she heard what had happened, she wanted to weep. She wanted to throw herself at his feet and beg his forgiveness because she felt that she had committed some sin and she wanted to be reassured, told that it was not so, forgiven.

Her mind darted about, frantic and hopeless.

She longed to press herself against him, simply to be close to him again, so that she could comfort him in this loss. But when she saw the firm set of his jaw, the hardness in his eyes, she knew that in his heart he had already moved miles away from her. Trembling, she held herself back from him with iron control.

'You,' he said to her eventually, calm and cool so that her blood chilled in her veins. 'You have done this.'

'No!' When she heard his nakedly brutal accusation, she crumpled. How could she carry such heavy blame? How could she bear it that he should accuse her so cruelly?

'You believe in the power of the mind,' he observed coldly. 'How many times have you told me?'

'That doesn't make me guilty of what has happened,' she protested. But it was no more than an automatic response to defend herself. When she heard him voice her own doubts, when she heard him accuse her, and command her to bear blame and carry guilt, she believed him. She loved him so much that whatever he said to her must be the truth.

François gazed down at her, hard and unrelenting.

She felt them being pulled apart from each other even as they spoke. She was going to lose him.

'I have to go now,' he said speaking in English again, as though all the important things had been said, as though everything vital was now over and done with.

She wanted to go with him. To be there for him, a steadfast consoling figure in his loss. And to be there for Leonore.

She saw in his eyes that she was the last person he wanted to share in this tragedy.

'There are things I have to attend to,' he said formally.

'Yes. Of course.' She picked up his jacket and handed it to him.

In previous times, when they had been so tenderly bonded, they had played little lovers' games. She would hold out his jacket and help him into it like the perfect

207

butler. He would smile and thank her very formally. Then swinging round, he would seize her with such possession and passion that she would gasp with the pleasure of it.

Today she simply handed his jacket to him. Desolation was washing over her, a cold swamping wave.

As silent as a stone, he went through into the hall. Took up his crash helmet and his keys from the table.

'When will I see you?' she dared to ask.

He turned, amazement on his face. He paused for a second. He did not speak. Softly he moved to the door, opened it and slipped through.

Zoe stood transfixed. A great black void opened within her. An unfurled black wing of grief. She sensed the breaking of bonds. She sensed endings and emptiness. Already she ached and ached for him.

Her mind would not work. It was not possible to think. Only feel. She told herself that, through some brutal primitive survival mechanism, she would manage to live through the next few seconds and minutes. Without François. And after that she might be able to think of living through the endless hours and the days. Without François.

Slowly she sank to her knees on the silky Turkish rug covering the cold marble floor. She bowed her head.

Charles returned to full consciousness with a little jerk. He had been lightly dozing. On the snooze button, as he liked to refer to it. The radio had cut in after the disc finished. Now it sang softly, some gently soothing night music. A serenade for a sweet seduction.

He saw Zoe's door open, a narrow strip of light

broaden out into a wedge through which François Rogier stepped. Tall and ramrod-like in his leathers and helmet, he was something of a sinister figure.

Charles snapped into acute alertness. He watched with intense concentration as François Rogier ran purposefully down the steps, hauled the cover from the bike in one sharp movement and then threw his leg over the exposed saddle.

The bike's engine activated instantly, and the machine veered away from the pavement and roared away down the road in a literal cloud of blue smoke.

Charles tapped his fingers on the steering wheel, pondering. Was this the dashing exit of the lover empowered by a magnificent performance in the bedroom stakes? Charles recalled roaring away from one or two of his own especially successful assignations, feeling the thrust of his car's high-powered engine echoing his own lusty performance.

Or was there another motivation behind the dashing getaway?

He had only managed a fleeting glimpse of Rogier's face. But he fancied there had been something there that suggested another emotion than triumphant elation. And there had been no looking back, no final wave of farewell.

Could this have been an abrupt exit fuelled with anger? Could he have been witnessing a flight from a lovers' quarrel? Charles remembered a few of those also. Good heavens, yes!

Excited speculation fizzed through his nerves.

He slid out of the car, zapped the central locking and watched the car wink its lights at him in response.

Standing on the broad step outside Zoe's door, he

considered his plan of action. He raised his hand to bang on the door and then lowered it again. This was no time for bullishness, he decided. Delicacy was the keynote. Softly, softly. Slowly, slowly. Like stalking a deer.

Placing his nose close to the glass, he peered into the hallway. The overhead chandelier was switched on, illuminating the place like a stage-set.

And centre stage – oh, dear God! – there was his fey-like little Zoe. Kneeling on the carpet, hands covering her face, her body shaking. Oh heavens, the poor wretched darling. Hearing the hollow wrenching sobs that came out of her, his heart somersaulted.

He tapped with his fingernails on the glass, but she gave no sign of noticing.

He pressed the bell, very lightly. Just once. But nothing happened.

He supposed he could put his fist through the glass. He'd have to wrap a protective handkerchief around his hand first, of course. These were not the circumstances in which one wanted to be troubled with slitting one's arteries and bleeding to death.

He looked hard at the glass, assessing the Victorian sunburst design and the heavy ground glass background. Obviously authentic. Christ! She'd be pissed off if he shattered that little lot. It must be worth four grand at least.

Knocking rather more forcefully, he discovered that the door was not fully closed. It swung back at his touch and he was able simply to walk in.

He walked right up to her and still she registered nothing.

Her grief filled the hallway, echoing in every corner,

floating away into the rooms beyond and up the staircase. Terrible moans of primitive pain.

He bent and touched her shoulder.

Her body stilled and her chest heaved as she took huge recuperative breaths.

She turned slowly and tilted her face upwards. Her eyes, flooded with shiny tears, looked at him uncomprehendingly for a moment. A light of desperate hope flickered and was snuffed. And then she gave a great gusting sigh. 'Oh, Charles!' she murmured.

He pulled her to her feet, revelling in his own gentleness, in the delight of holding her again.

She rested against his chest, shuddering still, the sobs not yet subsided.

'Oh angel, angel!' he muttered, stroking her hair, massaging her shoulders, rubbing his hands up and down her spine.

Her body was so tiny and frail. Her vulnerability stabbed at him and he made a sudden vow never to hurt her.

She crumpled against him, and the trembling through her body both touched and aroused him. Holding her so close, he was acutely aware of the spicy fragrance she always wore; it inserted itself into his senses, exotic and teasing. And beneath it were sensual notes of warm human femaleness.

Strong animal desire surged up, as he had expected it would, but he knew that he must control it.

For there was something other than that with Zoe tonight. As he held her very close to him, the words 'to have and to hold' ran repeatedly through his head.

CHAPTER 20

François felt the wind against his face. A raw, unforgiving wind springing out of the darkness. Street lights shone in his eyes, dazzling him. Behind his eyes there was a picture of Poppy. Sharp and vivid. Poppy as a girl of twenty. Utterly devastating. A mischievous, wilful, delightful brew of femininity and ferocity.

She had seemed to him a little wild when he first knew her, and he had told himself that if he should ever win her as his own, he would never try to tame her.

Tears streaming down his face in diagonal streams, he allowed himself to believe that he had been true to that silent pledge.

He winced to recall the unkind thoughts that had crept into his mind about Poppy in recent weeks. He would not think about them, would crush them to dust. But, cruelly, the words rose up defiantly to reproach him, despite his resolve. Words such as wilful, selfish, grasping. Those were the words he had used as captions to illuminate the pictures of Poppy in his head.

Ever since Zoe . . .

He swerved suddenly, so as to avoid a box lodged against the kerb. He had only just noticed it in time.

Fool, he told himself. He could have been thrown off, injured, killed. Swearing softly, he forced himself to think of nothing except getting back in one piece to Leonore.

Marina was standing in the open doorway, her hair like a huge furry halo around her head under the light.

She drew him inside. 'Leonore's fast asleep. She's fine. She knows nothing.'

'Then I'll leave her be.' He took off his helmet and tore open the snap fastenings on his jacket. 'Have you any more news?'

'I'm afraid it seems rather bad. There's a number for relatives to ring.' She handed him the pad on which the digits were jotted, went through into the sitting-room and left him to himself.

She heard his voice, a low flat murmur.

When it was over, he came to sit opposite her. He put his head in his hands.

Marina sat and watched him. There was no need for him to say anything. The message in the set of his body and the bleakness of his features made everything quite clear.

'They've found her body,' he said. 'It must be Poppy. She had a gold locket I gave to her . . .'

Marina sat and nothing. Waited.

'They need positive identification. I have to go as soon as possible tomorrow.'

'Yes.' She got up and poured him whisky. Gave it to him neat. 'François, you must contact Liam.'

'What?' He looked up. 'Liam. Oh, God.' He heaved himself upright again, moving heavily, wearily like an older man. At the door he turned. 'Why did she have to

213

come? Poppy. What on earth made her do this crazy, crazy thing?'

'If I knew the answer to that kind of question, I'd have discovered the secret of life,' Marina told him.

'Yes.' He sighed.

He was gone for ages this time. When he came back, he threw himself down once more and closed his eyes.

Marina sat and watched him. There had been a number of scenes like this in her past life. Grief and unspeakable anguish. A parent dying, a husband betrayed. She felt a still clear calmness inside her, knowing that it was possible to survive pain and, in time, rejoin the mainstream of life.

She poured him another whisky. One for herself.

They drank in silence. Then, suddenly, François wanted to speak.

'When someone dies,' he said, 'you think about that person for a while. And then you start thinking about yourself. You're all choked up with regrets. You start punishing yourself because of all the mistakes you made. And all the things you should have done that you didn't.'

'Yes,' Marina agreed.

'And you can't help it,' he said.

'No.' Marina agreed. 'If you have any humanity at all, you'll never be able to help punishing yourself.'

He took a long drink of his whisky. He tilted his head back, closing his eyes in a kind of frantic and despairing concentration.

Marina, watching him, had the irreverent thought that if she had been younger, and he had been hers, she would probably have been prepared to go to the stake for him, he was so beautiful and finely drawn and sensitive. So conflicted and desirable.

'There's something else,' he said, screwing up his eyes as though someone were taunting him with heated needle points.

'Yes?' Marina tilted her head, curious.

'Punishing others as well as yourself,' he said quietly, his eyes still shut.

'Ah,' said Marina. 'Well, I'm sure you're right about that. We all of us do it all the time, don't we? In my experience, anyway.' She waited. Ready to hear more. To listen, consider and respond.

But he had said as much as he was able for the present. He was not ready for further revelations. For a few moments he had escaped from his cage of raging guilt and despair and been able to see a pinprick of rational light at the end of a long tunnel of distorted and poisoned thinking. Now he was firmly back behind the bars, his barricades up, his defences watertight.

'I'll give Leonore her breakfast tomorrow, take her to school,' Marina said, mindful of practicalities. 'Will you speak to her first?'

'Yes. Ah . . .'

'She still has you,' Marina said in a businesslike way. 'The parent who's been looking after her for the last two years.'

François gave a little start. He stared at her. 'Leonore's only six. Children shouldn't have to lose either of their parents when they're so young.'

'No. But maybe, for Leonore, Poppy was lost when she left you both.' She wondered how she dare say that to him, at this time. She supposed it was because she

215

thought it was true. And that it might help him.

'Do you think she'll be fit to go to school?' François asked.

'We shall have to see. I'd be surprised if she weren't. Children like the daily routine, for things to be the same. At least, as much the same as is possible. Don't you think?'

'Yes. You're right.'

In both of their minds was the thought that the thing Leonore looked forward to most on a Monday morning at school was Zoe Peach's language group. On no account should she be denied that.

But neither of them referred to it.

Observing François's dark expression, Marina understood instinctively that the subject of Zoe Peach had entered forbidden territory. Had become a taboo topic, a completely no-go area.

And for François, guiltily and doggedly battling to stop the mental image of Zoe intruding on that of the dead Poppy, the only way of coping was to push that beloved image away and try to hate it.

Leonore sat at Marina's table feeding herself tiny bits of croissant. Risk sat under the table, glued to her knee, discreetly devouring whatever dropped his way.

François had woken her very gently that morning and told her that Mummy had been in a plane crash. That Mummy had died.

Leonore had felt her father's sadness stealing through the room like a autumny mist. She had put her arms around him and tried to make him happier.

And then he had said goodbye to them and set off to

216

the station, because he had to go on a journey to a place far away. But he would be back that evening.

'Will Mummy ever come again to see us?' Leonore asked Marina.

'No.'

'I can see her in my head,' said Leonore. She screwed her eyes up tightly. 'A bit.'

'Yes.'

Leonore pulled another doughy lump from her croissant, and Risk's nose tilted up, quivering. She said, 'If I collect some of those pink petals that blow off the trees in the park and wrap them in a clean hanky with the watch Mummy sent for me and put them on that big stone in the garden and count to a hundred, would she come back then?'

'No,' said Marina gently. 'Can you really count to a hundred?'

'Yes! And in French, too.'

'Good for you.'

'Do you want to go to school this morning?' Marina asked.

Leonore looked puzzled. 'I always go to school.'

'I know. But Daddy said if you'd rather stay here, then that's all right.'

'It's Monday,' said Leonore. 'Zoe comes on a Monday.'

'Yes,' agreed Marina.

'Can I tell Zoe about Mummy?'

Marina looked at the solemn, realistic child and felt tears spring up behind her eyelids.

'Of course you can.' Guessing at the ghastly scene that must have taken place between François and Zoe the previous evening, Marina seriously doubted that Zoe would, in fact, be around at school to be told anything this morning. Unless she were exceptionally dedicated, resilient and brave into the bargain.

As far as Leonore was concerned, however, Marina suspected that school would not be the hurdle François had feared. Leonore would welcome the reassurance of the familiar, of being busy. And François had said he would call the Headteacher from the train to explain everything so there would be no unnecessary extra hurdles to be cleared.

She and Leonore walked along to the school. It was a journey taking around ten minutes, punctuated by roaring buses and frantically revving cars. Each road crossing was a small nightmare, even with the aid of lights and the crossing patrols.

Marina kept a steadying hand and a close eye on her small friend. Leonore seemed to be bearing up pretty well, all things considered. But children's reactions to death were not like those of adults, mused Marina. Children still believed in magic. They believed in some kind of dreamlike, fantastical possibility of reincarnation.

But Marina had a strange feeling that, when Leonore had enquired about such magical methods of getting Mummy back, her reaction at being told of the impossibility of success had been tinged with relief.

Oh, poor Poppy, thought Marina. You left to make a new life. And lost your child in the doing so.

At the school gate Leonore turned and put up her face for a kiss. 'Daddy always kisses me on both cheeks.' She tilted her head. 'First this one and then the other.'

218

'That's because he's French,' said Marina, obeying Leonore's instructions with pleasure.

'And then I do it back to him,' said Leonore, nuzzling against Marina's face.

'I'll be here to collect you this afternoon,' said Marina. Leonore moved forward to join the throng. Suddenly she ran back and wrapped her arms around Marina in a swift fierce hug. Then she was gone.

Marina walked slowly back to her house, dabbing at her eyes and nose.

François returned just after seven. He looked tired and calm and strong. He swung Leonore up into his arms and put his hand briefly on Marina's shoulder.

'We've made supper,' Marina said. 'Mainly according to Leonore's directions, you'll be relieved to know. I take the prize for being the world's most disastrous cook.'

Her intention was simply to preserve a veneer of bantering cheeriness to lift the atmosphere of gloom. But François was instantly reminded of Zoe, light-heartedly regretting her lack of skills in cooking, oblivious to the disaster that was about to wrap itself around the two of them, choking their love for each other. His raw feelings screeched. He slipped back home, splashed his face with sharply cold water and got a bottle of wine from his store in the cellar.

If it were not for Leonore, he believed he would have been tempted to sit on his own and get very drunk so as to obliterate the memory of his most recent encounter with Poppy. A dead woman with a face bloated from being in the water for hours. Poppy all right, but very little to do with the Poppy he used to know.

He had felt curiously empty as he looked at her. And afterwards, sitting listlessly on the train as it hurtled south again, he had had to push away the image of Zoe, which kept creeping around the edge of his vision, trying to find a place. On no account must he fantasize about his former mistress, when he should be thinking of his former wife.

As a child, François had been brought up to have a strong respect for the dead. By the time the train slid into King's Cross station, he had done a good deal of thinking about both the dead and the living and come to the conclusion that he had no right to love a woman ever again.

He placed the bottle on the table in Marina's kitchen and drew the cork. '*Santé*. Cheers. Here's to life!' he said with a certain resigned determination.

Leonore looked at him with grave concerned eyes. But she said nothing, devoting her attention to cutting up her omelette with great care. She managed to eat almost all of it before Risk got a look in. All the time she was sneaking glances at François, as though to check that he was still whole, not about to shatter into little pieces.

'And how was school?' he asked her eventually.

'We did PE in the hall and then Maths. And then I went to Zoe's group.'

Marina felt a tiny current of electric feeling spark in the atmosphere. A pulse flickered in François's jaw and was then still.

'And how did that go?' he said evenly, taking a drink of wine.

'We did our reading first.' Leonore paused, frowning with effort of remembering and telling. 'I was all right and then all of a sudden I was crying. I couldn't stop.'

Marina and François looked at each other.

'Zoe said just to cry if I felt sad,' Leonore elaborated. 'And when the others went back to their class, *she* started crying, too.'

François laid his forehead against his hand.

'I sat on her knee and we both cried and cried.' Leonore said. She sounded sad and yet somehow proud too.

François had gone very pale. He laid down his fork, finding that his faintly revived appetite had all but vanished.

That night, long after Leonore had fallen asleep, murmuring about Risk and dropping hints about when she and François might be able to get a dog, he lay awake through the interminable hours, staring into the dark.

Zoe also found sleep elusive. She had spent the day swerving between hope and despair: unable to believe François would ever be able to look at her again without hatred, then immediately unable to believe that the precious love they had shared could be so swiftly and brutally wiped out.

When Leonore had come into the medical room for her lesson, her pale face so full of bravery and so transparent with feeling, she had thought she would break down completely. She had held on to her self-control like someone clutching at the side of a steep cliff with their fingertips.

When Leonore herself broke down, self-control was no longer an issue. She had taken the child into her arms and rocked her like a baby, stroking and kissing and soothing. Her own tears had wet Leonore's shiny hair and, for a few precious moments, they had been bound together in a shared steamy stickiness of sobbing.

When Leonore had eventually left to rejoin her class, Zoe had found herself exhausted. She had dragged herself through the rest of the day, her body leaden, her legs clumsy and disobedient as though her nerves had been severed.

Charles had telephoned. He wanted to come round, take her out to dinner. 'Angel, I have to see you!'

She had been grateful. Tempted even. But her mind was filled with François. 'I'm not fit company for anyone. Truly. I must get some sleep. Please, Charles! You were so good to me last night. Please understand.'

'OK, OK, I can take a hint.' With much affectionate chiding he had agreed to leave her to herself tonight. But he would be round to collect her the next evening. Absolutely no arguments. Yes?

Meekly she had agreed. What was the point of arguing? François was lost and so it didn't seem to matter particularly what happened in the forseeable future. Survival was her only goal.

And Charles had been very kind. Sweet and gentle. Just when she needed it. He didn't deserve rejection.

She turned from one side to the other under the bedcovers, unable to find comfort. Her hand crept out and felt the emptiness in the bed. The sheets were stiff, cold and unruffled.

After an eternity, dawn began to show, stealing into the room, light oozing back into her world from some mysterious other place.

She felt her muscles begin to relax, felt herself sliding

down into a soft soporific mental state. Suddenly she was alarmed as a new fear presented itself: the threat of dreams and visions. She struggled to stay awake.

Her conscious mind battled, furious with resistance, but another part of it fought back.

She was walking along a broad road. There was nothing to see, just darkness. Empty darkness, bleak and echoing.

She was alone . . . desperately alone . . . and very, very lonely. There was a fathomless hollow in the centre of the world filled with blackness. Then, ahead, she saw a flicker of light. It flared up, red and orange and warm, then was gone.

Black smoke billowed up, rolling towards her, choking her, blinding her.

A man came running from the smoke. His clothes were smouldering, and he was calling for help.

Zoe reached out her hands, but she could do nothing for him.

Then suddenly, like a miracle, there was a hose in her hand, cool water gushing. She turned the force of water on the suffering man and the flames licking around him shrivelled and died.

She wanted to run towards him, to comfort him and soothe his wounds, but her legs were leaden and wayward.

She was weeping uncontrollaby with despair and frustration; she saw that he was weeping too.

François! Oh, François!

CHAPTER 21

It was now Tuesday morning. Less than forty-eight hours since Poppy's death.

Zoe drew all her courage around her, got into her car and drove to François's house. She had no teaching appointments until the late morning. She knew that she must see him. If she could only see him before any more time passed, then somehow, something could be salvaged from the wreckage of Sunday evening.

She felt sick with anxiety as she parked the car. Her heart was a lump of pain throbbing in her chest.

The moment she looked at the house, she knew that it was deserted, that he had gone. The anticipatory shrieking in her nerves slowed. Her heart steadied, stilled. Became cold and heavy.

Knowing that hope was hanging on a very frail thread, she nevertheless swung herself from the car and went up to the front door. She could see the outline of her figure distortedly thrown back at her from the thick black oiliness of the fresh paint as she pressed the bell and then waited in resignation.

There was nothing but silence.

Desolation overtook her and she leaned her head against the painted wood.

A woman's voice startled her. 'He left early this morning. He'll be away for a few days.'

Zoe raised her head. The owner of the voice was addressing her across the spiky hedge dividing the two entry paths. A strikingly tall woman, her dark brown eyes full of life and sympathy. And a strange unusual knowingness.

'Oh, I see,' Hope finally dropped away.

'Are you Zoe?' the woman asked.

'Yes.'

'I've heard a good deal about you,' the woman said. 'From Leonore.'

'Ah.'

'I'm Marina. The helpful neighbour – at least, I hope that's the case,' she said in a dry, self-mocking way.

Zoe gave a faint smile. 'Yes. I've heard of you, too. Also from Leonore.'

'Well, since we're already so well acquainted, I think you should come in and have a little chat. You look as though you could do with a listening ear.'

Zoe hesitated, not knowing if she could cope with anyone or anything just at this moment. She looked again at the shrewd yet sympathetic face of the inviter and capitulated.

Following Marina down the hallway of her house, Zoe admired the length and slenderness of the older woman's legs, her lean yet feminine figure shown off to perfection in classic black Levis and a cream linen shirt.

How old would she be? Zoe wondered. There had not been time to assess her face properly and silver hair wasn't a particularly reliable indication of age. She had a friend who had gone grey in her twenties.

225

Marina beckoned her to the kitchen: a marvellous haven full of natural waxed woods and the lingering smell of a garlicky supper washed down with full red wine. Perhaps a supper François had shared . . .

'Please, make yourself at home.' Marina indicated a sturdy semi-circular chair of pale oak. She reached for the coffee pot, which was gently warming on the top of a deep rusty-red Aga, and placed it on the table beside two delicate white china cups.

There was something reassuringly genuine and comforting about this faintly battered, yet most elegant, room. Absorbing its welcoming atmosphere, Zoe allowed herself to feel soothed. A dog's soft wet nose nudged gently and insistently at her knee and she bent to stroke its silky ears. She recalled Leonore's eager descriptions of a white-muzzled mongrel who was so clever he could almost speak. 'Hello, Risk,' she said to him.

Bending to take milk from the fridge, Marina found it impossible not to keep staring at Zoe, peacock-bright in her sharp lime-green and canary-yellow suit, starkly edged with black. Such imaginativeness with one's wardrobe made her think that it was perhaps time to make an effort and stop slouching around the house in the monochrome uniform of jeans and shirts.

Mariana's curiosity was silently simmering. Looking at her guest, she had a sense of having captured an exquisite and exotic bird. *I am the birdcatcher, tra, la, la!* She smiled, recalling Leonore's piping voice struggling with the words, first in English and then in French – as encouraged by her tutor.

'Milk?' she asked Zoe.

'Milk, please. But no sugar.' Zoe's voice was ripe and low and attractive, but with no merry lilt of life in it.

So then, Marina mused, a wounded bird. Not yet grounded, but definitely struggling.

She placed the filled cup and its saucer in front of her guest, then sat herself at right angles to Zoe, close enough to observe all that was necessary, not so close as to be intimidating.

So this was the mysterious and fabled Zoe Peach. Mysterious as far as François had been concerned, for he had never given Marina any indication as to the personality of his lover. Fabled in Leonore's view, who had described her so vividly as an adored fairy-tale style figure, all lined up to take the place of Mummy.

Marina found herself enchanted. It was not so much the younger woman's individual style that caught her imagination – although the startling contrast of dark hair and pale skin with the glowing vivid clothes was certainly arresting, all attributes that were instantly eye-catching and would clearly excite general admiration – it was the haunting, ethereal quality about her which particularly fascinated Marina.

And there was something more; perhaps the most significant aspect of all in Marina's view. Sitting close to Zoe Peach, breathing the same air as she did, receiving glances from her strange acquamarine eyes, Marina had a keen, thrilling sense of being in the presence of one with a finely developed extrasensory ability. A hidden force Marina was able to pick up on, because it was one which she herself had once possessed.

She wondered if Zoe was aware of this and, if so, whether the force was seen as working for good or evil.

Offering the biscuit tin, the contents of which had increased in both quantity and variety since Leonore had begun to visit, Marina told herself to concentrate on the here and now and stop indulging in wild speculations.

Zoe did not take a biscuit. She said, 'Do you know where François has gone?'

'Yes. He's gone to New York.'

The aquamarine eyes flared with feeling: dismay and a sharp stab of alarm.

Marina wondered whether to elaborate further. But how much did Zoe know? Marina had no idea. And when in doubt, it was her policy to keep her mouth shut.

Zoe looked down. Her hands trembled when she next lifted her cup.

Marina sipped her coffee. She recalled François, two evenings before, sipping his whisky and talking about not being able to help 'punishing others'. It was quite obvious to her now who he had been punishing.

'A death causes many ripples,' Marina said eventually. 'Especially a sudden and violent death of someone still young.'

Zoe looked up. She nodded. 'I knew something terrible was going to happen. I've known for weeks.' She put up a hand to her eyes. 'I know you'll think I'm crazy and unhinged. I couldn't help my thoughts, you see. I truly did know there would be a disaster. But I'd never dreamed it would be that. Disaster for Poppy.'

Marina took some time to consider this impassioned statement. 'Then for whom? Who did you think would be struck down by disaster?'

Zoe flinched as though an insect had flown at her face. She stared at Marina as though a challenge had been issued. 'It was not my fault,' she said simply, as though that remark would be perfectly comprehensible to her companion.

Marina stirred her coffee. 'I think you'll have to help me out a bit to understand that.'

'You'll think I'm mad.'

'Maybe we're all a little mad sometimes. I'm prepared to listen, I'll try to understand, not to judge. Trust me.'

'I have these dreams,' said Zoe. 'I get these pictures in my head about disasters and dying. Terrible premonitions. And I know that they're going to happen in real life.'

See! Marina told herself. Your wild speculations are invariably right.

'Now you *do* think I'm mad,' said Zoe into the growing silence.

'No. I've had similar experiences myself,' she said evenly. 'A very long time ago.'

Zoe frowned. 'What sort of experiences?' she asked cautiously.

'My pictures didn't come in the form of dreams,' Marina explained. 'I saw them when I was awake. And they weren't pictures of disasters like the ones you've experienced. They were images that gave me the ability to predict future happenings in people's lives – a marriage, a move of house or job. That kind of thing.' Harmless, really, thought Marina, certainly compared with what Zoe was experiencing.

Zoe slanted a swift glance at her, checking that she was not playing some awful joke.

'François believes that my dream is to blame for

229

Poppy's accident,' she said dully. 'I suppose he thinks that, in some strange way, I willed it to happen.'

Marina said slowly, 'He's had a terrible shock. He'll be grieving and feeling guilty and angry. It's natural then to look around for someone to blame. And, also, you have to remember that a lot of men tend to be sceptical about the "power of the mind". They shy away from that kind of thing, reject it.'

'Yes.' Zoe's voice was dull, unconvinced.

'His view will soften,' Marina said gently. 'In time.'

'No,' said Zoe, sharply, finally.

'Why do you say that?'

'I can't see a way back to him,' she said. 'I can't see a way through to him. The pictures in my head are full of darkness. He's there. I can see him there quite clearly and he needs me – but I can't get to him.'

'The pictures could alter,' said Marina.

'Do you think so? I don't.'

'You have to remember,' said Marina gently, 'that the pictures are of your own making, after all, and like your conscious thoughts, they too can be shaped and bent as time passes.'

Zoe seemed not to be listening. Or perhaps not wanting to hear. Her thoughts were still with François, with the awful loss she had suffered. 'He loved me so much,' she told Marina quietly. 'Deep, true love – even though we've known each other for such a short time. And now he hates me. In the pictures in *his* head, I'm nothing more than Poppy's murderer.'

'It will pass. It will change,' Marina said.

Zoe was silent. Immovable. She turned her head, looking away from Marina. Her eyes fell on the pack of Tarot cards, resting on their silk scarf, not yet wrapped up.

'My mother used to go for Tarot readings,' she told Marina. 'Once a year in January. She had such complete faith in the readings, it was almost frightening to see.' Zoe lifted her cup to her lips, her eyes faraway and reflective. She put the cup down again without drinking. 'Mother believed everything she was told, the poor darling. Even when things hadn't come true for the past year's forecast, she'd still believe the next year's one. It was quite a worry on January the first, wondering if she'd come home laughing or crying.'

'Didn't anything from the readings come true?'

'Yes. One or two things. They always told her she'd be travelling a great deal and have minor problems with her health.'

'Go on.'

Zoe smiled. It was the first time she had smiled properly since entering the house. 'My mother always took several holidays a year and she was something of a hypochondriac. It wasn't too surprising that the cards got those things right.'

'So, once upon a time, you were a sceptic?'

'No. I was . . . open-minded,' Zoe said.

'Maybe it's only those who are truly open-minded who can receive pictures and premonitions,' Marina observed. 'Is your mother still alive?'

'No.' Zoe was startled, suspicious. 'Why do you ask?'

'Because I'm interested. Because it might be relevant to what's happening to you now.'

Zoe paused, thinking, wondering how much to reveal. 'She was killed in a car crash. She saw a magpie flying towards her in the garden and then she went out in her car and was crushed by a tractor.'

Marina said nothing.

Zoe stared at her. 'You didn't need to ask that, did you? You knew the answer to that question before I answered it?'

'I had a feeling about it. In my younger days I had quite an aptitude for clairvoyance.'

'And now?'

'Less so. But it's still there.'

'I wish it would leave me alone!' Zoe said, her small face fierce. 'I have to . . . live again. Even if I've lost François, I must have some life back.' The passion in her voice was startling, seemingly almost too great to have come from her delicate frame.

'You mustn't keep saying you've lost François. You must have hope,' Marina told her.

'You didn't see his face,' Zoe said quietly. 'Whilst you were telling him the news on the telephone, his face told me everything. Something in him was dying. And it was his loving feeling for me.'

She got up. 'I have to go now,' she said. 'I'll be late for work.'

Work! thought Marina, her heart sinking to be reminded of her promise to the shop that she would be in again this afternoon, following the time she had taken off to care for Leonore.

She stood at the door, watching Zoe opening the door of her car. She recognized that firm set look on the younger woman's face. That huge determination that would guide her destiny into the paths she decreed. Not those she wanted, but those she decided were meant for her.

She thought of herself in the past, doing something of the same kind. Although she doubted that even she had had quite the fatalistic resolution and strength of gazelle-like Zoe. And certainly her mate at the time had had nothing of the magnetic steely qualities of François.

She watched the bright yellow car slide away and meandered her way slowly back to the kitchen, Risk tracking her every move, almost tripping her up in his eagerness to be close. She bent to him, running her hand along the wiry coat. 'You know everything, don't you? Especially when I'm going to get myself into bother?'

She cleared away the stained cups, found a clean one and poured herself fresh coffee. Sitting at the table, staring out into the garden, she had an extraordinary conviction that the time had come to cease coasting, to pull herself out of the ruts she had been digging herself into, and take her life by the scruff of the neck once again.

In these past few days, being there for Leonore and François, and briefly also for Zoe Peach just now, she had felt herself shifting to a harsher yet sharper level of existence. She had felt herself moving back into the mainstream of life, being of real use again. Needed.

She had an urgent sense of time going on. Hours and weeks simply being passed through rather than *lived*. There were things she had to do, past knowledge she must explore so as to help those struggling in the present. She had to expand her thoughts, to grow again.

'I can do it,' she told Risk, who instantly came alert, sitting up very straight, his eyes bright, his tail vigorously brushing the floor.

'See, you agree with me, so it must be all right.' Flourishing the receiver with flamboyant purpose, she

233

telephoned her employer at the fashion shop and gave in her notice. There was little concern in response: it seemed that people were queueing up for a nice little job like hers.

Dizzy with a sense of escape, she reviewed her scrappy savings and things she might have to sell if her frail finances starved to death. The antique clock? Colin's stereo system?

As excitement and panic jostled for supremacy, she reassured herself that something would happen to rescue her before the money ran out. Something good, something positive. She had just gained her freedom; penury was not the price she was prepared to pay for it.

She would *will* it not to be so.

All would be well.

Shadowed closely by Risk, she went upstairs into her tiny junk room and searched through the ring-binder files she had kept from her student days.

Human Learning, Human Perception, Experimental Study of Sleep . . . Good grief, did she really used to know all about that? Tossing aside these unwanted materials, she rifled through the remaining files more urgently. Surely it couldn't happen that the one she wanted wasn't there. But wasn't that always the way of things!

'Aha. Got it!' she exclaimed to a worried Risk. She turned to the front page. There was a long title, painstakingly written in flowing script. And beneath it her name, because she had been the one to compile the file. 'Listen,' she commanded a quiveringly watchful Risk. '*Unexplained Phenomena in the Study of Human Experience*. Impressed, huh?' She looked at the subheadings:

The paranormal, telepathy, clairvoyance, precognition.

Ah, yes, this was the one.

She took the file down to the kitchen, sponged the dust from the cover and the yellowed edges of the paper and settled down to read.

An hour passed. Two. Three. Risk pawed her reproachfully. Walk time. Dinner time. Anything!

She stretched her stiff legs. 'Yes, yes. OK.'

They went out together into the sunshine. Little jewelled birds darted in the trees. The new season's leaves decorating the branches swayed and sparkled.

Marina smiled. All *would* be well.

CHAPTER 22

Charles was standing at the top of the steps, leaning up against the door frame when Zoe got home later on. 'Angel!' he exclaimed, bringing her masterfully into his arms and kissing the crown of her head, which was all she was prepared to offer him just at that moment.

'Charles! I thought you were calling for me at seven-thirty!' She was not displeased to see him, but unable to hold back a slightly jarring note of protest from her voice.

Charles heard it, and was not in the least dismayed. He recognized that it would take time to wean her from her lovesick state and banish François Rogier from her thoughts. But he judged himself well up to the challenge. In fact, her loyalty to the other man rather impressed him, made him keener than ever.

'I couldn't wait another minute to see you,' he exclaimed. 'I sometimes have the feeling you'll fly away if I don't keep a very close eye on you.'

Zoe unlocked the door and invited him in. The morning's mail lay in the wire cage beneath the letterbox opening. Her eyes darted to it instantly, hoping against hope there would be something from François, some sign that he had not cast her away from him for ever.

With elaborate casualness she removed the envelopes from the box and went through into the sitting-room. 'Sit down, Charles,' she said politely, although a shade too formally for his liking. 'I'll make us some tea.'

'A g & t would be nicer,' he drawled. 'And then you won't have to disappear to the kitchen.'

'Help yourself,' she invited him, indicating the cupboard containing bottles and glasses. 'because I do have to disappear to the bathroom for a moment. I'm sure you'll survive for a few minutes on your own.' She recalled the way in which she had been denied any choice to conceal her grief from Charles when he had suddenly reappeared in her life, just at the moment François had departed. She had been stripped naked as it were, utterly helpless and exposed. Now that she had had time to wrap a blanket of protection around herself, she was determined never again to reveal her wound site to him.

'Not too long,' he warned, teasing her very charmingly, 'or I shall come and get you.'

Zoe gave him a warning tap on the top of his head as she passed.

Locking the bathroom door, she scanned through the envelopes. And yes, oh joy, there was something from François.

Just to glance at the exquisite italic lettering with its long strong strokes made her faint with longing.

The paper flickered in her unsteady fingers as she unfolded it.

My dear Zoe,
I am flying to the States, taking Poppy's body back to

237

New York. I thought it best not to come and tell you my plans. You will know why.

I think you will know, too, that there are many things we should have said to each other. But perhaps these are things it would be best to leave unsaid.
François.

There was an added line, an afterthought clearly, but so heavily crossed out as to be unintelligible.

Zoe stared at the words, so formal, so cold. Words of final farewell with no glimmer of hope.

She touched the paper his beloved hand had rested on and longed and longed for him. Despair overwhelmed her.

She found her legs weak and quivering. Stumbling and about to crumple, she threw out her hands to steady herself against the wall.

I am falling apart, she whispered to herself in horror.

Beyond the locked door, she heard sounds from downstairs. The movement of feet, the crackle of a newpaper being turned and re-folded, the fizz of sparkling tonic water as a cap was released from the bottle.

Life and breath. The here and now. Reality. Charles.

Slowly she straightened her spine, threw her head back and breathed deeply. Her hand tightened on the paper she still held. It buckled and shrank into a tiny ball, warm and damp from the heat of her hand.

A calm stillness crept into her heart and mind.

She crossed to the mirror and brushed her hair back into gleaming shape. She stroked fragrance on the pulse points of her skin.

Holding herself very steady, she returned to the sitting-room.

Charles glanced up. 'More gorgeous than ever.' He patted the space beside him. 'Come here.'

Zoe sat down. With careful concentration she focused the whole of her being into putting the haunting picture of François from her mind. At least temporarily.

She turned to Charles and gave him a long slow smile. Her complete attention.

'I want to take you for a drive into the country,' he announced.

'What, now?'

'Uh huh.'

He wants me to meet his parents, she thought with sudden intuition. The thought struck her as curious rather than disturbing.

'I'd like to show you off to Charles senior and my mother,' he said grinning. 'Come on. They're expecting us.'

In the car she said to him, 'Let me put you right here, Charles. I'm very happy to meet your parents. I never had a proper family. I like the whole idea of families.'

'Really! Excellent, excellent!' He sounded utterly delighted.

'But I'm not prepared to be "shown off" like a trophy.'

'Ouch. I keep forgetting you're not a girl to be trifled with. Sorry, Zoe darling. A figure of speech, slip of the tongue.'

'Forgiven.' Tentatively, she reached out and touched the back of his hand with fleeting fingertips. Flesh that was firm and warm and dry. Flesh that was not François's. She drew in a sharp breath, was about to snatch her hand away, before instantly wrenching herself back into control.

239

Looking out of the window, she watched London gradually fall back into the distance, the peripheral suburban sprawl dwindle away and eventually give in to the dominance of the countryside. Huge sprawling fields spread themselves on either side. The trees became ever more imposing, the roads ever more narrow.

Soon, they were passing through wooded terrain interspersed with walled parkland, indicating the borders of considerable country estates.

Zoe became increasingly curious to know what she would find at the end of the journey. She knew very little about Charles, having previously simply accepted him as an agreeable and amusing escort. Charles had spoken hardly at all of his parents and his home. He had made casual reference to his job in his uncle's merchant bank. She had gained the impression that his working hours were both flexible and undemanding and that he probably did not take his work very seriously. She had also gathered that, when he was in London, he lived in a small flat in a leafy terrace of Belgravia.

And that was about all.

And because her mind had been taken up then with other things, and her feelings had been swept away by another man soon after she first came to know Charles, she had never bothered to enquire further.

Charles made a swift sudden turn to take the car through tall iron gates. There was a long dead-straight drive leading up to very substantial house built of grey stone with a distinctly Gothic frontage. A country house. A small stately home.

'Orignal building dates from the time of Queen Anne,' Charles commented. 'Substantial extensions in the Re-

gency period, and again in Victoria's reign.' He said all
this with an air of studied nonchalance, but it was easy to
tell that he was deeply proud of the family house.

'It's called Percival,' Charles told her grinning. 'Don't
ask me why. There's some ancient and complicated
reason. I could never remember all the historical stuff
Mother used to spout at me.'

'It's beautiful,' said Zoe. She reflected that she and her
mother had always lived in large and comfortable houses,
beautifully maintained, plumply furnished, upholstered
and draped with all the best that a good deal of inherited
money can buy. But Charles's house was something very
different. A house speaking of history and ancestry. And
most likely of very old and very serious money gained in
a rather different manner from the way her father had
acquired his in a small-town building company.

Turning this over in her mind, and looking up at the
splendid house, Zoe felt neither excitement nor intimi-
dation. She had never been poor. She had never needed
to worry about the payment of bills, the ability to make
purchases, employ help in the house, take holidays. But
she had never been acquistive or greedy for more than
she already had. She had enjoyed her cushioned life-
style, her vast wardrobe and smart little car. She had
recognized that her job, too, was something of a play-
thing, something to interest her and provide a focus for
the days because there had never been any need to make
money. She was not, however, materialistic. Her ambitions were directed elsewhere, in her heart and her spirt.
And, if François had asked her to give up everything and
go and live with him in a tent in the desert, she would
have gone.

241

She gave her head a vicious little shake. Snapped her eyes shut against François.

'I thought you'd like it,' Charles said with satisfaction.

He held her arm as she swung her legs from the car. 'God, you're so exquisite,' he whispered. 'You're like a mysterious queen in an old Egyptian painting.'

'I thought history wasn't your strong point,' she said drily.

Charles Pym senior, master of Percival, turned out to be an older, more wiry version of his son. His once-blond hair had lost its buttery yellowness and turned to a pleasing thick milky white. Wearing baggy corduroy trousers and a very hairy old sweater, he came down the panelled hall and looked at Zoe with intense curiosity.

Charles was all delighted exuberance. 'Father, this is she – Zoe. The elusive maiden I've told you so much about.'

Zoe extended her hand and felt it clasped briefly and then released.

'Good journey?' Charles's father asked her politely. 'Charles keep to the speed limits, did he?'

'Yes. And no,' Zoe smiled. She looked around the hall, admiring the high arched and latticed windows, the great solid oak staircase branching into two halfway up and leading to a graceful carved gallery.

'Hmm,' said Charles's father.

'Where's Mother?' Charles enquired.

'Somewhere out in the garden. Where else?'

'Mother is utterly devoted to her lupins and peace roses,' Charles explained to Zoe.

'Indeed she is, I hardly ever see her.' Charles's father

was observing Zoe carefully, making no attempt to disguise his continuing curiosity.

She turned, looked him straight in the eye and gave an enigmatic smile.

'You're going to have to change, my dear,' Charles's father informed her. 'Your clothes, that is, before you venture into the garden. My wife will have you grubbing about in the flower beds and the greenhouses, showing you what's what before you can say marsh marigold. And I must also warn you that she has two frightfully undisciplined labradors who will wreck that delightful little outfit of yours in two minutes flat.'

'Oh, dear,' said Zoe. 'I see I've been cast in the role of poor little town girl woefully ill-equipped for the rough rigours of the country. Perhaps you could loan me an all-enveloping mackintosh and some galoshes?'

'*Touché*!' Charle's father patted her shoulder in a congratulatory fashion as though she had cleared some sort of hurdle. 'I'll get them right away.'

'You see,' Charles told his parent. 'Girl of spirit and wit. What did I tell you? She's a miracle.'

Dinner was served at eight punctually in the huge, hushed dining-room whose walls were crammed with family portraits done in thick oils. A vast mahogany sideboard stretched almost the width of the room, laden with Georgian silver.

At dinner Charles's father was the perfect English gentleman, a genial and perfectly mannered host, steering the conversation skilfully along and allowing for no awkward pauses. His mother, joining them a little late and rather breathless, was brisk but friendly. Around

243

sixty, she struck Zoe as a woman who would have been wholesomely handsome in her youth, but was now somewhat ruddy, wizened and weathered from being continually outdoors.

She had made an effort to dress for dinner, wearing a smoky-blue cocktail dress in figured brocade of the kind Zoe recalled her own mother wearing when she herself had been a very small child. Any glamorous effect was entirely obliterated by the sagging and bobbled beige cardigan she had put on over the dress, in defence against the deep chill of the Percival dining-room even in the early summer.

'You're a teacher, I hear,' Charles's mother said to Zoe in a blunt, down-to-earth manner. It sounded like a faint reproach.

'I teach English as a second language to young children.'

'And are there many who need that kind of teaching?' Charles's mother asked. 'Children of school age who know no English?'

'Quite a few.' Zoe smiled.

'She's not really a career girl,' Charles cut in, reaching for the wine coaster and refilling his glass.

Zoe turned to him. 'What makes you say that?'

'Because, my angel, I've been out with one or two girls who certainly were. And you're not one jot like them.'

Zoe looked at him with fresh interest. He was right in his judgement, she decided, although maybe not for the right reasons. She had always liked her job. She liked the challenge of motivating the children, and she loved their company. But she had no ambition for climbing the promotion ladder. The idea of being a Headteacher, bound to a desk and a mountain of paper and endless meetings, held no attraction whatsoever.

And also, at the back of her mind, there had always the shining image of a perfect love, a passionate yet deeply solid marriage. Children.

Her mind flew to Leonore. Ah, if she had any responsibility for the love and care of Leonore, she knew that the job would be pushed very firmly into second place.

Oh, Leonore! Leonore!

'More wine, darling?' Charles put his hand to hers and unwound her wine glass from her fingers. He glanced sharply into her face. 'Angel! Are you all right?'

She looked down at his hand. Gently it had grasped hers and turned it palm-upwards. Red weals showed on the pale skin. She had been clutching the fat stem of her wine glass so tightly that the chiselled cuts had almost pierced the soft flesh.

She turned to face him. 'Yes. Yes. I'm perfectly fine.' Oh, dear sweet Charles. She fancied that he understood very little about her, but he seemed to have a knack of stepping in when she needed comfort and solace.

'I never wanted a career,' Charles's mother said. 'I never wanted anything except a husband and children. A quiet country life. And a garden.'

'Mentioned last but rating no means least,' quipped Charles.

'And,' Charles's mother continued determinedly, fixing Zoe with a stern eye, 'I have always been terribly proud of my husband's career. When a man has the responsibility of sitting on the board of several international companies, I believe he would prefer his wife not to be out there in the world competing. Men like a little female docility and support, you know, whatever they tell you in the news-papers and on TV. Even in these modern times.'

'Of course.' Zoe smiled diplomatically. All this was so familiar, just the kind of conversation that used to go on at her mother's little supper parties for her comfortably off friends.

She wondered what François's view would be. A huge stab of longing leapt in her at the thought of discussing the issue with him. His ideas were always so clear, so logically thought out. And yet passionate. And never prejudiced.

Except on one issue.

She took a long drink of wine. Stop it, stop it! Stop thinking of him! The pain was flaring up all over again. She didn't know if she could keep on withstanding it when it struck without warning.

She raised her body slightly in her chair. She moved her head to look at Charles, quite unconsciously showing off her lovely swan-like neck and thrilling him. 'What do you think, Charles?'

'Mmm? What? Oh! Women working!' He grinned. 'Always support my mama. Wouldn't do to argue with her at her own dinner table.'

'I rather admire the kind of work you're doing,' Charles's father said. 'I'd imagine the children you work with are not the easiest.'

'I suppose not,' Zoe agreed. She looked at him with new interest. 'But I've found that children are usually pretty co-operative if you can just find the right way to get their interest.'

'Keep the little devils busy?' Charles's father suggested.

246

'Exactly.' She smiled, warming to the older man.

'We've never found the secret of keeping *this* little devil busy,' he continued wryly, looking pointedly at his son.

'Not with work!' Charles's mother commented with brutal frankness. 'I'm afraid he's been exceedingly busy playing instead. Usually with beautiful blonde girls.'

'Yes, I did used to have rather a thing about blondes,' Charles agreed, unabashed. 'But I rather fancy I'm becoming a changed man.' He gave the sable-haired Zoe a long lingering look.

At the end of the meal, Charles's mother escorted Zoe to the drawing-room, leaving the two men to drink an obligatory glass of port. 'We're very traditional here,' Charles's mother said with peppery irony, 'as you will have noticed, Zoe.'

'Yes.' Zoe smiled, accepting the cup of coffee offered her in the tiniest of bone china cups.

'I like tradition. I relish the progress of the seasons, the rhythm of my garden here at Percival.'

Zoe nodded, understanding exactly what was meant.

'Do you think you could?'

Zoe looked up slowly. 'Are you asking me if I could live here at Percival?'

'Yes.'

Zoe stared at her.

'I think I like you,' Charles's mother said. 'You're very different from the girls he's brought home before.'

'How?' asked Zoe, no longer surprised by Charles's mother's bluntness.

'More . . . grown up,' Charles's mother said eventually. 'And . . . deeper.'

'Ah.'

'Charles is rather a pup still. He needs responsibilities to make a man of him.'

'I see,' Zoe said.

'Yes, I rather think you do.' Charles mother stood up abruptly and approached the coffee tray once again with an air of grim purpose. 'Well, that's enough of that. Have more coffee, my dear. Do you enjoy liqueurs? I have some very nice Italian ones I brought back from Rome last autumn. Now tell me about your family. Your parents. Is your father in the City? What committees does your mother sit on?'

'I think I've been given the full parental scrutiny,' Zoe told Charles as they walked round the garden together in the dusk. 'What did you tell them about me?'

'Hardly a thing. Well, let's face it, what do I know about you, my angel? You're a delicious mystery.'

'Your mother was very frank. I almost expected to be asked if I had good child-bearing hips.'

'Oh, yes. The gateway for the son and heir to Percival. The poor parents are getting desperate. And do you, angel?'

'Have the right sort of hips?'

'Mmm.' He wrapped his arm around her shoulders. 'I really wouldn't know.'

'We can't go back to London tonight, sweetheart,' he said squeezing a little more tightly. 'I'm too pissed to drive.'

And I'm over the limit, too, thought Zoe. Charles had made sure of that. 'I need to be in school for eleven tomorrow morning,' she said sharply.

'You will be. So – you'll stay the night at Percival.'

'Thank you. That's very kind.'

He turned her toward him, pulled her face up and put his lips on hers.

Zoe felt warmth, breath, the contact of another human being. Nothing else.

Too soon, she told herself. Oh, much too soon.

'Charles, I'm not going to sleep with you,' she warned, disentangling herself.

'Angel! I wouldn't have dreamed of presuming.'

They walked back to the house. They parted in the hall. Charles went to the library for a nightcap with his father. Zoe went to the guest room in the west wing.

It was very charming, painted all in cream. The bed was a walnut four-poster, curtained in heavy paisley silk.

She lay beneath the covers, rigid and still. Reviewing the events of the evening, it struck her that all the correct formalities leading to an alliance had been set in motion by Charles's parents. The initiation of a proper wooing and courtship. And Charles seemed to be playing the game with a will.

All entirely the opposite of what had happened between her and François, that instant knowledge that they were twin souls. Bound together for always.

Don't think of it!

Tears glistening on her face, utterly exhausted from the effort of keeping up a brave front, she slid down swiftly into a deep sleep. There were no dreams.

Autumn into Winter

CHAPTER 23

'François – I'm so terribly sorry.' Mary Cartland was shaken. 'I really hadn't expected this!'

'You surprise me,' François responded drily. 'I would have thought you'd have seen it coming.'

'Woman's intuition?'

'Something of that kind.' He smiled at her, his eyes not unfriendly, but unmistakably detached.

He is giving away even less than before, Mary thought. She spread out the brilliant set of pictures he had brought for her inspection. 'Oh, sweet heaven, François, these are simply fantastic!'

Mary placed a finger on each of the prints as she looked more closely. These were François's recent shots of a household-name TV presenter, photographed glossily in the popular tradition of glamour combined with wholesomeness. In her expensive penthouse, clad in variety of gorgeous clothes, face impeccably made-up, hair arranged just so, the celebrity radiated beauty, success and assurance.

At first glance, that is. When you looked again you could see that, in some curious way, François had gradually peeled away the the woman's outer coating of triumphant complacency and captured doubt. Effectively stripped her bare. He had, quite miraculously, in Mary's view, highlighted aspects of his subject's personality that the discerning viewer would find highly intriguing. Especially in the light of the recent scandal concerning the woman's equally famous boy-friend.

'What can I say? Except stunning.' Mary swung round and faced him. 'So, this is it. The last lot. No more celebrity shoots. Never again?'

'Well . . . never say never again,' quipped François.

'So, what will you do?'

He raised his shoulders. The smile came again. Not quite a whole smile.

'Ha! The Gallic shrug!' Mary laughed. 'You don't fool me, François. I'll bet you know exactly what you're going to be doing.'

François's expression was tantalizingly unrevealing. 'In truth, Mary, no.'

She assessed him through narrowed eyes. He was lean and tanned from the hot summer, honed up to athletic fitness. Lots of swimming and racing about with his daughter, no doubt, thought Mary.

His face seemed to her quite meltingly adorable, with the tiny and utterly beautiful lines of grief etched around his eyes and his wonderfully kissable lips. She caught herself wallowing in adolescent-style yearning. Oh, for heaven's sake, Mary! 'I'm talking about work,' she informed him. 'Not . . . life.'

François turned his head slowly. 'You're a very perceptive woman, Mary. Which is probably why you're doing the job you do, with the gargantuan salary to match.'

Mary snorted. 'Very well, I can see you're going to keep your secrets to yourself. The life ones, anyway.'

'I'm going to do some shoots in the post-industrial north,' he told her briskly. 'Just a reconnoitre, I've no definite ideas on what theme I want to focus on.'

'No definite commission?'

He gave a dry laugh. 'Not yet.'

'Brave,' Mary said. 'Maybe foolhardy.'

François shook his head. 'I don't need the big "celebrity-style" fees any more.'

Mary had understood for some time that a huge financial burden had been lifted from François's shoulders with the death of his ex-wife. Other kinds of burdens had replaced them, of course, emotional pressures being the main source. He had sometimes looked on the point of utter desolation.

'I've got enough requests trickling in to keep the wolf from the door,' he added drily. 'And the paintings are going very nicely.'

'Ah yes. Poppy's collection.'

'Liam let me have the whole lot – at a crazy giveaway price. I didn't want to take them at first – well, you can understand my reservations. But I could tell Liam was desperate for me to take them off him. He could hardly bear to look at them.'

François moved to the window, positioned himself for his favourite view along the docks to the Dartford Bridge. 'Liam and I got on really well. I liked him. I didn't expect to. I thought the visit to New York would be hell, but oddly enough it wasn't.

'A ghost was laid?' Mary asked.

'In a way.' François drummed out a soft but urgent

rhythm on the glass. 'I've discovered one or two really promising artists up in the north. More to the point, I've managed to squeeze some funds out of various organizations to help them support themselves whilst they experiment with different styles of work.'

Mary could see that the likelihood of any more celebrity shoots from François's camera were well and truly knocked on the head. She was disappointed on her own behalf, but glad for François. This was the kind of work which truly engaged his talents and motivational drive.

'I'm thinking of setting up a gallery in one of the big northern cities. Bradford, most likely.'

'Ambitious. Exciting, too. Will you move there? A bit bleak, surely, for a Frenchman?'

'We have our gritty bits in the north of France! Ever been to Lille?'

'Quite.'

'No, I don't want to move. For a start, I don't want to uproot Leonore. We've got some good friends in London. And she loves her school.' The drumming had slowed to a gentle pulse whilst he talked of his new projects. Now it started again. Restless and insistent.

When he left, Mary sent a prayer up to whatever deity might be around to hear, asking for François to be offered the gift of true and consummated love in the not-too-distant future. He had surely earned it.

François took the tube going west. After two stops, he got off earlier than he had planned and walked along to the road in which Zoe's house stood.

The autumn was throwing a mantle of gently sorrowing browns and golds over the leaves on the trees. The sun glinted on the very clean and polished windows of the elegant houses. Ochre and burnt sienna flashed in a repeating sequence as he passed by and the angle of the light shifted.

The image of Zoe lingered in his senses: sight, hearing, smell, taste, touch. He had a simple need just to be in the vicinity of her habitat.

At first his disbelief in Poppy's death, his confusion and his need to blame someone, had prompted him to direct the stream of his cold anger to her alone. And because of that mysterious quality in her thought processes which was alien and unknown to him, he had been able to sustain his disdain and fury over a number of weeks.

When life came softly seeping back into his veins, the anger had begun to melt. He began to see things differently.

He had looked through his vast photographic collection and assembled all his photographs of Poppy. He had stared at them, with curiosity, with old dead love, with bewilderment. And, recalling Zoe's feverishly described images, he had looked at Poppy's bright shining face and searched it for some sign that she herself might have guessed at the tragedy that would end her life.

Liam had shown him snaps he had taken of her the day before the crash. He had insisted on François having one as a keepsake. François had scoured it for clues. Could there be something here? The tiniest hint of a suggestion that Poppy had some intimation of impending disaster. But he could find nothing. She gazed back at him, a triumphantly successful young woman purposefully looking forward to the new life she had manufactured for herself.

And maybe that was the fundamental difference between Poppy and Zoe. The one supremely sure of her own self. The other pricked by doubts, but gifted with a certain conviction which she had had the huge courage to share.

When he remembered the raw cruelty with which he had thrust Zoe from him, he shuddered with self-disgust.

He had not dared approach her again. He had felt himself entirely unworthy. A scarred and tainted figure. At least in the role of lover. As a father, he felt himself to be doing rather better. And through the summer he and Leonore had begun to shape a new life for themselves.

He had been acutely aware after school finished for the long break that Leonore, usually so chatty about her favourite tutor, had gradually lapsed into silence on the subject of Zoe.

Just once, when they were on their way to fly Leonore's kite in the park, she had asked François when Zoe was going to come again for Saturdays and suppers. He had pressed Leonore's hand and said that he couldn't tell her because he didn't know. Adding that he thought perhaps he and Zoe could not be friends any more.

In a child's instinctive way, Leonore had understood all that was necessary. She had not questioned further. François was pretty sure that she was biding her time. Quietly but relentlessly hoping.

Approaching Zoe's house, he slowed his pace. The 'For Sale' sign swung gently in the light breeze. It had been in place for a few weeks now. He wondered how things were progressing, how many interested buyers had been to view.

He knew all about the swerve in her life plans. Her engagement to Charles, announced in *The Times* at the same time as the appearance of the 'For Sale' notice, had been accompanied by a very attractive photograph and an informative piece about the couple's plans. A wedding to take place in the spring. Renovations now in progress at the family residence, Percival, in preparation for the young couple's taking over the main wing of the house after their marriage.

François had read with grim fascination. A honeymoon on some exotic and exclusive island, he had added to himself. The patter of a little heir's feet some time in the year following.

François forced himself not to stop in front of her house. An image of Zoe's dark head resting against Charles's blond one rose up to taunt him.

The pain of loss and the pain of wanting her stabbed at him without mercy.

CHAPTER 24

The radio in Marina's kitchen sang out with tuneful conviction.

'. . . *in our lives, we have walked some strange and lonely treks . . .*'

The voice was ripe yet metallic. Mournful and yet magnetic. Abba. Unmistakably seventies. The ideal music to accompany the washing up of the breakfast things, not to mention the stragglers from supper the night before.

Marina, standing dreamily at the sink, picked up a sudsy fork, idling beating out the dogged four/four rhythmn of the song.

'. . . *slightly worn, but dignified and not too old for sex . . .*'

She plunged the fork back into the foaming hot water. Hah. The cheek of it. She'd be willing to lay money on it that the Swedish foursome were singing about poor old decrepits just turned forty.

She nipped across to her radio on the dresser (very seventies and slightly worn) twisted the knob and spun through the channels. Various squeaks and protests followed.

There was more music, soaringly sentimental. Rodgers and Hammerstein? Ivor Novello? Then a clipped voice talking listeners through the ins and outs of a national minimum wage, emphasizing the need for specific government pledges. 'Yeah, yeah, agree,' Marina told him, spinning on.

She loved her new freedom. She studied and wrote down her discoveries, she listened to the radio and pottered in the garden. She read novels – in the mornings, when all worthy people should be working!

During the hottest part of the summer, in between drinking iced white-wine spritzers on her little sun-trap of a terrace, she had painted every single wall in the house white, sandblasted all the floors and waxed the boards to a soft honey-coloured sheen.

Risk had looked on with initial horror. Had she lost her wits? But then she seemed always to be there for him these days and he liked that. He had retired with grace to the kitchen to sleep through her bursts of frenetic activity and then rose to greet her with elderly dignity when all the bustle was over.

Marina had also relished having time to give to Leonore when François was out working on his photographic assignments. Or when he was up in the millstone-grit cities of Yorkshire, forging new ground in his career.

'What do you do up there?' she had challenged him. 'Besides grub about in muck in the name of art?'

'I thought you'd approve,' he'd said. 'Anyway, it's enterprise. Creating new career opportunities for myself. Isn't that the current jargon?'

'Thankfully I couldn't say. How long can I have Leonore, then? Two whole days?'

261

'Yes.'

'Bliss.'

'Marina, are you sure I'm not presuming . . .?'

She had stopped him. 'No, François, you are not presuming. Having the benefit of Leonore's company is utterly delightful to me. A true bonus. And don't worry, I'd be the first one to say if anyone dared to presume.'

He hadn't made any further comment.

Leonore had insisted on being taken to see *The Magic Flute*.

'All of it in one go?' Marina asked. 'It's very long. A whole afternoon long; lunch until tea. Are you sure?'

Leonore had withered her with a knowing six-year-old look which warned against any further cautions.

They had sat together in the packed auditorium of the English National Opera. Leonore had been bewitched and enraptured.

'It's lovely,' she had exclaimed in delight as the first Act finished, adding sympathetically, 'Don't cry, Marina, it's not a bit sad.'

And, in and amongst all that feast of free-reined gladness, Marina had had the added pleasure of getting to know Zoe Peach a little better.

Despite the persuasiveness of Marina's telephone invitations, Zoe would not come to the house again, shying away from any confrontation with François. So, instead, she and Marina had met at a variety of delightful bistros and shared a number of piquant and dainty lunches embellished by glasses of sharply chilled white wine. And they had talked of love and life. And of dreams.

So that, all in all, Marina was learning a great deal.

She feared, however, that she had not been as helpful a friend to Zoe as she would have wished. Much worse, Zoe had taken into her head to handcuff herself to a great blond hunk of a chap who looked as though he would crush her delicate sylph's bones to dust if he turned over too hastily in bed.

And now it was the end of a summer idyll and, as the weather slowly turned colder and wetter, Marina's money supply was slowly drying up.

This morning, spinning the radio knob, she looked ahead to the day rolling out in front of her, aware that her marvellous freedom might be short-lived, the need to generate more income crowding in ever closer.

The radio squawked and then settled on a channel as though of its own accord.

'. . . at every stage in the history of scientific investigation facts have emerged which can't be explained, according to the accepted theories of the time . . .'

Marina stilled her finger, tuned in the channel to full clarity. It was not just the subject that had caused her mouth to drop open in a gasp of surprise, it was also the sound of the speaker's voice, curiously familiar, a jolt from the past.

I know those dry clipped tones, Marina murmured, frowning.

'Perhaps you could give us some concrete examples from your research, Professor Penrose,' an interviewer's voice interposed with perfectly timed helpfulness. 'For instance, in your new book, you have some interesting things to say on the subject of extrasensory perception.'

A dry little chuckle. 'Thank you. I'm delighted to hear

I've managed to arouse some interest somewhere.'

Marina snorted. She recalled Professor Penrose as a young man: his wit, his spiky sarcasm, his thumping self-satisfaction.

'Indeed you have,' the interviewer responded smoothly. 'Now, can you tell us, Professor, what exactly *is* extrasensory perception?'

'Quite simply, it is the ability certain human beings demonstrate to have access to information that doesn't appear to have come to them through the channels of the normal five senses.'

'Which, as I recall, are sight, hearing, touch, taste and smell,' the interviewer volunteered.

'Well done! Now, this information is remarkable in that it doesn't come through any of these sensory channels, at least not in the way we are used to experiencing in normal life. And so we have to consider the possibility that it must come from some other, *unknown* sense. An extra sense.'

'And this is what is happening when a person claims to have telepathic or clairvoyant abilities?'

'Exactly.'

'Tell us a little about these abilities. Just what do they involve?

'In simple terms, they refer to a person's capacity to *detect* things about other people, or about external events.'

'Things that couldn't be discovered by the usual means, clearly understandable means?'

'Exactly. In other words, these people have made their detections by *unknown* means.'

'Fascinating.'

264

'You'll have noticed the word "unknown" cropping up a good deal in this discussion of extrasensory perception. And this goes some way to explaining the feeling of mystery and magic surrounding these particular abilities.'

'Disbelief? Scepticism – maybe hostility?'

'Oh definitely. And these were issues that particularly interested me. I felt it was my job as a scientist to attempt to examine and describe the phenomena under examination in a way which would take the mystery out of them, and hopefully neutralize the negative feelings around them.'

Marina stood very still. A prickling wave of sensation ran over her scalp.

'There is another type of ESP I should mention,' the professor continued. 'Perhaps the most curious one and, for some people, the most spine-chilling. It's called *precognition*.' He paused.

Marina leaned forward.

'Could you explain that for us?'

'Precognition is the ability to demonstrate prior knowledge of future happenings. The person concerned has access to knowledge which cannot possibly have been gained through the five senses. Nor by guesswork, either. Or even simple logical "working it out".'

'Truly amazing. Could you give us an example?'

'I suppose some of the earliest examples we can point to come from the Old Testament with the proclamations of the prophets.'

'Yes, indeed. Historical figures are of interest, of course. But what about the present day?'

'That was exactly my question when planning my

research. What about the here and now? What of the *facts*?' The Professor stopped again, a master of the dramatic pause.

Marina bit on her lip. Come on, come on!

Risk stirred in his basket, growling sleepily, then leaped up in preparation for doing his utmost to defend the house against the invasion of the post.

'Shut up, shut up!' pleaded Marina, pressing her ear against the cold steel of the radio.

'The starting point of my research was to take a critical look at reported evidence about ESP. To look with a scientific eye at the facts.'

'In your book you quote a quite remarkable story of a woman . . .'

'Not a story,' Professor Penrose interposed, charming and razor-like at the same time. 'This is first-hand evidence given to me by a highly qualified and intelligent woman in a prominent position in the medical field. Her record of professional achievement and integrity are impeccable.'

'And the evidence?'

'This woman – I shall call her Dr A – suffered the loss of her sister in a car accident when she was in her twenties, just at the time Dr A was about to qualify as a medic. Exactly a year later, whilst she was sitting on her own, quietly reading, she became conscious of someone sitting beside her. She turned and saw her dead sister. Her sister looked exactly as she had remembered her, except that she had a vivid red scratch on the side of her face. When Dr A relayed this experience to her parents, her mother became extremely distressed. It transpired that, when she had been to see the body in the mortuary, she had put a rose into the coffin and the thorns on the stem had scratched the dead girl's cheek. No one else in the family had seen the body afterwards. No one knew of the infliction of a slight wound. And the mother had never told anyone of the incident because she felt guilty about it.'

Marina gave a little shudder. She was not suprised at Penrose's choice of story. He had always been a bit of a showman, liking to tease a little with tales of the grim and gruesome.

'Is this, then, an example of communication between the living and the dead? Of an extra sense that transcends mortality?'

'Perhaps.' Professor Penrose sounded noticeably dry and detached in comparison with the mounting excitement of the interviewer. 'Or possibly it could be an indication of telepathy between the living mother and daughter. There are a number of options to consider when reaching a conclusion, as there always are in science, as opposed to mere speculation.'

'Indeed. And you have several other equally remarkable pieces of evidence which are quoted in the book,' the interviewer commented. 'Quite rivetingly intriguing, in my opinion.'

'Thank you.'

'So, Professor Penrose, does all this point to scientific proof of extrasensory ability?'

'The evidence is strongly suggestive, certainly.'

'Proof?'

'These reports are so vivid and arresting that they cannot be ignored. As regards scientific *proof*, however, one must keep an open mind.'

'No doubt those listening will be keen to read your book and make up their own minds.'

'I most certainly hope so.'

'Professor Penrose, thank you very much for talking to us this morning. And for those who still have questions, *Unravelling the Mysteries of the Mind* is published today, available at all good bookshops.'

Marina moved slowly to the window and stared out into the garden. After a time, she curled her hand into a fist and punched it against the wooden frame. 'Right!' she proclaimed with huge purpose. 'Right!'

CHAPTER 25

A few weeks following their engagement, Charles bought Zoe a puppy. A red setter with ridiculously long ears and an even longer pedigree.

'Got to get you into the way of being a country girl,' Charles joked. Sometimes when he glanced around and caught a glimpse of her talking to his mother in the garden, or observed her wandering through the wood in one of those vividly colourful outfits that marked her out as special, he felt a jolt of unease.

By the side of his amiable sturdy mother, Zoe was like an exotic bird of paradise. Charles was infatuated with her. In his book she was utterly gorgeous and so different from the hearty horse-mad country girls living on the neighbouring estates. He loved showing her off at the country-set dinner parties: her delicate charm, her wit, her sense of style. But would she ever manage to fit in? He knew that his parents liked her, that they were overjoyed to see him 'settling down' at last. But he was pretty sure they were starting to have worries too.

There was some quality of Zoe that eluded their understanding. Charles had decided that it was her delicate physique and seeming fragility that concerned them. But for himself, it was perhaps her giving off vibes of great purity of mind and spirit that was a bit bothering. Charming, of course. And, on the whole, unique in his experience. But maybe she was just a little *too* pure. And maybe having a dog would be just the thing to move her on to matters more . . . sensual.

As far as Charles was concerned, a dog was a symbol of earthiness, of country living and damp walks over carpets of rotting leaves. He fancied that a dog would be the very best means of drawing Zoe into that world.

He told her nothing of his plan. Early one Saturday morning, at the start of a full weekend of social engagements at Percival, he slipped out to the breeder's he had contacted earlier on, and collected the eight-week-old puppy he had ordered.

Although he had been brought up with dogs and had been used to them always being around at Percival, Charles had never had the responsibility of the actual care of an animal. That side of things had always been dealt with by his mother or the servants. Charles would take the dogs for walks if he felt in the mood, or hurl sticks for them to chase in the woods. In the evenings he liked to see them lying by the fire, their coats gleaming and faintly steamy.

It was a long time since there had been a puppy at Percival, and Charles had forgotten just how wayward they were. A mixture of unbridled energy and very little sense.

This particular specimen was all piston-like legs and fizzing enthusiasm for life. Once in the car, it refused to sit still for a moment; in the end he had to force it down against the seat by the scruff of its neck, keeping it firmly pinned there whilst he drove with one hand.

Scooping it into his arms when they arrived back at Percival, he ran up the stairs, bound for Zoe's room in the west wing. Holding the elastically squirming puppy in his arms, he knocked sharply on the door.

Waiting for some answer from within, Charles was jarringly reminded of the curiousness of his relationship with Zoe. He would never have believed such a set-up possible if he had imagined it a few months before.

They had been engaged for some weeks now – properly and very publicly engaged. There had been announcements in all the quality papers, a solitaire-diamond ring to seal the bond and a huge celebration party in the ballroom at Percival, which had been kick-started into life from beneath the dust sheets shrouding it in recent years.

And still he did not feel that he was permitted to intrude on Zoe's privacy in the bathroom or the bedroom. He sometimes saw himself in the position of his father, whom he had often mocked for standing tapping tentatively on his mother's door, calling out gruffly, 'Are you decent?'

Zoe opened the door. She was barefoot, simply dressed in beautifully fitted jeans and a cream silk shirt. Her hair was newly washed, gleaming around her pale face. She looked at the puppy. She looked up at Charles.

'A present for you, darling,' he said.

Zoe put out her hand and touched the puppy's ears. 'Oh, heavens!' she said.

'Well, what do you think?'

'She's beautiful.'

271

Charles gave a bark of disbelieving laughter. 'How did you know she's a bitch?'

Zoe shrugged, smiled. 'I can't say. I just felt she was a she.'

The puppy was wriggling like fury now, panicking to be set down, set free.

Charles dropped her lightly to the ground and she immediately dashed into Zoe's room and squatted on the carpet. A small shiny puddle appeared from between her legs, growing to the size of small plate.

Charles strode into the room, grabbed the puppy once again by the neck and rubbed its nose in the small mess.

The puppy made a gulping choking noise, straining to get its breath.

'No!' exclaimed Zoe. She wrenched Charles's hand away from the small quivering animal. Wrenched it with a strength that surprised him. '*No!*'

He stared at her and laughed. 'Animals have to learn the hard way. They soon get to know the difference between right and wrong.'

Zoe gave him a level stare which made him take a small step backwards. My God, there was just the odd occasion when he wondered if she was made of platinum rather than flesh and blood.

'You have to be a little cruel to be kind,' he volunteered. 'Come on, darling, stop looking at me as though I'm the one who's just made a mess on the carpet!'

Zoe sat on the floor. The puppy gambolled up to her and put its paws on her chest, making little brown marks on the cream silk. She laid her hand on the frail tube of its neck and stroked it with a tenderness that made Charles ferociously jealous.

272

'They learn by encouragement and praise,' she said quietly. 'And kindness.'

'For God's sake, Zoe, I was hardly brutal!'

She looked up at him again and he felt that he had made a terrible mistake, revealed to her some facet of himself that perhaps should have been kept secret.

Charles was suddenly infuriated. Why the hell should he have to put up with feeling so guilty? He had done absolutely nothing out of line. Quite the reverse. He had been spectacularly thoughtful, imaginative and generous.

He looked down at the puppy, nestling close against Zoe's breasts – an intimacy which *he*, her fiancé, had not so far been permitted. Damn dog! He wished he'd never dreamed up the whole daft scheme of getting an animal for Zoe. He could see nothing but trouble ahead.

'I think she's hungry,' Zoe said, tickling the puppy's ears as it nuzzled against her.

'Well, it won't get much joy there, will it?' Charles remarked with sarcasm, staring pointedly at the swell of Zoe's breasts.

'Hardly.' Zoe laughed. 'Poor little thing,' she crooned to the puppy, 'only just left your mother.'

Good God! thought Charles. This puppy's going to get more tender loving care than me.

'What does she eat?' Zoe enquired.

Charles was well and truly caught out. He smiled appealingly like a naughty little boy. 'God only knows. Oh, dear!'

'I'll go give her some warm milk,' Zoe decided, standing up with the puppy still cuddled against her.

'And then I'll drive into the village and get whatever else she needs.'

Charles watched her walk towards the staircase, a tiny perfect figure, exquisitely vulnerable. He sometimes fancied she was almost shatterable, like a china figurine.

He loved Zoe's physical fragility and the way in which it contrasted with a certain steely secretiveness in her personality. Even now, she still seemed to him as deliciously mysterious and unfathomable as when he had first met her. It often struck him that whilst he had captured her, he in no way possessed her.

Yet.

He sat on her bed, running his hand along the scarcely rumpled sheet, pondering. Wondering how much longer she was going to make him wait.

Zoe came back after a while. The puppy was cradled in her arms, drowsy and on the point of sleep. Zoe smiled down at her, wiping the lacing of milk from her soft puppy lips with a gentle finger.

She laid the puppy on the bed, on the sheet where she herself had recently slept. She stroked the puppy very softly and it was soon asleep.

Charles was reminded of the sleeping arrangements of his parents. How his mother's pongy old labradors snored the night away on her bed, whilst his father slept alone in the room next door.

He looked at Zoe, somehow eternally unattainable. Desperately desirable. Things are going to change, Charles proclaimed to himself.

He stepped up to the bed. Zoe turned up her face to him and smiled. 'Thank you, Charles,' she said simply.

'You like her?'

'Oh, yes.'

'You're sure? You know I'm a bit of a blunderer sometimes . . .'

'I'm sure – ' there was a tiny pause ' – that I like her.'

'Do I get a reward?'

There was a very long and silent pause and then she stood up. She moved to stand close to him, put her arms around his waist and laid her head against his chest.

Charles stroked her neck. It felt creamy and luscious under his fingers like heavy sueded silk. 'Zoe, do you love me?' he asked.

She said nothing for a while. Her hands moved over the bones of his back, exploring him in a way she had not attempted before. She raised her head. Her lips were parted slightly. The tip of her tongue flickered in the opening between.

Charles decided that this must be her answer. He threw out his arm behind him and gave the door a shove so that it shut with a sharp click.

The puppy raised its head and whimpered.

'Bloody Christ!' Charles muttered, then sighed with relief as the puppy, having made a few contented chomping noises, allowed its head to drop back on the sheet.

'Do you love *me*?' Zoe asked, her face still hidden against his chest.

'Angel, I don't think I've ever wanted a woman so much in my whole life,' he breathed. Adding to himself that it was a very long time since he had endured interminable weeks without getting laid. Not so much wanting her as reaching the point of desperation.

Her head still lay on his chest, her body rested unresisting against him. He would not go so far as to say that her body was relaxed, but at least it wasn't tense, poised as though for flight, which was far too often the case.

He moved his hand from her neck. Holding her close with one arm, he allowed his free hand to stroke the hollows in her collar bone. Insinuating his fingers downwards, very softly, oh so slowly, he made contact with the V-shaped divide of her shirt.

She made no move. Breathless with hopeful anticipation, he allowed his fingers to slide down the bluish shadow of her cleavage, exploring, teasing, assessing.

She sighed.

'Oh, angel!' His fingers fumbled at her buttons like those of some clumsy, uninitiated adolescent. He parted the silk. Beneath it she wore nothing but a white lace bra. One of those glorious complicated creations that was a fantastic mixture of fairy-tale gossamer, precision engineering and bony scaffolding that did miraculous things to boobs.

Charles bent to caress them. She tilted her head back as his lips made contact with her skin. He flicked his tongue around a nipple, took the tiniest, most fleeting of nibbles. A trick that never failed to please.

Zoe's eyes were still closed, her features peaceful. She moved a hand around his ribs and slipped it inside his shirt, caressing the bones of his chest.

Charles thought that he might explode with long pent-up lust. Throwing caution to the winds he reached down and unzipped her jeans, pushing his hands inside the stiff cotton and making contact with some very intricate and lacy fabric. Moving down, he felt her take in a breath. Jabbing and sharp. God! She wanted him as much as he wanted her. Intoxicated with desire, he wrenched down her jeans, pulled off her panties and plunged his hand between her legs.

'Ahh,' she cried softly.

For a fleeting moment it occurred to him that this was a cry which could indicate either intense passion – or alarm.

He could not bear to consider the latter possibility. He was too near the edge now, driven to press on by some relentless internal engine.

He swept her up in his arms and carried her to the plump little sofa beneath the window. Settling himself in it, he placed her so that she was straddling his thighs. He reminded himself that a less than sexually confident woman was often overwhelmed to be covered by a man. Such a woman felt reassured to be on top herself, with the illusion of having some command.

Zoe stared at him unflinching, her eyes open and direct and yet, somehow, quite distant.

'Heavens, angel. Have pity!' he begged. 'I've been living the life of a bloody monk.'

'I know.' She spoke very tenderly. 'And I'm sorry,' she added, and then leaned forward and pressed a somewhat nun-like kiss on his forehead. At least, that was how it felt to Charles.

He couldn't possibly hold back any longer. The sight of her naked; the perfect porcelain body, the contrasting and thrilling dark animalness of sable pubic hair, set the blood pounding and roaring through his veins. He began to fear tht he might disgrace himself utterly and reach his climax before she had even felt him inside her if things did not move on more speedily.

277

His eyes connected with hers. He took her hand and guided it to his zip, under which the frustrated bulge was frantically throbbing to be free.

Zoe felt the hot urgency of his desire beneath her fingers. The reality of what she was about to do suddenly hit her with the force of a swung iron bar. Her brain reeled, her heart contracted. In her head an image of Françoise's face rose up to fill her vision. She saw his beautiful long lips, his dark eyes full of hurt and deep reproach.

She stiffened, drawing back, tensing like an animal in danger. No, she could not do it. She would not do it. No, no, no!

The puppy suddenly raised its head, letting out a volley of high-pitched barks as footsteps approached down the corridor and there was a sharp rap on the door. 'Charles!' came his mother's low but imperious voice. 'Charles, are you there? You're wanted on the telephone. I've been calling and calling for you.'

'Jesus!' said Charles. 'Bloody effing damn, damn, damn!' He smiled ruefully at Zoe, lifting her from his knee whilst making a swift check on the state of his trousers and his zip. 'Angel, I'm going to have leave you for a minute. When Mama calls, one must obey!' He winked at her. 'Don't run away.'

Zoe stared at him, amazed. He had no idea of the turmoil she felt inside. No inkling that he had been about to be well and truly repulsed. As he slid through the door she was not sure whether to be grateful or sorry to have been saved the drama of an immediate confrontation. She felt herself filled with panic and confusion, a sense of having trapped herself in a locked cage.

She tried to be calm, to offer herself rational explanations for the revulsion she had felt in anticipating sex with Charles. She told herself it was simply too soon. She was not ready to give herself yet. Maybe she would not feel ready until they were married. Within marriage sex was proper and right and dignified. Yes, surely things would work out then.

Willing herself to be convinced, she wriggled back into her clothes, lifted the puppy into her arms and carried her out into the garden to show to Charles's mother, knowing that in the company of that redoubtable lady she would be utterly safe from any further amorous advances.

There was a dinner party for twelve in the Percival dining room that evening. The old rules of the English upper class still prevailed there. The men were all wearing dinner jackets, the women dressed in elegant gowns of silk or wool crêpe, cut low at the neck. Charles's mother had gone so far as to dispense with her beige cardigan in view of the log fire burning in the vast dog grate.

The table was polished to mirror-like brilliance and an ornate crested dinner-service set out. Flames from the fire glinted on the delicate Georgian silver cutlery.

Charles's mother insisted on Zoe and Charles taking the host's and hostess's place at the head and foot of the table, making no secret of her plan to groom them up for their eventual role as master and mistress of Percival.

Zoe, a tiny perfect figure in bright scarlet with black and silver jewellery, smiled hesitantly at her fiancé across several feet of mahogany. He raised his glass, smiling back at her, jubilant with the pleasures of the morning, looking forward to a hearty helping of fully consummated passion later on. It occurred to him that he must go easy on the claret. There was the muscat to accompany the pudding and then the port. He didn't want to be half-cut when it came to the point and unable to deliver the goods.

Zoe pricked the fish on her plate with the tip of her fork. It looked overcooked and unappetizing.

Charles's mother disapproved of 'fancy cooking'. The woman she hired to provide the food when guests were invited was instructed to keep things plain and simple. And so there was not a herb, nor a whisper of garlic to be found anywhere in this meal. The grilled turbot was curled up at the edges and presented on the plate quite naked, apart from garnishing wedges of lemon. The main course was a traditional English roast; wild duck served with apple sauce and game chips which were, in fact, fried potato crisps from a packet.

Zoe took a sip of wine and had a sudden flash of remembrance of François's deliciously imaginative and sensitive cooking.

The very reverberation of his name in her head made her momentarily dizzy.

Don't think of him. Don't, don't, don't!

She tried to catch Charles's eye. He was leaning across to the woman on his left, his cheery glance flickering between her strong big-boned face and her heavy-duty cleavage.

Zoe watched him, her gaze magnetically held. She laid down her fork. Charles is a basically decent and good man, she told herself fiercely, fresh panic rising in her throat.

Placing her napkin carefully at the side of her cutlery, she got up and walked around the table. Dropping a light kiss on Charles's head, she excused herself for a moment and went into the kitchen where the puppy dozed on a pile of old coats beside the door.

The cook, pink-faced and painstakingly putting the final touches on a sherry trifle, smiled as she entered. 'Little thing,' she said, nodding towards the puppy. 'I had to put her out while I cut the birds up. She's not too young to know what a good roast is!'

The puppy came suddenly to life, gambolled up to Zoe and scrabbled at her leg, creating an instant ladder in her glossy black tights. She shook her ears with a great flap and swiftly squatted down with the intention of relieving herself.

Zoe scooped her up and dashed outside into the garden. The puppy stood on the earth, looking puzzled. Zoe smiled at her. The puppy looked up. She became interested in the smells of the evening garden and wandered around for a while exploring, her previous need apparently forgotten.

Zoe waited patiently, sniffing the fresh earthy air, breathing deeply. She felt as though she had been sprung from some kind of captivity.

'Good girl! Good girl,' she told the puppy when eventually the desired performance was completed.

She gathered the warm furry body into her arms. Charles had said she should call the dog something noble like Circe or Miranda. Zoe did not think so. What name then? She didn't know. She didn't seem to be able to make even the simplest decision at the moment.

Not since she had said 'yes', when Charles asked her to marry him.

Hugging her dog close, she could feel its heart beating, rapid and urgent. A surge of love for the small creature welled up within her.

I'm starving for love, she whispered in sudden and terrible understanding.

She recalled the events of that morning. She had almost made the ultimate contact with Charles. He had touched her in the most intimate places. He had touched her but not moved her. And she had stood on the brink of betraying the only man she had ever loved.

She put the puppy back to bed beside the still warm oven. She returned to the ritual of the extended dinner in the Percival dining room. She touched Charles lightly on the shoulder. She glanced down the table and noted which wine glasses required replenishing.

She sat down at her place opposite Charles, leaned towards those on her right and left with smiling comments.

No one noticed her inner turmoil. Her public mask was quite perfect.

When the guests had all gone, she went to her room and splashed cold water on her face. Returning to the ground floor she found the place already in darkness. Creeping into the drawing room she found Charles stretched out on one of the sofas snoring softly. She placed tentative fingers on his forehead.

'Pissed,' he murmured sleepily. 'No damn good, angel. Be fine in the morning.'

Her heart swelling with massive relief, she crossed the hallway and made her way once more to the kitchen where her puppy slept like a baby, totally and utterly blissful. Zoe smiled.

Her eyes moved to the phone on the wall, placed there for the benefit of the staff. It was one of the two-tone grey variety that still had a shrill ring and a circular dial. Carefully she lifted the receiver. Her heart began to accelerate as her finger traced its way around a familiar sequence of numbers, long neglected, because she had not trusted herself to use it.

As the connection was established and the rhythmic purrs began she pressed her free hand against her frenziedly pulsing heartbeat. She felt herself move into another sphere. Begin to live on a different plane.

His voice sounded in her ear. 'Yes?' Low and sensual. Rich with sensitivity. Very, very male.

François.

Zoe drew in a long breath. She found herself transfixed, unable to speak. That he was still alive, still there for her, still *him*, made her want to throw back her head and howl like a vixen, prowling the wood tracking the scent of her mate.

'Darling!' His understanding was instant, his tone filled with urgency. 'Darling? It's you, isn't it?'

She swallowed. Her voice died in her throat.

'Zoe. Listen to me, it's all right, darling. Talk to me. Say something. Please!'

'I shouldn't be doing this,' she murmured.

He started to speak in French. 'Don't hang up, Zoe. Just stay. Let me talk to you, darling.'

Zoe found tears filling her eyes, dazzling her with a curtain of silvery liquid. He was no longer angry. He loved her again. He had always loved her.

She understood all of that now.

But it was too late.

'You don't have to speak, darling. Just listen. I was a fool and I hurt you terribly. I've been crazy with worry, wondering how you were.'

'Yes,' she breathed softly, tuning in to his thoughts, a perfect mirror of her own.

'I've been giving myself hell, thinking of you hurting as badly as I've been.'

'François,' she breathed. Simply saying his name was a precious luxury, as though she were caressing him, moving her fingers with slow reverence over the beautiful bones of his face.

'I've been going out of my mind, racking my brains for some means of finding my way back to you.' He paused. 'Say something, Zoe. For God's sake!'

'I never blamed you,' she managed at last.

'I was in shock, raging and hitting out.'

'Yes.'

'Do you forgive me? Do you still love me?'

'Yes.' Ah, the relief of simply speaking the truth. 'Of course I do.'

She heard his sharp intake of breath. 'Then let me come for you. Now. Tell me where you are.'

She sighed.

'Zoe!' His voice was suddenly harsh and insistent. 'Don't slip away from me again. I couldn't bear it.'

Zoe lifted the receiver a little distance from her ear and stared at it as though it held a secret she had been desperately seeking but unable to find. She had an unshakeable conviction that the link which had been so cruelly broken between her and François was now whole again. A miraculous reconnection had been made.

And that must be enough.

'Zoe! Zoe!' he pleaded.

There was nothing she could say.

'There's something else, isn't there?' he said softly, with his disturbing intuition. *'Isn't there?'*

'Yes.'

'You can tell me,' he said. 'Anything, darling, anything. You can . . .'

'No,' she said softly.

Fighting back her distress, feeling that she was plunging a rapier into her own heart, she gently replaced the receiver.

His voice echoed in the silence.

CHAPTER 26

Marina went by tube, southern-line train and taxi in order to get to Professor Penrose's house in one of the most expensive and inaccessible pockets of rural Surrey.

Edward Penrose lived in a converted windmill, which stood alone on the edge of a common bordering an exclusive village.

Wouldn't he just? thought Marina grimly, irritable after a two-hour journey from north London and outraged by the taxi fare from Redhill station.

Walking up to the comical, conical windmill, she tried to picture Professor Penrose as he would be now, almost thirty years on from when she had last seen him. Then he had been a truly innovative thinker and somewhat untamed, she recalled. In physique, memorably tall, big with it and rather rumpled and frayed-looking. Clothes always baggy and shapeless, as though he might have slept in them. Hair thick and ruffled.

He opened the door. Still tall, and most impressively big with it. He was wearing baggy worn corduroys in a rather fetching shade of forest green and his hair was a great mop of wilful grey, reminding Marina of pan scrubs when the pink soap had worn off.

'Marina! Did you have a foul journey?' He did not look like an academic. He had the worldly, chunkily handsome features of an elderly TV soapstar. And grey eyes like razors.

'I did, Professor Penrose. Does it show?'

'Yes. Do, please, call me Teddy. Come in.'

Marina looked around her. White brickwork, stone flooring, beautiful faded Indian rugs, a curling iron balustrade corkscrewing its way up a spiral staircase, also of solid stone. And everything confined within curved walls, a perfect sphere.

He watched her as she assessed his lair. 'I wanted something really eccentric,' he said. 'You know, a fallen-on-hard-times citadel or a redundant cooling tower. But Lizzie liked this. So!' he shrugged.

'Lizzie? Your wife.' Marina vaguely recalled a vivid and skittish redhead telling jokes at the sherry bashes in the psychology department. 'How is she?'

'She died two years ago. A heart attack.'

'I'm sorry,' said Marina.

'Stress of living with me, probably.'

Before she could reach up to unfurl her swirling cape, he deftly removed it from her shoulders and laid it over an oak bench.

She was aware of the razor-sharp eyes making a rapid appraisal. She felt a spark of pride in her long legs and still slim figure, her abundant long silver hair. She was glad, too, that she had opted to wear her beautifully faded 1980s black Levis and her long black boots lovingly preserved from Harrod's Christmas sale of 1963. Kinky boots, they called them in those days.

Not too old to revel in a spot of masculine appreciation, she thought, amused at herself. Even from the satirical Teddy Penrose.

He ushered her into a quirky semi-circular room, painted in billiard-baize green. Drawings and paintings almost obliterated the walls. Picking his way through tottering heaps of academic journals, newspapers and open books, he eventually reached a sofa. A chocolate-point Siamese cat slumbered in the one small available space amidst back-copies of *Nature* journal and Sunday supplements.

Teddy Penrose woke the cat with large gentle hands, lifted it from its pride of place and poured it carefully onto the floor, where it protested crossly.

Marina duly sat. A cloud of fine white hairs rose up around her.

Teddy Penrose flicked them away with an energetic sweep. 'Sorry! This place is truly disgusting.'

'No. I like it.'

He went away and, on returning, presented her with a large glass of whisky and very cold soda water. It was what she would have requested if he had asked her preference. But he hadn't.

The cat, having assessed her with a critical eye, now reached a judgement and leapt on her knee, turning himself around twice and nestling down, his throat throbbing with purrs.

'Er – do you mind about this?' Teddy Penrose looked at Marina and then at his cat, vaguely concerned.

'Not one bit.'

'Well, now,' he said, getting straight down to the nitty-gritty. 'I was highly intrigued by your telephone call.

Tell me some more about this young friend of yours with the premonitions.'

Marina took a long sip of her whisky. In the absence of a conveniently placed table on which to rest it, she propped it against the base of the sofa on the floor. Then she began to tell her story.

She spoke with great clarity, selecting her words with the utmost care. Whilst she was by no means intimidated by Teddy Penrose, she was nevertheless highly alert to his intense and undivided concentration. She recalled him as an up-and-coming academic all those years ago. Teddy the Brains had been his nickname. A shaggy Rupert Bear with the mental capacity of a mainframe computer and an IQ in the stratosphere.

This was a man who did not suffer fools gladly.

As she told him about Zoe's chilling premonitions, she knew that he was absorbing every word she uttered, weighing its meaning, allowing his agile mind to leap off on nimble feet; conjecturing, devising theories, searching beyond the words for further illuminating clues

She closed her tale with a brief account of the way in which Zoe's premonition of a fatal air-crash had driven a rift between her and her lover and had subsequently driven her into the arms of another man. Rather unsuited to her, in Marina's opinion. And with marriage in mind.

Teddy Penrose sat in silent consideration for a few moments. 'So, what is your question, Marina? In what way do you expect me to help you in your crusade to save your friend from a fate worse than death?'

'Don't mock!' she warned.

'Indeed, I don't. A bad marriage must be a living hell.

I had a very happy marriage. It was one of life's most precious gifts.'

'I have a sense that these premonitions Zoe has experienced are preventing her from making the kind of decisions she would normally be able to make.' Marina frowned, wondering if she was explaining herself adequately.

'In what way?'

'By stopping her from using her natural gifts of good sense and rational thinking. Zoe is an intelligent woman. She speaks several languages, she knows how to handle children with all sorts of problems. She's very dedicated in her work.'

'A capable and normally level-headed woman?'

'Yes. I believe so. But, in some way, at the moment, she seems to be driven by some curious force out of her control.' Marina looked up and caught Teddy Penrose's eyes resting on her with quizzical interest. Damn, she thought, annoyed with herself for using words such as 'curious force' with a man such as him, who only had truck with 'hard facts'.

'You're saying that if this young woman could be helped to understand something about the way precognition works and how other people have experienced premonitions and dealt with them, then she might be able to view them in a more detached way.'

'Yes!'

'*She* would be in control of her extrasensory power, rather than the other way around?'

'That's precisely it.'

'Don't look so astonished,' he chided her, looking mildly offended. 'You make me feel as though you had expected me to be less than human! Just because I'm an experimental scientist doesn't mean I'm not interested in people's feelings and motivations.'

'So *can* you help, Teddy?'

He reached for a note-pad and pencil. 'Let's look at the facts. First of all, some basic biographical detail: age of your friend, background, parents, upbringing.'

Marina told him as much as she knew.

Teddy scribbled away, although Marina doubted that anyone, even him, would be able to make any sense of the resultant hieroglyphics.

'Right,' he said eventually. 'So we have here a young woman who was an only child. Her father died before she had really got to know him. And she was very close to her mother.'

'I have the impression it was that kind of relationship where the child takes on the care of the parent. A sort of reversal of roles.'

'Mmm. And the mother was highly superstitious?'

'Apparently. As a child, Zoe was never allowed to wear green. It was drilled into her that she must never walk under ladders or look in a shattered mirror. And as for magpies! Well, from what Zoe told me, it was all hell let loose if either she or her mother ever spotted one on its own. You know the old saying about magpies: "One for sorrow, two for joy."'

He nodded. Sighed. 'And one single magpie was sighted by her mother just before her sudden tragic death. Zoe included that information in her account to you.'

'It was obvious to me that the sighting of the magpie had some terrible significance for Zoe's mother.'

'I entirely agree. And, perhaps, for Zoe herself that tragic incident must have ensured that all of her mother's theories and superstitions took on a new and grim ring of truth.'

'I had come to just that conclusion.'

'Mmm. Now you say that Zoe's mother was interested in clairvoyance and fortune telling?

'It sounded to me to be more than simple interest. More like fascination. A bit of a hang-up.'

'Perhaps an obsession.' Teddy Penrose squinted down at the wild scribbles on his pad. He drew heavy rings around one or two of them.

Marina took a further sip of her whisky and waited for his brain to process the information so far.

He said, 'I've been asking you for all this detail because, in my researching, I've discovered a strong link between certain early life experiences – especially highly charged ones of the type Zoe described – and the subsequent demonstration of extrasensory incidents.'

'And what have you concluded?'

'Conclusions!' Teddy Penrose echoed thoughtfully. He shot her a razor-like glance. 'You know the pitfalls in this kind of work, Marina. In any branch of science, the researcher has to work hard to back up theories with clear factual information. But, when you're dealing with areas such as the paranormal, squeezing the kind of hard evidence that would allow you to promote your hunches to the dignified rank of "conclusions" is rather like the proverbial getting blood out of a stone.'

She laughed. 'Sorry. Perhaps you'd better tell me about your hunches, then!'

'I'll tell you something about my new book,' he said,

leaning forward, his face alight with merriment. 'My book is uniquely brilliant in managing to quote respectable research, give entertaining examples and outline my "theories" in such a way as to appeal to popular taste and give satisfaction whilst not offending the hard-nosed scientist brigade.'

'Ah, I see,' Marina exclaimed, suddenly understanding. 'You've written a sure-fire best seller. But in the end you've found no real proof? Reached no conclusions?'

'I don't give away my secrets as easily as that, Marina. You'll have to read the book and find out.'

'Oh, don't worry, I will. And I won't be afraid to say what I think.'

His eyes glinted. Then his features stilled into seriousness. 'What I will tell you is this. I've interviewed over a hundred apparently sane people who claim to have powers of telepathy or prediction. I've taken lengthy personal histories from them and I've subjected them to endless questioning about their abilities and experiences in the realm of extrasensory perception. It makes fascinating reading.'

'But all that is no more than anecdotal evidence, isn't it? Intuitive, personal accounts from people with a point to demonstrate.'

'Good, good. You haven't forgotten all that work you did years ago. Of course, you're right. And I didn't just talk to people and take their word for it. I also carried out tests in carefully regulated laboratory settings with observers present. No trickery. No mirrors or white mice up sleeves.'

'How do you test for ESP?'

'The tests were very simple. They had to be. If you

start getting complicated, then you're not able to record your results precisely. These tests were based on human behaviour that was easily observable and could be simply scored. You could probably guess the kind of thing I did; getting a person to predict the way a coin will fall, or to correctly state the sequence of five cards laid down behind a screen out of their vision.'

'And then you compared the results with what would be expected to happen by the usual laws of chance?'

'Exactly. That's just what I did.'

'Well? Come on, don't keep me in suspense.'

'I regret to say that, in the laboratory setting, the results were disappointingly negative. I had a number of subjects who had reported some quite remarkable ESP phenomena, as astounding as the example I will give you in a moment. But none of my subjects' predictions in the experimental laboratory were significantly better than you would expect to occur by chance.'

'So you emerged from your research something of a sceptic regarding ESP?'

'Not at all. I started out entirely open-minded. And I still am. I proved no positives, but I proved no negatives either. Moreover my subjects were all able to show great integrity and sincerity. There was not a trace of deliberate trickery or hoaxing.'

'But then, dealing a few cards and tossing a coin are hardly the stuff-of-life drama such as predicting a death or a large scale disaster, are they?'

Teddy Penrose nodded in agreement. 'I'm afraid they're not. Besides my actual experimental work, I also looked at confirmed records of reported cases of precognition. There are one or two very dramatic and moving examples. A woman in Kent dreamed of the 1966 disaster in the mining town of Aberfan. It was a very clear dream, very clearly told. She saw coal hurtling down a Welsh mountainside. She saw a little boy at the bottom of the hill looking terrified. She saw rescue operations taking place. She had this dream seven days before the disaster. Two friends confirmed that she had related this dream to them four days before the disaster.'

Marina felt a cold crawl of unease.

'So you see,' he said, 'I'm no sceptic. But, unfortunately, such clear and confirmed reports are rare. Reliable, unbiased witnesses are extremly thin on the ground. In a nutshell, the whole area is maddeningly problematic.'

'You spent a couple of years on painfully laborious research which turned out to be inconclusive?' Marina suggested with a wistful smile.

'That's the lot of scientists. But I had hoped for more definite results. And between you and me, I retired from the fray decidedly disappointed with the lack of hard-nosed evidence.'

'So did you actually unravel any mysteries of the mind?'

His eyes sparkled. 'Maybe not. I wrote a cracking good book, though!'

'Have I wasted your time?' Marina asked.

He shook a warning finger at her. 'I haven't finished yet. Along the way I learned a huge amount about human personality. The way in which the strength of evidence about those who claim telepathic or clairvoyant powers is influenced by their personal qualities.'

'And?'

'Basically the more ordinary, normal and sane seeming is the person concerned, the stronger is the evidence for ESP, rather than some distortion of personality which makes that person want to attract attention to themselves by making extravagant claims.

'I see.' Marina allowed herself a few moments of consideration. She recalled Zoe's distress that first morning they had talked together.

You'll think I'm mad . . . Do you think I'm mad?

'I'd rate Zoe as pretty "normal" in personality terms,' Marina said. 'Sensitive, but by no means neurotic.'

Teddy got up and stretched, back arching, chest expanding, arms shooting up into the air like the chunky paws of a great bear. He stared down at Marina for a moment. 'For what it's worth, Zoe's disaster premonition sounds like a valid example of ESP to me,' he said bluntly.

'It's worth a good deal, Teddy. And if she has this ability for ESP and it's causing her trouble, what can she do about it? Anything? Nothing?'

Teddy shrugged. 'Look into her personal history. That's about all I can advise. Get your friend to look into her past, her childhood years. Somewhere there, she'll find a clue.'

'The key to unlock the mysterious secret of her psyche?' Marina suggested drily.

Teddy roared. 'That's enough of ESP. Let's talk about you,' he said. 'You'll stay and have some supper, won't you?'

'Thanks, and that's really nice of you. But I've got a dog to go home to.'

He smiled. 'Another time, then?'

'Yes.' She started to think of getting up to leave, but his level gaze in some way pinned her to the sofa.

'You gave up your own research, if I remember?' he commented.

'I left the university in disgrace, tail between my legs.'

'Disgrace? Did you? I don't remember that.'

'I was a very insignificant research student. You were professor-designate, at what – twenty-eight, twenty-nine? Shooting stars are not renowned for remembering scuttling mice.'

'What happened?'

'I made the classic error of professional life. I got over-involved with my subject. I was investigating the paranormal. Clairvoyance, telepathy . . .'

He chuckled. 'Now she tells me.'

'Instead of standing back coolly investigating, I started practising the art. I was rather good at it. I used to get these pictures in my head. Just sometimes I could see things happening to people, things that would happen in the future. Crystal clear.'

'Then what happened?'

'The university stopped my grant. Colin, my husband, was furious with me. My confidence collapsed. And suddenly I was yesterday's news all round.'

'What did you do?'

'I stayed at home and had babies.'

'An utterly noble calling.'

'Yes. I got quite hooked on it, in fact. I manufactured two lovely kids and adored introducing them to life.'

'Well, then?' he said gently.

She felt suddenly free to make revelations. 'I hated the research work. The grind of it, the restrictions. Setting up theories and attempting to prove or disprove them. Academic life made me feel like a bird in a cage. I wanted to fly. Tell stories, dream dreams.'

'Why didn't you? You could have become a writer. Poetry, novels.'

'No. I hadn't the discipline. I could never put my mind to anything for long enough. Apply myself, as Colin used to say. Still can't.'

'I remember your Colin. Research team leader, wasn't he? Senior lecturer in behavioural psychology.' Teddy Penrose suddenly checked himself. 'Good God, you're not still married to him, are you?'

'No.'

'No. He was a cold and clinical smart-arse, as I remember it. Albeit extremely bright. Mind like a rapier, blue eyes like icy fjords. One glance from them used to set all the female knees in the department trembling.'

Marina made a little show of wincing. 'I think you've just about netted him with those few damning words.'

'He was good at his job, though.'

'Mmm.' She sighed.

'And you're very good at putting yourself down.'

'It's probably what I deserve.'

Teddy Penrose declined to comment. He pinched the edge of his jaw with his thumbnail. 'You and your friend Zoe seem to have something important in common.'

'Yes, I think we do.' She looked up at him. She hadn't expected this kind of understanding.

'You both have a sense of being ruined by ESP. As though you were in its power, instead of the other way round.'

'Possessed. That's how I felt for a time. And I know that Zoe feels the same.'

'Possessed,' he said, turning the word over in his mind.

'Invaded by pictures of other people's secret lives,' she elaborated. 'I'm sure your subjects will have told you all about it.

'Oh yes,' he agreed. 'And what happened?'

'For me? The pictures simply stopped coming.'

'That is quite common. Many of my subjects reported the same – experience.'

'I was "possessed" for a time, in a mild sort of way,' Marina elaborated. 'But that wasn't what ruined me!'

'Ah. Are you going to tell me what did?'

'Not today,' she said, smiling provocatively.

He chuckled. Then he surprised her by reaching out and stroking his hand briefly over her cheek. Suddenly he looked almost wistful.

And lonely.

'I really would have liked to stay,' Marina said. 'And I really do have a dog who's been on his own far too long already.'

'Your life is ruled by your dog?'

'Oh, yes. I'm an extremely foolish woman.'

'An extremely honest one, though.'

Teddy Penrose drove her to the station. He gave her a copy of his book. 'And when we meet for our next discussion, I shall expect you to have read it. Every word.'

CHAPTER 27

Zoe named her puppy Elle. A simple and apt name. 'She' in French. François would have been entertained, if he had known.

Letting herself out of Percival's small east door, Zoe felt her body tense, bracing itself against the raw hurt that always came when the sentinel on guard in her head slumbered and allowed thoughts of François to come stealing back. *Don't! Don't! Don't think of François.*

Since the madness of her impulsive midnight phone-call, she had embarked on a fresh campaign to close her mind to him. The intense sensation of shared closeness that had instantly sprung up between them in those few precious moments of communication had almost seduced her into agreeing to leave Charles. And there lay danger.

'*Let me come for you,*' François had pleaded. '*Tell me where you are.*'

Too late, my darling! she cried out silently. Too late and too dangerous.

She had got up very early that morning, telling herself that the puppy needed to go out to relieve herself. Which was, in fact, the case. Zoe knew, however, that her main motivation in getting out of the house was to avoid

Charles and any danger of a further bedroom confrontation, following that first jarring incident.

She raised her head, scenting the morning breeze, the mingle of earthy damp fragrances rising from the ground. Looking up, she saw that sky was a cold hard blue. The intricate wooden skeletons of the trees were beginning to show clearly now that their leaves were almost gone. Looking back, she saw that she there were sets of dark wavering tracks in the dew, marking out the paths she and Elle had taken.

Elle was well in front now, gambolling along on her ludicrously long and floppy legs, her movements so fluid she could have been swimming.

They walked along by the side of the fence enclosing the paddock. Neither Charles nor his mother rode currently and she had offered the use of the unoccupied paddock to a neighbour whose grey mare had foaled in the summer. Mother and child stood side by side, grazing with steady concentration, their teeth rhythmically tearing at the wet grass.

When Elle spotted these strange, enormous creatures, she leapt back in amazement, her body rearing away from potential trouble. Her head dipped down in fear and submission, then poked forward as curiosity took over.

Zoe squatted on the ground beside the quivering puppy and talked to her softly. The mare looked up and approached the fence, her foal following. Gravely they observed the woman and her small dog.

Elle's quivering gradually subsided. Then suddenly she had lost all interest in the horses and was springing off in search of new entertainments, scuttling squirrels and the odd strutting pheasant.

Her life is just beginning, thought Zoe. For Elle, everything is enchanting and wonderful. It seemed to Zoe that Elle's boundless and fizzing enthusiasm simply for being alive was almost intoxicating. Nothing was too insignificant for Elle's delighted attention; a blown and spinning leaf, a beetle crawling along the ground. The puppy's insatiable desire for new knowledge and sensation made Zoe smile, warmed her chilled heart.

But the chill was cutting in deep now. Zoe felt her zest for life spiralling downwards into a frightening and monotonous resignation as she became more and more convinced that some cruel force of destiny was working day and night to ensure that she was denied the bliss of spending her life with the one man she loved.

It was the tyranny of the dreams. Like stalking intruders, they penetrated her sleeping mind. And when she was awake and her own person again, the memory of them held her a helpless captive. She could see no way out of the bewildering maze created by her dreams. If she had tried to explain her feelings to any sane and sensible person, they would surely brand her as deranged. A foolish and hysterical female at the very least.

And yet, only a few months before, she had used to consider herself a perfectly normal, rational and together person. In fact, she had never really considered it, she had simply taken it for granted.

The two premonition dreams had changed all that. But there was a new and sinister facet to the latest dream. It kept recurring. Not every night, but with a random frequency that kept her in a state of suspense. She could never be sure when it might come; spiking her sleep with fear, demanding that she should heed its insistent message.

The dream terrified her, not simply because of its drama, but because of the message it contained, telling her that her hopes of happiness were all dashed.

Foolish and hysterical, she mused. Is that what I am? In some ways, she wished that were true. If her dreams were simply the manifestations of a neurotic turn of mind, then maybe she would have some chance of dealing with them. She could get some shrink to sort her out. These people delved back into your past, didn't they, digging out all the ghostly skeletons from the cupboard and drawing their fangs?

Foolish and hysterical. The words kept repeating in her head. She stopped and stood quite still for a moment, concentrating. Elle ahead stopped, too, observing her mistress with attentive and puzzled eyes.

The words in Zoe's head were spoken in a man's voice. The tone of voice was ironic, yet gentle and affectionate. She smiled in sudden recall: it was her Uncle William she could hear, her father's younger brother.

She remembered how he used to tease her mother quite shamelessly, mocking her endless stream of superstitions, her incurable addiction to fortune tellers and clairvoyants. And yet he had never been unkind, never put her down.

The connection with Uncle William had dwindled over the years. After Zoe and her mother moved south, they had seen him only rarely on occasions when there had been special family celebrations. Thinking it over now, Zoe judged that four or five years must have passed since she had seen her Uncle William.

Elle bounded back to her, interrupting her reminiscences, floppy paws stretching up and scrabbling against Zoe's thighs. *Come on, come on!*

Zoe fondled Elle's lovely warm velvety ears. Her mind was active with a new speculation – a strange and hopeful flicker of light glimmering at the end of a dark tunnel. Quite what this meant, she was unable to say. She simply had a spark of intuition that Uncle William might be the spring to activate some lever on her behalf, to transform the frail flicker of hope into a flame.

She looked at her watch. It was approaching eight and time for her to be returning to the house. If Charles woke up and found she was out, he would create a great deal of fuss and noise, wondering where she had got to. Charles was continually under the impression that she was on the point of escape from him. And maybe he had reason to worry.

Zoe wandered back down the length of the paddock, Elle making bounding circles in pursuit. The mare and foal came up to investigate, companionably walking along beside her on the other side of the fence.

She was becoming more and more convinced of the need to go to Yorkshire to talk to Uncle William. There was a rapidly growing belief that he might be able to help her. Maybe, just maybe, he might be able to give some clues to work on, some signposts into the past which would help her to fight the demons of the present.

Excitement surged within. New hope.

She considered practicalities. She guessed that she could get to Bradford on the train in less than three hours. That meant she could see Uncle William, have a long talk with him and still be back in time to meet

Charles in the West End for supper. Charles need never know a thing about it.

She let out a tiny sharp moan of pain. How was it that she felt the need to employ such dealings with the man she was going to marry? Concealment and deception – she had always considered those kinds of behaviour tawdry and cheap.

In addition, and more to the point, why should she keep the Yorkshire trip secret from him? It was an entirely innocent enterprise. Charles would understand perfectly that she might want to go and look up a long-neglected relative, especially at a time when she had an engagement and a forthcoming marriage to report.

Zoe had, in fact, every reason to believe Charles would strongly approve of her plan. For in getting to know Charles in recent weeks, she had been interested to discover that under his boyish bravado Charles was a thoroughly traditional man with solid old-fashioned views on the value of family connections.

What is to stop me, besides fear of what I might discover? she asked herself. Charles would have no objections. There were no other commitments claiming her. It was half-term. She was free to do what she liked . . .

By the time she and Elle reached the house, Zoe had made a definite decision that she would go and see her Uncle William that day, providing he could be contacted.

But who would look after Elle? Not Charles, she decided. Quite apart from the fact that he would consider looking after Elle amounted to shutting her up somewhere and telling her to be good, she remembered that Charles had mentioned plans for lunching in town at his club with clients that day.

There were Charles's parents, of course. She liked them, and they liked dogs. But she hesitated to ask them for favours. There was something about Charles's father and mother that made her want to keep a slight distance, preserve her independence.

Charles was standing at the front door, surveying the garden and grounds in the leisurely manner of a man who owns the land rather than works it. He raised his arm to her in greeting.

Elle bounded up to him and deposited muddy paw marks over his clean beige chinos for which she received a few sharp smacks and some extremely rude language.

'You'll have to teach this little bitch some manners!' he commented cheerily to Zoe, wrapping an arm around her and bending to kiss her lips.

Zoe stiffened. Automatically she turned her face slightly so that his lips made contact with her cheek. 'I shall teach her everything necessary to make her socially acceptable. You don't have to worry on that score, Charles.' She spoke with careful politeness.

'Angel! You're mad at me!' He threw back his head and guffawed. 'For tapping the bloody dog's bottom. God! I didn't know you could look so thunderous.'

Zoe forced herself to smile. She told herself for the hundredth time that Charles was basically a good man. And that he was harmless.

He regarded her with cheery, good-natured lust. 'Mmm, angel-sweet, I could really fancy a good screw when you're looking so fierce.' He awarded her a smile of pure sweet seduction. His long lazy grin. 'Could fancy tapping your lovely bottom, too. A whole lot more entertaining than spanking the dog.'

306

Zoe stared back at him. She felt her features tighten.

He surveyed her through half-closed lids. 'You might like that, angel. Apparently, many ladies do.' Charles's clear blue eyes gleamed and his thick front lock of yellow hair fell enticingly over his his forehead.

Ah yes, there were plenty of women who would be only too willing, Zoe was absolutely sure of it.

She looked down, focusing every shred of her concentration on her puppy. Elle looked up, her treacle-coloured eyes filled with trust.

Marina, thought Zoe in a rush of inspiration. Marina would be just the one to care for Elle whilst she dashed up to Yorkshire. Marina knew all about making dogs happy and she would love to take care of her. Eccentric old Risk would be ecstatic. Elle would be cossetted and reassured. There'd be happiness all round in fact.

Moreover, Marina would be just the one to offer some good advice before she finally set off.

Last but not least, Marina's house was just next door to François. Zoe would not see him, of course. But for a few moments she would be there in the vicinity of his house. She would breathe the same air that he breathed. Look out on to the same street, the same trees and sky that he looked out on.

Zoe breathed deeply. For the first time in weeks she felt as though she were driving her destiny instead of the other way round.

Smiling up at Charles, she linked her arm in his.

'I've decided to go up to Yorkshire,' she told him crisply. 'To see my Uncle William.'

There was not a moment of surprise or hesitation.

'Splendid! Excellent! I just wish I could come with you, angel. But you know how it is . . .'

'No, no. You've a busy day in London. I'll be perfectly fine.' She squeezed his hand. 'And I'll be back this evening.'

CHAPTER 28

Marina and Risk returned from their early morning walk, a round trip of two miles through north London's residential streets and a small nearby park adorned with dusty shrubs and weary-looking rose trees.

It had been nothing but brickbats and hassle. Marina flung down her keys on the kitchen table and blew out a heavy sigh of relief. She felt as though she had gone ten rounds in a boxing ring.

Risk, the cause of all the bother, demurely lapped up the milk she had offered him and stepped into his basket, turning himself in a series of spiralling movements before settling with a contented grunt. He tucked his front paws beneath him and hung his head over the side of the basket, smug and well satisfied with the results of his various skirmishes in the great outdoors.

Marina filled the kettle and switched it on.

There were a number of well-known hazards on her walks with Risk, mainly consisting of rowdy confrontations with other terrible-terrier-types with whom he liked engage in a deeply fulfilling snapping and snarling session before being dragged away by Marina with the growls still choking in his throat.

Other pitfalls came in the form of cats lurking wickedly in gateways, just waiting for a dog on a lead to make the kind of vicious unexpected lunge likely to bring its owner flat on their face, nose to the concrete. The cat would then nip gracefully up into the security of a tree, leaving the earthbound dog panting and straining beneath.

This morning had been fraught with all of those snares and nearly every other peril Marina could possibly have imagined. She was sure that Risk was becoming ever more combative and energetic as his muzzle became ever more grizzled.

'I've heard it said that keeping a pet helps to relieve human loneliness and stress,' Marina informed Risk, wagging an admonishing finger.

Risk looked up. His tail twitched with pleasure to be spoken to so kindly by his mistress.

Marina spooned coffee granules into a china mug and poured on boiling water. 'As far as I can see,' she continued to Risk, 'the main thing that keeping a pet does for you is *generate* a lot of stress. I just pray that you haven't actually drawn any blood from any of your adversaries this morning.'

Risk gazed at her enraptured, sighed with doggy happiness and allowed his eyes to close.

Marina spread out the morning paper and turned to the pages of job adverts. 'Ugh!' She pushed the paper to one side and reached for Teddy Penrose's book, by now almost half-read. Instantly she was engrossed.

When François called a little later, it took a few seconds before she was able to pull herself from the fascinating information in front of her eyes and register the gentle knocking on the front door.

François came through into the kitchen. He was hollow-eyed and gaunt-looking.

'Coffee!' Marina said to him. 'And a nice squidgy chocolate biscuit. That's a command, not an offer.'

He gave a dry laugh and sat down at the table.

'Where's Leonore? Isn't it half-term?' Marina put coffee and biscuits in front of him.

'She's gone to stay with a friend. The family are all going off to Brighton for a few days. Seaside holiday.'

'Nice.'

'Yes.' A long silence.

'You're not out on a shoot today?'

'The bike's in for a service. I thought I'd have a day at home, catching up on the accounts and so on.'

'Ah,' she said.

Another long silence followed. It seemed a huge effort for him to speak. Marina could see that his mood was dark and bleak.

He crumpled a biscuit on to the plate. He sighed.

'François,' Marina said with gentle urgency, leaning forward to him, 'you look as pale as death, you look as though you haven't eaten properly for weeks. You look as though someone has slapped you so hard you can hardly breathe.'

He turned to face her, his beautiful dark and watchful eyes full of hurt. 'Zoe's been in touch with me. Just this weekend.'

'Ah.'

'She telephoned. It was well after midnight. She sounded so – alone.'

'Ah.' Marina got up and made a show of preparing fresh coffee. This was difficult for her. Zoe had been

311

in touch with her also. By telephone. Zoe would, in fact, be arriving at the house with her puppy any time now.

Marina had assured her that François would be out working. Well, wasn't he always? And, if for any reason, he was at home, then of course the bike would be parked outside as usual, marking his presence. In which case Zoe would have to make her own decision about taking the risk of seeing him once more.

Marina glanced across at François. A lion in pain. What should she tell him? Anything? Nothing? Perhaps she should attempt to manipulate the situation in some way. Speak to François and try to persuade him of the benefit to be gained from a meeting with Zoe. But then she reflected that these two lovers were deeply wounded people. Maybe a surprise meeting would be harmful at this point. Maybe she should go as far as trying to prevent it?

Her decision was instantly reached. She sat down again, strong and sure of her conclusion that there was nothing to be done except allow events to take their course. There was only so much one could do on other people's behalf, only so much one should even try to do.

Since her meeting with Teddy Penrose, since reading his book, Marina had found her own mood increasingly buoyant and positive. Maybe this wouldn't last. But for the moment it felt very good.

All shall be well.

François was flicking through the pages of Teddy Penrose's book. He looked up at Marina, a question in his eyes.

'The author's an old contact from my student days,'

she explained. 'We both have an interest in the para-normal. His is proper and scientific.'

'And yours?'

'Mine – isn't.'

He stared at her.

'A long time ago I used to fancy I had some powers of extrasensory perception. Clairvoyance, that kind of thing.' She smiled, shrugged.

'No! You, too?'

She smiled at his weary, disbelieving face.

Into the following few moments of contemplation the door bell sounded and Risk exploded from his basket, a wiry bundle of risen hackles and frenzied barking.

'Excuse me,' Marina told François, pursuing her dog down the hall and seizing him by the collar. Taking a deep breath, she opened the door.

A scene of doggy mayhem followed as Risk reached ignition point at the idea of another canine daring even to consider entering his domain.

'Oh, my God!' gasped Marina, hanging on for dear life as Risk struggled to get at Elle.

Zoe was having similar problems, her puppy thrashing and bucking on the end of her lead like a frantic hooked trout.

'Come in, come in,' said Marina, grabbing Zoe's hand and pulling her through the doorway. 'Everything will be all right in a minute. Just let Elle go. As soon as Risk finds out what sex variety she is, all hostilities will cease.'

Zoe was pink with all the excitement and confusion. Her dark hair swung against the collar of her bright lime-green coat. Her slender ankles, in their shiny tights, gleamed above navy suede shoes.

Marina thought that, if she had ever had any skill in portrait painting, she would have moved heaven and earth to get Zoe to sit for her.

A sudden heavenly silence fell as Risk's nose informed him that he was in the presence of a delightful and playful young female. His rumbling growls turned to little squeals of pleasure.

The two canines progressed down the hall, all capering legs and frenziedly waving tails.

Zoe began to move forward, her gaze following her puppy.

She stopped dead. She inhaled sharply as she saw him, a long still figure, darkly outlined against the light from the far window overlooking the garden.

She saw the stunned wonder on his face. Pure, dazzling joy. A perfect replica of her own feelings.

Sliding past the dazed couple, Marina shepherded the ecstatic dogs to the back door and through into the garden. 'There are times,' she told Risk and Elle, settling herself on the wooden bench festooned with glistening golden leaves, 'when three is most definitely a crowd.'

Zoe moved towards François, dreamlike and compelled. His opened arms enclosed her. His lips caressed her hair, her forehead, her cheeks.

After a time he held her away from him. His fingers traced the path his lips had taken. 'The real you,' he breathed. 'Not just a voice. Not just some picture in my head. Really you.'

Zoe gazed and gazed at him. He had spoken words echoing exactly what she herself had been thinking. 'Your hair has grown,' she whispered. 'So silky and thick.' She reached up and stroked the shiny strands. 'A mane!' she laughed.

'I needed *something* to keep me warm,' he said meaningfully.

He reached out again and gathered her to him. 'Zoe, Zoe,' he murmured over and over.

Zoe sighed. She hardly knew what she was hearing and seeing. She was blind and deaf with happiness.

Moments passed. Timeless. Filled with sensation.

Slowly she pulled back from him. 'I have a train to catch,' she said with rueful appeal.

'What? Where the hell are you going? Good God, Zoe, you don't imagine I've any intention of letting you out of my sight, do you?'

Zoe laid her hand flat against his chest. She could feel his heart leaping beneath her palm. She began to explain to him about going to see her uncle in Yorkshire. Embarking on some journey into her past. Hoping, hoping.

She looked up at him. Not fearful any longer. Defying him to be angry.

There was concern in his face. Incomprehension for a time.

As she spoke, she noted the ghostly whiteness of his face and knew that he had been in terrible pain and that he was still hurting.

She was keenly aware, too, that she might have no choice but to hurt him further. And yet some strange vital hope for their future was still there. Frail but glimmering.

When she finished speaking he responded simply, 'I shall go with you.'

'No! Oh, François, I don't know!'

'I'm coming,' he told her. 'You can't stop me. Can you, darling?'

Outside in the garden, in her thin shirt and jeans, Marina chaperoned the cavorting dogs and shivered.

The few remaining leaves on her cherry tree shivered, too. There were no more than a handful of them left now, but they were hanging on grimly. The wind was sharp and raw, insistently rattling branches and whipping around chilled hands and arms.

Marina wrapped her arms around herself and rubbed her hands over her ribs.

The autumn wind was truly predatory and bitter, yet somehow filled with promise. The crisp air, pungent with the scent of rotting leaves, smelled also of freshness and damp, of dark earth, of smoke and petrol and rain. The complex scent of a living breathing city.

Marina breathed in deeply.

She looked at the dogs; one old, one nearly new. They had rapidly established a ritual of play, pleasing to both of them. First they pranced together in a wild frenzy, and then they stopped dead, eyeing each other, teasing and testing, preparing for the next bout, their hot breath curling up from their muzzles like white smoke.

Marina smiled.

She imagined the couple inside. Would they, too, be testing and teasing? Preparing for the next bout?

Life, she murmured. Life.

But please God Zoe and François didn't take too long to come to some kind of decision.

She would prefer not to die of hypothermia. And Teddy Penrose was coming to supper at the end of the week.

CHAPTER 29

They spoke very little at the beginning of the journey.

It was enough simply to be together, to be in each other's presence, side by side, fingers loosely twined.

Zoe felt François's gaze on her face. Through his silence, she could hear in her mind the questions that he must be longing to ask.

She tightened her fingers over his. Smiling, she turned away from him, staring out of the window. His face seemed to her so beloved, so beautiful, that she could hardly bear to rest her eyes on it.

We are together, she thought. Our hearts and minds are perfectly in tune. We must live just for now. Today. These few precious moments. What we had in the past has sunk back into memory. And as for the future . . .

The train was beginning to gather speed, hurling itself forward and carving its way up the spine of England. With the extra surge of acceleration, the carriage began to rock from side to side. Passengers returning from the buffet car clutched their giant-sized plastic beakers of coffee more tightly, trying to avoid slopping the hot liquid over the sides.

François swore softly as scalding drops fell on his free

hand, the one not interwoven with Zoe's. *'Merde!'*

She swung round to observe his expression. A succession of feelings moved rapidly over his features. There was a sharp fleeting register of tension, a snap of annoyance, and finally a rueful self-mockery.

Watching those emotions cross his face brought their joint past, those shared moments of rapture in the spring, suddenly roaring back. There was no way of stopping them.

She remembered how it had been for them in the kitchen of his house as he prepared the supper. That sense of sheer happiness and content. She and François and Leonore forming the beating heart of a loving family. She remembered how the soft evening light from the garden had lit François's carved features, how Leonore would swarm up on to her knee with a book to read with her before the supper was finally served.

She recalled the evenings at her own house, too. Ah, yes. Just she and François. How it had felt when he took her into his arms.

'Leonore?' she said to him softly. 'The schedules were changed around. I don't visit her school any more. Does she . . . does she ever talk about me?'

'No,' he said shortly, 'but I think she hopes.'

She knew that he had said the words deliberately, to manipulate her feelings and make her change her mind. She tore her gaze away from him again and stared fixedly out of the window, vaguely registering fields and cows and a huge stretching sky.

'Are you sorry?' he asked quietly. 'Sorry that we came together again like this?'

She parted her lips in distress, struggling to find a way

to explain to him the hundreds of different things that she was feeling.

'If you'd seen the bike parked outside my house and known I wasn't at a safe distance working, would you have turned around and gone away?' His eyes rested on her, cool and quizzical.

Zoe was silent. A dark shadow passed over her face. She was not entirely sure of the truthful answer to his question.

What *would* she have done, if she had suspected there was some danger of meeting François face to face?

'I think I would,' she said eventually.

'Have gone away? Avoided me?'

'Yes.' She unwound her fingers gently from his and pushed aside a strand of hair that had fallen over her cheek. 'You know why, François.'

'I'm not sure I do.' He thrust his hands into his jacket pockets, his face tight and closed.

'Because our lives have changed.' She hesitated. 'After Poppy's death, everything changed for us.'

'Yes. I was a crass, cruel, insensitive fool,' he said violently. People across the aisle turned, stared for a moment.

'No. You were in shock and grief. And you were very, very angry.' Zoe traced a line down the window with her finger. The glass squeaked under the pressure. 'You were angry with fate. But you thought you were angry with me.'

'Yes, yes, you're right,' he agreed. At the same time as admiring her clear-minded summing up of what had happened, he was impatient to make her see what led on from it. 'But we have no choice but to live with fate, go

319

on forward into the rest of our lives. We have to simply accept what fate deals out.'

Her eyes sharpened. 'Exactly.'

His fingers gripped her arm. 'Accepting fate doesn't mean we allow it to ruin the rest of our lives.'

'Things have moved on far beyond that,' she said softly.

He threw himself back against his seat, pushing his hand through his hair in that gesture she knew so well. Every tiny gesture seemed to her delightful, reminding her of how deeply drawn to him she was.

No! I mustn't let him persuade me, she told herself in panic. I mustn't let everything start up again between us and then have to go through all the agony of parting from him again.

'Things have certainly moved on,' he said bitterly. 'For a start, you've promised to marry a man you don't love. A man who's shallow and grasping and can't possibly have any idea of how to appreciate you.'

She flinched. 'That was brutal, François!' She felt her innards tighten, her body brace itself in self-protection.

'Why, in heaven's name, Zoe? Why did you do it? I couldn't believe it when I found out. I still can't. Surely what we had together . . .'

'Stop it!' she whispered fiercely. 'You know perfectly well how much I loved you.'

'Well, then?'

'When you left me that night Poppy died, you looked as though you hated me. As though I were a stranger to you.'

His face drained of colour. A tiny blood vessel at the side of his mouth flickered.

'You looked as though you'd have preferred it if I had been the one to die, not Poppy.'

'Dear God! Now who's the brutal one?'

'You thought because I had dreams and premonitions, that a tiny part of me was slightly crazy.' She stared at him, her eyes shining, sharp and blue.

He said nothing.

'You thought it was weakness at first. Human weakness. Feminine frailty, perhaps?'

He heard the strong accusation in her voice, her complete rejection of the guilt she had been willing to carry on his behalf following that terrible night of Poppy's death.

'Yes, I admit it,' he said slowly. 'Your dreams and visions – whatever they were – they seemed to be a part of you which was secret and closed to me. I could never make myself understand it, so I rejected and despised all those things. I told myself they weren't a part of you. Not the real you.'

She gave a huge deep sigh. 'And then, when she died, you thought it was some kind of wicked witchcraft. You thought I had worked some evil magic?'

The people across the aisle had their ears pricked now. Zoe was talking in a very soft voice, but her tone was urgent and her sharply defined features were contorted with feeling. Certain words chimed out. Evil. Witchcraft.

Curious faces turned once more.

François glared back at them with such ferocity that the would-be observers blushed with shame and returned swiftly to their newspapers.

He took Zoe's hand from her lap and placed it once

321

more in his own. 'Yes. I admit all of that. I need to be forgiven,' he said simply.

Zoe felt cold ripples run across the skin of her scalp. Tears surged into her eyes. She tightened the pressure of her fingers around his.

François's mind seethed with more questions about Charles. And, even more urgently, he longed to know what it was Zoe had partly conveyed to him in her desperate phone call that night. Something highly significant for them both. That had been quite obvious.

'Let's just talk about today, the here and now,' he said practically, with massive self-control.

'You'll like Uncle William,' she told him after a brief pause.

'I won't intrude, Zoe. I'll just wait for you if you'd prefer to see him on your own. There are plenty of things I can entertain myself with.'

She gave a little frown. 'Oh!' she exclaimed, remembering. 'Your artists and the plans for a gallery. Of course! Marina told me about your new work.'

'Marina seems to have been a marvellous means of communication between us. I'd no idea! Well,' he added with a shrug, 'I don't know that I want to be involved in any art-empire building today. But I can always while away a few hours on the streets with the Nikon.' He smiled, raising his eyebrows. 'Real hands-on work.'

'I want you to come with me,' she said, very clear and definite. 'There are things that I need to ask him that will be easier for me if you're there with me.'

'Truly?'

'Yes.'

An announcement from the conductor came over the

intercom system. 'The next train stop will be Doncaster.'

'Why do they say *train* stop these days?' François enquired moodily. 'What other sort of stop could it be, for goodness sake?'

Zoe had a think about it. 'The sort where you stop in the middle of some fields because of a points failure,' she suggested.

They looked at each other. Mutual amusement surged up.

'Oh, darling!' François leaned over swiftly and kissed her very firmly on the lips. As he straightened up, she watched him with great tenderness.

They sat together in silence once more. Close. Two people in total harmony.

As they approached their destination, and the train braked hard, bracing itself for the approach towards the buffers, Zoe touched his arm, demanding his full attention once more.

'When we were together before,' she said, 'I sometimes kept things secret from you. It was because I was afraid.'

'There's no need to be afraid. Not now. You know that, Zoe darling.'

She gave a brief knowing smile. She shook her head gently. 'Perhaps. But whatever else,' she said, 'no more secrets.'

William Peach lived in a small flat over a bakery in one of the maze of tiny streets, close to the city centre.

Paying the taxi driver and looking up at the huddle of small houses, François was surprised. He had imagined that Zoe's relatives would all live in suburban affluence.

323

The entry to William's flat was at the top of a narrow flight of steps built against the outer wall of the side of building. William was waiting for them in the open doorway at the top.

'Little Zoe!' he exclaimed, grasping her hand and kissing her cheek. He looked over her shoulder. 'Aha! What have we here? You didn't tell me you were bringing the lucky man along too.'

Zoe turned, grimacing. 'Sorry,' she mouthed to François.

He smiled. Leapt lightly up the remaining steps and took William's outstretched hand. 'François Rogier,' he said briskly. 'I'm very pleased to have been able to come.'

William led them through into a small sitting-room. A large gas fire glowed on one wall. Everything was neat and tidy and polished. A small round table under the window was laid out with a dainty afternoon tea. There were tiny triangular sandwiches, freshly baked scones thick with butter, and slices of fluffy sponge and rich fruit cake.

Zoe was instantly taken back to the Sunday afternoons of her childhood. Uncle William had lived in a little bungalow on the other side of town then. He and his wife Jean had run a very successful bakery and tea rooms. Sunday had been their only day off. The only day for 'entertaining', as her mother used to refer to it.

Zoe recalled how close Jean and William had been. Jean had died within a year or two of her own father, and for a while Zoe had assumed, with a child's logic, that William and her mother would marry each other.

'Sit down, sit down. Take the weight of your poor travelling legs,' William told François, who had been standing at the window looking down into the street, assessing the possibility of some interesting shots.

William went into the kitchen and there were sounds of spoons and a teapot lid clinking.

Zoe walked around the back of François's chair and ran her hand lightly over his hair. She sat down opposite him. Their eyes met. He raised his eyebrows and gave a slow half-wink.

William reappeared almost immediately. 'Always like to have everything ready and waiting when company's expected. Sugar and milk, François? Zoe doesn't take sugar, if my memory serves me correctly.'

'It does,' François smiled. 'And she doesn't.'

'Ooh! You and me are going to get on just fine,' William said, chuckling.

Watching her uncle whilst she sipped her tea, Zoe could detect very little difference in him from when she had last seen him. He was one of those people who hadn't changed much at all since he came into middle age. And now he would be about sixty, she thought, a small and wiry man with a mobile leathery face, deeply grooved with laughter lines. His thick hair was a brilliant silver white, but his brows were still thick and dark. Sable, like her own.

'What's she told you about me, then?' William asked François. 'Black sheep of the family, eh?'

'Not at all.'

'No, I was just having you on. I was never rascally enough for a black sheep. Bit of a plodder, me. That's why I'm at the poor end of the family, you see, François. There are rich Peachs and poor Peachs.'

Zoe and François laughed.

'But we've all got hearts of gold.' William guffawed, delighted at his little jest. He flourished a plate in front of François's nose. 'Come on then! Have another scone. I baked them myself.'

François obediently took one. William poured more tea. It was good tea, thought Zoe, thick and strong.

Zoe felt herself relax. Since telephoning her uncle out of the blue, she had wondered how William would react to this sudden and impulsive wish to visit him. She had imagined some sticky moments, especially with François unexpectedly coming along, too.

She realized how little need there had been for concern. William was clearly delighted to see her and would happily chat away for hours, plugging any awkward gaps in the conversation, had there been any to plug. And François, for all his tense and critical alertness, was the kind of man who would get on with anyone, regardless of style or wealth, provided they were solid and genuine in spirit.

She tried to imagine Charles in the same situation, wondering what his reactions would be. Outward politeness, and a humorous hatchet job in the car later?

'You know,' William mused, 'it's a funny thing when people start thinking of getting married. They seem to have this need to get back to their roots and talk over old times. Isn't that what you were after, pet?' he demanded of Zoe.

'I suppose so.' She smiled, her mind running over her thoughts in Percival garden, the motivation for this visit. The *seriousness* of it.

William leaned towards François, conspiratorial, man to man. 'She's a deep one, is Zoe, you know. You'll have to have your wits about you, taking one like her on.'

François raised his eyebrows eloquently. *Go on.*

'Zoe's like my brother, her dad, oh yes,' William said. 'He was deep, too. You could never really fathom him – he was a bit of a law unto himself.'

William reached for another piece of cake and offered the plate around. He frowned, reflecting. 'And determined. You couldn't budge Zoe's dad once he got an idea in his head. That's how he made his tidy little fortune, most likely.'

'You look rather determined yourself,' François remarked, taking a piece of sponge cake and breaking it deftly into two equal pieces.

'No!' William said dismissively. 'I'm just a plain solid grafter. Zoe's dad had that extra "go-for-it" instinct. He was special. One on his own.'

He stood up, dabbing at the crumbs on his trousers with a rose-printed paper napkin. Crossing to the small bureau standing against the back wall, he picked up the box resting on its top.

'Look,' he said. 'I dug out the family snaps. You'll be interested in these.'

The box was large and shiny gold, tied with a brown satin ribbon. Zoe recalled such boxes being exchanged in the family at Christmas time. Boxes crammed with luxury chocolates, to stave off the pangs of hunger between the turkey dinner and the pork pie supper.

William placed the lid carefully on the floor and started sifting through the glossy prints within. The majority of them were older ones in black and white, and a few more recent ones in colour.

'Now, then. Here's you when you were a baby, Zoe.

And there's your Aunty Jean on the sands at Whitby.' He peered at the image of his former wife. 'By, she's making a brave job of looking happy. It was nigh on freezing and blowing a gale, if I remember. And that was June.'

François leaned across. 'May I?' He dug out a small handful of photos and leaned back, leafing slowly through, observing intently.

William continued his commentary, unstoppable like a faulty tap. 'See, Zoe, here's your dad with one of his new Mercedes. He changed them every year, you know. Must have cost a bomb. And here's your mum all tarted up for a wedding. Your mum was a real looker when he first met her. And always so well turned out. Like she'd just stepped out of band box, Jean used to say.'

He looked up. He eyed Zoe. 'And I think my Jean might have said the same about you, love. Snazzy frock!'

He inspected the photograph of Zoe's mother more closely. 'I had a very soft spot for your mum. Of course, we used to have our little set-tos. I never could go along with all that mumbo-jumbo about fortune tellers and the like.'

'You teased her unmercifully,' Zoe said. 'You even called her hysterical.'

'I do believe I did. And it's nothing I regret. She needed to be told.'

William turned to address François, who had put the photographs on one side and was now listening intently.

'Zoe's mother was a real sucker for these charlatans. She'd pay over good money to anyone to have her fortune told. Gypsies by the road side. Those women on the pier with the greasy crystal balls and the dog-eared Tarot cards. She went to the posher ones, too. The sort that hire the lounges in hotels in Harrogate to ply their trade. Same old crystal balls, of course. But not nearly as greasy.'

Zoe nodded, tender and regretful. Yes, it was all perfectly true.

'I've nothing against all that sort of thing, if you keep it in perspective,' William assured her. 'But your mum . . . Dear, dear. You see, love, she believed all they said. Swallowed it hook, line and sinker. And when you were old enough to toddle, she started taking you along, too. Do you remember?'

Zoe frowned. 'Vaguely.'

'Your dad never liked it. Thought it could be dangerous. And – ' Suddenly William stopped and checked himself. 'Well, there came a time when he had to put his foot down with a firm hand, so to speak.'

François's eyes were snapping with speculation. He glanced at Zoe, a slight frown on his face.

Confronted in this way with her childhood and youth – the photographs, her uncle's bluff comments – Zoe found her eyes suddenly swimming with tears. 'I'm sorry,' she said, getting out a handkerchief.

'Ahh, lovey! I didn't mean to upset you.' William swept the photographs back into their box and crammed on the lid. 'I should have thought before facing you with this lot. You're just a poor little orphan when all's said and done, aren't you, love?' He patted her knee. 'Never mind, you've still got your uncle William.'

François stared at her. 'Darling, are you all right?' He reached out a hand to her.

'Yes. Yes, truly.'

He paused for a long moment and then got up. 'I'm going to leave you two on your own. You might want to have a private chat between yourselves for a few moments. Will you excuse me, William?'

'Most certainly. But there's not much exciting to see around here I'm afraid. Not for a Frenchman of style who lives in London.'

'You'd be surprised!' François smiled mischievously. He picked up his neat travelling case. 'I never go anywhere without my Nikon.'

William pulled a wry face, catching on instantly. 'If I'd known you were in the big league, I'd have kept my little snaps in the cupboard.'

François paused by Zoe's chair. She lifted her face up to him and he kissed her lips gently. His eyes were very tender. *Don't worry about anything*, he seemed to be saying. *And I'll soon be back.*

The door closed softly behind him.

William looked hard at Zoe. 'That young man. Hang on to him. He's a diamond. And he's not after your money.'

'Why do you say that?'

'You should think on, lass, as your old grandma used to say. You must have inherited a tidy pile from your mum. There's plenty would be panting for it.'

Zoe considered and then smiled. Her money had never been one of her problems. But she had never allowed a man to get very close before François.

'The way he looks at you,' William said. 'That's real love.'

'Do you think so?'

'Know so.'

'Uncle William, what was it that made my father "put his foot down"?'

William sniffed, then cleared his throat. 'Your mum took you with her to see this clairvoyant in Leeds. She was just a local housewife, seeing people in her poky back parlour. But she'd caused bit of a sensation. Articles in the local papers about her miraculous powers and so forth.

'Well, love, when your mum came back from seeing this woman, she was in a terrible state. Ranting and raving, carrying on. Completely hysterical. Your dad couldn't do a thing with her. He rang us in the end and Jean went round to see what she could do.'

Zoe waited, tense like a wire. 'Well?'

'From what Jean could gather, this clairvoyant had told your mum something about you. Made some prediction.'

'Can you remember what Jean said?'

William raised his eyes and looked hard at her. He shook his head. 'I've never had any patience for that kind of thing. I only half-listened. Is it important for you, love?'

'It could be.'

He rested his head on his hands, pushing his lips forward as he concentrated. 'It was something to do with you coming to a time in your life when there'd be some . . . negative force over you. I think that was it.'

'Oh, God!' whispered Zoe.

'There was something about you bringing bad on yourself, bringing on a lot of unhappiness.' William shook his head in resigned disbelief. 'It's wicked, if

331

you ask me, for perfect strangers to be feeding women like your mum that kind of dangerous rubbish.'

'Was that all?' Zoe asked. 'Wasn't there anything else?'

He hesitated, looked highly uncomfortable. 'I seem to remember there was a death along the way in all this. But then there always is with these fortune-teller people. They like to shock. It pulls in the punters.'

'Did Jean say anything to suggest that my mother had been told I might be the cause of a death?' Zoe asked with slow emphasis. 'Either directly or in some other kind of way?'

William flinched visibly. He looked terribly shocked. 'No!' he cried in fierce protest. 'No, no, no!'

He's protecting me, Zoe thought. I've asked the one question no one in the family ever wanted me to ask. And the reason they didn't want me to ask was because the answer was 'yes'.

It was at that point that François came back. Zoe knew that William had said all that he would ever say on the subject.

She smiled in greeting at François, attempting to conceal her mood, which had suddenly turned darkly thoughtful and subdued.

'Any good pickings?' William asked.

'One or two. What I'd really like to do is take some shots of you,' François told him.

'Go on with you! Here? Shall I comb my hair? Do you need any special lights?'

'Nothing. Just you and a dark background and this little anglepoise I've got in my bag.' François began to assemble his equipment.

William stood against the wall bolt upright, as though he had just escaped from an army parade ground.

'So,' François said conversationally, pointing his camera, 'were you always a baker, William?'

'Man and boy,' said William.

'Training?'

'Training! You must be joking. I started at the bread factory in Wakefield. Sweeping the floors. Ten-hour day. A real sweatshop.'

'Came up the hard way, then?' François was almost dancing as he spoke. Rocking from one foot to another, falling gracefully on to one knee, springing up again, twisting his body from side to side to get an angled shot.

And all the time he was talking, questioning, listening, drawing out.

The tension seeped out of William's ramrod spine. His flow of talk started again. He forgot about the visual impression he was creating. He simply became himself again – a man who liked to talk about life.

Zoe had not seen François engaged in his professional work before. Now she began to understand the secret of his artistry, his ability to allow his subjects simply to be themselves. She looked on, transfixed.

As they left to catch the train back to London, William grasped her by the arm and whispered urgently in her ear.

'You just hang on to him, love. You won't find another of that calibre in a hurry.'

CHAPTER 30

It was cold as they walked into the station. Rain was driving down, mingled with sleet.

Zoe shivered. She turned up the collar of her coat.

François had his arm around her shoulders, warming and protecting.

He settled her in a seat on one side of the table and placed his jacket and camera equipment on the facing seats so that other passengers would be discouraged from taking up a place there and shattering their privacy.

Reassuring her that he would be back instantly, he went along to the buffet car to get coffee and brandy.

The queue was already extensive. Customers ahead of him were requesting complicated orders that seemed to be taking forever to process.

Leaning against the gently rocking wall of the train, he stared unseeingly ahead of him. His thoughts were entirely of Zoe, and the afternoon they had spent with her uncle, sharing a brief journey into her past.

He had not yet confronted Zoe with any of the pressing questions that repeated themselves in his mind. He knew that he must do so. The journey would be over in less than three hours.

An image planted itself in his mind: Zoe parting from him, walking away. There was a flare of sheer panic as he contemplated that bleak moment.

They had been so close today, springing together like magnets, cleaving to each other. One minute he had persuaded himself, been convinced even, that the chasm which had opened up between them in the spring was now firmly closed. The danger was over.

Then, in the next minute, he had felt hesitation, had realized that he could have been deluding himself. Magnets could be torn apart if the dividing force was strong enough.

It struck him that he had been through this before; struggling in the dark lonely pit of shattered relationships. It had been at the time he had begun to understand that Poppy really meant it when she said she was leaving him.

And Zoe had been in that dark pit, too. He pictured Zoe, anguished and deserted in her house as he roared away on his bike into the night after their quarrel. Zoe broken, wounded and alone, with angry words echoing all around her. Zoe totally vulnerable, ready to fall into the arms of another man who had simply been biding his time waiting.

Frustrated and impatient, he shifted from one foot to the other. The whole notion of this other man in Zoe's life was hateful to him. An invasion of body and spirit.

Little images flickered behind his eyes to taunt him. That man, Charles, touching Zoe. Possessing her.

He gave a vicious little jerk of his head as if to clear the pictures within.

When he got to the front of the queue he was astonished to hear himself speaking in French.

'Sorry, squire,' the steward smiled cheerily. 'No speak the lingo.'

'Miles away,' François apologized, instantly repeating the order in immaculate English.

Balancing the plastic cups with elaborate care, he made his way back to the carriage where he had left Zoe.

Through the windows, he could see nothing but the reflection from inside the train. Beyond its pale yellow overhead lights, the darkness was intense.

Her seat was empty. He felt instant alarm. Placing the plastic cups on the table, he moved rapidly up and down the carriage, wild-eyed and intense. As he roamed the aisle, scanning each set of seats the other passengers looked up, their glances revealing curiosity and concern.

She was nowhere to be seen. His heart began to race.

He sat down at their table and threw back one of the brandies in a single gulp.

The door at the end of the carriage swung open and she came through the doorway. Softly gliding in her flared swinging coat, she looked graceful and calm. He would almost say serene.

He gazed at her, the panic rising again.

She took off her coat, folded it deftly and laid it on the seat. She sat down and smiled at him. She reached across for a cup.

'What is it, François?' she asked, suddenly catching his mood.

He drew in his breath and held it for a moment. 'I thought you had gone. Left me.'

She shook her head. 'Darling François! Where could I go to from a train?'

'God alone knows.'

She tilted her head on one side. 'Oh, François.' Her voice was gently chiding.

'Yes, I know, I know. It's stupid.' He threw back his head like an animal in pain.

She reached out and put her hand on his, a gesture filled with deep tenderness.

He sat forward. 'No, it's not stupid, is it? Because you are planning to leave me when we get to the final stop. Aren't you?'

She looked down, avoiding his eyes. It was all the answer that was needed.

'Christ!' he muttered.

Zoe simply sat in quiet contemplation. Her seeming calmness drove him mad.

'Explain!' he commanded. 'Tell me why you're going to do this incredible thing. Make me understand.'

'I don't know if I can explain. I think we're looking at this situation through different eyes.'

'Situation! You call two people coolly planning to tear up the roots of their happines together a "situation"?' he asked coldly.

'I didn't mean to sound heartless,' she protested.

'Very well. I accept that. So, go ahead, Zoe. Give me a good sound reason why you're going to leave me and go back to Charles when we get to London.'

'Ah!' She tightened the muscles of her face in an instinctive gesture of pain. That, at least, gave him a small particle of comfort.

'Go on,' he said, merciless. 'You said there would be

no more secrets for us two. So tell me the very worst, feel free.'

Her hand, curled around the cup, began to tremble. She jerked it in a protective gesture towards her body, then thrust it beneath the table.'

He seized her other hand and held it within his own. 'Oh God, darling. Forgive me, I simply can't bear what's happening between us.'

'No, I know. Dear François, I truly know how you must have been feeling. And I want to tell you everything,' she said simply. 'I don't want any more secrets.'

She turned towards the window and began to speak, resting her gaze on her own pale reflection. But she hardly noticed it; what she was seeing was a memory of the pictures inside her head. 'For a few weeks now, I've been having this same dream. Over and over.' Her eyes flickered towards his, cautious, anxious.

He nodded, gave a faint smile of encouragement. This time he would really listen, try to tune in with her feelings.

'Try to imagine it. I have this sensation of being in water. I'm in some great lake. I'm swimming and I feel so free. It's a beautiful marvellous feeling, like flying; perfect freedom.' She looked up. 'It's how I felt when I was with you, François. When we were making love.'

Their eyes met. There was a shiver of pure communication.

She went on. 'There's a man with me, swimming ahead. His legs in the water are very long and graceful. He looks around to make sure that I'm following. That I'm safe.'

'And who is he, this man with the graceful legs?' François asked with a wry smile.

338

'I can't see his face. He's wearing a diver's mask, just as I am. All I know about him is that I feel that I want to follow him anywhere he goes.' She paused. 'So it must be you.'

She looked hard at him, but he said nothing.

'We're in a lake where there used to be a village. As we swim down and down we can see houses and a road. And a drowned church with a tall pointed spire. The man ahead of me is swimming down towards the ruins. He has some kind of torch on his mask and there's a golden beam of light coming from it. The beam draws me on. I'm like an insect drawn to a flame.

'This man's a very strong swimmer. He goes very swiftly and then he turns because he senses that I've fallen behind. The two of us are becoming further and further apart.'

She stopped and rested her chin on her hands. She frowned, trying to recall exactly, to paint the clearest of pictures for him. But it was at this point that the dream became cloudy.

'Why have you fallen behind?' François prompted softly.

'My legs begin to feel heavy. Like lead. The more effort I make to move them, the more deadened they feel. They become so heavy they're like huge tree trunks. Immovable. I want to go towards the light, but I've no more power of movement in me than a stone.

'I see a dark shadow pass above. It blots out all the light. It's the hull of great ship. Its propellors churn the water and black smoke pours out of a pipe in its side. I feel terribly frightened, paralysed with fear. A man's body falls from the ship. He's wrapped in a sack, struggling and shouting. The sack is tied very tightly so that he can't escape. There's only me to help him. He knows I'm there. He shouts to me in terrible fear. "Zoe!"

'My legs are still very heavy, but because this man is in such need I manage to swim to him. I start to untie the sack so that he can be free to swim up to the surface. The man inside is Charles.'

She finished her story. She bowed her head.

François clenched his hands beneath the table. The nails dug into the flesh so that the knuckles shone bone white.

She dared to look up. 'Do you understand?'

His eyes blazed.

'Please, please, François! Don't you see the meaning of this dream?' she insisted.

'I think I know the meaning that you see in it,' he said slowly.

'Then tell me,' she whispered.

'You see two men in your dream. You see myself and Charles. You're drawn to me, but something holds you back. And that something is Charles. You see that he needs you. He's in danger and only you can be his saviour.'

She leaned back and let out a huge sigh. 'Yes, yes, yes.'

'It won't do, Zoe. It won't do as a reason. It's simply a dream.'

'No. My other dreams were prophecies of some sort. And they came true.'

'*No*! They did not come true in the literal sense. Neither Leonore nor I were harmed as you had feared we would be. And whilst the little boy Stefan was hurt in a road accident, his injuries weren't fatal.' His eyes challenged her and he made a quick, furious gesture with his hands.

'Listen to me, François.' She grasped his wrist fiercely. 'You *will* listen to me.'

'Very well.' His eyes were icy.

'I understand now that my premonitions are not literal in terms of precise detail. They are *warnings*, sketched out in my mind.'

He shook his head. 'These are utterly irrational conclusions to come to.'

'The foolish imaginings of a hysterical woman?' she cut in. 'Perhaps you would like to believe that I am like my mother. Or at least that part of her personality that William described?'

He shook his head in denial. He struggled to keep his temper. 'I'm sorry. Go on.'

'I told you my dream of an air crash in detail. I told it to you weeks before it happened. I warned you again just days before the fatal flight. And my prophecy of disaster came true.' Tears of frustration glittered on her eyelashes. She wanted shake him. Why would he not see? Why would he not accept?

Again he shook his head.

'Yes! Oh, for God's sake, François. Poppy – your wife, Leonore's mother – was killed in a terrible air disaster. She was killed just at the time I had dreamed there would be exactly that kind of tragic crash. What more proof do you need?'

'Your dream was prophetic, I do accept that. In a general sense. But . . .'

'You insist on denying the truth before your eyes.

You're stubborn and obstinate because you like to believe you're a realist!' She felt herself grow hot with the effort of trying to convince him.

He remained silent.

'Very well, then, if you didn't believe in the power of my dream, François, then tell me this – why did you blame me for what happened?'

He turned away from her.

'If my dream was nothing more than a mere flight of fancy, then why did it lead to our splitting up?'

Still he was silent.

'You did have some belief, didn't you? You weren't quite the sceptic you liked to make out.'

'Perhaps not. Although I don't pretend to understand any of these things you describe.'

She leaned back, drained and exhausted. At least he had stopped fighting with her.

He said, 'Are you saying to me that because of this latest dream, you feel compelled to return to Charles?'

'Yes.' Her eyes were dull and weary.

'That if you don't, then he might be in some sort of danger; some terrible disaster might befall him?'

'Yes. That is exactly it.'

'My God!'

'I haven't had this dream just once, François. It keeps coming. A recurring dream. A *warning*.'

'What can I do?' he demanded. 'When you say things like that, I'm powerless.'

She shook her head in a gesture of resignation he found utterly terrifying.

'There must be some way I can make you change your way of looking at things. Please, Zoe.'

342

'How can I choose my own happiness when it involves taking the risk of exposing someone else to danger? How could I live with that, if something dreadful happened to Charles?'

'This is madness,' he warned her. 'I'd bet on it that Charles is virtually indestructible.'

'He's a vulnerable human being like all the rest of us.'

François felt so angry and helpless that it was painful for him to breathe.

'I simply can't believe you're going back to Charles,' he told her, 'after this precious day we've had together'

She would not look at him.

'What do you see in Charles, for heaven's sake?' he burst out finally.

'He's offered me stability and permanence. He was there when you pushed me away.'

'Very well, you had a moment's weakness. You can't let a life hang on that.'

'I was wrecked that night you left. You wrote me a letter that made my heart feel as though a stake had been driven through it.'

François felt himself freeze inside. There was a growing realization that he would have to accept Zoe's intentions. That there was nothing he could do to stop them.

He got up and went to the washroom cubicle. His legs were disobedient and liquidy and he had to clutch at one of the seats to steady himself.

Locking himself in the cubicle, he splashed cold water on his face and took deep, long breaths. He stared at his face in the glass above the basin: haggard, drawn and desolate. Hope draining from it even as he looked.

343

He returned to Zoe. She smiled at him with huge love and compassion, like a mother comforting her child who has suffered some cruel rejection or disappointment.

He sat down. He felt cold and hard and cruel. In the mood for very straight talking.

'Have you made love with Charles?' he demanded.

She said nothing. A dark flush crept up her throat and neck.

'Do I take it that your silence means yes?' he wondered with icy disdain.

She turned her head very slowly in a swan-like movement. 'Oh, François,' she protested with deep reproach.

François felt a churn of nausea. Gripped with raw jealousy, her response seemed to him nothing more than a simple affirmation of the question he had asked. The jealousy fired him and then burned him, a torturing flame running back into his past and flaring through into the future.

He put his head in his hands. 'I don't think I can bear this,' he said bitterly. 'It makes me feel sickened. It makes every crevice of me ache.'

Zoe rattled his arm. 'You never let me answer,' she told him sharply. 'You simply believed the worst of me.'

He looked up. 'So you haven't . . .?'

'No.'

'Oh, darling! Oh dear God, I'm so glad. And so sorry!' He took her hands in his. 'Forgive me, *chérie*!'

Recalling what had passed between her and Charles on

344

the morning when he had so nearly forced the issue, Zoe bowed her head.

Sensitive to her thoughts, François frowned. 'But he touches you. He kisses you . . .'

'We are engaged,' she said in horrible distress.

'Sweet Jesus, and soon you will be married. Then you will have to let him make love to you. Have you any idea how that makes me feel?' he burst out.

She was unable to speak. Her throat was swollen with grief.

François sighed. 'So, what is going to happen when we get to London? Are you going to leave me?'

She looked him straight in the eye and said nothing.

'Oh, I see. I put you in a taxi for the West End and I go home to my empty house? Is that it?'

'Yes.' She looked away and bowed her head under his weariness and anger.

François considered the nature of love. He thought of Poppy. He thought of Leonore. He recalled a sonnet of Shakespeare that he had learned at school as a young boy:

> Let me not to the marriage of true minds
> Admit impediments. Love is not love
> Which alters when it alteration finds . . .

He stood up. He went to sit beside Zoe and took her in his arms. He stroked her hair and her face. 'Whatever else, I shan't stop loving you, darling. Even you can't make me do that.'

At the station he put her in a taxi. It gleamed oily black beneath the bright lights on the concourse, the reflections on its roof stretching and contracting as it moved away from the kerb and merged into the traffic.

François turned and walked towards the underground.

He had made a decision. He would not cease to hope.

CHAPTER 31

Zoe sat in the taxi, cold and numb.

In London's central streets, in the clutch of a deepening winter, all was light and warmth and gaiety. The Christmas decorations were already in place and the black darkness was spiked with a mass of coloured lights, strung out over the roads. She looked up and saw a giant iridescent teddy bear bobbing gently, and further along a huge and grotesque clown's face in sparkling silver, grinning down at her through mocking blue lips.

Brilliant wedges of brightness flared from the shop windows. Gesturing mannequins in gowns of glowing reds trailed holly and tinsel from their stiff dummy fingers. Christmas trees dotted all over with robins and snowy glitter stood at their feet.

Couples strolled together through the freezing streets, arms linked. They paused by the gleaming window displays when something caught their eye. Zoe imagined them discussing the presents they would be buying for their friends and families – for each other.

She opened her bag and felt around for the small box

containing the ring Charles had given her. She slipped it onto her finger, relieved to have remembered, in the nick of time, how she had quickly slid it off that morning before she and François boarded the train.

Charles had a keen eye for that kind of detail, he would have noticed immediately that his ring was not in evidence.

He was waiting for her in the restaurant. He was on his third g & t, because Zoe was very late.

He stood up. He looked annoyed, rather than worried. But then, she told herself, worry often has that effect on people.

'Angel.' He leaned down to kiss her. 'I've been hanging around a hellishly long time waiting for you. I began to think I was being stood up.' He laughed as he spoke. Being stood up was as unthinkable for Charles as being prevailed on to take a monk's vow of celibacy.

'I'm truly sorry, Charles. I had to get a later train than I'd planned.' She felt herself flush slightly. The lie was distasteful to her. Talking smoothly of 'I' when it should have been 'we'.

'You should have called me from the train,' he reproached her mildly. 'It doesn't do a lot for a guy's ego sitting around on his own, looking a bit of a lemon when a cosy little table for two's been ordered.'

He was leaning back in his chair, smiling at her lazily. His tone was fond and indulgent, but Zoe did not miss the hint of warning running beneath. He would not be at all pleased if she did this to him again.

'You're quite right. I should have called from the train. I really am sorry.' Zoe accepted the glass of chilled dry wine offered by the waiter and picked up the menu.

348

'I've already ordered,' Charles informed her crisply. 'I was simply famished.'

'Oh!'

'I've asked for melon for you, angel, and the grilled sole to follow. OK?'

She glanced across to him. 'Yes, of course. OK.'

Charles tossed back what was left of his g & t. He looked around and clicked his fingers. A waiter hurried up to pour out the claret. Charles took a long gulp.

Zoe felt sweat prickle beneath her armpits. The nasty sense of shabby deception was tightening its grip. To come in such a short time from the arms, mind and heart of one man to the company of another – the man she had promised to marry – made her wince with discomfort and shame. She felt as though she were a traitor to both of them.

She picked up her glass and tilted it to her lips. A wave of aching longing for François gripped her with the sharpness of a spasm of physical pain. She took quick breaths, steadied herself, sipped at the wine with delicate grace.

'You look a tiny bit glum, angel,' Charles remarked. 'Did the day turn out a bit hard going? Not what you'd expected?'

She stared fixedly into her glass. 'I suppose, when you make impulsive arrangements, you have to be prepared for things you didn't quite expect. All kinds of eventualities, in fact,' she said.

'I suppose so.' Charles felt a twinge of irritation. Her careful thoughtfulness and her refusal to succumb to the cheap snappy retort were qualities that had always impressed him. He reminded himself that, from very early on in their getting to know each other, he had marked her down as an unusually thoughtful and sensitive girl. Fragile, but by no means a lightweight.

But sometimes her silences and her deeply considered remarks bugged him a little. Why couldn't she just respond to a simple question with a simple answer?

'What did your uncle think about us getting married, then?' he wondered.

She put her glass down.

Charles saw her begin to consider again. He saw the anxiety in her eyes as she weighed up what she should say and the way in which she should say it.

'I'll bet he was surprised, mmm?' He fingered his glass and stared at her, amusing himself with some lazy speculation. 'You know, I'll bet the men in your family saw you as a bit of nun-like figure. Your Uncle William probably thought you'd never take the plunge.'

She opened her eyes wide. Charles watched a slow smile illuminate her face. There was even a hint of wickedness.

The sight of her like that made him feel extremely horny. He bolted his devilled kidneys and set about making inroads into his steak.

His mind raced on ahead. He began to plan the evening's seduction programme. Zoe might be his fiancée, his bride-to-be, but she still required seducing. He had spent many a day bemoaning the fact, asking himself what the hell she thought she was playing at, being so . . . unavailable. But just at this moment, the contemplation of masterminding a seduction scene was decidedly pleasurable. In fact, he couldn't think of any prospect more arousing.

He decided he would take Zoe back to his own pad. He had the feeling she was somehow less of her own woman when she was off her home ground. And thus much more likely to be *his* woman. As any sportsman worth his cricket pads knew, an away game always created vulnerability in the visiting opposition.

His desire flared up. He caught her eyes, pushing out his lips in a gesture indicating that there would be a hearty lustful kissing for afters when the dinner was completed.

He inserted his serrated knife into the steak. The flesh parted under the pressure, the inside becoming exposed: pink, luscious and tender.

Charles made a solemn resolve to be very gentle with her, very patient. He saw himself slipping some enticing love music into the disc player, drawing Zoe down onto his knee. He imagined their deep kisses, saw his hand sliding over the roundness of her breasts, slipping inside her shirt . . .

He looked up. Ah! She was wearing a dress. Rapidly he made adjustments to the mental scenario. Now his hand moved to the top of the zip fastener at the base of her neck. It had to be said that a dress had advantages. The whole thing slipped off in one go.

He pictured her in her lingerie, recalling that she chose to wear superbly scanty little bits of nonsense underneath. He saw himself unfastening the lacy bra, teasing a nipple with his tongue and a tiny nibble of his teeth. He saw her arching her back, moaning.

Idly, with the luxurious anticipation of desire soon to be gratified, he allowed himself a fraction more licence. The half-naked Zoe was turned in his arms, laid gently across his knees on her stomach. The soft globes of her buttocks, framed in a skimpy white garter belt and lace topped stockings, gleamed in the dim lamplight.

He saw himself languidly stroking the silken skin of those gorgeous jutting mounds. He felt the softness of her belly beneath his hand as he raised her hips towards him, his head bending so that he could apply his lips to the trail his fingers had blazed. He would be superlatively leisurely and gentle with her, and he fancied she might enjoy herself a lot more than she expected.

Charles was not often so lengthily engaged in his head. He was a man of action. Go, go, go. But the roads down which some thoughts dashed off were too interesting to leave alone.

He sliced more beef flesh. He took several gulps of wine.

He looked at Zoe, who was quietly sectioning her grilled sole.

Zoe was one of those rare creatures: a true sexual innocent, he told himself. Well, a novice at any rate. She had such a lot to learn, so many wonderful discoveries to make. There was a whole world of delights he would show her. And he, as her self-appointed teacher, would be only too pleased to make a very thorough job of her education.

He reached across the table and covered her wrist with his hand. 'Happy, angel?'

She nodded.

'Come on, eat up. You'll need to keep up your strength for later on!'

Still she was silent. This time she did not look up. He saw a rosy flush steal up her neck.

Whoa. Take it easy, Charlie boy, he told himself. She's not in the mood yet. Change the subject. Get on to safer ground.

'I've been doing a bit of talking with the parents.'

She looked up. 'Oh?'

'Don't look so worried, angel. Just boring money talk. There's a general feeling that you and I need to take a little advice.'

'Financial advice?' She laid her fork down.

'Yeah. Before we marry. Sort things out a bit. Protection for both of us. After all, we're neither of us short of a bob or two.'

She frowned, digesting his words. 'You mean, that in case we should ever split up, then it makes sense to have it in black and white who gets what?'

She flashed him such a look. Charles never stopped being astonished at her occasional displays of iron-hard determination. Feminine assertiveness, that's what it was. One or two of his other girls had had it really badly.

'You make it sound disgracefully calculating,' he said, keen to sound low-key and reasonable. 'It's simply good sense. Come on, angel. Money's my profession. You can't expect me to close my eyes to all the implications involved when a marriage is in the offing.'

'No, you're right.'

'Good! So will you come with me to see a chap my father recommends?'

'When?' Her tone was sharp, suspicious.

'Not right away, angel. In a week or so.' He raised his arm, summoned a waiter, requested the bill. 'Come on, my lovely one,' he chivvied affectionately. 'Smile!'

As they stepped from the enclosed warmth of the

restaurant, the freezing night air hit Charles like some huge swung icicle. He staggered slightly, almost losing his balance. For a moment he thought he would fall and take quite a knock. A passing car swerved sharply, anticipating trouble. Christ, thought Charles, I was nearly a goner.

Zoe ran up behind him. She grasped his arm. She started to shake it, staring up into his face, her cheeks ghostly white with anxiety. 'Oh, dear God! Charles. Are you all right?' She was breathing hard, as though she had been truly terrified on his behalf.

Charles was deeply gratified. 'Absolutely fine, angel. Only half of the nine lives gone. If that.'

Zoe persuaded him to leave his car in the road outside the restaurant. He could pick it up in the morning.

He allowed her to fuss. 'All right, all right. But I'm perfectly A1 OK. And I'm not half-cut, if that's what you're thinking.'

They took a taxi to his flat. He saw Zoe watching him with solicitous eyes. He took her hand and squeezed it hard.

He could hardly wait to get her on her own.

He was relieved to find his flat much more orderly than he had left it. It must have been one of the days for his little treasure Maria from the Philippines to dash around with duster and detergent.

He poured himself a whisky. 'Drink, angel?'

She shook her head. He looked up and saw that she was standing in the centre of the room, staring into space. Her face was utterly still and as white as chalk. Poor sweet must have had a frightful shock, seeing him about to go down in front of the the wheels of a four-litre Jag.

He sat down. 'Come here, my sweet. You look bushed. Come and let Charles take the strain.' He opened his arms.

Obdiently, as though sleepwalking, she came towards him and allowed him to draw her down on to his knee.

The scene which had run in Charles's head was now ready to play in reality. And it started off most satisfactorily. She made no protests when he started to unpeel her from her clothes. She simply rested quietly in his arms, her eyes faintly drugged-looking.

They got as far as the part where Charles administered a variety of caresses to her breasts. He was pleased to hear some very satisfactory moans in response. He was just about to turn her body to lie in a different postition, when she jerked herself into a tight ball, clasping her hands around her stomach.

'Christ, angel!'

She was panting slightly, her lips parted. It was a very similar picture to that of hot, lusty passion. But it was not long before he realized there was something entirely different from passion at the root of her moans and contorted features.

Gasping apologies, she dashed suddenly from the room, a small distressed figure, naked apart from her stockings and garter belt. He heard the bathroom door snap shut.

Then sounds of dreadful sick wretching.

Poor pet, she must have eaten something that disagreed with her. On the train, most likely. Transport food was notoriously dodgy.

He sighed. Fate seemed to manage to intervene at the most hellishly inconvenient times. What rotten luck. For this to happen, just when he thought he was in, so to speak. He settled down with his glass of whisky and resigned himself to the temporary role of comforter and brow mopper.

Still, with any luck, she might have snapped out of it in the morning.

François paced the ground floor of this house. He dare not go to bed. He could not contemplate the torture of lying awake seeing pictures of Zoe as she had been on their two journeys – Zoe moving through a whole rainbow of moods. From shining gold to indigo. Zoe wistful, sitting in a little room in Yorkshire and being united with her past.

And now – Zoe with Charles. The idea of it sickened him. It made him go cold with fear and revulsion.

As he pictured her in Charles's arms, the pain was like lightning striking. He found himself looking on at some moment in the future when Charles placed his hands on Zoe's breasts, spread her thighs.

She had told him that he, François, was the only man who had touched her soul. And that was something he must hold on to, to survive the re-awakened agony of parting with her and standing back whilst she walked into the arms of another man.

But he feared that Zoe did not understand that, for a man, the thought of his woman being *bodily* touched was more indescribably painful than could ever be conveyed in words.

He felt so intimately bound with Zoe not only spiritually, but also bodily. It was as though each part of his body knew each part of hers.

356

He recalled the sight and sound of her. The touch and smell and taste of her. He remembered the way her pupils dilated as he entered her, the rapt expression on her face, the registering of a tiny exquisite shock to feel him inside her. He recalled the rising and falling of her body against his, the way in which her lips parted and then closed as he changed the rhythm of his thrusts.

And at the end, when they were tranquil again, she would lie against him and their breathing would synchronize. He would lift the damp strands of dark hair from her cheek and kiss the white skin beneath.

He told himself that she was not his creature. Not his 'thing' to possess. He had always despised men who thought of women in that way, as though they were bitches on heat, to be hotly defended from eager sniffing rivals.

But with Zoe, it had simply been a feeling that she was his, in just the same way as he was hers. That any other man should possess her, or any other woman claim him, was simply unthinkable.

But the unthinkable had now become reality, and the jealousy was of an intensity he had never before experienced. It stabbed through his body like a rapier, lacerating his heart, piercing his groin.

He stopped trying to shut the pictures out. Charles and Zoe. Zoe and Charles. He would let the pictures come, do their worst. If you ran things through in your mind for long enough, over and over, then they lost some of their power, didn't they?

He went through to the kitchen and examined the contents of the fridge. He would do something tangible and practical. He would make preparations for the

357

supper he and Leonore would share when she returned from her short holiday.

He picked up a knife. He sliced an onion and put it on the oven to soften in a pan of warmed butter. He peeled a clove of garlic, chopped it very finely and added it to the onion. Then he got out tomatoes, looked through his pots of herbs.

Later on, at the sink, he very carefully washed the kitchen knives and wiped down the chopping board.

Focus on the here and now, he told himself. Take notice of the shape of this knife, the shine of its blade, the dull black of its handle.

He waited for himself to grow calmer.

CHAPTER 32

Marina browsed in the High Street bookshop and splashed out on a new cookery book. She had been attracted by its title: *Friends for Supper*. It sounded like cannibalism, which must be less bother than *haute cuisine*.

She was alarmed when she opened out the book on the kitchen table and gave herself time to consult it fully. The titles of the dishes were decidedly alarming.

Saffron-Scented Sea Food Stew with Tuscan Bean Purée. Marina shook her head. No, I don't think so.

Artichokes with Shallots, Lemon Grass and Green Goddess Dressing. Oh, dear!

Everything was meant to be put with everything else and something extra besides. The preparation methods, described on the cover as 'stunningly simple', appeared to Marina to be stunningly complex.

She leafed through. The pictures of the food were beautifully artistic. She felt like cutting them out, pinning them up on the wall and then rustling up a couple of simple scrambled eggs.

She found herself spending quite a bit of time wondering what sort of food Teddy Penrose would most enjoy. When it had dawned on her that she was actually quite anxious to put on a good show for him, she had had a hearty chuckle at her own expense.

She had never used to be worried about cooking for guests. In her young days she had been an instinctive and imaginative cook who could whip up dainty dishes with the minimum of effort and have her guests gasping with admiration.

'Ah, how have the mighty fallen,' she told Risk, balancing her new book in one hand whilst prodding a red pepper which was sweltering in the grill pan. The idea was for it to obligingly roast to the point where the skin could be gently levered from the flesh. But at this particular point the vegetable appeared to be a volcanic eruption of charred black swellings wreathed in blue smoke.

She threw it in the bin and had a frantic re-think.

'Friends for supper, indeed,' she muttered ferociously, tossing the book on to the dresser.

Risk looked up questioningly.

'Friends for supper,' she explained to him. 'You'd like that. I'll bet you'd be only too happy to devour some of your canine friends at any hour of the day or night, if I gave you a chance.'

Teddy Penrose arrived punctually to the minute. He stood planted in her doorway; a huge, smiling hulk of teddy bear-man, carrying a bottle of chilled champagne and a horde of long-stemmed roses. Red ones.

Marina shook her head wonderingly. 'Teddy!' she chided. 'What's all this?'

'They were all that was left,' he said regretfully, eyeing the small spiky dog cavorting beside his ankles. It seemed

360

intent on rousing the entire neighbourhood with its virtuoso barking performance. He bent down and patted it affectionately, bringing about an instant and welcome silence.

'I don't believe you for a moment!' Marina laughed.

She led him through to the kitchen, a startling figure in her original 1970s' burgundy velvet flares, topped with a loose 1990s' black open-knit top, purchased the day before at an expense completely at odds with her means.

Teddy opened the champagne whilst Marina attended to the serving out of gently grilled sausages sprinkled with chives and creamy mashed potatoes enlivened with a squeeze of garlic purée.

'Bangers and mash!' he exclaimed in delight. 'My mother used to give it to us for supper every Thursday evening. It was a real economy dish. And now people pay a fortune to eat it in smart clubs in the West End.'

He poured the champagne and they raised their glasses to each other.

'I've read your book,' Marina told him. 'I was impressed.'

'Ah. Good. Thank you.'

'You'll make a fortune, Teddy. That book is a supremely cunning mixture of carefully researched information and pure entertainment.'

'Good, good!' Teddy's eyes lit with pleasure. 'Now, tell me,' he commanded, 'how is your young friend with the gift for extrasensory perception?'

'In a most awful mess,' said Marina, recalling Zoe's ravaged and strained face when she had called to collect Elle the day following her journey to Yorkshire with François.

361

Zoe had been ominously subdued and withdrawn. She had lifted the puppy into her arms and buried her face in the furry warm body as though she would have liked to melt into it. She had smiled wistfully at Marina, and thanked her most gratefully for caring for the dog. But beyond that she had said very little.

François, however, who was usually such a private man, holding his feelings to himself, had been much more communicative.

He had given Marina a vivid and detailed account of Zoe's latest dream. His face had been contorted with pain as he came to the end of the story she had told to him. And its damning conclusion.

'I don't seem to have any power to do anything to change her mind,' he had said bitterly. 'I simply have to stand aside and watch her link herself with a man I know she doesn't truly love.'

The hurting in his eyes had been dreadful to see. *Help me, help me*, he had been calling out silently.

But Marina had been as powerless as he.

'I've thought a good deal about what you told me when we met before,' Teddy said reflectively as they prepared to eat. 'Zoe's first premonition – the dream of the air disaster – strikes me as typical of a genuine extrasensory experience. It fits very snugly with the accounts of those of my subjects who could provide independent confirmation of their dreams or visions.'

'You mean the ones who could prove that they had reported the premonition before the event?'

'I'm always wary of that word "prove", as you know. But yes, those with apparently reliable witnesses to confirm the prediction.'

'Zoe certainly had that. François is highly sceptical of the paranormal. I'm one hundred per cent convinced that his report of what Zoe told him before the crash took place was both genuine and accurate.'

Teddy forked up some potato. He paused, caught up in his thoughts, fork poised in mid air. 'Yes, yes. Quite. Now the other issue we have to consider is how the events of the premonition match with those of the real event. The two need not be mirror images, but they must be close enough to be recognizable as linked to each other.'

'And in this case?'

Teddy made a small balancing movement with his hands. 'Maybe, maybe not.'

'Too much of a coincidence, surely to be ignored? A young woman dreams of an air crash and sees in her dream the man who is the ex-husband of one of the victims.'

'Highly intriguing, certainly. If Zoe had been inclined to tell all to the tabloids, they would have had a field day,' Teddy said drily.

Marina smiled.

There were some moments of silent reflection as Teddy devoted himself to eating more sausage before it became completely cold.

'But you see,' he said, laying down his fork, 'this business of Zoe "seeing" François in her dream bothers me a little. She seems to have seen him with great clarity: his facial and bodily characteristics. That kind of detailed and specific imaging of the characteristics of people who have never been seen before by the "dreamer" are pretty rare.'

363

'All right. But what other explanation could there be besides ESP?'

'That's a fascinating question.' Teddy dabbed at his mouth with his napkin and took another sip of champagne.

Quietly, Marina stacked the empty plates and replaced them with dishes of fresh fruit salad.

'Let's consider Zoe,' Teddy said. 'Think about her past, her history. Her father dies when she's very young, leaving her in the care of her suggestible and superstitious mother. A pleasant and sociable woman, but psychologically fragile, from what one can gather. This young girl soon finds herself feeling responsible for the welfare of her mother. Mother and daughter become very close. They have a rich social life, but they are, in the main, dependent on each other. Or should I say that the mother is mainly dependent on the daughter and perhaps unconsciously wants to keep her for herself.'

Marina sighed. Nodded.

'Zoe is coming up to twenty, but she doesn't have serious relationships with men . . .' Teddy looked up. 'That's right, isn't it? You didn't actually tell me that there hadn't been a significant man for Zoe before François, but that's the conclusion I reached when I started thinking about it.'

'Absolutely right, from what Zoe told me.'

'Because ..?'

'Because she feared that, if she became too involved with a man, her mother might feel supplanted. Zoe saw her mother as someone who would always need caring for. To have a serious love affair, to consider getting married, would be like a betrayal of her mother. A kind of desertion.'

'Precisely!' Teddy beamed. 'We are of two minds,' he told Marina, his eyes sparkling.

'And then the loved and needy mother suddenly dies, leaving her daughter free,' mused Marina. 'But a lonely figure, cut adrift. She gets herself a fulfilling job. She keeps herself busy, being a social butterfly in her leisure hours. But, basically, she's still alone.'

'Exactly, exactly. Now, what happens then?'

'She directs her affections to the children she teaches.' Marina shrugged. It was so obvious. So sad. 'One child in particular. Leonore Rogier.'

Teddy smiled. He topped up Marina's glass. Then he topped up his own and leaned back in his chair. 'It seems to me that there lies a possible explanation to François's appearing in her dream before she had properly met him.' He raised his eyebrows in a question.

Marina nodded. 'It's possible, I suppose, that at some time before the dream Zoe might have caught a glimpse of François, without knowing it. She could have seen him as one of a crowd of parents waiting in the play area after school . . .'

'Just what I had thought. Or, alternatively, she could have "seen" the father in the child's face. Are they alike?'

'In bone structure, yes. But very different in colouring.'

Teddy shrugged. 'Ah well, all we're doing is concocting hunches. And they probably don't affect the authenticity of the reported premonition, when all is said and done.'

'Really. I'm intrigued,' Marina smiled. 'Come on,

365

then. Let's have some conclusions! I bet you've got some. Does Zoe's premonition stand up to the severe Teddy Penrose scrutiny? Your words won't go beyond these four walls.'

Teddy paused. Suddenly he looked deeply serious. He said, 'All right, then. My assessment is that, on balance, Zoe's disaster dream deserves to be quoted alongside the other bona-fide reports of premonitions based on ESP.'

'Well, well!'

'So there you are. But does any of this help the star-crossed lovers?' Teddy asked mischievously. 'ESP is one thing. Love is quite another.'

Marina raised a warning finger. 'Young love is *very* serious,' she admonished.

'All love is serious,' he agreed mildly. 'But I truly doubt if any of what we've talked over will be any help in that respect.'

'Wait a moment!' Marina said sharply. 'There is one more thing.'

'Yes?'

'Zoe is reporting a current dream. A recurring dream.'

Teddy listened attentively as she repeated, as accurately as she could, what François had told her about Zoe's new dream.

Even before she finished, he began to shake his head.

'That's not a premonition,' he said firmly. 'Premonitions rarely recur with such frequency. And the content has a strange kind of beauty about it. The way you've described it makes it seem lyrical, almost romantic'

'That's how it was told to me,' Marina said. 'But then the woman who dreamed it and the man who told it to me are quite desperately in love.'

366

'It's a classic dream based on perfectly normal human anxiety. We all of us carry around worries,' Teddy said. 'And most of us have dreams about them at some time or another.'

Marina glanced across to him. So Teddy Penrose had anxious dreams. She was beginning to think he was human after all. Very human, in fact.

'Which reminds me,' he added. 'With regard to Zoe's other dream about the little boy Stefan. That seemed to be less of a premonition experience than another anxiety dream, surely. Poor Zoe was probably in a highly and suggestible state at the point she had this dream. Besides which, it was quite reasonable and rational to be concerned about that particular child, who clearly had a number of problems, being separated from his parents and living in a strange country. He was difficult to control, impulsive and he came to school every morning on busy roads. It doesn't take much of leap to get to Zoe's unconscious worries about him, which eventually came out in her dream.'

'Hmm,' said Marina, inclined to agree. 'I suppose there's a marvellous symmetry about our hidden thoughts and our dreams.' She stopped. Sighed.

'Marina,' Teddy said gently, 'François and Zoe will find their own salvation. For one thing, Zoe's ESP experiences are very unlikely to persist. My research clearly points to that.'

'Yes.' She smiled at him. 'I'm sure you're right.'

They took their coffee into the sitting room. Marina poured Teddy a large whisky.

He looked around him. 'Nice room. Clean strong lines and colours.' He bent to inspect the hi-fi system. 'Good

367

heavens. Genuine 1970s, untouched. It must be a true collector's piece.'

'No doubt. Maybe that's one of the compensations of getting older,' she commented with irony. 'Becoming collectable.'

She wondered if he would think that sounded a touch flirtatious, and decided that she didn't mind if he did. 'It was Colin's,' she said.

'Ah,' said Teddy. 'So, you've hung on to his treasured hi-fi! Could this be a touch of sentiment?'

She shrugged. Unaccountably, tears pricked her eye-lids.

'It was right for us to get a divorce,' she said. 'But when it actually happened, it was like having some vital organ removed.'

'Yes.' Teddy spoke very softly. 'Oh, yes.' He looked at her and his face under the shaggy grey mop was inde-scribably sweet and tender.

'I was shamelessly besotted when I married Colin,' Marina told Teddy, softly stroking Risk, who was snuggled at her feet. 'When he looked at me I used to go all warm and liquidy inside.' She sighed. 'In those days, you had to get married to be allowed to go to bed with someone. They wouldn't even let you go on the pill if the wedding bells weren't about to ring.'

He laughed. 'It was another world.'

'Yes,' she agreed. 'It was. And looking back at the hot, panting Marina who dashed into marriage with her cool, grey-eyed Colin, she seems like another person.' She sipped her whisky, in the rare mood for confiding. 'You know, Teddy, people often say that whilst your body changes over the years, the person inside you remains the same. Not for me! I sometimes feel it's quite the reverse; as though another person had squeezed under my skin, making short work of the former inhabitant.'

He chuckled. 'So, what happened?'

Marina rested her head on her hand. 'Oh, we were fine for a time. Then came the business I told you about, how I had to give up my work. And after that I had the children, which was nice. And then Colin started to get himself a reputation as the Don Juan of his research department, which was not at all nice. He actually believed I was blissfully ignorant. The cheek of it. He used to appoint a new junior assistant each year. And before the first term had gone by, he would have got her into bed.' She paused. 'Eventually I had enough.'

'And?'

'Oh, I behaved with splendid drama. I cut out the crotches from his underpants and his trousers. And then I cut the sleeves off his jackets. And then I hacked the whole lot into tiny pieces and presented them to him in the lab, at work. In the presence of the girl of the moment.'

Teddy winced. 'My heart does bleed a little for any chap on the receiving end of that.'

'Mmm, it was pretty off-limits stuff.'

'Splendid stuff!' He rubbed his hands, his eyes twinkled.

'We chugged along for a few more years.' Her face stilled. 'And then a young man joined Colin's team. Very bright, very charismatic, very sexy. He was rising thirty and I was rising forty. He made me feel like the most desirable woman in the world.' She stopped. She looked into Teddy Penrose's intriguing crumpled face and felt the twitch of some thread long broken.

'And?' he prompted gently.

'I threw up everything and ran off with him. And therein lay my ruin.' She shot Teddy a wry and rueful glance. 'The idyll lasted less than a year. He went out one morning and didn't come back. I fell to pieces. I felt so useless and inadequate, and so foolish to have been taken in.' She gave a dry laugh. 'I had hardly any money and no job. I'd lost all confidence in my own judgement. Well, think of it this way, I'd virtually thrown away my career and made two disastrous choices with men. Not the most glittering of track records!'

'What then?'

'Colin gave me half the proceeds of the house, so that I could buy a place of my own, which meant that at least I wasn't on the streets. After that there was a succession of unskilled jobs. And here I am. Getting steadily older and perhaps no wiser.'

He shook his head. 'It seems that, like Zoe, you need a good man and true,' he said.

She looked at him. Yes, she thought. There was a small fizz of pure excitement.

'I remember you being an exceedingly bright and compelling girl,' he said slowly. 'And now you're an able and compelling woman with all the benefit of life's experiences. Formidable.'

She flashed him a sharp glance. 'And you were a brilliant and bumptious young man, Teddy. And now you're a brilliant, highly successful and patronizing middle-aged one!'

'Patronizing! Am I? I suppose I am.' He roared with laughter.

They talked more. It became late.

He got up to go.

'You could stay. I have a guest room,' Marina said.

He smiled. 'I have a cat to go home to.'

'Ah. Of course.'

He bent to pat Risk. 'What will happen when our two animals meet?'

'A good deal of snapping and hissing, I should imagine. They'll soon get over it.'

'Yes.' His eyes moved over her. 'Will you and Risk come for Christmas?' he asked with low urgency. 'Say yes.'

Marina stared into his face and saw his tenderness and humanity. Also his loneliness. She felt warmth steal through every nerve. She smiled and nodded. She said musingly, 'Teddy, I came to find you in order to help a friend. But now I think I'm going to help myself.'

She put up her arms around his neck, and then felt herself most deliciously enclosed in a great bear-like embrace.

CHAPTER 33

When Charles went to wake Zoe on the morning following her sudden sickness, he found her already dressed, perched on the edge of the bed, pale and forlorn.

'You poor pet,' he said, sitting down beside her and putting his arm around her shoulders. 'You look decidedly rough.'

She nodded. Her face looked dull and chalky, all the life drained from it.

'Should I call the doc?' Charles asked.

She shook her head. 'I am sick,' she told him, her voice low and shaky. 'But I don't think a doctor can help.'

'You just need time, eh?'

'Yes.' Gently disengaging herself from his protective hug, she stood up. She reached out and touched his cheek. 'I'm going to go home for a while,' she said.

'You could stay here, angel. No problem. My little treasure who comes to clean will keep an eye on you, I'm sure.'

'I'll be better at home,' she said. 'And less trouble all round!'

He called a taxi for her and kissed her as he handed her in.

She looked up at him as the taxi set off. Her eyes were huge and full of wistful tenderness.

For a moment Charles felt slightly overwhelmed. As though he had bitten off far more than he truly wanted to chew.

He went back into his flat and paced about for a minute or two. And then, rather to his surprise, he found himself leafing through his telephone book, idly going through the list of former flames. He placed his hand on the phone. And then lifted it up and pulled out the aerial.

Zoe directed the taxi to drive to Marina's, from where she collected Elle. She was glad there was the excuse of the taxi waiting, so as not to run the risk of another encounter with François. Also to have a genuine excuse not to stay and talk. Sometime in the future she would like to talk to Marina. On and on.

But not this morning. She was so exhausted she felt she could barely speak. She needed to be alone with her thoughts.

She took Elle into the park, keeping the dizzily gambolling puppy on the lead, close to her heels. They walked for an hour or so and then made their way back to Zoe's house.

After she had fed Elle, Zoe cut some slices from a loaf of bread and forced herself to eat them with some butter and honey. She made strong hot chocolate and sat down to drink it at the table in her kitchen where she and François had enjoyed shared precious moments.

She thought of her Uncle William and the things he had said to her the day before. She thought of what she had learned from them: how her mother had interpreted

373

the words of a fortune teller on the pier and taken them to heart as some sort of prophecy. A prophecy of doom concerning her daughter. Her mother had become convinced of some future unseen force that would brood over her innocent daughter, causing untold damage and distress. It seemed to Zoe that the story was reminiscent of the tale of the Sleeping Beauty and the threats of the wicked fairy concerning the needle that would prick her finger.

Over time her mother's anxieties had driven her to wrap her daughter in a cloak of protectiveness. A mantle of illusions and half-truths, fantasies and dreams, irrational fears. Seeing danger everywhere.

And because she was her mother and Zoe had truly loved her, the power of her influence had been awesome...

Zoe looked up, surprised to find that the room had grown dark. She must have been sitting in exactly the same position since the late morning. She was chilled and stiff, her limbs and spine aching. She got up and crossed to the window, realizing that many hours must have passed during her waking reverie. The setting sun was no more than a huge incandescent glow, almost completely swallowed up now behind the dark horizon. A beam of silver moonshine came through the window, laying itself across the length of the dark shape of her table like a great silver sword.

Zoe stared into the darkness, pulling at the threads of her thoughts, trying to draw them together into a knot of conclusion. I have gone some way down the road which was marked out by my mother's footsteps, she told herself. My mother called and I followed. When I started out I was a child. And then I was a young woman, struggling to find a path of my own. But now I am grown up and I have found the path I want. And I must take it.

Suddenly the way ahead was clear and illuminated with brilliant light.

Without any further delay, with no trace of fear, only a marvellous, blissful anticipation, she picked up the phone and dialled François's number.

Leonore got out her little red case from the wardrobe. She put in her toothbrush and toothpaste, her brush and comb and her nightie. She paused to think.

François came silently to stand in the doorway. 'Can I help?'

'Clean socks, clean vest, clean pants, change of shoes,' recited Leonore. 'That's what you always say, Daddy. And I've done my tooth things already.'

She set about gathering the articles she had mentioned.

'What time shall I come and collect you on Sunday?' he enquired.

'Melanie said four o'clock. And her mummy and daddy said you have to stay for a cup of tea and a cake.'

'Very well. I'll be there.' François smiled at her very tenderly. He felt a surge of love and protectiveness. 'Melanie seems to be a good friend,' he commented.

Leonore looked up at him. 'Yes,' she said.

François hoped to God that her quick, instinctive child's understanding would fail to penetrate to the medley of strong emotions currently swamping him. Perhaps the only positive feeling was his pleasure for

Leonore to have become a regular visitor to the home of a proper family. Melanie had two parents, a brother and sister. Her house was full of noise and bustle. François had often wondered if Leonore felt lonely and cut off, with only a sad, troubled father for company at her own home.

'You're a very well-organized girl,' he said, watching her lay her clothes neatly in the case.

'I'm very old in my head,' Leonore told him.

'What a strange thing to say, darling.' He smiled. 'But I think you're right.'

'It was Zoe who said so.' Leonore's hands were still for a moment. She did not look up. Then she continued her packing.

'Ah. I see. Well, then, Zoe was right.'

Leonore turned. 'You said Zoe's name – out loud!'

François felt a jolt. 'Yes.'

Leonore sat on the bed. She bowed her head and rubbed her hands over her knees.

'Daddy?'

'Yes?'

'Can Zoe come at Christmas?'

François's heart gave a great buck. He had not expected this.

He sat down beside Leonore. 'My sweet one, I'm not sure,' he said.

'I want her to come. And you'd like her to come, wouldn't you, Daddy?' Leonore burst out with great feeling. 'Wouldn't you?' she insisted.

He could not speak.

Leonore turned and put her arms round him. Not seeking comfort, rather offering it.

He felt a tightening in his throat. A swollen tenderness. 'Oh, *chérie*,' he said.

'Will you ask and see what she says?'

François sighed.

'Daddy?'

They heard the sound of a horn outside. They went down the stairs together, François carrying Leonore's case. She turned back to look at him. The question was still in her eyes. It was a question François had already answered for himself. Quite a few hours previously, following his agitated and sleepless night.

Zoe heard the tone burring rhythmically in her ear. She stood, the phone pressed against her face, just letting it go on, sure in her conviction that a connection would be made.

Minutes passed. She imagined him, out on the road somewhere. On his bike or in the underground. Walking through the streets, making his way home. Getting nearer, closer.

Through the regular burrs of François's phone, she heard the ring of her own doorbell. Elle stirred in her deep puppy sleep, made a little whimper. Stood up, alert and listening.

'François!' Zoe cried out. 'François!'

She ran to the door, almost falling over the puppy in her haste to get there. She saw the tall black figure through the glass and her heart leapt with joy. Catching Elle in her arms lest she dash out into the road, she greeted him, pulling him inside with her free hand. Putting up her face for his kiss.

'Oh, my poor darling. My poor wounded darling,' he

exclaimed, seeing the white face, the crumpled clothes and the ruffled hair.

'No, no. I'm not wounded. Not sick any more.'

He held her away from him. 'Something has happened,' he said slowly. 'Something quite new.'

'Yes.'

'Tell me. Whatever it is, darling, you know you can trust me now.'

She laid the palms of her hands flat against his chest. 'I've discovered for the first time, who I really am, and who I want to become.'

François felt sweat break out on his forehead.

'And it's because of you, Françoise,' she added softly. 'It's you I have to thank.' The words were said with quiet determination, with sweet simplicity.

His eyes moved over her face.

'You have me to thank! I felt that I was the one who had almost killed you.'

She shook her head slowly. 'Your being there with me when I went to see my uncle – it was your presence and your thoughts all around me that made it possible for me to understand things about my past that have always been hidden and mysterious before. And it was knowing that you would always be there for me that helped me to see why things have happened as they have in the present. And the way ahead into the future.'

'Thank God, thank God,' he breathed. He drew her to him and kissed her until they were both dazed.

When at last they drew back a little, gazing and gazing into each other's eyes, he ventured to ask, 'The dreams? Are they still coming?' He felt himself hardly daring to breathe. Did the change in her way of seeing things mean that now she would come to him forever? That Charles must become a figure of her past? Or simply that she had learned to be at peace with herself whatever new obstacles were to be endured. Oh, dear God!

'Zoe?' he whispered, laying his hand on the top of her arm, exerting just a little pressure.

'I was becoming a slave to the images of my sleeping mind,' she said. 'A prisoner of my dreams.'

'And now?'

'It's time for me to believe in my waking mind and the reality in front of my eyes and ears.' She reached out and touched him with her fingertips, his eyelids, the hard straight line of his nose, the warmth of his neck, the firm broad shoulder bones. 'This is real,' she breathed.

She took his hand and placed it on her throat, and then pulled it lower to carve out a path over the contours of her breasts and her waist and hips. A slow heat rose within her at the thought of making love once again with François.

'Darling,' he gasped. 'Please! Now! Before anything else.'

She pulled his head down to hers. 'The usually immaculate Zoe is creased, sticky and sweaty and quite unfit to be loved by her wonderful François,' she teased.

A slow smile lit his face. He took her hand and led her to the bathroom. He switched on the taps.

She kicked off her shoes. She stood watching him. Giving her fullest consent for him to do whatever he wished.

'Come here,' he said. He enclosed her in his arms, then turned her and slowly pulled down the zip at the back of her dress. As the fabric slithered down into a brightly coloured puddle at her feet, he reached his hands around her and gently held her breasts. Slowly he undid her bra and it, too, dropped to the ground.

This was the moment for which Zoe had longed. She shut her eyes, feeding on the touch of his fingers, savouring the feast of exquisite pleasure as the months of longing for him came to fruition at last.

Steam was rising from the bath, wrapping them in a moist haze. Zoe rotated herself in his arms, raising her arms to place around his neck, offering her lovely breasts to his eyes and his lips.

Lingeringly, he kissed her salty shoulders. Then his lips moved down across the tender membranes of her neck and the hollows of her collar bones. Now his tongue was teasing her swelling nipples. A low moaning was sounding in her throat. The contact between them was electric.

Gently pulling off her lace panties, he lifted her into his arms and stood her in the bath. As she reached out to unbutton his shirt, he began to caress her with wetted soapy hands. His fingers slipped and slid all over her – arms, neck, breasts. Slowly, slowly, they worked, sending the water cascading over her arms and hips and thighs in a shower of piercing thrills. She arched in ecstasy as his fingers finally slid between her legs, parting her flesh. She felt him coax the tender folds so that they began to unfurl and swell like flower petals in warm summer rain.

Swiftly he pulled off his own clothes. Lifting her from the water, he laid her on the carpet. 'Come to me,' she whispered, and instantly his beautiful shaft was enveloped deep within the secret darkness of her femaleness.

For long, wondrous moments they moved, locked together in an urgent dance of pleasure and love and deep commitment.

Later they lay in bed and stroked each other with long sweeps of their hands. And then made love again, until at last they were exhausted and fell asleep.

The next day they lay in each other's arms, not wanting to get up and get dressed, reluctant to do anything which would curtail their newfound intimacy.

'You must go, darling,' François said at last. 'You must go and tell him today.'

'Yes. I must. He'll be at Percival. He said he wanted to spend more time there.'

'He'll be expecting you, then?'

'Yes.'

'Shall I come, too?' His dark eyes were full of concern. And a raw dark streak of jealousy also.

Zoe smiled. 'No.' She leaned to kiss his eyelids. 'I would rather as little blood was shed as possible.'

She dressed swiftly, putting on a thick Aran sweater and furry cord trousers. Country wear. Charles's parents would at least approve of her choice in that respect.

On a raw and sullen December morning, Percival was framed by a lowered winter sky that formed a soft grey lid over it.

In the garden where the mist was like tiny particles of ice, Charles's mother was plodding through the dormant flower beds. Pausing by the holly hedge, she got out her secateurs and began to clip short branches, dropping

381

them in her wicker trug. She spotted Zoe arriving and raised a hand in greeting. Zoe slowed the car and waved back, then drove on to park beside the front door.

In the hall a huge spruce tree was decorated with dangling wooden figures of animals and birds. No glitter or tinsel here, just swathes of dark red ribbon. And hanging from the huge dangling chandelier overhead was a mass of unadorned misletoe.

Zoe looked around her, contemplating the beauty and symmetry of the gracious hall. Suddenly she had an image of another woman standing in just this spot in the future. Some unknown woman who would be brought to this house by Charles. Someone who could love both him and the house.

She found Charles in the dining-room. Alone, much to her relief.

'Angel!' He stood up, came forward and kissed her. He drew back, sensing something about her, something different and telling.

She sat down at the table with him. She took his hand. And very quietly and honestly she told him all that was necessary.

She told him that she could not marry him because, although she was fond of him and always would be, he was not her true and only love. She explained to him that she had unwittingly used him to comfort her at a time when she had been undergoing great turbulence and been in great need. And for that she was deeply sorry.

As she spoke she saw his expression change from one of concern, through to disbelief. A rusty stain appeared in his cheeks. He got up, turned sharply away from her and went to stare out of the window. He thrust his hands into his pockets jingling the coins.

'Christ!' he muttered shakily after a time. 'This is a bit of a facer.'

'Yes.'

'Are you back with him? *The French lover.*' The last three words were said with sarcastic emphasis.

'Yes.'

Charles gave a sharp braying laugh. It grew louder and stronger. He swung round. The flush in his face had cleared. He was himself again. 'So, angel, you've come to tell me I've lost my fatal hold over you? Is that it?'

'Yes,' Zoe said smiling wistfully at him. 'I suppose that's exactly it.' *Oh, Charles, if you only knew the whole story.*

'If you ask me, my pet, I'd say I never really had it. And things haven't been exactly tickety-boo lately, have they? I'm not a complete fool; I know the writing's on the wall when the girl you're going to marry has to run to the bathroom to throw up when you lay a finger on her.'

She would not be drawn on that point. It was true, so what was there to be said? She laid the diamond ring on the plate beside him. 'Can you forgive me, Charles?'

Charles picked up the ring, turning the gold hoop through his fingers so that needles of light flashed from the stone. Relief was flooding through him in great waves, enlivening him, astonishing him. Normally he hated to be the one given the push. Moreover, he had fancied Zoe was indeed the girl for him. But now, watching her beautiful intense face, the huge seascape

383

eyes searching and penetrating his, he felt as though he had been sprung from a velvet-lined trap.

Vaguely, he thought of a future when he would bring a sexy, big-hipped and horse-faced bride to Percival. She would bully him unmercifully, be a lioness in bed, have sturdy babies and turn a blind eye to his occasional wolf-like prowling.

In the meantime, whilst he would enjoy the renewal of his freedom, he thought he would make a New Year's resolution to steady down a bit. Rather more work, a little less play. His parents would be as pleased as a box of monkeys.

'Charles?' she prompted. 'Say something, please.'

'You've astonished me, angel.' He faced her head on, and now she could see a rakish gleam in his eye.

She saw that, far from being dismayed, he was becoming gradually more and more exhilarated with the notion of the return of his old bachelor freedom. She slumped against the back of the chair. Oh, thank God!

He sat down again, and pulled his chair to nudge against hers. 'Have I been an absolute sod?' he asked.

'No.'

He took her slender hand and patted it.

'No hard feelings?' she asked with concern, thinking how shallow those words sounded in the circumstances.

'None.' He shot her a wicked glance. 'And for a randy bastard like me, that's quite a confession to make.'

It was an hour or so before Zoe finally drove away from Percival. She had wanted to see both of Charles's parents, to explain things to them with honesty and simplicity.

As always, they had been grave and kind and understanding. They had expressed, not anger, but regret. They had shaken her hand and kissed her cheek with great sincerity. But she knew that, deep down, they had been relieved.

She felt a huge and urgent need to get back to François. As she made the turn into the main road, the car swung round to face due south. A shimmering winter sun broke through the clouds, striking against the windscreen, dazzling her.

She pulled down the sun visor, her eyes blinking against the brilliance.

Whatever threats had darkened her past, or might beset her in the future, when it came down to it she found there was no choice but to go where the light beckoned.

CHAPTER 34

In Teddy Penrose's windmill, the enticing fragrance of roasting goose and lemon stuffing stole from the kitchen and curled itself around the vast cone of the hall and the stairway.

From either side of the oven a small wiry dog and a languid Siamese cat occupied themselves in soaking up the bliss-making smells emerging from the oven. From time to time one of them would shift a paw or twitch an ear, whereupon the other would stiffen, eyeing the opposition with renewed suspicion.

Following a ragged start, Marina's dog and Teddy's cat had reached a state of truce-like tolerance.

Whilst the animals sat on guard beside the oven, Marina and Teddy flew around the dining room, clearing up the remains of their delicious tête-à-tête Christmas Eve supper, and setting the table for the Christmas Day dinner.

Teddy had served her baked ham with mustard sauce, crispy roast potatoes and creamed spinach. Warmed mince pies and cheese afterwards.

'A man who heads up a prestigious research department and writes best sellers really shouldn't be able to cook like a wizard as well,' Marina had chided with a wry smile of appreciation.

Afterwards, they had sat on the floor beside the spitting and crackling log fire, had sipped whisky and talked until the logs sank down into a grey and rose mesh of ash.

'I think you know what you'll be taking on, if we become lovers,' he had said very gently, taking her hands in his as the hands of the clock moved towards midnight.

'I think you do, too,' she had replied. Already his face was becoming very dear and familiar. She supposed it was because the two of them had a tiny particle of shared past from so many years before.

Ignoring Risk's mounting indignation, she had thrown her arms around him. 'I can't believe this!' she had laughed, kissing him.

'I don't want "living together",' Teddy had said after a while. 'I'm very old-fashioned.'

'Yes,' she had agreed fondly.

'I want marriage,' he had said.

'Yes,' she had agreed.

And at that moment the clock had given a small whirr and begun to chime out the arrival of Christmas.

'Four adults, one child, two dogs, one cat,' said Teddy with anticipatory satisfaction as he polished the glasses and set them out. 'Last year, Christmas dinner was just a lonely man keeping company with his mournful feline.'

Marina smiled across at him as she twisted twigs of bright shiny holly around red candlesticks and set out multi-coloured crackers on each plate. She thought of the presents waiting in place under the huge tree in Teddy's sitting-room, where the carpet was already showered with a thousand fallen needles. She felt an almost childish thrill of expectancy at the magical prospect of seeing the expression on various faces as each one was opened.

For Marina, too, recent Christmas Days had been wistful and forlorn affairs.

Zoe, François and Leonore arrived punctually at one o'clock. Leonore was proudly and lovingly bearing Elle in her arms.

'Elle really likes me,' she confided to Marina. 'Zoe says she can be my special pet.'

She crouched down to stroke Risk, who was clamouring for his own share of love and attention. Teddy's Siamese, meanwhile, had leapt up onto the kitchen unit, surveying the scene from a lofty height, reserving himself a prime position for supervising the carving of the goose.

Much later, when they were all full and satisfied, dogs and humans set out for a walk on the common whilst the cat slumbered in deep contentment in front of the blazing logs.

François and Zoe walked with their arms entwined around each other. Leonore, who had been hanging on to Zoe's free hand, disengaged herself and fell back to walk with Marina, Teddy and the dogs.

'Daddy and Zoe are going to get married,' she announced, looking sparkling and triumphant.

'Good for them, and well done!' said Teddy.

'When I was very small,' Leonore confided softly, 'I used to think that, when I grew up, I'd marry Daddy. But now I'm six I know that's silly.'

Marina and Teddy nodded gravely.

'Daddy and Zoe and me are going to see my *grandpère* Rogier next week. He's French,' she explained. 'Daddy's French, too, and I'm half-French. And Zoe's English. But she can speak French nearly as well as Daddy and lots of other languages too. Is your cat Siamese?' she asked Teddy.

'He is. But I don't think he speaks French,' Teddy said.

Marina hooked her hand into the crook of Teddy's arm. He bent swiftly and kissed the tip of her nose.

He pulled her more tightly against him. 'By the way, don't imagine I didn't notice the Tarot cards lurking on your dresser,' he said.

'I got a very good reading last time I dealt. Excellent prospects all round.'

'Mmm, seeing your cards has set me thinking of a new book. You could help me in my research.'

'What will you call it?' she wondered. '*Pack of Lies*?'

He stared down at her, droll and wicked. 'I'd thought about *Tarot and Tea Leaves on the End of the Pier*. Who could resist that?'

Zoe and François walked on, gazing into the sky. There were no more than a handful of rose-tinted clouds, hovering over the horizon beneath a canopy of clearest blue and luminous gold.

She was conscious of a deep unspeakable happiness. And also a sense of wonderful release. A portent of freedom, of danger banished to a far shore.

François was full of renewed vitality and purpose. He brimmed over with plans of where he and Zoe and Leonore would live in England, of how often they would get to France. He was fired with a longing to rediscover his homeland. With Zoe.

'My father will adore you,' François told her. 'He has a beautiful house in Provence, at the top of a long steep track. And in the village there are little cafes where you can sit out in the evenings.'

'And the air smells of the countryside and cooking and red wine,' Zoe said, smiling at his surge of new enthusiasm for life.

'Ah, yes! And at night it is so dark. There are pale hunting owls flying over the hills.'

Already the sun was sinking towards the dark line of the horizon. Across the bluey-gold brightness of the winter sky, a single magpie dived in a decisive arc, speeding menacingly towards them, veering off at the last minute.

Zoe took in a sharp breath.

'Don't you want to look for its mate?' François asked, tender and amused.

She smiled. She pulled his face down to hers, blocking out every other vision.

THE EXCITING NEW NAME IN WOMEN'S FICTION!

PLEASE HELP ME TO HELP YOU!

Dear *Scarlet* Reader,

As Editor of *Scarlet* Books I want to make sure that the books I offer you every month are up to the high standards *Scarlet* readers expect. And to do that I need to know a little more about you and your reading likes and dislikes. So please spare a few minutes to fill in the short questionnaire on the following pages and send it to me. I'll send *you* a surprise gift as a thank you!*

Looking forward to hearing from you,

Sally Cooper

Editor-in-Chief, *Scarlet*

*Offer applies only in the UK, only one offer per household.

QUESTIONNAIRE

Please tick the appropriate boxes to indicate your answers

1 Where did you get this Scarlet title?
Bought in supermarket ☐
Bought at my local bookstore ☐ Bought at chain bookstore ☐
Bought at book exchange or used bookstore ☐
Borrowed from a friend ☐
Other (please indicate) _____

2 Did you enjoy reading it?
A lot ☐   A little ☐   Not at all ☐

3 What did you particularly like about this book?
Believable characters ☐   Easy to read ☐
Good value for money ☐   Enjoyable locations ☐
Interesting story ☐   Modern setting ☐
Other _____

4 What did you particularly dislike about this book?
_____

5 Would you buy another Scarlet book?
Yes ☐   No ☐

6 What other kinds of book do you enjoy reading?
Horror ☐   Puzzle books ☐   Historical fiction ☐
General fiction ☐   Crime/Detective ☐   Cookery ☐
Other (please indicate) _____

7 Which magazines do you enjoy reading?
 1. _____
 2. _____
 3. _____

And now a little about you –
8 How old are you?
 Under 25 ☐   25–34 ☐   35–44 ☐
 45–54 ☐   55–64 ☐   over 65 ☐

cont.

9 What is your marital status?

Single ☐ Married/living with partner ☐

Widowed ☐ Separated/divorced ☐

10 What is your current occupation?

Employed full-time ☐ Employed part-time ☐

Student ☐ Housewife full-time ☐

Unemployed ☐ Retired ☐

11 Do you have children? If so, how many and how old are they?

_____

_____

12 What is your annual household income?

under $15,000	☐	or	£10,000	☐
$15–25,000	☐	or	£10–20,000	☐
$25–35,000	☐	or	£20–30,000	☐
$35–50,000	☐	or	£30–40,000	☐
over $50,000	☐	or	£40,000	☐

Miss/Mrs/Ms _____

Address _____

_____

_____

Thank you for completing this questionnaire. Now tear it out – put it in an envelope and send it before 30 June, 1997, to:

Sally Cooper, Editor-in-Chief

USA/Can. address
SCARLET c/o London Bridge
85 River Rock Drive
Suite 202
Buffalo
NY 14207
USA

UK address/No stamp required
SCARLET
FREEPOST LON 3335
LONDON W8 4BR
Please use block capitals for address

WODRE/12/96

Scarlet titles coming next month:

WILD LADY   Liz Fielding
Book II of 'The Beaumont Brides' trilogy
Claudia is the actress sister of Fizz Beaumont (heroine of
WILD JUSTICE) and Gabriel MacIntyre thinks he
knows exactly what kind of woman she is . . . the kind
he despises! But Mac can't ignore the attraction between
them – particularly when Claudia's life is threatened!

DESTINIES   Maxine Barry
Book I of the 'All His Prey' duet
They say that opposites attract . . . well, Kier and Oriel are
definitely opposites. She is every inch a lady, while Kier
certainly isn't a gentleman! And while Oriel's and Kier's
story develops, the ever-present shadow of Wayne hangs
over them . . .

THE SHERRABY BRIDES   Kay Gregory
Simon Sebastian and Zack Kent are very reluctant bride-
grooms. So why is it that they can't stop thinking about
Olivia and Emma? Emma and Olivia don't need to talk to
each other about the men in their lives . . . these women
know exactly what they want . . . and how to get it!

WICKED LIAISONS   Laura Bradley
Sexily bad and dangerous to know – that's Cole Taylor!
Miranda Randolph knows she should avoid him at all costs –
until she looks into his blue, blue eyes. Miranda is different
to the other women in Cole's life and she's determined not to
let him add _her_ name to those already in his little black book!